BREATH

a novel

BREATH

a novel

VICTORIA DOUGHERTY

BREATH

Published by Bloodwilde Press
Printed in the USA

ISBN (hardcover)   978-1-9550390-1-7
(paperback)   978-1-7342234-3-9
(ebook)   978-1-7342234-2-2

Visit the author at www.victoriadoughertybooks.com

Bridegroom, let me caress you,
My precious caress is more savory than honey,
In the bedchamber, honey-filled,
Let me enjoy your goodly beauty,
Lion, let me caress you.

— at 4,000 years old,
this is the oldest known
love poem ever discovered.

Each of us has a before and an after.

BEFORE, I WAS JUST A GIRL. A lucky girl, you could say. One born to a good family. I lived in comfort and even some style. Was certain of my place in the world. Sure, it was thousands of years ago, but rich girls haven't changed that much over time.

Neither has love. Or lovers for that matter. The sting of pleasure that burns through your every cell from that first kiss. The venom that is love. Deadly beautiful. You'd die a thousand times to feel it again. I have.

That's what brings me to my after.

Because after love, I was everything. And nothing. A pawn, a slave, a witchdoctor, a street urchin. The leader of a revolution. Even a queen, once. Only once.

But a Nin'ti always. Evermore.

Nin'ti. A mighty contraction of a word coming from the most ancient language known to mankind. Nin means "to live" and ti "to die." Over and over. Quite simple on the surface of things.

Nin'ti. As rare as an angel or a demon.

If you look up the word, you'll find that Nin'ti was a Sumerian goddess—a Lady of Life. But that's only the surviving interpretation.

I'm not a goddess. Most of the time I'm quite human, actually.

Nor have I ever been Sumerian.

Nin'ti.

If I were whispering what I am through a pair of lips, my hands would be dancing along with my sentences. That's been my custom in any body I inhabit, talking with my hands, I mean.

Nin'ti.

That's me. Sounds strange to say it even after millennia. As strange as it must be for those few, wretched creatures who find themselves staring into a mirror empty of their reflection to say, *I am a vampire.*

But it's what I am. A Nin'ti. That is all.

Forever young, eternal even.

Forever moving and starting over.

God's idea of a celestial military brat. Always the new kid. New school, new parents, new culture and time. Always a new death. And always before the sun sets on my seventeenth year. I've never lived a day beyond it. Don't know why I can't make it to eighteen. Must be a reason, though.

I've never watched my face age into a richly lined map of my life—a testament to my joys, jealousies, tears, and humor. My very humanity.

And I've never been a boy.

Always and never. The story of my life. My lives.

And one more thing—the most important of all. This one's an always. An always is always the most important thing of all.

Always the same love.

Fierce and exquisite.

Warm and consoling. Imperfectly perfect.

Never a never.

The sort of purity that can only be conceived through fire.

That fire will be lit again very soon. I hope.

RARELY DO I GET more than a few glimpses of flesh and blood people when I'm still on the other side. A free soul and metaphysical whatchamacallit, if you will. Most of the time, when I try to look into the lives of friends and loved ones who are still among the living, it's as if I'm watching them through a piece of gauze. No real details, just shapes and fuzzy smears of color. I'm lucky to hear a few sentences from a conversation.

It's only before a rebirth that my vision into the living world becomes crystal clear. And it's thrilling. Like the movie trailer for a sequel you've been dying to see. I'm able to haunt places I've been to, people still tied to my destiny, who I might see again. Even things. Like an old, little statue.

A bird's head.

A lion's mouth.

Once red wings, still flecked with the faint remnants of paint in some areas, but mostly worn to clay.

A strong, thin body.

Clawed feet clutching a flower.

The man who holds this little statue is leaning against an effigy of the Sphinx near the entry of the Egyptian Museum of Antiquities in Cairo. He is wearing a keffiyeh, of sorts. It's square and white, flowing down to his shoulders, and topped with a blue Chicago Cubs cap. The rest of him is all Indiana Jones in his prime. Rumpled cotton shirt—probably white once, but now somewhere between beige and gray, with large, wet ovals around the armpits. Soft worn khakis held up by an oiled, leather belt that's genuinely old—his grandfather's, if I'm not mistaken. Only on his feet, instead of the weatherworn brown oxfords Indy would have worn, are a pair of Nike Air VaporMax Flyknit utility shoes. Black. He squints up at the sun, takes off his baseball cap and wipes his face, also black, with his makeshift keffiyeh.

The heavy doors to the museum groan open and a young man, barely five feet tall and sporting the most outrageous curly, chestnut hair, scampers over to him.

"Dr. Neville!"

"Not another bomb threat," Neville says, pocketing the statue.

"No, no," the young man insists.

Neville laments that his lecture at the museum has already been postponed twice.

"It's still on, I think," the young man tells him. "But, but . . ."

"But what, Jordie?"

Jordie Mostafa jumps up and down like he's riding a pogo stick.

"You're needed in the desert!"

Neville's hand goes straight to the statue in his pocket. He swallows hard.

"Are you saying what I think you're saying?"

Jordie nods wildly.

"You were right. Just where you said it would be. The palace gates. Beautifully preserved, considering. Superb in its artistry."

Neville covers his mouth with his palm. Big hands, like his grandfather's. He curls them into fists and looks up at the sky.

"We did it!" he says. "You hear me, Dad?" Tears stream from his eyes.

If I had eyes right now, I'm sure tears would stream from them as well.

"We leave tomorrow—before dawn," Jordie says, inhaling a deep lungful of air. The air in Cairo, usually thick with pollution, is clearer today. Cleansed by a late northern wind. The kind that normally visits in the dead of winter.

"Why not tonight, after my lecture?"

"You need rest, Dr. Neville. And traveling in the desert at night is dangerous—you know that. Not even the Arabs do it." Jordie slaps Neville on the shoulder. "Tomorrow will be a big day. If it is the oldest civilization ever discovered, it's been there for thousands of years. Hardly going to go away in the span of one night."

"The most ancient city in the world. The Palace City of the Rah'a." Neville says it like he still can't believe it. "Makes the pyramids of Giza look like a brand-new subdivision."

Cornelius Rodin Neville. Neil, to his wife. Neville to his friends. "That lucky bastard" to his envious colleagues. I do love him, but not like that. I've loved his family for generations and watch them every chance I get, which isn't nearly often enough.

"May I see it again?" Jordie asks.

Neville nods, taking the statue out of his pocket and laying it in his assistant's outstretched hand. Jordie caresses its lines. He has long fingers for such a small man. "Not Sumerian after all. Much older. Your great-grandfather was right all along."

Neville turns and paces near the fountain just a few steps from the museum's entry. He stares past the lily pads that float in its murky, gray waters. That statue has been passed down in his family for over a hundred years, from archaeologist to archaeologist.

"Nin'ti are born for the love of only one, but to the virtue of us all," Jordie says. "At least that's what you said your grandfather told you."

"That's what the ancients tell us, anyway," Neville affirms. "At least according to my grandfather."

"Let me make sure I've got this right. Each one has a divine quandary—a quest they must complete for the good of human kind. It's why they're born over and over again, your grandfather said, did he not? I guess one life isn't nearly enough for that."

Jordie scratches his head, contemplating the statue. "I wonder if Nin'ti are destined for their fate or simply stumble upon it, the way one might chance upon a large fortune, or a killer on a darkened path?"

"Nin'ti are a myth," Neville says. "Though a much older myth than anyone knew. Anyone but you, Granddad," he says again to the heavens.

"Uncover the past or die trying," Jordie says. "Isn't that your family motto?"

Neville laughs.

"Not literally. At least I hope not."

"But your father, and his father, and his father before that. They all died trying."

Neville looks down at his assistant, towering over the fellow. At well over six feet, he's taller than any of his forefathers. I should know.

"I suppose they did."

Neville wraps his arms about his chest, contemplating those lily pads again. "You know, my grandfather thought he'd met one. A Nin'ti, I mean. My dad told me."

Jordie chuckles. "Ah, yes. But your grandfather's people hailed from Senegal, and he was a creature of science and superstition. Like any archaeologist worth his salt, right?"

A big, white slice of a smile spreads across Neville's face. "You oughta know, Dr. Mostafa. Superstition is like a hereditary disease in your family."

"But it skipped me! Swear!"

The north wind blows again. So light, like an infant's breath, but just strong enough to make Neville's shirt stick to his sweating torso. A strong back for an academic. He keeps fit to feed his addiction to the dig.

"You know, my ancestors traveled up from sub-Saharan Africa to Egypt to uncover the past. My great-grandfather came to America right after the First World War to study what he'd found. A partial tablet carved in a sophisticated language, one part word, and one part hieroglyph. Looked like visual music. Indecipherable. At least that's what everyone said. Everyone but him. There was this statue, of course. Little else. Only trinkets. A myth here and there. His endless talk about the Nin'ti. It's all we had to go on."

Neville, with that faraway look on his face, turns his head to Jordie. Strong, straight line of a nose, irises like blackberries. It's the head of a raven.

"Granddad said you know a Nin'ti by their eyes. They're supposed to be unusual, gem-like. Something out of a dream."

Jordie punches Neville's arm and starts to dance. "David Bowie was a Nin'ti! I knew it! Cha-cha-cha-changes!"

But Neville is paying no attention to the Bowie homage. He starts to pace again, cracking his knuckles. "He said being a Nin'ti was sort of like having a specific genetic trait—being vulnerable to a certain illness. You might be a carrier, in which case nothing really happens and you live your one life. Or you may have a real susceptibility to becoming a Nin'ti, and all it takes is dying with another Nin'ti to get that ball rolling, so to speak. Or dying at the hands of one."

Jordie stops his song and dance routine and studies his mentor.

"Do you believe?"

Neville cranes his neck and looks right at his assistant, blinking. "In Nin'ti? God, no. But I loved my grandfather. And I love old myths."

THIS OLD MYTH knows she became a Nin'ti in her first life.

It was the life that gave me the memory of my mother's voice, soft and mellow like a prayer; my favorite pair of slippers—covered in raw linen the color of lilacs and molded comfortably to my toes from day upon day of wear. Whatever body I inhabit, I tend to have a weakness for shoes—and lilacs.

That life also gave me my eyes, ones like Neville's grandfather described. A ripe green, they're the color of an emerald flecked with rust, or so I've been told. A French sailor once said they reminded him of a sea flower that grows in some of the deepest parts of the ocean, then floats daintily to the surface once it has detached from the sea floor. My eyes, too, follow me from body to body.

My first life introduced me to the putrid scent of death— the way it came to hang in our living room in place of the musky incense my mother used to light every morning. And later, after those early tragedies had healed—clumsily, like a jagged scar—I had my first taste of love.

If my spirit were within a body right now, I would breathe deeply. You might hear me sigh. My skin would burst into a tapestry of goose pimples, and a warm shiver would begin in my heart, then spread unbound to every part of my being.

That, for me, was how love began. With a breath.

And I'll never forget it.

Not if I live a thousand more lives.

Just as I'll never forget that first death—even if a hundred of my deaths have been more agonizing, or more memorable—historically speaking. It was the slowing of my heart—a dying battery. Fear and restlessness choking me, the claustrophobia of being trapped in the failing shelter of my body while the storm around me raged on. "No," I kept repeating in my mother tongue.

And of course, ultimately, I surrendered. Little choice in that.

There was no light, as I've heard some people describe. At least not for me. There was so much more than merely a light. An infinite threshold spread before me, but not into another world, the way it is for most beings. For a Nin'ti, a cosmic sojourner like me, it is a wide step onto another long and twisted road.

"WE SHOULD GO to your hotel, first," Jordie tells Neville. He looks him up and down, wrinkling a nose that's wide from his father's Arab roots and all freckled with his mother's Irish ancestry. "We've got enough time before your lecture, and you could use a bath, if you don't mind my saying."

Neville takes the statue from Jordie, but he doesn't pocket it this time. The figure always feels light in his hand when he first holds it, but seems to grow heavier by the second. A trick of the mind, he thinks. Feels as strong as if it were made of metal. It's not, though. It's made of clay, but of a sort that has never been found anywhere except in the land I was born. The statue has survived all these years, and except for its missing paint, it looks much as it did when it was first made.

"Yes, let's do that." Neville takes a deep sniff. "You could use a bath, too, if you don't mind *my* saying."

He looks up at the museum. Pink as salmon, it's a colonial oasis in the midst of a city pock-marked by cinder block buildings. His favorite place in the world.

"This is where all of this began for my family," he says, though not to Jordie. Not to anyone, especially.

It's where, more than any place on earth, Neville has always felt the spirits of his ancestors. They've visited him, talked to him in his dreams all his life. Told him his destiny lies in the desert.

I've told him a few things as well here and there.

That a soul is not a stagnant thing. It is as evolutionary as a child. As the destiny that has ensnared us both. One that was put into play long before what his history texts call the first civilizations. When a man was sent to fight a war even if a single hair had yet to grow beneath the belt at his waist. And a woman put away her girlhood to face birth and dying at the first drop of blood that fell from her sex.

This, I know from experience.

As I know that forever, no matter what my name, or my station, whether I look like a troll or a fashion model, if I am famous or live in obscurity, I will always be Sherin of the Rah'a.

Chapter 1

The Sultan of Rah'a's Kingdom.
Before the Bible, even before the Sumerians.

YINA WEARS A NEW TUNIC of indigo, a slave's tunic that flatters her albino pallor. It moves with the sway of desert brush blown wild by a restless wind, and makes her look like she's dancing.

"You are so like a woman, Sherin."

She sighs, hands resting just under her full bosom. I think she might cry as she kisses my forehead—the only part of me that can't be smudged, wrinkled, or otherwise messed up with a small gesture of affection.

"Wumum," my younger brother says, imitating her.

"Three years old and already spicy," Yina tells him. "Maybe that's what we should call you when it's time for your naming ceremony: *Gul*, after the pepper." She sticks her tongue out and blows.

"What do you think of that, *Gul?*"

I pull his nose and he giggles, then continues stacking clay blocks on a soft, citron play rug my mother made. His hair, full of loose, black curls, tangles over his face like vines, but he doesn't seem to care.

"I guess it's a more interesting pastime than watching his older sister get dressed up like a dolly." Yina's teeth are clenched, holding a pin of polished bone. She plucks it out of her mouth and slides it right under the base of the coil she's made of my hair, pulling my eyebrows up into a look of surprise.

"It'll relax," she tells me, but I'm not so sure.

I nudge her and stick a leg out, admiring the way my tunic pours along the length of my body. It's been beaten to a silken finish that is at once fine as onion skin and strong as wool.

Yina clears her throat and puts her finger to her lips. She lifts a disk of polished copper from behind an arras of snake skin.

"You didn't!" I say.

Yina widens her soft pink eyes, urging me to hurry up about it and get a good look at myself.

And I do. Pressing my shoulders back, I bite my lip, studying my reflection.

At thirteen, I'm tall for my age. Olive skin, deep and dark from the sun. If I yank out the pins and let my hair fall to my waist, it'll be straight like a girl from the northern tribes—thick, with the glossy sheen of obsidian.

"Nice," I say, admiring the twist Yina has made of it.

She holds the plate closer to my face. Even through the rosy tint of the copper, my eyes look startling. Nearly everyone comments on them, since they're such an oddity. Certainly nobody I've ever known has green eyes. In fact, apart from Yina, everyone in the Rah'a seems to have some variation of brown. Mostly dark brown or near black. And Yina's eyes don't count anyway, since she's been touched by the god Mazal and made in the image of his wife, the moon.

Yina retreats and I become smaller in the copper plate, but at least I can see the whole of me.

Upright and slender. Two lumps no bigger than plums on my chest. There's a good handful of curly hairs between my legs, too, but obviously I can see those. And engaged to be married.

The copper plate is a bit warped in places, and I wish I

could run to our wading pool and catch my reflection there. But that won't do at all. Narcissism is considered bad luck for a waiting bride, and I'm not supposed to be looking at myself at all until the night of my marriage.

Of course, that doesn't mean attention isn't going to be paid to my appearance. From the moment a betrothal becomes official, everyone becomes involved in the way a bride looks. I'll be watched closely by those who know my future husband's family and, since he's rich, those eyes will be many.

And their attention will be especially important today. On the day of my engagement party, all eyes will be on me. A girl from the Rah'a marries in the week after her first menstrual cycle begins, so the engagement is the real party. The wedding is put together in haste.

My brother looks up at me quizzically, taking in my appearance.

"Boring, I know," I say.

He scratches his tummy, then picks his nose, eating what he finds there.

"If any of the guests got a look at you, they'd turn right around and march home."

He goes ahead and eats another one.

Piggy brother or no, if things go as expected, I'll be called "Mala" from now until my marriage is consummated. It means womb, but not any womb; the womb of a high-born woman or, in my case, a woman who will give birth to high-born children. A woman of lesser station doesn't get a formal title. Just the name her parents give her.

And I'll be judged as a girl with smooth, unpitted fingernails, a confident laugh that puts others at ease, a face free of pimples, breath that is sweet, and soft, pretty feet that cause no one to look away in disgust.

"It may seem like petty gossip," Yina reminds me. "But at

a commitment feast, these morsels of information become everything."

Having been married three times now, Yina should know. Each of her husbands died not long after the marriages and no children ever came of them. It's believed the god Mazal is jealous and won't let any man have her, which is how, of course, she ended up with us. It was either that or be drowned under the light of a full moon to honor Mazal's equally jealous wife. At least, as a slave, the gods will let her be. We hope.

"Nineteen of them in total," Yina says, mouthing our guests' names and counting on her fingers.

Neither my future husband nor his parents will be attending my feast. It would be bad manners for him and his immediate family to attend the event, and would demonstrate an embarrassing lack of trust in my father, not to mention their own judgment. My would-be in-laws will instead send a league of family representatives to report on me and my home. It is, in most respects, more vital to hear the opinions of others about a proposed marriage. Trusted busybodies, whose findings hold tremendous esteem. A feed of friends, neighbors and business associates all weaving a rich tapestry of information that my new family will have to absorb.

How much did she eat?

Can she sing, play an instrument?

Does she show her parents the proper respect?

Is she serious?

Humorous?

Was the food any good?

Will she age well?

You get the idea.

It's why things must be perfect. You never want to give a groom and his family any reason to back out of an arranged marriage. Particularly when, like me, you're marrying up.

Yina unrolls the addax hide over my window and pours a cup from a cheerfully painted ale pot I made when I was five.

My fiancé's representatives have been spotted on their approach and it's time to get moving. She swats at my brother, shooing him off to his nursery, and promises him some dates dipped in spiced honey. Then she turns her full attention to me.

"Your mother and I worried about having your feast so close to tempest season, but the sky is perfection."

Brows pinched together—two furry white caterpillars—and looking very serious, Yina re-ties my tunic. She pulls hard, making a perfect square knot.

"Of course that could change in a breath, and the wind could pick up, bringing with it a sandstorm. Ruining everything."

"Damn the wind, and damn this knot. I can hardly take a breath given how tight you've made it," I say. She *tut-tuts* me.

"Mala's don't curse."

"I'm not a Mala yet."

Yina hmmfs. Her hands, paler than ivory, run along my lapels, smoothing non-existent creases.

"Your mother did a handsome job on the dye." Yina walks around me, tipping her head this way and that, sucking on the tip of her thumb. "When the light strikes you just so, it looks as fresh as the skin of a newborn."

She helps me kneel on my perch, a grooved olive wood stool my father made for my mother soon after they were married.

My betrothment dress is snug, unlike my usual clothes, as it's supposed to show the arc of my figure. It does suit me very well, if I do say so myself. How could it not, having been made by my mother? She's a master and has made sure the garment flows like water, each ripple accentuating the few curves I have to brag about.

I crouch on my perch, and Yina covers me with a blanket of soft blue, like a cloudless sky.

"Nahoor," Yina says. It's the Rah'a word that joins the words eternity and today. A word of promise, but so much more. It's a blessing given to a bride and groom, in hopes that a love so strong as to be infinite will grow between them. A lot to ask.

Next to me sits the goddess Kujuh—made of goat and fish bones—her arms held wide as if ready to take my husband in an embrace. A feral smile on her lips. Kujuh will possess a bride's heart on the night of her wedding, opening it to her mate. Making her want to bear his children.

As I sit under my wedding blanket, I pray to Kujuh that I can love my husband, and that I will one day want his children. It's not that I don't want a family, it's just that I already have one, and as far as kids go, my brother seems quite enough for me.

Kujuh, a cold bitch of a goddess if there ever was one, remains as silent as the dead goats from which she is made.

"Damn the wind, damn my knot, and damn her," I say.

I can make it on my own.

Chapter 2

The Feast

I'S A COOL NIGHT, and our hearth is blazing, sparks whirring up into the black, and vanishing like magic. Part of me wishes I could vanish into the night sky. My palms are damp and cold and my fingers tingle unpleasantly. I place them on my lap and force a cheerful smile for our guests, which they return along with a nod of respect. I must look alright, then.

The train of my mother's tunic, all rosy, ripples behind her as she makes her way across our roof garden. She takes a goblet from Yina's hands and shares it with an elegant, long-necked woman who I will one day be calling auntie. This woman tells my mother how excited her nephew is about the prospect of taking a wife, assuming all goes well tonight. My mother laughs and waves her hand with an impressive aura of confidence.

The night is overflowing with garments made of bold desert hues. Jugs and platters are arranged on our finest eating cloths; ones embroidered with pretty images of grapevines outlined in delicate gold thread. The musicians play from our central courtyard three stories below, stomping their feet to a beat on a patio of mud brick built by my father's hands. The sounds of harps and reed flutes waft up along with the strong perfume of the royal purple lulas I've been growing for the occasion. Those are just beginning to blossom, and haven't yet unfolded into the decadent flowers they'll become. When they do, their scent will be stronger than smoke and reach all the way to the ziggurat, I'm sure.

We lounge on pillows, as our guests pick from an array of barley cakes, mustard greens, goat, fowl, and mutton. Sauces that hint at sweetness, but are overcome by the taste of blood. I know them well. Pastes of organ meat and crushed nuts are smeared over flatbread. My favorite! Mulberries and pomegranates spill over clay bowls painted with symbols of fertility—horses, hunters, gardens, breasts the size of engorged udders. I look at my own bosom, and sniff. Can't imagine they'll ever be like those.

A chorus of women—lizard-skinny and full of gossip—are rolling cuts of roasted meat in finely chopped herbs that leave a green, furry ring around their lips. Splaying around our hearth fire, they point their toes as they stretch, cupping their breasts and giggling. My new clan. I wish I could like them a bit more, but every new bride feels that way at first. Or so I'm told.

"Godly, just *godly*," one of the ladies says, chewing with her eyes closed in rapture. Her nostrils flare explosively as she speaks, and even more so when she takes a deep sniff of roasted flamingo.

The strum and pitter of good conversation conceals the growls from my stomach. So I lay back, like the ladies, pretending I'm accustomed to a life of leisure. Yina, taking pity on me, sneaks the odd bite of heaven into my mouth as she rushes by, filling cups, replenishing platters. She doesn't trust the other slaves we borrowed for the occasion.

All along, my prospective husband's uncle watches me. One of his eyes is larger than the other and he fixes it on the buds of my breasts, not at all taking care to be subtle. Dressed in fine linen, bone white, he seems safe and dangerous all at once, like a garden snake.

"*Sahjaloh*, Uncle," I say, nodding.

A bride never uses the names of her would-be husband or his family until the wedding. It's considered very bad luck. But it's so hard in this case since his name means "one-sided" and has a peculiar connection to his face. I say his actual name to myself only once—Arik—to keep it at bay.

"Mala, your father tells me you make linens as fine as your mother's."

A dare, a test. Every little thing is. I lick my lips and take a good swallow.

"Only because my mother is such a fine teacher, *Uncle*," I say, but the name Arik keeps rising up like a ghoul.

I blink hard, trying to gauge how well I played it, and meet eyes with a young man on Arik's—*the uncle's*—right. His son, I think. Well-built and a full head bigger than most, with fresh skin, smooth like mine. It's possible he's only a couple of years older than me. With long, wavy hair that falls down his back and eyes the color of a golden ripe apricot, he seems out of place. Like he belongs to another world, another people. He smiles and I glance away before I'm tempted to smile back. That wouldn't do.

"And you garden, I'm told. A wishful pursuit for one who lives on the edge of a desert," the uncle mentions casually.

"A girl's life is made of wishes."

"That it is," he says. "It'll be a wish fulfilled if your womb makes life as readily as your hands."

I realize I've been speaking with those hands and fold them into a tight ball at my waist.

"Is it also true you kick stones with the boys and run like a gazelle?"

The uncle crows and crams a soft lump of mutton into his mouth, its juices running the length of his forearm.

"If I'm being chased, Uncle," I tell him.

He stills for a second and I can't even breathe. I'd wanted

to sound sure of myself, but with enough modesty and regard for my elders. No one wants to invite a diva into their house, then have to whip her into shape. Literally.

I'm tempted to apologize for being too offhanded, but Arik's eye twinkles and he roars with amusement. Even the gossiping ladies start to hoot, shielding their mouths with a swathe of linen, like they're so dainty. The young man looks at his lap, biting his lip. I try on a grin—not *too* pleased with myself, I hope.

The uncle unfolds, stretching and groaning. Sitting up tall, he slaps his hands on his ribs. It's his job to set the tone of the evening, which he does with a wordy speech about the many virtues of my would-be husband. He begins—incredibly—with a flowery monologue about the qualities of the top of my husband's head (round like a melon, with an abundance of hair).

He moves from there, as thorough as any man who loves to hear himself talk, and expounds on the merits of my husband's face and neck (handsome and foxlike, aquiline nose, and so on) then his broad shoulders, chest, hard belly, and strong hips.

He doesn't shy away from describing a remarkable set of genitals—in detail, his big eye boring *straight into mine the whole time*! No one dares to snicker, especially me, although when he describes the gem quality jewels pierced into my husband's foreskin (at the very tip of a member the size of a calabash, he tells us, giving a big wink while stroking the neck of a jug of wine, no less!), the ladies struggle not to fall to pieces. I only survive the ordeal by imagining the uncle squatting over a chamber pot, just as Yina advised me. She's been through this ritual three times, after all, and has suffered through all manner of innuendo—including a detailed description of her parents' wedding night once! She knows how to fight fire with fire.

The uncle keeps his comportment, staying deadly serious, and I have to admire him for that. His son strums his fingers along his thighs and glances away. I pinch my thigh hard to keep it together—an eager, enthralled look upon my face, I hope. An expectant bride never wants to look like a prude.

After a long and hearty clearing of his throat, the uncle continues to describe a pair of sturdy legs—like the trunks of a tamarix—all the way to my future husband's feet (stronger than the most well-made sandals, he says, and I think he could have done better than that) and finally, his toes. Seeming to grasp for something properly marvelous to say about those, he ends by assuring us they were the most beautiful and manly toes he's ever seen.

"Nahoor," he says, concluding the speech with his blessing.

Nearly everyone takes a deep swallow of wine, some downing their entire goblet and pouring another, because his are only the opening remarks. As ready as a rainstorm, my husband's representatives begin talking all at once—over one another, grabbing at me to get my attention. One woman even pulls on my hair, making me yowl and Yina go stone cold with fury. They charge at me with stories of my would-be husband's courage and athletic abilities, his handsome features, strong mind, and yearning for a wife.

It's called the stirring of the bride. And once the stories begin, reaching ridiculous proportions—like the way my husband hunts animals with his bare hands, *"Not only did he snap the leopard's neck, but then ripped into the fur with his teeth and skinned it right there!"* I know I have my marriage sewn up. A betrothal party would never be so excited about selling a prospective bride on her husband if they didn't approve of the match.

This reassurance gives the whole event a second wind.

Miriam, my mother—I can say my own family's names without any fear of ill luck—begins dancing with a fever, and in a way I've never seen before. I'm one part mortified, and another part impressed.

She's graceful and alluring, pressing each of her fingers lightly to her lips and sending her kisses off with the flick of her wrist.

My father sinks into his cushion and takes to smoking aromatic leaves with the men, holding the drag in his mouth, before gently letting it whistle from his lips. The plumes curl into the air like written language, and smell of sepi petals—a pungent fragrance calling up cardamom, strong cheese, and fresh mango all mixed together.

But between the laughing and the storytelling and the gorging, the chimes and the dancing, the thick soup of incense all around, a sadness visits me. It's as if all the flutters in my belly have come together to form a ball of iron so heavy I can barely move.

I start to see my life as it will be, not as it's been. And once that starts, I'm lost. Because the reality is that I'll no longer spend my mornings at my mother's feet, learning to make clothes and weave carpets. Or my afternoons with my hands worming through the sandy soil of our garden. I won't get to watch my mother's fingers glide across a ribbon the color of a freshly picked fig—not the skin, but the inside. As I did yesterday. And I'll no longer live in my father's fine home. Tall as two palms and as square as his shoulders. Smoothed with a thick layer of plaster that's the color of fresh goat's milk.

I think of the way my father feeds me pistachios as we walk into town. How they crunch between my molars, sounding like percussion to my father's light hum. Always the "Songs of the Desert Wind." My mother's favorite.

"There is a wind in the desert that murmurs; there is a wind in the desert that speaks of secrets." Crunch, crunch, crunch.

My husband's family might be kind, but they can't possibly love me the way my parents love me. While their home is far grander, I'm sure, it won't match my parent's taste and artistry. They know how to live with a grace that mere opulence can't touch. Everyone says so. Even the skinny ladies lying all about our pillows have admired our house, remarking on its elegance and charm.

And I won't get to follow Yina on her errands and gossip with her, giggle at her biting observations about people neither of us like. I think of the squat, little brick-maker who still reminds us—any chance he gets—that Yina should have been drowned under moonlight. She calls him *Pudi*, "the pucker of a pig's anus."

Quite horribly, it occurs to me that, when I marry, my baby brother won't be coming with me either. My sweet, chubby boy, who has a special smile that I know is just for me.

My eyes tear up and my fingers quiver like palm fronds in a breeze. It's terrifying. If my in-laws' representatives see me falling apart, it will jeopardize everything my father has worked so hard to secure. A whiny bride can expect no respect from her husband's family.

"Mala, won't you join us in the courtyard? My cousin has promised to sing a song." The young man, son of Arik, stands before me, as if he just appeared there. He talks to me directly, not even bothering with a *sahjaloh* of greeting. It's his right, I guess.

I nod and rise from my cloth. The embroidery leaves its imprint on my thighs—vines, snakes coiled among wood avens—and I rub at them as we walk.

I can't for the life of me remember the son's name, and I hope that's a good omen, especially as his father's name has been splashed all over my thoughts. I do know that he's one of those rare creatures chosen to be trained as a soldier for the sultan. At this point he's been away from his family for years already, but he has been allowed home because of the importance of this occasion. A growing man who is tapped as a soldier for the sultan's army is most definitely asked to judge a would-be bride for his cousin.

I follow this young man down two flights of stairs, past the rooms where a few young couples have ducked in for a little privacy. It's uncomfortably quiet, except for the occasional giggle and sigh, making me feel like an intruder in my own house.

Every step I take bears the weight of doom. The aromas of minted lamb, apple tea, and jasmine-laced sweat seem to sneer at me. Even the tapestry at our front gate—streaked in the colors of sunrise and boasting of good times ahead—mocks my father's dreams for my future.

"Would you like a chew?" the young man asks me.

I swallow and nod. My throat feels tacky, like I've thrown up.

He holds out the piece of boiled, marinated bark and I take it. Tastes like wet earth and sweetened wine.

"Where's your cousin?" I ask. "The one who's meeting us."

The young man smiles a little. "Oh, I don't know. Inside I guess," he says. "Probably hiding away somewhere with his new wife."

The wind blows, caressing his hair.

"You've been lucky with the weather," he tells me. "The tempest seasons have been getting stronger in recent years. Especially as they draw to an end and the hot air of the fire season overtakes the cooler winds that still linger on nights like tonight."

"Isn't he going to sing for us?" I ask him. I've always hated talk of the weather.

"Who?"

"Your cousin."

"No, he's a pretty terrible singer."

I stare at his feet. Wide and straight-toed. The sandals in

which they're wrapped appear as if they can barely contain them. Tipping my head up, I face him. Might as well. Our eyes, both of them unexpected and strange, meet in what feels like a sudden clash.

"All of my cousins are terrible singers, actually," he says. "Come to think of it, so am I."

His little jest takes me by surprise and I press my lips together. It feels good to suppress a giggle. I glance to the ziggurat, which sits in the distance like a giant scarab. It's lit with torches and is festive, but I notice the road is empty.

"We're alone?" I say.

He puts his hands on his hips, and for a moment I see the full effect of the rising soldier in him. I wouldn't want to meet him on a battlefield, that's for sure.

"Hardly alone," he tells me. "There's a house full of people only a few steps away."

Of course there is. I don't know why I asked. Maybe because of the way he keeps looking at me. Like we know each other or something. I suppose that in a way, we do. We are going to be family, after all. And there's no shame in having a few moments alone with a prospective family member.

"Would you like more?" He offers me another piece of the sweet bark, and I accept.

We stand there, chewing in complete silence—the moon shining on us.

When the chew has lost its flavor and begins to crumble, the young soldier suggests we rejoin the party. By this time my eyes are dry and no longer streaked red with the threat of a cry. I've found my smile again.

He leads me upstairs and to my perch, leaving me there.

"Aren't you going to bless my union?" I ask him.

"With Nahoor?"

I nod.

"I think I've done quite enough to bless your union."

I can't deny that. Taking me away from view just as I was about to burst into tears. Taking my mind off having to put my happy girlhood aside. I smile at him and mean it, but he doesn't return the gesture.

Instead, he turns from me and walks away, blending seamlessly into the party. As if nothing happened. Watching him nod in courtesy, making polite conversation, I try to imagine how he'll look in a few years' time. When his body hair will be gone—plucked or shaved, as is the fashion for all of the sultan's fully grown soldiers. He will have become another head taller, perhaps, his muscles swollen with hard work. A dangerous man, I think. An asp. Not a garden snake, like his father.

NEVILLE IS SLEEPING. Dreaming of me, though he doesn't know who I am exactly.

The night of my betrothment feast, I had a dream, I tell him.

I dreamed of the back of a young man's head. Dark, sinuous hair touching the base of his neck. He was naked, and his skin looked blue in the moonlight.

In my dream, I felt a tremendous love for this young man—a love I didn't understand.

I never saw his face.

I also dreamed that night of a fall. It seemed to go on forever and was at once terrifying and exhilarating. When I awoke in the morning, I felt a sense of destiny—as if, for good or ill, my life was about to begin.

My first life. My first name. Neville's life's work. The obsession of his ancestors.

I say my name to him—Sherin—and he twitches in his sleep. No matter what life I'm living, I always turn my head when a name like Sherin is called—Sharon, Cherry, S'urrah—no matter who I am or what I'm doing.

And I always love a boy named Nif.

"Nif," I whisper to him.

I've come to tell Neil about Nif, in the hopes that he can find some clue—anything—that would lead me to him. Our last few lives have left us mired in a tangle of long accrued secrets. Ones that have torn us from each other as surely as death. And those secrets can be found beneath the desert floor. In the Palace City Neville's research has uncovered. I'm sure of it.

That's why I've come to tell Neville a little bit about my death, too—the first one. Not my actual, physical death; the process a body goes through when it shuts down and a soul gets evicted from its home. I want to tell him about facing death.

At the hour of my first death I sat lonesome, parched in a desert between tempest and fire season. My lips were cracked and my head was pounding from the hard rays of the sun; I felt as rational as a human being can feel. Hopeless, faithless, blind to all magic.

My journey had been hard and bitter and I saw very clearly that it was coming to an end. Save for a miracle, there would be no one who could come and save me—give me water and shelter, take me far, far away in their caravan. In a few, short hours at the most, my body would be beyond help anyway—so unforgiving is the desert. So vindictive was the one who had brought me there.

I looked out onto the expanse—my last view of the earth would be of a wasteland—and I couldn't, in that moment, see any beauty in the surf of sand before me. Nevertheless, I found myself staring into the distance. I don't know how long I did so, stiff as a statue with sun-blistered hands resting lightly on my knees. The ripe odors of fear and abuse wafting up from under my shredded tunic. It was hard for me to judge time in that moment, when every minute seemed like an hour, every hour an eternity.

My breathing was shallow, my shoulders hunched, but still I held my gaze, until on the horizon I saw what looked like the figure of a man. I couldn't believe it and thought it must be a mirage. White robes fluttering in the sandy wind, head down, conquering one grueling step after the next. I truly thought I was going mad on top of it all.

As he came toward me, he turned into animals and

acquaintances—a camel, an owl, a leopard, my father, a sultan. But he was none of those.

The one who came to me was Nif. My always. In my weakened state, the sight of him almost killed me—or maybe it helped me hang on a little bit longer. It's hard to say. I do know that my heart just about stopped and I began to breathe so hard, sighing audibly with every exhale. Breaths of absolute joy and despair all at once, because I knew Nif had not come to save me. No one could save me—not here, so distant from help. Without a single camel. Too remote to carry enough provisions for basic needs.

He had come to die with me. To hold my hand and stroke my face—distorted, inflamed, awful. My body reeking of my own frailty, and the brutal impulses of ruined men. To slip into infinity at my side, so that I would not have to go this terrible road alone.

A gift like no other.

One of many he's given me throughout the ages, but without question the most dear.

Nif had followed me and my tormentors into the desert, knowing he would be stranded there. As he stood before me, I shook like a dog. Kneeling, Nif took me into his arms.

"Look at the dunes," he said. "They glow with the majesty of the sun." Leave it to Nif to find splendor in such a moment. And I did look out. What had been a barren wilderness to me now blazed in a way that was glorious. I have never seen anything so beautiful.

There, cradled in the desert sand, would be the only time Nif and I would die together.

"Nif," Neville mumbles, turning over.

Yes, Nif. He was, perhaps, the last person to see the Palace City before it all went to hell. Just as I was the last person to see my home, my life, before it was ripped out from under me.

Chapter 3

The Stranger

A S EACH DAY PASSES, I remain a girl.
Yina ties my tunic extra tight this morning, as if she thinks she can squeeze the blood out of me. I crack a nail down to the quick trying to loosen one of her knots. No go.

Forced to move with the short strides of a thick-bellied lizard, I can hardly keep up with my parents as they enter the marketplace—a round of stalls furbished with an over-abundance of goods and a riot of opposing smells. I hold my nose at a truly foul bouquet of luxury perfumes, salted fish, animal waste, and citrus.

Acacia and juniper trees surround the footprint of the market like standing stones, a reminder of the abiding power of the gods. Old and upright, shivering in a light breeze, their branches are spread wide and open to an infinite sky while we scuttle about in their shadows. Nearly every vendor is swarmed by shoppers employing vigorous gestures, as laughter and furious arguments volley from one end of the bazaar to the other. I love it.

"Aba, you evil spirit," my father calls to a grizzled tent-maker.

They chuckle, exchanging greetings and a kiss, and my mother and I exchange glances. We know it'll be a while. He gives a firm but kind assessment of the tent-makers inventory, and the man slips him a corked pot, quite tiny, full of perfumed oil. An item likely to be passed as a gift to my new family. An engagement is all about gifts, especially to the richer of the two families. They will, after all, be sharing their wealth with me and mine for a long time to come, and it's important to show gratitude. But my father has had quite enough of expressing gratitude. Especially as my engagement has dragged on for nearly a year now.

"Are you sure you're a girl?" My father teases me. "Too pretty to be anything else, I suppose."

"Ha-ha," I say.

"I was a late bloomer, too," my mother reminds him.

Late bloomer. Terrible thing to be called. The crusted soil beneath my feet dissolves into ash as I kick at it, watching the neat tips of my lilac slippers become coated with its powder. My mother made them for me and they are perfection, but a bit too new-looking for my taste.

"Beast!" She chides.

My mother bends over to beat the dust off my slippers as if she's giving them a good spanking. I wave to Ibbi, once a playmate of mine, but now a married woman. She bites on her knuckle to keep from laughing, and I bug my eyes out at her. She gestures for me to meet her at a tea stall and I nod. Her husband Kirin stands next to her with his hands on his hips like he's trying to be all man of the house, but even he can't stop himself from snickering.

"Act a bit more like a woman and you might just become one," my mother says. She puts her nose to the air, inhaling deeply, then pulls the sleeve of a spice merchant. It looks like she's ready to purchase yet another gift to send to my fiancé's family. The merchant, his braided beard as stiff as a daisy stem, unrolls a reed mat, presenting several precious sticks of cinnamon.

"Only Sultans have need for cinnamon," my father intervenes, waving the offering away.

Seeing my opening, I drift back to my mother's side, sniffing the various array of allspice, sumac, and baharat.

"I'm going to the tea stall," I tell her, but she's minding the spice merchant. His braid is tipped up, his eyes narrow with concern. Travelers like him can be twitchy, attuned to changes in the air. My mother drops her satchels of spice on the man's table and turns around.

At first, we hear only gasps, but those quickly turn to screams. I want to see what's happening, but my mother grabs my elbow hard, digging her nails into its crook.

"No, Sherin." She says it as if she *knows*.

The crowd parts for a man, a stranger; stooped-over, gray-skinned with blackened lips, gaping wounds from being beaten. He stinks of urine and spoilage. I know enough to understand that this man is suffering from plague. And not just any plague, but the Death of Vara. It's obvious by his symptoms, so long have they been part of our mythology. Many times, we've heard stories of entire regions being destroyed by this merciless contagion. They've always seemed far away, an unfortunate affliction for the poor and unlucky.

"Help me," he says, vomiting a mixture of blood and bile onto his six remaining toes. He clutches my mother's tunic and she does something I could never, not in a million years, imagine her capable of doing. She kicks him hard in his gut, sending him reeling into a cluster of shoppers. The sick man pins Ibbi to the ground, and she shrieks, pushing him off her. Kirin, her husband, pulls her up off the ground and stands before her like a shield.

"They're coming," he says, pointing his crooked finger at me. "They're coming for you."

Without even a grunt, the spice vendor drives a great sword through the man's heart, pinning him to a foot mat of thick red yarn like a shriveled date to a cube of raw lamb.

We're all winded from the horror. Not of his death—the

man was near death anyway, and the spice merchant has done him a kindness. A death by Vara only gets worse by the hour.

It's the realization that we've breathed in the man's vapors. Some of us have touched his person, while others have only witnessed his oozing sores and fetid appearance. But it's no good. We've all been exposed. Just as the dead man was exposed. A man who could have walked among us only days before, with no sign of what was to come.

Ibbi's hand goes to her belly. She must be pregnant. Her servant girl begins to pray aloud, but no one joins her. Not even Kirin, who comes from a devout family. The spice vendor sets his jaw and walks away. In the dead man's chest, he leaves behind a sword that must have been in his family for generations. With a curved blade and elaborate carvings that look at once floral and military, I've never seen one so fine.

With a jerk, my mother takes my hand and leads me out of the marketplace. Past the dazed shoppers and the shivering trees. We say nothing on our walk home. Normally, we would take a rickshaw, but we've left our spices behind—not caring that they're paid for.

Once home, we barely speak.

Yina's prepared a fish stew with a delectable aroma of dill weed and garlic, but none of us have an appetite. Only my young brother finishes his bowl, licking the juices off his fingers, and leaving his cheeks glazed with broth and spotted with green, feathery wisps of herb.

My father arrives home just before sunset and I can see that he'd been in our bathing pool. His hair is damp and his linen clings to him as if he's passed through a light rain. He's come from burying the man in the marketplace. I know it. No matter what the danger, he'd never leave a man to rot in the street. When he passes my mother, he kisses the top of her head, inhaling her scent. He smiles at me and squeezes my toe between his thumb and forefinger.

"Yina, your stew has a fragrance that was made at the feet of the gods," he tells her. Yina, who has been seated near the hearth, hushed, full of woe, fills a bowl for him. Her fingers tremble.

And my father eats with a gusto that rivals my little brother's—picking every morsel from the bottom of the bowl, then patting his stomach and asking for another. When he's finished, he retrieves his flute from a basket beneath our long bench and puts it delicately to his lips. Blowing a sweet whistle, he plays *Song of the Sun, Fire Song, Songs of Rain* and *Songs of Love* for my mother, he begs us to dance for him.

And we do.

Kicking. Spinning. Whirling with our hands in the air. And yes, laughing. We point our toes and make our fingers move like the tiny, lapping waves the wind conjures in the Tigris River.

The wind.

Finally, my father plays the *Songs of the Desert Wind*, and my mother sings. Her voice like raw silk. Her lips wet and the color of claret.

We stay up into the late hours that night—drinking ale, star-gazing, loving one another. And when we are finally too tired to go on, we make our beds by the hearth and sleep in each other's arms. Only Yina goes to her mat. And my brother to his nursery behind the house. I kiss each of his toes before putting him to bed.

An exquisite night. I've only known one that was better.

Chapter 4

The Vara

MY MOTHER'S SICKNESS makes itself known with an unbearable headache.

Her joints swell, blooming in umber and mulberry like great blood blisters, making her every move a misery.

At her insistence, Yina and I shuttle my brother off to his nursery, leaving him with some toys and enough food and drink for a couple of days. We try to seem light in our manner as we go, telling him we big people have much to do right now and he'll have to take care of himself for a while. Quietly, we tie his door closed with some thick twine.

From then, it is an affliction of threes. Three fevers, three people twisted, fouled, mutilated by illness. Three days until the first of them goes.

Yina, even as she succumbs to her own symptoms, nurses my mother until the very end, cradling her forehead in her palms, holding her as her body shakes and bends with spasms. My mother vomits blood and bile, just as the man in the marketplace did. My beautiful mother, her toes and fingers turning black.

Yina weeps, holding her mistress to her breast. I crouch behind her, wrapping my arms around them both, and sob like a child.

Yina thinks she's brought this on us because we wouldn't let her be drowned in the moonlight, but I fear it was me.

Arik, my fiancé's uncle. For saying his name to myself. I didn't say it out loud, but it was there in my mind like an omen.

"Arik!" I scream. It feels like nobody hears me.

Yina's pains are so ferocious that she begins scratching her face.

"Stop it!" I say.

But she won't.

I grab her wrists, and Yina tears away, pushing me down with the pure strength of desperation.

She attacks herself until bloody trails lead all over her cheeks. Her nails rip at her eyes, and tear at her lips till they hang from her face.

"Slay me," she begs.

I can't.

Her skin, so white, is smeared with blood. Like rose petals thrown onto the snow that falls on the very tips of the mountains. She looks unearthly and dazzling and terrible. I crawl to her feet and kiss them, begging her forgiveness.

My father is watching us. Lying on Yina's mat, holding my mother's limp hand.

Somehow, he finds the strength to stand. Teetering, burning with fever, he makes slow steps over to us, taking Yina's face in his hands. He kisses her white brow and, with one last, mighty gesture, wrenches her head around, breaking her neck. He falls with her body, collapsing on top of her in prayer. They lie together like fallen soldiers, their limbs splaying over a woolen rug as blue as a field of hyssop. And I join them, aching for sleep. It's been so long.

But there is no sleep with the Vara. When all those you love are succumbing one by one to a ruthless, pitiless death, and all you can do is sit and wait your turn to become like them!

Days go by in seconds and years. Every hour brings a new onslaught of horrors, as my father suffers worse than I can imagine it's possible for any man. His limbs curl in agony, his flesh seems to boil, turning sickly shades of pink before shading into gray. An inhuman color that speaks only of ashes and dark, stormy skies.

"Alehlah," my father whispers.

I crush my hands over my ears and shake my head. My eyes are screwed shut, but I can't close them to the visions in my mind's eye. Those are worse, because they're not only made of my father's ordeal, but of my memories of him when he was healthy and strong. Just three days ago. I see him whistling as he feeds our animals; I watch him toss me into our fish pond and jump in after me, coming up with a handful of the slippery silvers cupped between his palms. And there he is with his arm around my mother's waist, his thumb absently stroking her rib. She turns to him and goes up on her toes, kissing his earlobe.

I rise from the floor and go to our pantry, feeling as distant as a ghost. My body no longer belongs to me. High on a shelf is a pot filled with poison from the alehlah flower. It's sweet smelling, like tea, and the color of a red moon—tempting as a bad woman, my father once joked. We use it to keep away vermin and predatory animals that prey on our livestock.

For a moment, I think of emptying the entire pot into my mouth. It's a sweet moment that promises so much. No more grief, no dying alone of Vara while my parents and Yina molder next to me. Most of all, it promises freedom from what I know I must do.

But the moment passes.

I spoon some of the mixture into a small cup of wine, watching it fade like a light mist, careful not to let it touch my skin. My hands, to my surprise, don't shake. There's plenty left for later, I say to myself, and that sweet feeling of relief visits me again.

I carry it to my father, setting it next to him. Craning his head, he sniffs the contents, and I see on his face the first trace of pleasure that I've seen in days. Raising the cup, my father tips it toward his mouth, letting the poison spill onto his tongue.

The moment I see him swallow, I begin to weep.

"I've always wondered how alehlah might taste," he rasps, softly smacking his lips. He takes my hand in his and brings it to his lips.

"How?" I ask him.

"Like cherries without their sugar."

He closes his eyes and nestles his head into the crook of his elbow, while I stroke his hair—thick, black, as soft as a well-beaten patch of linen. The only part of him that's still like before. His breath becomes ragged, like an old dog's, then slows. I pet him.

"Sherin," he says as he dies.

Somehow, it is beautiful to hear my name on his lips. Maybe just because it's the last time.

⊢——⊣⟨◇⟩ ⟨◇⟩⊢——⊣

THEY'VE ALL GONE. But for hours I continue to sit among them. Their souls have moved on and their bodies are becoming stiff, bruised with the torpid greens of decay.

I can't stop shaking. My teeth chatter so violently that I think they might chip and crack. On a side table, there's a pack of playing discs that my father and I had amused ourselves with just a few days ago. He'd held one behind his back and asked me to guess which symbol was carved into it. "The sun," I said, but I was wrong. It was a bird.

I crawl over and try to pick them up, but it's difficult. At first they spill onto the floor because my hands won't obey me. I concentrate hard, picking up each one, and it seems to take a long, long time. But in the end, it's good. Something to do. Helps me take control over my body again. When I finally manage to stack them neatly, making each one align with the next, I look at them, and think about all the times I watched my father and mother play together. Drinking wine and nibbling on flatbread and chutney. Laughing at jokes only the two of them understood. These simple discs, made of shell and clay, given as a gift on my parents' wedding day, hold the memories of my family from its first day to its last.

All at once, I notice I've begun to play, matching pairs by suit and symbol. Marking my wins against myself, I dip a finger in pomegranate syrup and swipe a series of lines across our stone floor. I listen to myself breathe and watch my hands pick up disc after disc, amazed at the way my fingers can move at will once more. Only a few feet away from me, my mother's hands are clenched in rigor mortis.

In flickers, my thoughts return to me again. They're distant, impersonal at first. I think about being hungry, and this leads me to think about Yina's fish stew. Then I take a deep breath in through my nose.

The stench hits me like lightning and I gag, barely managing to hold on to the little food I've eaten. I should be dying of plague myself, my body reeking of waste and rot. Only I'm not dying—at least not yet. As far as I can tell, I don't have any symptoms at all. My head doesn't ache; my joints haven't swelled to the size of oranges. The only thing I feel is hunger and nausea. And I'm feeling most impersonal, even though I was wracked with sobs when my mother died. Then Yina and my father. Somehow it seems like a long time ago now.

From outside, comes a noise. One of our goats bleating. I stop playing cards and hold my breath. There's something about the sound that isn't right. It's too high-pitched and has a curious melody. With each passing second it grows more familiar.

My brother!

In my grief, I'd forgotten about him. I'd brought him some more food the day before yesterday, I think, and he seemed all right. Of course by now he could be dying—or at the very least, hungry and soiled.

I scramble from our living room floor to our courtyard. There, I undress, and step into our wading pool, letting the cool water wash the stench of death from my skin and hair. There's been no reason to keep me away from my parents' sickbed. After all, I'd been in the marketplace, too. If the plague is going to get me, it's going to get me.

But for reasons that can only be defined as hope against hope, my brother has been kept in his nursery away from us all for the most part. Maybe my parents thought some kind survivor might take him in the unlikely event that he doesn't die. Parents will try anything to save their children, and in this case they might have been right. After all, I'm alive. *I am alive.*

Wet and naked, afraid to don any of my fouled clothes, I enter his nursery. It's quiet and my heart beats in deep, thirsty gulps. He's gone hushed all of a sudden and I'm filled with panic, afraid that his chubby body has turned gray and black like the others. I creep to his mat, pulling aside the woven fronds of his curtain.

And there he is, looking up at me.

Confused and vaguely unhappy, but none the worse for wear. His hair, brown as a horse's eye, is matted in parts and sticks to his forehead. The air smells of damp linen and pee.

"Mir?" He croaks, calling for our mother.

"Shh, she's gone," I say. "But I'm here."

I smooth his hair to his temple with one finger. Then all of a sudden, I pull him up into in my arms, unable to stop myself from kissing him everywhere. It's an awful assault to put a dazed and hungry child through, and he struggles with me.

"I'm sorry," I say.

"I'm hungry," he whispers.

I lead him out of his nursery and to our pantry. Dug into the ground, it's cool in there and I light a small bowl of kindling to see where I'm going. Its glow comforts my brother, and he runs his finger through the flames. There, hunched around the crackle and burn of a small pile of woodchips and brush, I'm able to calm him with some goats' milk, which he gobbles down as if it's any other day.

When he's sated, I let him blow out the last lick of flame and lead him up into the warm sun. I pull on a clean shift, find my favorite pair of lilac slippers, my new ones, and sit with him on a soft pillow that Yina and I had embroidered with starlings. I begin humming, "The Songs of Desert Wind."

I can't bear to look at him right then, because I think I might lose my mind and start to cry. I know once I start, I won't be able to stop, either, and a girl can't take care of a child when she's walking around crying all the time.

Instead, I tell him everything will be well. That we have each other, and I'll find a way to care for him. I'm sure that the family of my future husband will take us in. What's one more mouth to feed in a house filled with forty slaves?

We have to wait, that's all. Wait until the plague has done what it's going to do. Wait until others from the kingdom will dare to come see what's left of us.

"What do you suppose we should do now?" I say to my brother.

His liquid eyes, earthen, nothing like mine, search my face—landing upon my lips as I murmur comforts to him.

I can't take him into the main house. At least not until I've burned Yina and my parents and cleaned everything up. He doesn't deserve that. And he doesn't deserve to be called just 'little brother' either. It's hardly a name for a child of his grace, one who will grow into manhood in a few short years, with any luck.

In the Rah'a, a male child isn't named until he's much older and has demonstrated some kind of trait or skill. My future husband is named Rahnemezek for his propensity to look up at the sky. It is thought he has high ambitions. Rahnemezek. It's the first time I've said his name, even in my mind. It's fine, though. I figure our luck can't possibly get any worse.

Rahnemezek. My young brother should have a name as forward looking and I decide right then that even though he's barely past being a toddler, he's already displayed the amazing skill of staying alive despite some pretty grim odds.

I take my brother's dimpled hand and lead him out to the wading pool.

"It's time for your naming ceremony," I say.

He furrows his brow, pushing out his bottom lip. "Not *Gul*," he says with a stomp of his foot. Gul has stuck ever since Yina nicknamed him so.

"No, of course not," I say.

Unwrapping his dirty tunic, I lower him into the clean water.

"Whoosh-whoosh!"

He giggles and kicks his feet, flapping his arms as if trying to fly.

"Call me hawk!" He loves birds.

I splash water over his belly.

He hooks his arms around my neck and presses his lips to my cheek, all slippery.

"Grateful for the bath?" As of days ago, he hadn't liked them.

He squeals as I rub his bottom with soap. When he's as clean as if Yina bathed him, I massage him with oil—something he's always loved—and wrap his loins in a soft piece of linen.

"Big boy," I say.

I pick him up and carry him to the daybed in his nursery, where I lay him and sprinkle more oil on his face and limbs.

"Shrim," he says, and I smile.

"This isn't about my name, we both know my name. It's about yours," I tell him.

Then, I speak the name I've decided to give him—Salan.

It means, rather simply, *to be*, but so much more than that. It's what we tell our heroes who survive a violent battle. It's what we tell a mother who has survived childbirth. It's what we tell those we love, when we are sure that we will never stop loving them no matter what.

Salan, Mama.

Salan, Father.

Salan, Yina.

Salan, Salan, Salan.

Chapter 5

The Intruder

BATHING IS BY FAR the best part of my day. Salan's, too, I think. We splash in our wading pool until our fingers prune, then I chase him naked into the garden. There we lie down, baking good and hot in the heavy afternoon sun. It's the only time everything seems like before. As if any moment now our mother will finish with her weaving and join us, our father will return from the market center, Yina will ply us with snacks.

The love I feel for Salan now is something different than what it was. In a few short days he's become everything to me. We live together in our house as if it has always been this way—me feeding him, singing to him, bathing and clothing him. Playing a game where we try and squeeze into the tiniest spaces. Last night I managed to get him to fit into our earth oven and he came out covered in ash, a fishbone stuck in his hair. Had to bathe him again, but that was the point.

We dry quickly and the sun grows unpleasant, so Salan and I dress and move to the stone floor. We perch on pillows touched with heavy dyes of scarlet and indigo, stuffed full with horse hair. Made by our mother's hands. I cuddle him and think through our predicament, humming a soothing song for him that feels at odds with the way I feel. Staring out onto our lands, it's as if I'm seeing them like a newcomer.

Our yard has four goats, a dozen chickens, a sow named

Beel—not the smartest sow, but a good girl—and a pond where Yina farmed the tiny, silver fish, hardly bigger than my fingers, that my father was so fond of. I wish Yina was here to help me. She could stretch the stores in a pantry better than anyone. And always hummed the prettiest songs while she worked. There's no use in wishing, though. Wishes only bring more tears, so I chase away my more tender thoughts of our good servant and friend, thinking instead of what I learned from her about running a household. I count up our grains in my head, our spices and preserved fruits and vegetables. Salan and I are lucky that these were replenished just a moon ago. As far as food goes, we're all right for the time being. And I'll certainly have no problem growing at least some of our needs in the garden. It's the one thing I could do better than anyone in our family.

What unnerves me most is that one day—sooner rather than later—I'll have to leave our house to see what's happening on the streets. There will be other survivors, too, I'm sure of that—but I have no notion of what state they'll be in. Grief and desperation can do all sorts of things to people.

I remember my grandmother beating her chest when her son was killed by a roving band of thieves. She rolled on the floor, pulling her hair out, and screaming like she would never stop. Eventually she did, but after that she wouldn't speak, and remained silent for two years.

My mother was sympathetic at first, but then began to view her as a bit of a diva.

"The woman has responsibilities," she said of my father's mother. "But instead she indulges in nonsense and expects everyone else to dance around her."

My mother lost three children between me and my brother. Two at birth, and one, barely two years old, toddled into our wading pool and drowned. It happened when I was only four, so I don't remember it well—just that I didn't like that brother much. He was a nuisance, and he hadn't even been named.

Which makes me think of Salan again.

He's doing better than I am with our misfortune on most days, although I'm better at pretending everything's fine. While he misses our loved ones and begs for our mother at night, he seems alright much of the time. As long as he has me to give him what they no longer can. His needs get me through the day, too, and give me some small scrap of confidence in the future.

I don't know what I'll do with Salan when I go out into the streets. I can't take him with me. It's too dangerous. Leaving him behind will be no different than when he was left in his nursery while the Vara devastated our household, I guess.

What bothers me most, apart from the menaces I might find out there, are the comforts of heart and soul that I'll be leaving behind when I step out of our house. Even if it's only for a few hours.

Its walls and flat ceilings the color of skull bones, make it feel as if we live in the mind of a loving god here. The same god who made my parents, so that they could make a life for me and Salan. This house is all that's left of it. The lingering scent of Yina's fragrant chutneys is embedded into every tapestry, and infused into the very air we breathe. The bright linens speak of the happiness we were born into.

With great toil and trouble, I've been able to clear the house of its stench of death, lighting a funeral pyre behind our animal pens and wrapping our loved ones in fine cloth for their journey to the next world. One by one, I took them to the fire by rickshaw, letting Salan throw the strong, dried herbals onto their bodies as they turned to smoke and floated back to the heavens from whence they came.

"Will they ever be back?" He asked.

"No," I told him. "But one day we will go to them."

While Salan played in the courtyard, I washed our floors with salts, perfumed oils and wood ash. The stench of illness was strong, but the aromas of cedar and pasu flower were stronger. Both have faded quickly, and I thank the gods that Yina's good smells remain.

Our furniture, made of cypress, sanded and stained, are the finger bones of our house. The whorls in the wood a fixed image of raw nature, like a god's idea of a memory. My father made our furniture, and it gives me nearly as much comfort as my mother's linens. Those are the tissues of the place in which we live.

Going away from here, even for a short time, will make our loved one's deaths permanent. In our house, they're still with us, but I don't believe their protection extends to the streets of the Rah'a. The houses and the empty market. The abandoned ziggurat.

Salan, out of nowhere, begins to cry like a baby. He's been doing that on and off.

"Shh," I say to him. "What's the matter? You can't be hungry."

I fed him two eggs and smoked fish before we hung up our tunics and slipped into the pool.

"Mir," he says, and won't stop.

"Quiet," I say. "I mean it!"

I start to rock him as a sequence of thuds plod from inside the house. Shushing Salan, I stroke his hair.

"You really have to be quiet now. Please."

I'm positive I hear footsteps. Not sure footsteps, but erratic, distressed ones.

Salan breaks off from his fussing for a second or two, so I dip my thumb into his leftover goats' milk and shove it into his mouth, like when he was little.

There is no question now that someone is in our house. I can hear them distinctly, fumbling from room to room, picking things up, throwing them down, and rummaging through our belongings.

Tiptoeing, I tug Salan with me, my thumb securely in his mouth. Back in his nursery, I throw on a fresh tunic, then wrap him up in a long swathe of linen that makes him look like a chrysalis. Sliding my feet into my slippers, I creep to the linen pantry, emptying a wooden box where Yina keeps Salan's clothing.

"Let's see if we can fit in here," I whisper. If I make it a game, he might stay quiet.

I tilt the box over, letting him crawl in first. Pulling it upright, I step in leg by leg around Salan, then crouch with him and close the cover. With any luck, the intruder won't be looking for linens.

But luck has not been my friend of late.

Chapter 6

The Archer

HE TEARS the lid open and stands there, staring at us. His eyes are wild and dark, like he hasn't slept; his lips dry and cracked, bleeding everywhere.

"Kirin?" It's my friend Ibbi's husband.

His scream is shrill. His mouth opens wide, as if his jaw has unhinged. The spittle and hot steam of his breath overwhelm me as much as the foul, dead cat stench that comes with it. He's crazed with grief, thirst, or hunger. Maybe all of those things.

"Kirin, sit down," I tell him. "I'll get you some food and wine." I lift Salan from the box and trip out of it myself, knocking it over and falling on my face. As I struggle to my feet, Kirin shrieks again, this time pulling his arm back and making a fist. He comes at me fast, punching me in the shoulder.

"Kirin, please!"

Backing up into Salan's nursery, he reaches behind him, fingering a pitcher from top to bottom like he's trying to decide what it is. Next, his hand touches a few of Salan's toys, ones I like to put him to bed with—a carved wooden doll of our mother, a straw puzzle, a gourd with broken nut shells that pitter inside it. Those don't seem to please him. It's when he reaches under a pile of soiled cloths that his face lights up, as if he's got a great idea. Slowly, he pulls a fire poker out from under the pile. It's the big one I used in the funeral pyre, when I burned my family. Damn the wind, I forgot it was there.

With a look of deadly determination, Kirin raises the poker high above his head and starts walking toward Salan and me.

"Kirin." I keep repeating his name. "Do you remember, Kirin, the first time we met?"

If he does, he doesn't show it.

"On your wedding day."

A hot, blistering day. Ibbi fainted at their wedding supper.

"I always wondered if it was the heat that made Ibbi faint, or her excitement at becoming a wife," I say. "Your wife."

He grunts, his neck straining. It's as if he's forgotten our common language.

"I know I feel faint when I think of my marriage. And like you, I'll have to move somewhere strange and foreign—a distant part of our kingdom."

I speak quickly, trying to forge a connection with him. Kirin came from a settlement, too, but his wasn't as rich as ours. His marriage to Ibbi had been a boon to his family as my marriage would be to mine. I try to remind him of this.

"I can take you with me," I whisper.

But Kirin staggers toward us, gripping the poker like a spear. He's a terrible sight. Uncaring of me or himself.

"Shrim!" My brother yells.

Kirin continues his march, swinging the poker up and behind his head.

"Run," I tell Salan. But he doesn't! Instead, Salan throws his arms around my legs, making it difficult for me to move without tumbling over.

"Damn the wind!" I scream. "Don't do this!"

And Kirin stops. Dropping the poker, he falls to his knees and crumbles. A whistle escapes his lips and I gasp, clutching

Salan. In Kirin's back is an arrow. A long, skillfully made arrow that I know is not the property of a mere household armory.

Through the doorway comes a man, tall and lean and wrapped in linen—fitted and loose all at once like priest's clothes. Dark blue and dark gray, but fine colors. Well dyed.

"You killed him," I say. It's not an accusation, but a statement of fact.

"Yes," the archer says. "He had the Vara."

I look at Kirin and shake my head. My hands are trembling.

"Sometimes it only takes the mind," he informs me.

That seems even more monstrous.

"Do I have the Vara?"

"No."

Somehow, I knew that.

"Or my brother?"

The archer shakes his head. He pulls his hood off and runs his fingers through his hair—shoulder-length, black, tight curls—then scratches his beard hard. That is short and neat. Well cared for. Thick in parts, less so in others.

"Why don't we have it?" I ask.

"Don't know," he says. "It came through my lands some years back and I didn't get it either. Not then, or now."

He smiles and I feel strangely bare all of a sudden. As if my tunic has unwound.

"*Sahjaloh*," he says, extolling the most formal of Rah'a greetings. Seems odd coming from him. Then he bows and holds out his hand, as graceful as a wild cat. I don't take it.

"Is that why you've come all the way here? To plunder what's left?" I ask him. There's a bounty to steal from in our rich and ravaged part of the world.

"I have come for what's left. I've come for you."

He fixes his stare on me as he speaks. His eyes, the right one the color of meat gravy streaked with blood. A delicious color, a meal. The other flecked with amber, like a tortoise shell. Subtle and discerning. They seem gentle. Quite at odds with his purpose. I don't want to believe them.

"Why me?"

His cheeks flush above his beard, and he glances at Salan. My brother, guileless, breaks into a crescent moon of a grin.

"Did you fit into there, both of you?" The archer tips the box with his foot.

Salan nods with some pride.

"Impressive. You must have twisted yourselves in quite a knot."

"We can fit anywhere," Salan says.

"Anywhere you say?" The archer reaches over to Salan and starts to tussle his hair, but I grab his wrist, sinking my nails into his flesh.

"I should have asked first," he says. "May I?"

"No."

The archer raises his brow and almost grins.

"How about a bite to eat, then, for saving your life?"

Chapter 7

Tea time

"**T**HEY'RE COMING FOR YOU," I tell the archer. "That's what the man with Vara told us. The one in the market."

The archer is stoking our hearth, making the flames surge. I watch how he twists the poker that Kirin would have used to kill me, agitating the kindling. He adds more dried fauna and a single cut of wood, his fingers gliding through the tresses of smoke.

"It's hard to say whether that man would have volunteered to become infected, or had the sickness forced on him," the archer says, glancing my way. "He may have been taken from a region that already had an outbreak, then brought here."

"But who would do such a thing?"

The archer meets my eyes, clear and direct.

"Who?" He shrugs. "Anyone, that's who. Out of envy or greed. Desperation."

"How much--" I start, but stop.

"How much of the Rah'a has been affected?"

I nod.

"Have you been out on the streets at all?"

I shake my head. I hate for him to think I'm a coward, but then I don't owe him an explanation either. And he's not asking for one.

"All of it," he finally whispers. "All of the Rah'a has been blighted."

Words like a splash of well water. Cold from the deep. Not uncaring exactly, but as candid as his gaze.

"You have more family you were hoping to find?"

I help him stoke the fire, just to give my hands something to do. Keep them from shaking.

"I'm betrothed. He's from a western region."

The archer crushes a few more dried leaves, sprinkling them onto the fire. They spark up, dancing above the flames. "You're a mala, then." The archer looks around, his eyes landing on a mountain of linens I'd been meaning to wash. "Nice place."

"Not that nice," I tell him. "But yes. I *was* a mala."

The fire hisses, its blue core glowing under the new wood-chips. The archer scratches behind his ear, looking away.

"He's probably dead, of course. But whether he is or not," he shrugs, "you're with us now."

He doesn't mean anything by it. His mouth is set in a soft line—not unmerciful exactly. The archer is just saying what is. Acts of war are lucky for some and less so for others. Simple as that. My luck has taken a turn for the worse, and I'm now a captive of the archer. A piece of property—strong, resistant to the worst of plagues. A lucky find for an invading army. Or so he tells me.

"The Army of the Waterless Sea," he crows with an air of smugness. "A strong people."

I've heard of this kingdom. A neighboring one, not particularly impressive. If our kingdom is rich, the Waterless Sea is more or less surviving. The name in and of itself is the tip-off. What good is a sea without water? But what they lack in status and natural resources, they seem to make up for in courage and ingenuity. I have to give them that. At least if this archer is any indication of what they're like.

"Don't look so glum," the archer says.

I say nothing, but wrap my arms around my chest.

He's slaughtered Mita, one of our goats, and tied her over our hearth to roast. No cumin or urfa biber to bring out her flavor. Just plain. She ogles me with no feeling, as she did in life, and I swear to myself that I won't eat a single thing he's prepared no matter how hungry I get.

Salan is humming our mother's supper song to himself and I watch him throw rocks into our potted little pond of fish, watching them scatter and regroup with each plunk.

"Your fate could be worse," the archer tells me.

That is rich coming from him.

"The Prince of the Waterless Sea could have ordered his men to kill any survivors in the plaguing regions. But he's a reasonable man." He cuts into Mita's thigh with a sharp and impressive dagger. One he handles as if it were a third hand. He offers me the lump of meat and I shake my head, then watch him stuff it into his mouth. A piece of it clings to his beard.

"He sees the value in utilizing resilient individuals—like you. And he's better than your sultan, who's left you to your own devices."

"At least our sultan hasn't come to steal what remains!"

"Are you so sure about that?" The archer slices another chunk of meat off the bone.

"Could you please chew with your mouth closed?" I tell him.

He stops, looking me up and down. Amused at me this time. The archer crosses his arms and finishes chewing at leisure.

"You're not a princess-in-waiting anymore—a *mala*," he says. "I'm not sure what you are."

"I was never a princess," I say, moving further away. "Any more than your leader is a prince."

He scoots closer and I move again.

"Are you afraid I'm coming down with Vara?"

I shake my head, kicking a stone. "You smell."

The archer slides right up to me and raises his arm, pushing its sweaty underside into my face. I shove him away and gag.

"I think you're right," he says, sniffing himself. "I might have to bathe after we pack up tomorrow."

Tomorrow.

Somehow, I didn't expect that he wanted to leave so soon. It takes everything I have left not to burst into tears. My home. I'll be leaving my home. And my parents. And everything I've ever known and loved.

I won't be leaving to be a wife and to bring prosperity to my family. To bear children and run a household. I'll be leaving with a stranger, as a prisoner, going alone into the unknown.

The archer's face softens and he places his meat on an eating cloth he's selected from our kitchen. A fine cloth—thick and dyed aubergine. I'm sure he's never seen one as fine.

"Please," he says, offering me his supper.

"Not hungry," I say, right in tune with a low grumble that comes unmistakably from my belly.

I expect him to chuckle at my expense, but he doesn't.

Instead, the archer stands up and walks across our rooftop, disappearing downstairs. I don't ask after him. I don't want him to think I care. Nor do I even look at his supper, and breathe through my mouth to keep from smelling it.

Salan lands his rump on my lap. He squeezes my cheeks together and caw-caws before catching sight of the archer's meat. Swiping the still-warm chunk off the eating cloth, he tears into it with his tiny teeth, chewing with the single-mindedness of a dormouse. He slides down my outstretched legs, folding up cross-legged in front of the fire. Sated, his eyes getting sleepy, Salan curls up at my feet and drifts off into his dreams. I stroke his hair with the very tips of my fingers.

"Don't you worry," I say, and rise up slow, creeping to the edge of the rooftop. I can't see the archer down there, but I can hear his light footstep and whistle somewhere near the courtyard. Gathering Salan, gingerly, making sure not to wake him, I tip-toe down the stairs, glancing around on each empty floor just to be sure. At the front of the house, I wait for just a moment. A memory stops me cold, and takes me to the night of my betrothment feast, when I came here. The way that young soldier held open the tapestry for me and gave me a chew, saved me from myself. There's no one to save me from myself today.

Lifting up the tapestry, I walk outside, pinching my eyes closed, but steeling myself to make a run for it. I'll hardly be fast holding a sleepy child, but if I can make it to the ziggurat, we might be able to hide there. At least for a while. Cautiously, I open my eyes, my feet itching to move.

But they don't.

THE STREET IS LITTERED with death. People I've known all my life look unrecognizable to me. Some alone, others in the arms of their beloveds. All of them lying in stiff and misshapen forms, like my parents, and Yina. Faces frozen in torment, pools of vomit and feculence spread out beneath them. For a moment it feels as if I'm the only one left in the world. Even with Salan in my arms.

One breath, then a second, my knees nearly buckling.

I wish I could close my eyes again—unsee the future that awaits me and my brother. A future even more bleak than the death of my family.

"I won't let you die out there," his voice says from behind me. It's different to hear it when I'm not looking at him. Sounds all full of care and truth.

"Can't you just let us be?" I whisper. "Take what you want, and leave a few provisions, so we can survive."

"I can't," he says, just as softly.

"Why?"

"Because I'm not the only one who'll come through here. But I may be the only one who won't kill you, or worse." He reaches out as if to touch me, but doesn't. "Maybe you'd take the chance for yourself, but what about the boy?"

Salan takes a deep, slumbering breath as if on cue. I close my eyes and kiss his neck.

"Go back to the hearth and eat," he says. "We have much to do tomorrow. And in the event you do decide to try and run away from me between now and then, you'll certainly need to get your strength up for it. I'm not an easy man to escape."

———— ◆◆ ◆◆ ————

I SNUGGLE MY BROTHER into a cozy nest of straw not too near the hearth, but close enough that he can stay warm. I don't know how long I sit there, hungry, watching Salan sleep, but it feels like hours. When the archer returns from downstairs, he's holding a pitcher of ale, which I can smell on his breath. He takes his place next to me again, and notices the empty eating cloth from his supper. A light wisp of a smile touches his lips.

"It was Salan," I say, glancing up at him. I notice at once that he's damp and clean.

"It's a fine bath you have," he tells me.

Had, as of tomorrow. I almost sharpen my tongue to say so.

"You don't have a wife, do you?"

The archer swallows and shakes his head, picking up the eating cloth and shaking it out.

"You could use one," I say.

He sniffs and gets up, sauntering to the edge of our roof-top. I hear the rustle of his clothes and a drip-drop-splat on our floor as he starts peeing over the side of our house.

"Like I said," I whisper.

CAN'T CATCH A WINK OF SLEEP. I lay on my mat, memorizing my ceiling, the rough and porous facing of my walls, the night smells of the house my father built with his hands—wet clay, anise, fire-smoke. I roll and squirm on my linens—clean linens from Salan's nursery. I dressed my bed in them for one last night, and dressed Salan's, and even the archer's. They're soft and smell of dry leaves. Heaven.

But even they can't keep me in bed. Wrapping up in my blanket, I go to our rooftop and gaze up at a starry sky that seems indifferent to my plight. Why wouldn't she be? Later, I watch the sun peek her head up from the horizon one last time.

"I don't remember ever having slept so well," the archer tells me, his head popping up from the stairway. He stretches and goes to our hearth, easing in next to me on the bench. I'm making a tea of rosemary, honey and some other things, and ladle it into a cup, handing it to him.

We sit in silence for the most part, save for the occasional nod of thanks the archer offers for a piece of flatbread, some nuts and dried fruit. He chews with his mouth closed for once.

"Your tea will get cold," I tell him.

He takes a deep sniff off a tendril of steam floating up from his cup and smiles with pleasure.

"We wouldn't want that," he says. "Are you sure you wouldn't like to drink it?"

"Oh, no, I've had plenty. I awoke early."

"Perhaps we should save it for your brother?"

"Salan?" I say. "He'll want goats' milk."

Raising the cup to his lips, he drinks it down in one, large swig. "Delicious," he says. "Just what I needed."

I smile and offer him a second, but he declines.

Salan is the last to rise, and he comes tottering out of his nursery, ready for me to kiss his forehead, give him his milk and an egg or two. He yawns and wings out his arms, then grasps my hair in his hands like reins.

"There's much to do before the heat burns away our comfort," the archer explains. He says more like him will be joining us before the sun touches the dunes, and we'll have to have everything ready to load the caravan as we begin our journey to the Waterless Sea. He goes to stand, but not with his usual pluck. Taking a deep breath, he sits down again and extends his legs. Leaning back, I watch him. His eyes are still keen, but his body has slowed. The tafir leaves I put in his tea are starting to take effect. Later than I hoped, but they do finally seem to be working. The archer folds his hands at his waist and catches eyes with me. Or catches me in his eyes is more like it. I have to remind myself that this isn't uncommon. Truth is compelling and tafir is unique in its ability to tear down inhibitions, letting verity walk unchained to the tips of our tongues before putting us gently to sleep.

I square my shoulders and lick my lips. It's now or never.

"What are you going to do with me?" I ask him.

His face is at rest, almost lacking any expression at all. He takes a long time to answer.

"Nothing you won't want yourself."

"Is that so?"

He nods.

"And what is it you think I'll want?"

The archer takes a deep breath, his chest rising and falling like a frond in the wind. He lifts his hand, drawing a finger through the air as if painting my face with it. His finger traces the length of my body as his eyes flutter closed.

I SPRING UP from the bench and scuttle down the stairs, pulling Salan along with me. In the courtyard, there's a sack of dry goods, smoked meat, linens and water that I've hidden under my lula bush. The flowers are in full bloom and their fragrance is more than thick enough to cover any trace of the foodstuffs. I look through them one last time and add a bit of jerky for Salan. We should have just enough to take us to the next settlement, I hope. Salan follows me out back, like a good boy, and I start to untether Beezu, my father's mule. The one he always claimed would never let him down. He's been tied tightly to his post and I don't remember making such a knot—it must have been *him*. Tucked under our rations is a paring knife, and I draw it out and start sawing away at the braided rope around Beezu's neck. I break a sweat from the start as I try to sever the line—hardly frayed from my attempts—and Beezu hee-haws at me like I'm the one who's the problem.

"Shh, I'm saving us both," I tell him. "So, stop acting up."

He doesn't stop. In fact, he angles back, making it even more difficult for me. I have to pull on that rope hard, until he yanks his head to the side, causing it to slip out of my hand quick, burning my palm.

"Now see what you've made me do!"

"Bad mule," Salan says, and then he tries to take up the rope. Beezu goes to nip at him and I have to swat the boy away, so he doesn't get a finger bit off. Salan starts to cry and I'm *this* close to joining him.

"You look like you could use a little help."

I gasp and spin around, and yes, there he is standing as straight as a palm—as if he wasn't dead asleep when I left him. And he's not alone. A line of men on camels, four of them, are right behind him. Dark and shiny skin, humorless faces.

"He's, uh, temperamental," I say. "I thought I should get him ready for you."

The archer comes over and starts to untie Beezu's knot— and the beast is acting all chummy now. He glances down, and I realize I'm still gripping the paring knife like I might stab it into something, or someone. I squat, sliding it right back under the twine where it came from and offer a weak smile.

A loud throat-clearing comes from a strange looking fellow. A thin jaw and thick neck makes him look like an antelope. The archer nods and the antelope man gestures to the others. They get down off their camels and spread about the place, going to work. The archer himself begins leading the large animals, tying them together, clucking and cooing at them in the way of men who have a finesse with nature. I shoo Salan off to the pantry and ask him to gather our spices—good work for someone his size. He sniffles a bit, but goes.

"Now I could use some help," the archer says. "Unless you had too much of that tea you concocted."

I take a rather haughty breath and he notices.

"Tafir is difficult to grow," he notes, squinting his eyes.

"Just takes a little extra care." I pick up mine and Salan's package and begin tying it to Beezu, who has turned out to be quite the traitor. The archer smiles, stroking the creature like he belongs to him. Which, I suppose, he now does.

"You must have a talent for life."

"I like to garden," I tell him. "Any growth is precious on the edge of a desert. It's a gift from the gods."

The archer shrugs. "It's one thing to like to garden and another to grow tafir as strong as yours. Usually does little to me, but your one cup nearly put me to sleep. You yourself must have an impressive tolerance for it. Didn't you say you had several cups this morning?"

I bite my lip and call out to Salan, telling him to make sure to wrap the spices twice, as they lose potency fast otherwise. I turn back to the archer, trying to seem casual. Touching lightly upon the rope burn across my palm.

"Tafir is common for settled people in the Rah'a," I tell him. "We're used to it. Where would a man of the desert come across it?"

"He wouldn't," the archer says. "I drank tafir a long time ago. Before I ever came to the desert." Taking my hand, he lays it open, blowing softly on the enflamed wound. Makes me shiver. "My mother used to make tea just like yours."

THE REST OF THE DAY brings with it hard work, and I do my share for no other reason than to make sure our things are cared for. To pack up a house as well appointed as my father's is no easy feat. And it isn't just the furniture, the linens, the pottery, and the stores, but our untethered animals as well. The chickens and herding dogs. Then there are the leather goods, metal, and feed.

It's a parade of my father's accomplishments—the life he and my mother forged together. And it's oddly consoling to see that our many fine things will be put to use again and not burned or left behind, as is often the case during acts of war and looting, when only the essentials are given value. The archer, for all of his faults—and there are many—is a man of economy, who seems to hold a genuine appreciation for quality and, at least I hope, civility.

About mid-morning, another caravan full of thick-set men arrives. They're part of his regiment, I assume, and wear a similar get-up to him and the men already here. Only their clothes are not dyed anywhere near as well. Muted brown with rings and flecks of lighter hues spot their dress in an ad-hoc fashion. Nor are these men as polite as the early arrivals, who understand the basic role of pleasantries. But they aren't mean either. Salan ducks next to a desert rose in our courtyard, peeking out from behind it, keeping an eye on them and reporting to me their every exchange.

Working well and quickly together, they give deference to the archer, calling him *sam*, which is basically like sir among the nomads. Several of the vendors at the marketplace used to call my father *sam*. So, it looks as if this *sam* has distinguished himself with much more than an immunity to Vara. Having begun his time with his prince as a prisoner, like me, he's clearly moved his way up, if they're calling him *sam* all the time. If I can be useful, maybe I can work my way up, and they'll let me keep Salan close, even raise him. If it comes to that.

So I show them how to wrap the linens properly, to keep them from being damaged on the road. I feed them from our dwindling stores—not that it makes a difference at this point—and help load and pack and tether. I take several clay pots from our kitchen and fill them with embers, to take fire with us. Sparking one with flint or sticks is murder after a long day of travel through the desert.

"What are you doing?" I ask him.

The archer is leading a camel to the front of my home.

Strong and diligent, this one, with a fine trim of expertly pleated leather on his saddle. I saw one of his men ride in on it.

"This is a camel," he says.

Obviously, it's a camel. I must have one of those looks on my face because the archer—I will not call him *sam*, especially not to myself—seems like he wants to say something smart, but thinks better of it. Instead, he signals one of his men—a tall one with arms too long for his body—and tells him to help me and Salan onto the animal. It had been his camel, the lanky one's, but he doesn't protest at all. With arms like elephant trunks, he boosts me on, then lifts up my brother. Taking the camel by its lead, he begins walking.

"We're leaving later than I hoped," the archer says. "But we'll still pass a few hours by nightfall." He pats the camel's rear and the creature moves faster, making Salan bounce. Behind us, the archer mounts his own camel and trots to the front of the caravan.

"North," he calls out. It's only a direction, but his men appear to know precisely where north we're headed.

"Ny-ny," Salan says, nuzzling against my breast.

He wants me to sing his night song and I try. My voice, clear and in tune, has always calmed him.

Only my song can't catch any magic. My breath betrays me and my voice quivers, at times getting stuck and letting no sound come from my throat at all. Salan knows it's sadness choking me. As our home begins to fade into the distance, my brother holds me. Looking over my shoulder, he cries.

I never look back. Instead, I look at my favorite linen slippers, watching the sunlight dance upon their dusty lilac shell. One day, I promise myself. One day, I'll come back here. No matter how long it takes.

NIF. I WORRY EVERY TIME I can't feel him near, and hate to even consider if his destiny has changed—if he's moved on from this cycle of death and birth that we've been joined in since my very first life.

It's why I find myself returning again and again to that time, as if I can find him there.

I page through the memories of our other lives, too. Thinking about the first time my soul had matured enough to look upon him as more than my lover. As everything. Since my lives are so short, that did take some time.

Nif, on the other hand, has always known. Maybe not always, but certainly sooner than I did. But then he's had an advantage over me. Nif has not been constrained by a seventeen-year lifespan.

"It's a testament to the human spirit how much our souls shape our appearance," Nif told me during one of the times our souls overlapped before another birth.

"What makes you say that?" I asked him.

"I'm trying to understand why I think you're so beautiful."

I know very well why he said this, because in our previous life I had not been beautiful by any standard. I had survived small pox and there was hardly a portion of my body that wasn't hideously scarred.

"It's not just your eyes," he continued. "No matter what people you're born to or who you become, you look remarkably similar to me."

Nif has died in infancy and lived to be one hundred and eight. In my less virtuous moments, I'm jealous.

"Don't envy me," he once said. "I'm the one who has to live so many of my years without you."

When we're apart, I long for the way he caresses my face with his gaze. I've always loved how he looks at me. Even at my ugliest—deformed, blemished, damaged—he makes me feel that I am a thing of beauty. And when I'm lovely—blond, willowy, a face like the sun, or a black swan of a girl with lips as rich and vivid as red rose petals—he makes me feel as if I'm so much more.

⟶ ⟨⟨⟩⟩ ⟨⟨⟩⟩ ⟶

"IT MUST HAVE BEEN a much larger region than we thought," I hear Neville say, and it startles me. His voice is clearer now, though it still crackles a bit. Like he's speaking through a 1930s radio broadcast. "Spread out over parts of what's now Libya and Chad, maybe even into Sudan."

Jordie is nodding his head, contemplating various fragments of antiquity: the blade portion of a small dagger, a royal seal, a bone hair pin—mine for all I know. He picks up the largest of the artifacts—a chipped carafe that's beautifully designed, as if the potter had known what an egret might look like as it floats on the glassy surface of a royal pond.

"Better climate then, more fertile," Jordie observes. "Pockets of farmable soil within striking distance of each other. There could have been dozens of settlements of various sizes surrounding the main city. Some quite sophisticated. And all reachable to a people accustomed to desert travel."

Jordie stretches on the gold velvet of the sofa. He looks out at their view of the Nile and sighs. "I'm afraid we'll have to get used to desert travel again now that we've got a proper dating on these things. Goodbye Ritz Carlton, hello poly-cotton tent."

"Could've had city-states," Neville says, quite ignoring their posh surroundings. "Or more than one kingdom. The smaller ones would have had to have been subservient to the sultanry. Certainly dependent on it to some extent."

Jordie reaches across the coffee table, his fingers hovering over a large mezze platter. They finally land on a beef kebab studded with sundried tomatoes and Aleppo peppers. "How is it that you always get put up at the Ritz in Cairo? I didn't think University of Virginia went for that sort of thing. State school and all."

"Hmm? Oh, the Ritz. It costs less here than a Holiday Inn in New York. Or DC for that matter."

Neil Neville cannot stop pondering the artifacts, staring at them, putting them in context . . . placing them in the hands of the people of the Rah'a. He strokes the bone hair pin.

"A full thousand years before the Sumerians." He says, shaking his head. "Artistic, advanced. Traders and farmers for God's sake. A military. And all done in by a massive sand-storm that lasted for at least a few years. Maybe more."

Neville runs his fingers through his thick short hair, scratching his scalp with a weary abandon. Jordie watches him. Sinking his teeth into the kebab, he chews slowly, as Neville's eyes dance over the carafe.

"Maybe," Jordie says. "Or maybe they were already dead, and the storm buried what was left." He sits up suddenly, a visible shudder running through him.

"What's the matter?" Neville asks him.

"Nothing. It's . . . no, it's nothing."

Jordie goes to the picture window. Cairo is lit up, familiar and mysterious all at once, like any modern city at night.

"Such a powerful sandstorm," he says. "Must have looked like the eye of Jupiter if seen from above the earth."

Neville goes to his friend, watching the ghostly outline of his own reflection in the window. For a moment, he sees his father in himself. The way he held his arms at his sides, as if ready. The broadness of his shoulders and straightness of his spine. Neil Neville has never missed his father more than right now.

"Feels like a punishment to you somehow?" He asks Jordie. "God's idea of wiping the slate clean and starting over. Or the devil's idea of a joke."

"And we've uncovered it."

Neville puts his hand on Jordie's shoulder, nearly cupping the whole of it.

"You're starting to sound like my wife, Dr. Mostafa."

Inhaling deeply, Jordie turns around. His eyes meet Neville's—wet and wide.

"You yourself have said your better half is the wisest woman you've ever known. Not to mention the prettiest. We could use her around here, Neil."

Neville smiles, wishing the woman he loves was here and not back in Virginia, teaching a full course load of both classical and modern Hebrew and mentoring future Biblical scholars. He shakes his head.

"Come on, man. You think it should've stayed buried for some reason? That we might be unleashing something that should've remained beneath the desert?"

Jordie cocks his head. "I honestly don't know."

Chapter 8

Finally, a Woman

WE PASS PILES of bodies whenever we come near what was once a population—some corpses still burning, others a smoking jumble of ash and bones. The stench alone makes my stomach churn. Empty settlements, wandering loners. Some watch us go by, not even curious. Others beg to come along, to be whatever we need. A servant, a concubine, a slave. Anything to get away from what they've lost.

To make matters worse, every day seems to get hotter as the fire season comes closer. Our tunics cling to our damp skin and no amount of water can quench our thirst.

"I want to go home," Salan cries. And cries and cries.

Salan is miserable, and I'm in no mood to comfort him. In fact, I'm in the foulest mood I have ever been in. It's days into the journey, and we have days more left. I hate it. We've stopped at a small oasis, and I mean *small*. I'm filthy and my mouth feels like a discarded old snake skin.

I can't manage to make anything but a grimace as I take in our surroundings. This patch of greenery is so meager it can hardly be called an oasis at all. A few tufts of grass and a shallow well is all there is. A small mercy. I dismount the camel, stretch and stroll around, letting Salan toss rocks in the shade of the caravan. Every part of me seems to ache, especially my lower belly. I'm drenched in sweat.

"Sherin," the archer beckons.

He says my proper name, and I narrow my eyes at him. It isn't as if I've introduced myself. I certainly don't know *his* name, and don't really want to. He must've heard Salan calling me. Just the other day, Salan went from calling me Shrim, which means seaweed and is obviously not my name, but was the only way he could pronounce it, to Sherin. I imagine our circumstances have grown him up.

The archer pulls one of our linens out of its packing—it's a dark tunic, midnight blue—and holds it out to me.

"You might want to put this on," he says.

The tunic I'm wearing is drenched in perspiration and coated in sand dust. I must look unkempt even by his standards.

"I'll roast in that tunic," I tell him. Dark colors in the midday desert sun are little better than setting yourself on fire.

"You can change in the tented carriage," he says. "I'll keep watch for you."

His words are all politeness, but his tone is that of an order. I glower, tearing the tunic from his hands.

"Yes, *sam*." If he wants me to broil in the sun, then *fine*.

Inside the carriage, I light a lantern from one of the embers we took from my house, then proceed to undress. I feel wet everywhere, and sticky. Dropping my pale tunic at my feet, I step out of my slippers and peer down briefly at my naked body. My toes are bright pink, irritated, and my ankles swollen. My eyes trail up my legs, and when they find my thighs, I gulp.

They're smeared in blood, with tiny rivulets running down, making way to my calves. Snatching my tunic from the floor, I hold it up to the lantern. Sure enough, a large red stain marks my seat. Sinking down into a crouch, I hug my knees and start to shake.

If we had never met that man in the market, today would be a day of celebration. Word would go out to my new husband's clan and my mother and Yina would start throwing together a final party for my wedding. Within days I would be a bride and my parents would never have to worry or toil again. In becoming a woman, I would have become a wife, a lady of stature who had brought much to those I love. A nice trade for a happy girlhood.

I'm hardly ignorant of what it means to become a woman under my present circumstances, and don't have the luxury of indulging in what was. I take a deep breath to steady myself, fight back my tears. From this day on, I can become pregnant and birth a child. No matter what the kingdom, or the custom in our lands, a man wants surety of the children he's sired, and a bastard child and his mother are the most hated members of society. My virginity, a given before the onset of menses for a woman of my station, is now a prize, and one I have no intention of giving to anyone but a husband. To lose it by force or give it away by foolishness can sentence me to a life of poverty or harlotry. Even as a prisoner, if I maintain my dignity I can hope for a better future in the kingdom I'll be entering in a few days' time. A better future for me and Salan.

Only now I'm fair game as far as the soldiers in our caravan are concerned. There is no telling when the men in the caravan have last taken a woman. Maybe days, if they had the chance to woo or rape one of the survivors in our region. Or weeks, or months. Whatever the case, if any of them have seen the stain on my tunic, they'll know that I'm no longer a child, and as their prisoner they'll feel entitled to use me in any way they wish.

Even I know that.

Once we enter the Kingdom of the Waterless Sea, culture will be a governor on their behavior—at least if the gods are merciful. But until then, it's all conquest and spoils.

I peek my head out of the tent and look about. The men are talking or napping—very casual as they have been on other stops. The archer is standing with his back to the carriage, keeping watch as promised. It isn't lost on me that I owe him a great deal.

Inside the carriage, I rifle through the stores until I find some water pouches. They're not under any circumstances to be used for cleaning the body, but I pour some onto my thighs anyway and use my pale tunic to wipe down the blood. I smear my blood all over the tunic and then my upper lip to make it look like I have a bloody nose. Tearing two good strips from the linen—I hold one to my face, and stuff the other between my legs. I dress myself in the deep, blue tunic the archer gave me and climb out of the carriage.

When the archer sees me, he walks over and holds the crumpled strip of cloth away from my face, pretending to examine my nose.

"Much better," he says. "But keep your head tipped up until it stops completely."

I pretend to do as he instructs, but my eyes can't help wandering over his men. I watch the antelope-looking one—I think his name is Taran—spit his hard, yellow mucus onto the head of one of our goats. She bleats and ducks. When Taran laughs, it's like a hyena. He sits with another man who has short, stout legs and horrible acne. That one is called Karat and he picks at his pimples while he eats.

One by one, I study the men around me. Hard men—a lot has been asked of them. Gruff and vulgar when left to their own devices. Tough, unafraid, the grunts of an unpolished army made up from a hard-scrabble culture.

"Water?" the archer offers.

"Thank you," I tell him, and he nods. He knows I'm thanking him for more than the water.

"You should ride in the carriage, under cover," he says. "The high sun is no place for dark colors."

I try my best at a smile.

"You look well," he says, his eyes brushing my face. He then pivots and advances back to the head of the caravan, bringing Taran with him. His robes flutter while he walks, a contrast to the stillness of the vista. The deadness of the air.

I lead Salan from the shade where he's been playing and we clamber into the covered carriage. In there, it's cooler and I lie down, placing one of the water pouches over my womb. A cold sweat pricks my temples and I start to shiver again.

Despite the obliteration of what I've known as my life, the idea of being raped by a dozen men is a fresh hell, and one I can barely bring myself to contemplate. I turn my attention to Salan.

My brother is in much better spirits now, and takes to amusing himself. In the back, behind the linens, he uncovers the clay doll of our mother that I packed for him. He wanted it as we left our house, but I couldn't remember where I'd put it. Now, he holds the doll in his fingers, kissing it and making it walk along the floor. It's such a simple motion, one I've seen him perform a hundred times, and one rooted in our lives before the troubles began.

"Mir-yam," he says. It's the first time he's endeavored to say our mother's full name since I claimed him in his nursery after her death. Salan is all names today.

"Yes, Miriam," I say.

The carriage shuffles along and I watch my brother slowly get hypnotized by the motion. Eventually, his eyes flutter and close, and the clay doll of our mother slips from his fingers. I watch it lying there for a few moments before I pick it up. Such a sweet thing, it captures her essence with little more than a good sculptor's eye for true proportion. I kiss the top of its head and lift up the canvas, dropping the doll into the desert.

Chapter 9

The Prince's Bride

WHILE WE DID STOP to loot a couple of smaller settlements along the way, the archer's men destroyed little and took no liberties with the few remaining women we encountered. That, in itself, is a rarity I had thought exclusive to the men in the Rah'a's army.

The last settlement we traveled through was fairly large, but completely ravaged by Vara, with only a handful of dazed survivors meandering about the houses. An old woman, the last of her family, told us several of the victims contracted it in their brains. In their madness, they killed a good number of those who'd been left standing, before succumbing to death themselves. Awful to look into her face as she said this. So hopeless, heartbroken. Her cheeks pruned by hunger and a campaign of woe.

"Why haven't we taken more people with us?" I ask as we sit for supper. Salan plops onto my lap, while I make every attempt to steady him and pick the residue of daily grime from the corners of his eyes. When I finish, he nuzzles to my breast, peaking at the archer through his long, black lashes. He's stopped asking about the little figure of Miriam, and starts humming a song about a newborn lizard with a spiny tail. One Yina used to sing to him.

"Walking through the desert is no easy feat for people barely clinging to life," the archer says. He hands me some sun-warm flatbread and goat's milk cheese. "Not everyone is as strong as you. Or your brother."

Salan tries not to smile, but can't help himself. He pinches the muscle of my arm and sits up tall, going eye to eye with the archer this time.

"Sherin made the funeral fire all alone," he says.

"Funeral pyre," I correct him.

"That takes great strength indeed," the archer tells him.

I don't think of myself as strong, but I'm not going to tell Salan that. Or the archer. I'm simply doing what I have to do. There's a man we took with us from one of the settlements neighboring mine. He is strong. He calls himself Adamen and is angry all the time. Maybe if I was angrier, I could feel stronger.

"Were you strong when the Vara visited your home?" I ask.

The archer sips from his water pouch, offering some to me and my brother. His eyes soften, anointing his face with a tender sorrow.

"I was a boy," he says.

———— ◈◈ ◈◈ ————

ON THE EIGHTH DAY of our journey, the landscape changes. The dunes are less vivid, like a crumbling wilderness. Dirty-looking, inhospitable, unhappy is this new environment. I know we've reached the outer edges of the Rah'a and will be entering the Waterless Sea.

Well before sunset, we stop to camp near a series of caves. They're peopled with more of the archer's men, who come pouring out of every tunnel and crevasse like a colony of ants. The men stoke a fire inside the largest cave, oval and high like a giant egg. They're preparing for dinner. At the mouth of the cave, I sit on my heels with Salan at my side. The archer approaches, crouching beside us, which has become his habit.

"Are these your caves?" I ask him.

"My caves? The caves belong to the dunes and the dunes belong to themselves."

"Is that so?"

"That's the dune crescent." He points to a sorry series of dunes to the north. "I lived there as a child, not long after I came to the desert."

I try to think of something, anything positive to say about his boyhood home, but come up empty.

"They're easy to slide down in parts and climb in others, unlike the ones in the Rah'a. Those are handsome, but a boy can hardly play on them."

I know he's trying to be friendly and make conversation, but I can only nod in response. I'm plain exhausted.

"By noon tomorrow we'll enter my kingdom," he says. "Then it should only be two days' time until we reach the palace fortress." He looks at the ground, scratching his finger into the sand. "Are you still bleeding?"

"No," I say. And whatever blood I have left has found its way to my cheeks, where it burns.

"Good." He's as relieved as I am that this part of the conversation is behind us. "First thing in the morning, I want you to dress as a woman of your station. You can use some of our water stores to bathe."

"A well-dressed slave?" I didn't mean for it to sound as sharp as it did. But there you have it.

He shakes his head and looks out at the lonesome vista, then back to me.

"A bride for the prince."

He gets up and goes to the fire, leaving me dumbstruck. I thought maybe I hadn't heard him right at first. How would a prince, even a lesser one, know who I was? Unless he was somehow aware of my fiancé and his family, their wealth and status. That is a possibility.

Or perhaps he sent men like the archer to search for a suitable Rah'a bride? A bride who's immune to a plague that's already devastated his lands, leaving a strong group of survivors in its wake. A bride who will raise his status.

As I look out into the distance, out of the Rah'a and onto the lands that belong to the Waterless Sea, I understand why a girl like me could be a pick. Having never left the Rah'a, I've had no idea how rich we are compared to other kingdoms.

"Archer!" I cry out. I don't know what else to call him.

He's talking to Taran and turns briefly to me, then back again.

"Damn the wind!" I holler. "If you're right and I'm a bride for your prince of nothing then I think you should answer when I call you."

A hush comes over them and Taran glowers. As for the archer, his back turns to granite before he pivots and stomps over to me. I think for a moment that he's going to hit me, but he doesn't.

"Let me make myself clear," he hisses. "Until we reach the fortress, you're in my charge. I alone decide what to tell the prince if misfortune happens to meet you on our journey. And I alone decide if my men need comfort."

I try to look as if I can stand my ground, but in all honesty, I've turned to mush. Disrespecting him publicly, insulting his monarch. My damned, stupid pride.

"Forgive me. I meant no offense." I flit my eyes over to his men and they all glare back, hating me.

"*Sam*, I need to ask you something," I say, lowering my voice. I bow in apology to him, then the others. "Did you decide that I was going to be a bride for your prince, or was that his decision?"

His demeanor changes—I can hear it in his breath. Short, angry puffs before, but now the archer inhales long and deep, like a gust of wind. I don't look up, but I can feel him smiling.

"That was my decision," he whispers.

"What if he doesn't like me?" The words come tumbling out like spill from a grain sack. I steal a glance at him. "What I mean is, if the prince rejects me, what will become of me and my brother?"

The archer folds his hands in front of him. His fingernails have a layer of desert dust beneath them—reddish-brown, like the sky at dusk. He twiddles his thumbs, as if he's considering what to tell me, what not to tell me.

"The decision is final," he says. "You have my promise."

Taran beckons him, but the archer waves him away. He presses his lips together and leans in closer, to speak right into my ear.

"And my assurance that you'll go to him with your honor intact."

A waft of his scent—baked-in sweat and the faintest hint of rosemary from our meal—blows at me from the flap of his robe as he returns to Taran and the others. It's a comforting smell.

I know little of the culture I'll be entering into—marrying into, if I'm to believe this archer. In the Rah'a, decisions are made for others all the time. My own engagement wasn't my decision or my fiancé's. It's possible even the sultan has some of his wives brought to him, given as gifts.

I'll be one of many brides, probably, and from what I've heard, it's not uncommon in lands outside the Rah'a for a wife to be treated as little better than a concubine. If she's of a lesser station, she might even be regarded as a slave. But I don't have the luxury to contemplate what I like or don't like about any of this. All I know is that I'll be able to keep Salan and give him something resembling a good life, and I have to remind myself that's all that matters. Even if I'm one of a hundred brides, or a thousand, or if the prince is repulsive to me in both his person and character.

Because I don't have the luxury to dwell on that either.

"You're that bride, aren't you?" It's the angry one, Adamen. I think for a moment that he's referring to my conversation with the archer, but he's not. He recognizes me for what I used to be—a bride for one of the wealthiest sons in our region.

"I've been waiting for a chance to talk to you."

I almost ask why, but truth is, I don't want to know. Adamen's presence is oppressive and willful. He stands too close when he knows very well that a mala requires space around her. It's like he's doing it on purpose, letting me know the old rules no longer apply.

"You must want to cut him from throat to belly," he rasps. Adamen watches the archer move gracefully between his men.

He sniffs and flexes his biceps—substantial, that of a man accustomed to hard labor—and cracks his knuckles one by one. "That'll be my pleasure."

"He did take you with him," I say.

"After destroying the Rah'a."

The scent of Adamen's sweat is bitter, laced with fear and trauma. Not a comfort at all.

"You don't know that," I say.

"Don't I? He comes riding in soon after the Vara takes us—you think that's a coincidence?"

"I don't," I admit. "But even if it's true, it's hardly the man's fault if his prince is a warlord. Any more than it's our fault we have to go with these men."

Adamen tosses his head and cackles like a murder of crows.

"I just want to keep my brother safe," I tell him. The last thing I need is more trouble, and this Adamen is trouble.

"Safe," he snorts. "You'll never be safe again."

I RISE EARLY, well before the sun, and sit for a few minutes listening to the snores and grumbles around me. I slept poorly, but I'm learning to appreciate the quiet that comes with the night. It's the only time I have to myself, to ponder the sky, and bathe in my senses—the cool air at my back and the heat of the fire at my face. During the day, I can only think about Salan and survival. At night, there's still some small part of me that believes things can get better.

Rubbing my arms, I try to stave off the chilly desert morning. One of the men is dreaming and calling for his mother. Makes me smile. Especially since he's the biggest of the soldiers, with an abundance of hair on his head and face and back.

I pull a tunic out of the stores. It's my best—pink—and makes me look like a tulip. My mother embroidered its sleeves with what had always looked to me like droplets of rain, but Miriam insisted they were tears of joy. She made the tunic shortly after my birth and gave it to me only days before we met our fate at the marketplace. It was to be my wedding dress. I caress its fabric, one my mother touched a thousand times.

Untying a water pouch from traitorous Beezu, I get to work. The water is as warm as fresh urine, but does the job. I watch a thick film of dirt melt off my skin as I spill the water over my legs. I wrap my hair into a coil high on top of my head, securing it with a bone pin. Then a touch of dye to add color to my lips. No amount of pride or grief will be undoing me today. I have Salan to think of.

"You look very fine."

The archer comes up behind me, his voice mellow, like he had a good night's sleep.

"Your tunic," he says. "I've never seen one better. Your mother had a gift."

"What would you know of my mother?" I regret it the moment I say it.

"I've seen her work. What more do I need to make a judgment about her skills?"

I want to tell him that she was so much more than that. She was loving and brave and inquisitive. Wonderful company with a voice as clear as a wind instrument.

"You need to know nothing more about her," I say in my most pleasant voice, as if I'd slept well, too. "She was very skilled."

The archer looks out onto the horizon. There isn't a hint of the sun yet. "This is my favorite time of day." He says it like it's a confession

"It's still night."

"No," he says. "And that's what I like so much about it. Its deception."

So, he likes deception. Deception can mean surprise or duplicity and I don't know which he prefers.

"Why did you have me wash and dress if we won't reach your prince's palace for another two days?"

The archer puts his hands behind him. The firelight flickers over his face and I notice he's younger than I realized. Odd I didn't see it before, but then I've been making a point of not looking at him too closely.

It's his beard that gives him the appearance of an older man, but as I examine his skin and the subtle lines around his eyes, I see it's possible he isn't much older than I. The desert is harsh and ages a man who dwells in it. The archer should have a rougher edge to his face. Perhaps he grows the beard to age him, and hide the sweetness of his features.

Nobody likes to be ordered about by someone who looks like a boy.

"Will he be meeting us here—your prince? Shall we ride to his palace together?" I ask.

"Sherin," he says, letting go of his smile. "The prince has no palace. There is a fortress some distance away, where we keep weapons and stores, but otherwise we're not a settlement. Not as you know it. We're a desert people and we live under canvas."

Ah, the prince of less than nothing then. The prince of war and thievery and disease warfare, if Adamen is right. Of taking what others worked hard for, and stealing wives meant for better men. I want more for my brother, but choice is another thing I've been robbed of by the Prince of the Waterless Sea, with his boastful, oligarch's name. I look up at the archer and smile as graciously as I can. It isn't his doing that he has to bow to a man like that. He's an orphan of the Vara too, after all.

"Is that him?" A faint glow taints the sky, ushering in the day. Distant on the horizon, I can see what looks like another caravan approaching.

"What?"

"Out there," I say.

The archer's eyes follow mine and his face falls. Raising his hand high, he opens his mouth as wide as if he's about to bite into a roast. From his lips come a cry that has been only a legend to me until now.

"Kaji! Kaji!" he screeches. "Kaaaaa-jiiiiiii!"

Every cell in my body awakens. Every hair stands. Blood surges through my veins like a storm.

This is a war cry. I've heard boys in the Rah'a use it when they play at battle. But the archer's cry is nothing like theirs's. Not a hint of high adventure touches his voice. What his cry has is a guttural quality—animal—meant to block out fear and fuel adrenaline.

The men get to their feet. Many are groggy and confused, but the archer continues with the call until all of them are up and readying the camp. Some build fortifications, others prepare weapons. The archer, organized, used to thinking on his feet, gives orders, shouting a set of strategies indecipherable to anyone but his regiment.

Salan scuttles over to me, terrified and throwing a fit. His tunic has come undone. I tie his robes together and offer my back for him to climb on. We watch the men create makeshift ramparts, arranging the architecture of the battlefield to work to our advantage—whatever that advantage might be. I know nothing of fighting. I do whatever is asked of me, though—sharpen knives, fill water pouches. If my eye is true, we have less than an hour until the battle begins. It could be a tribal skirmish, against poor weaponry and badly trained fighters that the archer's small army can easily vanquish. Or it could be what I fear in my heart it is—the sultan's army come to head us off at the pass, slaughter each and every one of us as they defend what's left of their ravaged empire.

Chapter 10

Clash

IT'S EERILY QUIET before the battle. Birds don't caw, the wind doesn't blow, even the breath of the soldiers becomes so low it's as if they've stopped breathing altogether. It's a strangely comforting phenomenon, too, allowing body and mind to weave into one cloth. All of us feel it.

Salan and I are perched at the mouth of the central cave, the egg one, looking out over the battlefield. Below us is the Army of the Waterless Sea. They're in configuration, ready, and look surprisingly expert for a troop that's a band of desert nomads. The archer is to the right of his men, staring out onto a plum view of the advancing enemy. Those men are organized and in formation. Bigger in numbers. They line up a charriot's run from the men in the archer's front line, standing in stillness with an odd aura of etiquette, considering what is about to happen.

Despite the looming threat of the Vara, the sultan has dispatched his men to keep his kingdom intact. Perhaps they're a band that's immune, like the archer and his men. Like me and Salan. Covered head to foot in battle wear, their hairless bodies are protected by plates of armor and headdresses. Those are round and polished to mirror their bald heads. They wear fine lace-up boots. The way they march in unison; there is inevitability in each step they take.

I ball my fist and put it to my chest, feeling my heart pound.

I love the Rah'a, and I don't want it to fall. But I can't rejoice in the carnage this desert will see by the time the sun sets. Yes, the sultan's soldiers are my people, but I'll die by their hands if they win. Or become a purloined bride if they lose.

The archer looks up at me. I realize I've been staring at him this whole time. He nods, raising his palm. A familiar gesture both in and out of the Rah'a, as common as a smile, and means that he has my back.

I return the salute despite the fact that I'm essentially committing an act of treason by doing so. One unthinkable to me only a few weeks ago; as unthinkable as the prospect of being an orphan, a mother to my brother, a piece of stolen property for a desert prince, if he can even be called that.

But I'm indebted to the archer, and my father taught me that personal debts are always repaid. It's the way of the gods and takes precedence over the way of the world. I put my hand to my heart and feel my chest rise and fall with my breath.

"Salan," I whisper. But I'm not talking to my brother. I'm referring to the meaning of his name, "to be."

Rending my eyes away from the archer, I let them flow from man to man. They clutch spears and javelins, bows and arrows, slings, swords, clubs, maces, axes, and knives. The men are leaning in, chins jutted, shoulders squared. Their expressions are dogged, fierce. I look at Salan and he seems much older, a look of awe on his face.

From the battlefield comes a swell of voices. "Kaj-iiiiiii! Kaj-iiiiii!" The calls ascend to the heavens, as if beckoning the skies to part and summoning the gods themselves to join in the battle. Salan, too, mimics the sound, caught up in the building storm. The calls grow louder, shriller—a maddening noise that is neither human nor animal. I cover my ears. It's a song for death, rhythmic and disjointed all at once, imbuing the air with an unbearable friction.

Then, all of a sudden, the tension breaks.

A clash of metal against metal, the sluicing thuds of swords meeting flesh, and clubs crushing bone. Screams of pain, shouts of aggression—all playing a relentless concerto of violent purpose.

Will and rage kindle, cracking and spidering like lightning. Time runs forward and stumbles backward all at once. During some points, the men's limbs move sluggishly, their legs shaking in an endeavor to remain standing. Blood is smeared over faces, bodies lie on the ground—kicked, stepped upon, fought upon. Cries of agony. I can barely stand them. Pulling Salan close to me, I try to shield his eyes. I bite my lip so hard that it bleeds, but at least it helps me know I'm still alive.

In parts, the battle stops. But then the calls start again— *Kaj-iiiiii!*— I make the call too. It's impossible not to. The war song, as if casting a spell, revives the men who could not go on—the burned-out, the injured and dying. The frenzy begins all over again.

I find my eyes searching for the archer, catching a glimpse of him as he surfaces, then plunges again into the rough sea of battle. Thinking, ducking, spinning, shoving, swinging his weapon in a dance. He moves differently from his men, who are coarse and brutal. And so unlike the sultan's soldiers—who are all power and ferocity. The archer boils over the battlefield like a troubled river after a torrent of rain.

Salan starts to pull on my tunic. "Look," he shouts, as an axe cuts through a man's throat. It's one of the archer's men. He gave Salan a satchel of beans to use as a pillow last night. I pinch my eyes shut and open them again.

"You need to eat," I say to Salan.

"I'm not hungry," he yells above the uproar.

"Now!" I grab his elbow and pull hard, practically dragging him into the cave. He shoots me a look of defiance—cheeks all sucked in, nose twitching. Twisting his arm, he pulls away.

Neither of us has eaten since the crack of dawn. Not that I have an appetite. But Salan can't feed on the blood and fury out here. He's a child. Food, I hope, will take his mind away from death and remind him about living.

"Come on," I say, offering him my hand. He hesitates, but takes it.

"I want to stay."

"I know," I tell him. "In a little while. All warriors need to fill their bellies. Even future warriors. Like you."

We walk deeper into the cave, where a fire is still burning and there are stores of food. From a woven basket I pull out some barley cakes. Salan chews with no interest, stealing glances at the mouth of the cave. He's fidgety and his knees knock.

Here, the battle seems miles away. I feel remote and detached, like after the deaths of my parents. I matched suits on our floor then, and marked my wins with pomegranate syrup, although their bodies were so close that if I'd reached out, I could have touched them. Now, I'm doing something as mundane as stoking a fire, while men die only a few steps away.

Salan wrinkles his nose when I offer him our drinking pouch.

"It's sour fruit," I tell him.

He does put the weak wine to his lips and swallows dutifully. I'm hoping the wine will settle him some, but no. He starts running back and forth from the fire to the front of the cave, getting glimpses of the battle, despite my protests. He cries out whenever he sees the archer, letting me know all of his limbs are still intact.

The archer. While his army is making an impressive show, they can't possibly triumph over the sultan's professional soldiers and exemplary weapons. Even if the opposing battalions are similar in size.

Defeat will be slow, then sudden, the way men lose fortunes or wives. I may be young, but I do know that.

Salan puts his barley cake to my lips and I nibble off a chunk, chewing with no pleasure. I peer into the depths of the cave which, by the looks of it, goes on forever.

"It's just like the apartments," I say.

Salan looks up at me. He knows the apartments. They're a series of caves near where we grew up, and serve as comfortable homes for middle class merchants in our region. We visited them with my father only a few months ago. To buy thread for my mother and some fine pottery.

Lighting a torch, I take Salan by the hand again, but this time he wants up. Though he's getting too big to carry around, I lift him onto my hip, where he's content to eat his barley cake.

At the back of the cave, the path narrows, but does appear to go on. Some caves, like the apartments, have crooked passages that snake through to the other side. Others, of course, simply end.

"There is a wind in the desert that murmurs; there is a wind in the desert that speaks of secrets," I sing to Salan. *"There is a wind in the desert that bellows; there is a wind in the desert that wails with anguish."*

As we venture deeper into the passage, my torchlight glances upon several drawings—simple, but beautiful. They're of camels, cows, goats, and horses, with a few men, represented mostly by red-earth lines. Salan reaches out to touch them.

"Father," he says, running his little finger along the lines of a man who does, in fact, resemble our father. Our father, who on a day like today would be tending to our animals just as the line-drawn man is tending to his on the walls of the cave.

"You see," I say, kissing his forehead. "Our father lives on.

And he'll always live in this cave. Whenever you feel lonely, you can think of this place."

Salan is pleased to hear that. He puts his lips to my neck and blows, making a silly noise.

"The wind is a friend or a devil in the desert. You can follow him home, or be consumed by his hunger, walk in his path or eternally slumber."

I turn and start down the corridor again, Salan's arms wrapped around my neck. But instead of a free step, we walk straight into a man. I drop my torch and my brother gasps and hiccups, then begins to cry.

"Shut up," the man says.

The torch has fallen at his feet and its light glows upwards. It's Adamen.

"Shh," I tell Salan, and squeeze his hand.

"What are you doing here, Mala?" It's the first time in weeks I've heard myself directly addressed as Mala and it feels hollow, like a phony compliment.

"Same thing you are," I say.

Adamen smiles, but there's nothing light in his expression. It's a mean smile, drawn-lipped. He knows as well as I do that our hours are numbered.

Adamen picks up our torch and walks deeper into the tunnel. "Come on," he says.

I rise to my feet, pulling Salan up with me and follow. We can hardly stumble back to the fire in the pitch dark.

"Mala, you seem social with the man who leads this group of drifters," he says.

He uses the word "social" casually enough, but it stings of accusation.

"I didn't know him until he came to my home."

Adamen looks over his shoulder and licks my face with his gaze. "Neither did I. But I have seen him around."

"Where?"

"Around, as I said. In town, the marketplace." Adamen scratches at an island of hair above his breast, groaning with satisfaction. "His people were always coming to trade. They have few markets in their region. Not enough farms. Where else would they get their needs?"

"They've taken their needs this time," I say. It all seems like such a waste.

"And what are they going to do when they run out of stores?" Adamen asks. "Primitives. Without the Rah'a, they'll be left scraping to get by. Where will they trade, hmm?"

I have no idea. And I don't care. Our conversation is making me cross. At the Prince of the Waterless Sea, at Adamen for stealing our torch, and at the archer and his men.

"They'll probably die out within a generation," Adamen grunts. "Most of our surrounding regions depend on the Rah'a like children."

Adamen stops quite suddenly. His breath becomes faster and harder. Cramming my torch between two rocks, he kneels and starts moving rubble.

"Don't just stand there, Mala," he says. "You were all action before the sultan's army showed up."

He hoots and I finally see what he's excited about. Between rocks fitted in like mud bricks, there are a few, tiny specks of light. They must be coming through from the outside.

I kneel down and start to work with Adamen. Picking up a few small rocks, I put them in a circle for Salan, near the torch, so he can see and play. He isn't much interested in the rocks, but watches Adamen and I as we dig and pull.

"Beautiful!" Adamen crows.

He's made a hole from one of the tiny specks of light—one the size of an eyeball.

"Desert. It just goes on. No soldiers, no nothing. Look."

I lunge toward the little hole, surprised by my own eagerness. He's right. The rear of this cave leads all the way to the other side, well out of sight of the battlefield. It will take at least another hour to dig a hole big enough for us to crawl through. All we have are our hands, and those are already bloody and scraped. By then, the battle could be over and we could be prisoners again.

But hope is hope, isn't it? Even someone who seeks to end his own life does so in the hopes that his pain will end with it. And right now I hope that the desert will be kinder to us than a regiment of the Sultan's soldiers. So, I pick up a rock with a sharp edge and begin to dig.

"Come on, boy, you help, too," Adamen growls, throwing a rock at Salan's head, but missing.

"He's barely a boy," I say. My brother puts his arms around my waist, resting his chin, warily, between my shoulder blades.

"When I was his age, my mother put me to work."

"Carrying milk jugs, maybe, but not digging through a wall."

Adamen picks up a sharp-edged stone the size of a small melon. "You put that boy to work, Mala."

"If he works, I don't."

I bend and kiss Salan, smoothing his grime-stiff hair. He's tired and cranky and thirsty. I should've thought to bring more water.

"Lie down," I say. "Take a nap. It's dark and cool and we have plenty of time."

"No," he says. He's all bravado, but his eyes are droopy and he looks as if he's going to fall down.

"Salan," I say. "Take a short nap and you'll be of much better use to us. Then you can dig."

He gives Adamen an evil glare, but slowly begins to back down.

"Good little man," I say.

I arrange a bed for him out of dirt and sand and he curls

up into it like a puppy. Breath steady and strong, his nose cold. Then I pick up my rock again and begin to dig. I can feel Adamen watching me, but I don't look up. We work in silence, both of us hoping that when we meet the other side, a worse fate doesn't await us.

Chapter 11

An Old Acquaintance

"**T**HE DESERT IS WEEKS in that direction alone."
Adamen points randomly at the horizon.

After more than an hour of being hunched over piles of rocks, we're thirsty, wet and hot and cold all at once. Our fingernails worn down and broken. All to dig a hole just large enough for us to slither through. Now here we are—Salan, Adamen, and I—at the outside end of the caves. Separated by stone and sand and winding caverns, we can no longer hear the wild battle only a bull's run from where we stand. Assuming it's still going on. I do realize our efforts must be folly. An act of desperation, of hoping to return somehow to what was. I can't help thinking about the warm embrace of our father's house, though. How Salan and I, if we could get back there, might be able to survive.

"We're a good ten days from my home. Five from yours," I remind him, brushing the dirt off my fine dress. Does little good.

"And you want to go back there?" he says. "That's as sure a death as any. At least I know how to walk through the desert."

I, myself, do not. Salan most definitely doesn't. My brother is coiled around my leg, having just woken up. His sweet fingers stroke my calf.

"We were surviving fine until—"

"Until scavengers took you and every one of your belongings." Adamen squats and begins drawing with his finger into the sand. He's composing a map of sorts, portraying the Rah'a dunes. He marks where several small settlements have stood and depicts the sultan's palace with a square block.

"And what about the sultan's men?" he says. "Like the ones back there, who are willing to risk Vara to fight your friend. Men like that'll be coming through your happy settlement in a few days' time, if they haven't already. They'll burn whatever is left and kill any survivors."

I hate his mocking tone and the way he constantly refers to the archer as my friend. The archer is no more my friend than his, given our circumstances. And whatever favor I've received from the archer is because he's been tasked with choosing a Rah'a bride for his master, and figures I'm a pretty good find.

I mention none of this to Adamen, though. He's the type of man who can always find a way to use information for his own gain, or another's misfortune.

"How do you know what the sultan's soldiers will or won't do?" I ask him. "From what I've heard, areas that have been ravaged by plague are cleaned up over months and resettled. Especially where we're from—fertile runs of soil and water wells are better than gold."

Adamen spits, just missing Salan, and my brother pulls himself up, wrapping his arms around my waist.

"You think you're a lot smarter than you are," Adamen says.

"I could say the same of you."

He slaps me and I stumble, my head thumping against the cave wall. Salan screams, flailing his arms at Adamen.

"Stop it," I say, grabbing his scruff. "I'm fine."

Salan has never seen anyone hit me before. It isn't

something my father would've ever done. As for me, I know there's a lot worse that a man like Adamen could do.

"Shut him up," Adamen says. He rubs his hands together, itching to make a fist.

I lift up Salan and set him on my hip again, bouncing, kissing his cheek. But he's tired and thirsty and hungry on top of it all. He starts to cry and won't stop.

"Shhh," I keep saying. "It was nothing."

Salan snivels, heaving breaths.

"You might as well leave him here," Adamen tells me. He rolls his shoulders, grimacing and erasing the map with his foot. "It's either that or bury him on the way, and I want someone who can take care of herself."

And take care of him. I know exactly what he means.

Salan, growing more hysterical by the moment, buries his face into my shoulder. I hold him tighter, shutting out the wind that's begun picking up. Shutting out Adamen.

"I told you to keep him quiet!" Adamen squints his eyes into slits. His meaty lips twitch at the corners.

"You little hyena!" He snarls as he grabs Salan's wrist.

"Savage!" I take a firm grip of Salan by his collar and ankle, but Adamen is too strong. He smacks my brother's head with his palm, and twists his arm until the boy begins to holler. With his other hand, Adamen takes a fistful of Salan's hair, and yanks him to the ground.

My scream is so loud I can hear nothing else. Not my brother, or the string of curses firing out of Adamen's mouth. And certainly not the wind, which is now making the sand swirl.

The collar of Salan's soft tunic slips from my hand. In its stead, I grab Adamen's ear, trying to tear it from his head. Adamen hisses, letting my brother fall to the ground. In a single movement, one of startling grace and venom, he raises his foot high, preparing to stomp Salan's head.

"Die!" The word comes from somewhere deep within me. A curse on him. And I yell the word as the archer's soldiers had *"Kaji,"* the war cry. I almost sing it, savoring its every note. "Die! Die! Die!"

Something changes in the air. It's electric, undeniable. Then fades like a water stain in the hot, desert sun. Even Adamen feels it and steps back, his mouth open wide.

Salan seizes this opportunity and shoots up from the ground, dashing past me, fast, like a hare. And I follow.

"I'll eat him raw," Adamen bellows. "Then I'll kill you if you're lucky!"

I close in on Salan, pulling him up. His limbs wrap tight around my torso. Wheezing, my mouth dry as dust from the desert air, I fight for each step. The rocky plates surrounding the dunes melt away, and my feet sink into the sand. With every stride, my muscles burn and I slow, as if I'm wading through tree sap.

"Miriam!" Salan screams. Our mother isn't here and can't help us.

"Damn the wind!"

I know Adamen is closing in on us. I can feel it.

"Wa-ha-wa," the sound comes from our wake, muffled by that desert wind, which blows this way and that.

I fall to my knees, and Salan hangs about my torso like a breastplate. The ones the sultan's soldiers wear are inlaid with the image of a serpent's mouth, open and about to strike. Mine is a frightened boy. Flesh and blood, not metal. I'm so tired I can barely move.

"She's a traitor!" I hear Adamen call out.

Salan lets go of me, collapsing into a tuft of sand. There's an instant quiet, except for the wind, which continues to grow reckless and unruly. It barks threats at us like a drunken husband.

I turn around and there is Adamen, standing before a row

of the sultan's soldiers and pointing his finger at me. My heart begins to pound so hard it feels like it might burst.

"She helped him. I saw her!"

Nothing seems real. Not the hot squalls of air, or the form the sand takes when it blows up from the ground—a twisting stalk that puffs up high, then dissolves.

"She held her hand up like this," he says, gesturing as I had to the archer in Salan, *to be*. "They're good friends, I tell you. And from long before. She said so. She said they knew each other from the market."

He looks right at me as he lies.

"I bet she's the one who led him into the Rah'a, with his diseases and greedy hands!" He looks to the soldier at his left, a compact man with a neck of string and muscle. "You should have seen the men they killed on the way here. The women they took like beasts and left to die."

"No!" I say. "None of it's true!"

Adamen steps forward, and the soldiers let him.

"I saw her enter the caves with that boy and I followed her," he tells them. "It was like this hole was waiting for her. Dug before. She was going to signal him from here, that's what I say!"

Adamen stands wide-legged, assuming the posture of the sultan's soldiers like he's one of them.

"I think this whore was his lover from the start. And I bet you that boy—he's no brother, but their son."

Salan nuzzles closer to me and the soldiers take notice. He does look like my son. And I have been Salan's mother from the moment our own mother died.

"He's my brother," I say. "I'm all he has."

A cluck and "ha" breaks through the wind. It's the sound of attention for a soldier, I've heard it before. In the market, when shopping with my parents. The cluck is a loud smack of the tongue against the roof of man's mouth, and the "ha" like the crack of a whip. It's unmistakable. The soldiers fist their hands, putting them at the smalls of their backs. Right foot forward, eyes down, chin up. They "ha" once in position, then shift to the side, making way for a broad man who moves like water.

"Commander!" the stringy-necked soldier shouts.

Adamen fidgets. He holds his hands behind his back at first, then folds them across his chest. To copy the soldiers outright would be an insult. In the end, Adamen drops his hands at his sides, but stands in every other way like the men surrounding us. A wise move from a talented survivor. It shows his allegiance.

"Is this a party?" the commander asks.

He's impressive, strong. Closely shaved from head to toe, and bare but for a leather skirt across his loins. I catch myself staring, and look quickly to the ground. Breathing deeply, I take in the smell of urine on Salan's tunic, and the parched, fruitless perfume of the desert.

Hearing one of the men step forward, I glance up and see him point to Adamen.

"This one claims she's a traitor to the Rah'a," he says.

The commander pivots, leaning toward Adamen, looming over him. If Adamen is tall, this man is taller by nearly half a head.

The wind is coming closer, threatening to break into a storm, but the soldiers don't even stir. No one dares. Not even Salan, who might normally ignore the ways of adults. I put one hand up to my eyes, shielding them, trying to watch the exchange and listen for an opportunity to defend myself. My eyes are seared, raw, as weary as my legs. Everything's all a blur.

"Do you know this woman?" the commander asks.

"I know her."

Adamen swallows.

"Well?"

"Well enough, I think," he says. "She was friendly with that thief from the Waterless Sea. She's his and that boy is, too."

The commander steps toward me, turning his back to Adamen.

"Stand up," he tells me.

I peel Salan's arms and legs away from me, teetering up to a standing position. Salan gets up, too, hooking his hands around me from behind. I keep my gaze cast down to show respect, and hope my brother is doing the same.

"Take a good look," the commander says to Adamen. "This is the woman you mean?"

I clutch the fabric of my once beautiful garment, balling it in my fists.

"Yes," Adamen says.

"And you knew her before the other army plucked you from your home? Before the Vara?"

Now Adamen appears less sure of what to say, but he steels himself and answers that yes, he did. "And she was always flapping around that man in the market. I saw her. She was already with him when they picked me up—half dead myself, while she looked awfully good and well fed."

"Liar!" I cry out, but the commander shushes me.

"Do you know this whore's name?" He asks.

Adamen shakes his head. "A whore is a whore."

A few of the soldiers laugh, but the commander hisses them quiet with a ferociousness that has only been implied in his manner until now.

"What is your name?" the commander asks.

Adamen tells him.

"Well, Adamen, *I* know her name. Her name is Sherin of the Rah'a, and she is mala to my cousin, or at least she was until recent events."

Forgetting decorum entirely, I look up at the commander, open-mouthed like an idiot. Then I break into a sweat. But not just on my palms this time. Everywhere.

There is little recognizable about him from when we'd met at my betrothment feast. His long, midnight hair is gone, of course, and he's grown quite a bit, but it isn't only that. He, himself, has changed. Only a year ago, he had the easy-going grace of a young man, a prized apprentice with promise and prominence. Now, he's not only a man, but a hardening one. Like me, I suppose. We're all hardening.

"Tell me, Adamen, do you think my cousin is deserving of a whore who's borne another man's child—a man from the Waterless Sea no less? Is that what you're contending? That a cousin of mine would choose such a woman and think her worthy of him?"

Adamen seems to shrink by a head.

"Never," he sputters. "I-I must have mistaken her for another."

"Another whore who was engaged to my cousin?"

"No!"

The commander moves closer to Adamen, dwarfing him.

"Look at her. Is this how a whore dresses? In fabric like this?"

Adamen shakes his head. "My greatest apologies. I know nothing of fabric, and I must have overlooked her bearing. Hunger, you know. The horror of the Vara."

My fiancé's cousin pushes Adamen, making his stumble backwards.

"Show me your hands," he says.

Adamen hesitates, then lifts his hands up, holding them out flat.

"If you were a man of my skills of observation," my fiancé's cousin says, "would you not conclude that your hands look as if they've been digging? Digging something like this hole that you claim my cousin's mala had full knowledge of due to her adulterous relations with a traitor to our realm?"

Adamen is done even attempting to mount a defense for himself. At this point, any denials will lead him deeper down a dry well. He bends his head and falls to his knees in supplication to me. *"Sahjaloh,"* he says, too little too late. *"Sahjaloh,* Mala."

My fiancé's cousin, for his part, raises his hand in signal—fist and finger—and his men fall away.

"Get up and be of use." He kicks Adamen, who jumps up.

Not wasting a moment, Adamen helps the soldiers raise up some banners of canvas. With something of a barrier against the wind in place, the men begin wrapping linens around their noses and mouths in preparation for the coming storm. It's as if my brief trial never happened.

My fiancé's cousin turns to me and bows.

"Sahjaloh, Commander," I say.

"Mala," he replies.

He searches my face and I his. Can't stop myself. His cheeks are wide and firm, his lips set. If a woman were to kiss them, I think they would feel dry and loveless. His only feature that still resembles the young man I met at my feast—the night when my mother danced and I dissolved into self-pity—are his eyes. A fiery hue, they look more like a desert sunset now, rather than an apricot. They had once been a bold contrast to his long, black hair, and now they stand alone on his face as if they're all he has left.

"I fear I'm no longer that—a mala, I mean."

I want to ask if he's heard anything of my fiancée, but he urges Salan and me along. He's already wasted precious time, and with the wind blowing from the west, bringing with it a storm, he's not about to engage in conversation. It's a deadly storm that, by the looks of it, will fill the sky like thick smoke and bury our stores under a heep of sand in a matter of hours.

Such storms have been getting worse of late, and if the battle didn't kill us, there's still a good chance the desert will.

The commander sends a couple of his smaller men through the hole Adamen and I dug. They will meet us at the mouth of the largest cave and help the bulk of the army bring stores inside to wait out the storm. The rest of us are led around the long way.

Even now, in the storm's early grumbles, it's an arduous journey. Especially for Salan. I hold him close, tying him to me with a strip of linen from my dress.

"Seems like it's always tempest season," I hear one of the soldiers say.

I don't know what's happened to the archer and his men and no one speaks of the battle. I imagine they've been killed or captured. What's left of them tied up and waiting at the front of these dunes, guarded by the sultan's army. And I don't allow myself to think about what it will be like to see the archer again, especially after Adamen's demeaning accusations.

Adamen. As we trudge through the storm, I can barely make him out. He walks to the left of me, like a sand spirit. But I can feel his eyes. I keep my head as high as I can, letting the sand lash my face. I want him to know that I'm above him now, despite the fact that the wind has already told us, in no uncertain terms, that fortunes can change with just one powerful gust. Mine, in a matter of moments, has changed again, although somehow, deep in my marrow, I fear it's not for the better.

I CAN SEE NEVILLE as clearly as if he's standing next to me. His voice is sharp. As distinct as the ring of a doorbell. Even the tiniest beads of sweat that gather at his brow and hairline are visible to my essence.

The living world is so close now, which means I don't have much time left. I'm starting to feel that draw, the lust for birth that swells before one of my human lives. Soon my soul, in its endless wanderlust, will begin another voyage to another womb, another breath, another beating heart, another death. I'll learn to crawl, toddle, then run, and speak a new language. Or a language I've learned countless times. One that will come easily to me, perhaps. My new parents might comment to their friends on what an early talker I am.

I'll be lovely or plain and struggle with either. Rich or poor. And I will be loved, as my mother told me, and as our seer predicted upon my first birth.

"You have been destined to give life," my mother whispered. She took my hand to her lips and kissed it.

A mother is warned not to tell a child what her seer has foretold—at least not until that destiny has revealed itself on its own. It's true, some parents can't resist and it's considered very bad luck. Worse than speaking the names of your husband or his family before a marriage has taken place.

They usually regret it.

"Life and love are bound, our seer told me. People are drawn to a giver of life, but their intentions may not always be in your best interest. That's why I'm telling you this."

My mother then sang to me a verse from the "Songs of the Desert Wind."

"There is a wind in the desert that sighs; the wind of a thousand lovers and their children."

Lovers. Love.

I've learned in my many lives that love isn't always a gift of sweet kisses and a poetry of touch and secrets. It can be cruel, vindictive, corrupt, and malignant. It can look to utterly destroy the object it seeks. The seer was quite right about that.

And when I didn't have Nif's love to protect me, I fell victim to the other sort more often than I care to recount. It's a mercy that, when I'm human, I can't quite remember those times. But here, in this place between heaven and earth, I recall being berated by ugly words, locked in a cage, having my throat slit, being thrown from a window, driven off a cliff, shamed into suicide. All by people who loved me.

And, despite that, I still ache to be reborn so that my soul can experience the torment and ecstasy of another body. I hope against hope for another chance to love Nif, even if I can only be with him for a short time.

Life is a work of art that way.

"I don't think Michelangelo could have done better," Neville says, in awe.

I quite agree, although we're not talking about the same thing.

Neville's arms are folded across his chest, where he holds a flat tablet of stone. His sleeves are rolled up as high as they'll go. He's got his glasses on—oval silver frames that look scholarly and hip all at once. He looks as if he might just fall to his knees.

The air about them is filled with clouds of dust, still swirling following the collapse of a thin façade of sand and stone before them. After weeks of careful work, like with the care given an infants skull. After the tedious grind of excavation, and the brushing free of debris, all it took was the accidental drop of a felled pillar above ground to make a fissure form in the ancient casing of desert ground that covered this treasure. It fell away, revealing what Neville has been waiting for all his life. What I haven't seen in millennia.

Now, the doors to the Palace City tower over him and Jordie. Nearly perfect, apart from stubborn bits of crust that remain in some of their crevasses. They stand at the end of a deep tunnel dug by the people Neville has working for him. A bright light floods the tunnel, angled at those doors, which are tall as giants and intricately carved. Jordie coughs a bit, wiping his eyes and waving away the last wisps of floating dust.

"Good God," Neville gasps.

"This is an unexpected development," Jordie says. "I thought it would be a couple more weeks before we got a good look at them."

They both burst out laughing. Relief and joy and disbelief.

Neville steps up to the doors, his lips parted and legs shaking a bit. He runs his finger over a line of verse on one of them, and compares it to an identical line on the partial tablet of stone he's holding.

"Incredible," he says.

"What do you suppose it means? If you were to take a guess." Jordie steps next to Neville and peers closely at the script.

"A lot of these ancient entryways are festooned with boasts or stories." Neville looks the doors up and down and cocks his head. "I think they'd pronounce Rah'a the way the Egyptians do their sun god—Ra, don't you?"

Jordie considers this non sequitur while putting on his jacket. It's cold beneath the desert floor, a good fifty degrees colder than above ground. Neville seems to hardly notice.

"Or like Ray-ah," Jordie says. "The way the Sumerians might say it."

Neville shakes his head.

"Sumer was pretty far. I think I'll go with the Egyptians." He adjusts the light and points out a slight discoloration. "This might've been painted red right here. These people liked their colors."

It's almost like Neville is in a trance, talking out of a dream.

"Mmm." Jordie nods. "Sumer was farther away in distance, but closer in time. They popped up around 4500 BC, while the Egyptian civilization didn't really take off until 3100 BC with the unification of Upper and Lower Egypt."

"Really, Dr. Mostafa?" Neville snarks. "I had no idea."

"Well, of course you knew that," Jordie says. "I was thinking out loud is all."

Neville plucks his water bottle from the ground and takes a deep swallow. He wipes his forehead with the bunched-up sleeve of his shirt, another dingy cotton one with a frayed collar and breast pocket that's missing a button.

"For all we know, these people are direct ancestors to the Egyptians *and* the Sumerians. There are definitely traces of both cultures in the design elements we're seeing. What if Rah'a and Ra are essentially the same thing? If I were an early Egyptian and naming a god, I'd definitely consider something like this to be pretty heavenly."

Jordie leans in close to the face of a stone tiger flanking the massive palace door. It's only been partly uncovered and its face stands in relief. "Heavenly indeed," he grumbles.

"Dr. Neville! Dr. Mostafa!"

A frantic, young Australian rushes up all out of breath. Neville rolls his eyes and huffs. Interruptions like this have been going on all day.

"What is it, Pete?"

Pete stops abruptly and bends over, his hands on his knees.

"Slow down. Take it easy," Neville tells him.

"It's Nicho . . . he-he."

"He what?"

"He sank into the sand or something! He's vanished. Gone!"

Neville thrusts the stone slab into Jordie's hands and grabs Pete's shirt. He pulls him up. "What do you mean gone?"

Pete shakes his head.

"I don't know! Into a sink hole or something. Phillip and Louis are looking for him. Digging right where he disappeared. But it's like there's nothing there. Except . . ."

"For God's sake, man, spit it out!"

Pete swallows hard, nodding like a bobblehead. "We can still hear him. He's calling out to us, but we don't know where from."

Neville backs the Australian bloke up against the tunnel wall.

"What the hell are you talking about? You say he's calling out to you from under the sand?"

Pete rises up onto his toes to be eye and eye with Neville. "I know it sounds implausible, but I swear to God he's still there somewhere. We all hear him!"

Neville turns to Jordie.

"Get a long rope and another one of these lights. Let's hope to God whatever crevasse the kid fell into is a shallow one that's not going to collapse before we find him."

Chapter 12

The Commander

WE WAIT ALL NIGHT in the caves, Salan and I huddling to keep warm on the outer edge of the fire while the sultan's soldiers crowd around the blaze. My victory over Adamen's lies seems a passing one, as exhaustion and fear of what's next has not only taken hold of me, but all the Sultan's men.

The injured lie toe to head, like sardines. Bruised and scraped from the days' battle—some quite savagely. The others sit or stand, stoking the embers and giving water to the wounded. The dead have been left outside, given an unceremonious burial by the sandstorm.

As for my fiancé's cousin, their commander; he rests on a roll-out cot at their front. His body is in good shape—only a few welts, and a scratch running down his shoulder to mid-back. It looks like a tree branch, thick and heavy in the middle, with crisp lines veering from its center. It's been cleaned and the blood has clotted well. It's odd to watch him lie there—this man from the life I've lost—and I can't help feeling some affection for him. Maybe because he's the only one who knows me from before, besides Salan, of course. Or because he championed me in front of his men and Adamen. He didn't have to do that.

Adamen. He crouches alone on the ground—far from the

heart of the fire. On occasion, I can hear him cough, and it chills me.

The whole evening there's nothing but talk about the Army of the Waterless Sea and that prince of theirs. All in hushed voices and away from the commander. I stand up with Salan on my hip, pretending to hum his lullaby as I pace closer.

The wind couldn't have come at a better time for the enemy, I hear them mumble. It slowed the battle, and allowed the men of the Waterless Sea to duck and hide in the blowing sand. Like magicians, the sultan's men say. They confused the commander's regiment, becoming fewer each time the wind flared, disappearing like ghosts into the desert they know so well. Their footprints were blown away as if by the gods, and there's fear they're close by, waiting for the storm to die down so they can trap us. I should be happier that Salan and I are back with our people, but instead, there's a tempest in my heart. I'd grown accustomed to the archer's company and had begun to make some sense of my life again, only to have another change thrust upon me, a new set of dangers.

We have no choice but to wait out the storm in these caves, and it's made us vulnerable. But to stay out in the storm would bury us all. I look over by the fire and see the commander stir. His fingers curl at his sides, and I'm sure his eyes are open. He proves me right when he turns his head in my direction and we catch eyes for but a moment.

I go back to our place near the fire and lie down. Salan is cozied in my arms, blissful and inattentive to the stresses of the day or anything beyond it. I wish I could be.

In a single day, I've gone from being a bride for a dirt-poor monarch, the prisoner of an inferior army about to be slaughtered, to a mala once again, recaptured by my home army, a great army that's now in danger of being outmaneuvered by a bunch of nomads. The archer, if he comes again, might see little use for me in the light of a new day, a new battle. And the thought of meaning so little to him distresses me, too. Even if I know it's just the way of the world.

These thoughts of the archer take me a bit by surprise. I realize that in my loneliness, I haven't merely grown used to the archer, but I've started to look forward to our interactions. His humor and his confidence make me feel safe, or at least safer than I've felt since the Vara obliterated my family and my prospects. And now I've lost him.

Dozing in and out of sleep, I awaken for the last time a good hour before dawn. The storm is over and it's so quiet that I can even hear Salan, who still sleeps with the delicate breath of a baby. I cradle him, laying him softly on his side and kissing his ear before getting up to tiptoe to the mouth of the cave.

The moon casts an icy glow over the sand, and there isn't even a breeze left over from the violent winds that lashed us only a few hours ago. The stars twinkle and I feel the sort of peace that comes after a good, hard cry.

On the heels of the hoot of an owl, I hear a rapping sound, rhythmic, like two sticks striking to a musical beat. I can almost recognize the song.

Out in the distance, a shadow splays across the dune. It's a man's shadow, slender, his arm stretched out in *Salan*—to be, to endure, always. I bite my lip. The archer steps into the pale of the moon, the skin of his face aglow like a pearl. His beard as black as a panther. Even at a distance, his eyes kindle, lit by some trick of the desert. I step closer to the edge and hold out my hand, and he raises his, though not in *Salan* this time. He waves his fingers in a gesture of voyaging. The one the god Mazal used when he set his wife, the moon, into orbit around him. Forever.

"Mala," my fiancé's cousin whispers.

A shiver runs up the length of my spine. He comes up beside me and I rub my forearms as if I'm cold, glancing at his face with a faint smile—all I can manage. The desert is empty before us, and the archer is gone. Faded into its expanse. His escape brings an odd tickle of excitement and relief, yet I've never felt more alone.

"Commander," I say. I sense that a few years ago he might have laughed at the way I've greeted him, so formal, but today he lifts his eyebrows.

"I have nothing else to call you," I explain. "I can't keep calling you my fiancé's cousin, since I fear I have no fiancé anymore."

"No," he says. "You don't."

I'm surprised by how difficult it is to hear that the man I was to marry is most assuredly dead. The final blow to my life before the Vara.

"And his family?"

"Gone."

He says it factually, as if reciting the name of a recipe.

"They were your family, too."

The commander shrugs. "I've hardly seen them in years. Just the once when we met at your feast."

"They were still your blood."

The commander looks up at the sky, as I did before catching sight of the archer. My eyes dart out onto the dunes again, confirming the archer and his men are nowhere in sight. No matter how skillful they are at hiding in the desert, a commander for the sultan's army is highly trained and can certainly catch a glimpse of a careless movement.

"They're gone," I say. "The other army, I mean."

The commander scans the desert vista.

"Do you know where, Commander?" I ask him.

His eyes seem to land where I last saw the archer.

"Roon," he says.

"To Roon? I don't know that place. Is it far?"

The commander shakes his head.

"You asked what to call me."

I search his face, heart-shaped, hard-bitten, the creases that will define his expressions for the rest of his life already set.

"Roon is your name?"

"No," he says. "It's what you can call me."

I have the feeling he wants to smile, but he doesn't.

"Roon," I say.

Roon must be the name given to him when he came to the sultan. That's the custom. Who you were is gone; you belong to the sultan from that day on. You live and die for the kingdom.

But I can see that Roon has not forgotten who he is—was—after all. Why else would he have stood up for me with Adamen? A man like Adamen is strong and useful. A woman with a small boy hanging around her tunic is another mouth to feed.

"Sherin," Roon says. "Have you ever wondered why the desert is so cool at night, when we can barely stand his fever in the day?"

I shake my head. "My father said the air here has no fingers and can't hold the heat. It slips away."

"Like so many things," Roon says.

His breath is slow and he seems to empty his lungs fully with each exhale. And when he does take in a breath again, he swells a chest fraught with muscles and scars—the most prominent of which, and most recent, the tree branch, reaches toward me like a hand.

"But sometimes the wind can bring things back," he tells me. "Things lost. Things belonging to another. Things you never thought you could have for yourself."

Roon tips his head and meets my eyes. I'm unsure if, under the circumstances, I should look down in respect, so I do. But Roon puts his knuckle under my chin and lifts up my face.

"I wonder what my cousin would have thought of your eyes," he whispers. My eyes, green like a lime, like algae, like an emerald. Singular and aberrant.

"Did you know him?"

"Barely," he says. "But he would've been a good match for you, even if a lousy husband."

His eyes widen, brighter than ever. This time I can't help but look down. It's all I can do. In his eyes, the truth is explicit.

"You saw them, didn't you? After the Vara came."

Roon nods. Part of me wishes I hadn't asked.

"Theirs's was the first region we entered after the outbreak."

"Did he die well?" I close my eyes and hear Roon swallow.

"No one with the Vara dies well," he says. "But he died quicker than others."

"Quicker by your hand, you mean."

Not an accusation on my part. Who am I to judge? A girl who poisoned her father. I can see it in my mind's eye. Roon returning to his family at the onset of the Vara. Killing the infected—including his cousin, the man who would have been my husband. If not with his own sword, then by his order. Likely it was to end their suffering, the way I'd ended my father's, and my father ended Yina's. Or perhaps it was for a different purpose. I open my eyes and look up to see Roon watching me. Not just my face, as he had been, but my person as a whole. His eyes flicker over my neck and shoulders and down the line of my form, as if he's drawing me.

"Will we be hunting the other army today?" I ask, breaking away from that gaze.

"The nomads? No. They come and go like the Vara. They'll come back here a few days after we leave. They always do."

I smooth my hair, tucking it behind my ears. It's heavy, like winter linen, and I'm unused to having it loose, feeling it lie over me unbraided like a cloak.

"Will we stay here until they return?"

Roon huffs. "No. These dunes were for families not long ago, but they're fast becoming a den for thieves."

A light breeze blows, lifting up my hair. It's a cool one, but Roon seems not to feel it.

"Today we leave for the Palace City."

"The Palace City?" I can't help aping him like a fool. I've never been to the Palace City, but my father had business there once or twice. It seemed like a place made for gods. At least the way he described it. Full of soldiers, of course. Like Roon. Over one thousand of them guard the city, and hundreds more the palace itself. Opulent beyond belief, my father told me with a hint of disapproval—footpaths studded with rubies, solid gold columns, the finest hand-painted linens, and furniture carved into the forms of wild animals—lions, tigers, dragons, snakes. The furnishings even appear as if they're in motion, turning the palace into a wild and dangerous jungle at night. When no one is there, or when no one can see, the sculpted animals live, he said. The sultan's very throne is built in the form of a crouching leopard, and rumor has it that tens of thieves have been mauled by its claws.

Nonsense, of course. But a good bedtime story. My father always told the best bedtime stories—full of adventures that he and I conquered together. Only I'm going this one alone.

Chapter 13

The Palace City

AS WE MARCH closer to the sultan's Palace City, I wonder if I'm seeing a fantasy, except my own mind's magic could never invent something like this. If the Rah'a is rich compared to places like the Waterless Sea, then the Palace City is to the rest of the Rah'a what heaven must be to Earth.

Built deep into sandstone cliffs as tall as I've ever seen, the exterior is essentially a wall of sculpture, engraved by artisans from all over our realm. They're carved in relief, painted in bold colors of indigo and poppy, mustard and parsley-green. Also glittering ones of gold, silver, copper and bronze. Superb.

Instead of many discrete scenes, the way a hunt might be portrayed in clay paint on a cave wall, the sculptures tell one massive history. Of discovery, the growth of agriculture, building, conquest, celebration, prosperity. Breathtaking, the stone figures progress as my eyes follow the narrative— from a young man staking a claim and planting a seed, to a violent growth that spreads abundance and security to a large region. Animals hunted, animals tamed. Settlements conquered, then absorbed. Games and feasts. Generations of sultans in the embraces of their wives. The many children they spawned. The army—always the army—in every scene.

That army surrounds the Palace City. And, as we march

inside, through an arched doorway flanked by two ferocious stone tigers—each dressed in snakes—that army enters it.

"Your new home, Mala," Adamen spits as he passes me, scraping the chipped fang of his fingernail hard down my wrist. I gasp, cupping my palm over the scratch.

"We're here," I say, forcing a smile at Salan.

My brother cannot take his eyes off Adamen, who splinters off with several of Roon's men. They file down a hallway lit by torches. With so few healthy men, he's a prize, even if a tarnished one. I shouldn't be surprised that no one, not even Roon, cares much about his insult and treachery regarding one young woman and her brother.

"Ma-wi," Salan says, using his child's word for wound, bringing his finger gently to my wrist. Adamen has drawn blood.

"It's nothing," I say.

I crouch next to my brother and lick my thumb, using it to wipe some of the sediment from under Salan's eyes. But soon the soldiers are pushing and prodding us down another passage—this one wide and lined with grandiose pillars flanked by archways that lead into assorted chambers.

"It's not a place of subtlety," Roon says, brushing up alongside of me.

The palace, literally chiseled into a mountain, has single rooms that could fit ten of my father's house. Gems glitter from the walls, along with paintings and tapestries matching the purpose of the space. If it's a room for feasting, there are images of animals, hunts, rows of crops; if it's for leisure, palms, dancers, birds. Or if it's for love, well, there are illustrations for that, too.

Roon leads us all into a waiting area—humid and enormous—where the walls are plain, clean, and lined with benches. The soldiers unlace their boots and I follow in kind, taking off my lilac slippers and placing them on the benches with the other footwear. Then I go to untie Salan's sandals.

"No," he squeals, kicking his feet.

"What's the matter with you?"

I try to catch his heels, but he squirms and pushes me.

"Mine!"

"Well, of course they're yours," I say.

My little brother is sun and wind burned. His eyes are fierce as he bends to tie his sandals even tighter to his feet. He stops to rub a blister between his toes, then stands up again, doing his best to adopt the posture of the soldiers around us.

"It'll feel good to take them off," I tell him. I use my gentlest voice.

"No!" He stomps his foot, and then I understand. My father took him to have his sandals made. His first pair of big boy shoes.

"Come here," I say, taking his palms and kissing them. "You can keep them on for now if you want. If anyone objects, let them fight with you."

Servants scamper in from every orifice like bugs, carrying jugs of water, then pouring them over our heads. They enter one after another, soaking us, scrubbing, the men stripped to only a cloth covering their groins, while I'm bathed fully in my once exquisite tunic. The one that would've been my wedding dress.

Salan, poor Salan, is washed naked and howls as the lathered brushes attack his skin, cleaning under his arms, behind his ears, even beneath his fingernails. But they do not take off his sandals.

I should feel shy, being bathed so publicly and with so many men, but it's a strangely impersonal procedure. As standard as taking off your shoes before entering someone's house.

"The sultan," a servant girl whispers. "Is a man of many

preferences." A scrawny girl, she's rough skinned and short-haired, with a funny cowlick sticking up at the back of her head, like a claw. "He likes his people and his surroundings clean. If you are to live in his palace, you will need to get used to being washed."

I submit to holding up my arms, letting the girl pour more cold water down my tunic. The linen clings to me like seaweed, and her fingers go at me, scraping the sand away from my scalp. She then brushes my hair and wraps me in linen as soft as suede. I remove my wet dress from underneath it and hand it to her, securing the new linen wrap at my shoulder with an oval pin she's given me.

"Sherin." Roon puts his hand on my shoulder. "The desert's cruel for a child."

He gestures at Salan, who's being tended by one of the boys. My poor brother looks as if he could fall asleep standing up.

"He'll be fine," I say, but Roon dismisses me. He offers to have Salan brought to bed in our new chamber.

"I should go with him." I fear Salan won't take well to being separated from me, even if he is dog-tired.

Roon hands me my slippers. "Let me show you around. You'll see him within the hour."

He nods and a servant woman picks up Salan. My brother glances at me, his eyes heavy. I smile at him and he smiles back, but then dozes off on her shoulder as soon as his cheek touches it.

At Roon's signal, the soldiers file out of the bathing chamber. As silent as priests, they disappear into the bowels of the palace, with only Roon staying behind. He stands before me with a white cloth over his middle like the others, but his is longer, reaching almost to his knees.

"Come with me," he says.

Truly clean for the first time in weeks, and totally done in,

I'm not about to fight him this time. I follow Roon out of the bathing area and down one of the many corridors—this one leading to a room that's small by comparison. One painted not in stories, but in a splendid sunrise of hues befitting a royal wedding, each color blending into the next. The air is still in this room, and cool, like it has never seen the desert sun its walls are meant to imitate.

Roon's shoulders seem to float above the rest of his body as he walks. Broad and muscular, they carry his head gently and easily, like a silken pillow bearing a precious artifact. His face, once sweetly handsome, is set in a look of pure scrutiny.

He stops with hands at his sides and peers up at the ceiling. It's studded in yellow gemstones that look like stars dripping with honey. The large, new scar on his shoulder looks inflamed in this light. Red as a burst of veins on the white of an eyeball.

"This is my favorite room here and I wanted you to see it."

"It looks like a new day," I say.

"Tomorrow is a new day for you, Sherin."

A good one, I hope. One of food, water, and safety, whatever that means anymore.

"How long will we stay here, my brother and I?"

Roon tips his head. "You live here now."

That should be a relief to hear, but I know this is Adamen's new home, too.

"And what will we do in this place?"

Roon's eyes, wide and unblinking, are as golden as the gems in the ceiling. They have a terrible beauty, like a looming storm.

"You're an esteemed subject of the sultan," he says. "There's always a home for you here."

"There was no home for me and Salan when the Vara came," I tell him. "Only an invading army."

"From whom I rescued you," Roon reminds me.

"Adamen said that if we went home, the sultan's army, your army, would have burned our houses to the ground." I keep his gaze. "Burned us, too."

"Wasn't Adamen the man who would've had you killed as a traitor?"

I don't know what makes me smile, but I do. Roon's expression remains the same.

"No, Sherin," he says. "If my army had come to your house first and found you and your brother there, I would've taken you with me. We'd be standing here just as we are."

Roon raises his hand and takes a piece of my hair between his fingers, twisting its sable strands, but gently. The gesture gives me goose pimples. I don't know if I like it or not.

"You should get some sleep now," he says. "There'll be a great deal to do in the next few days, and you'll want to feel rested."

Roon summons a servant with a terse "ha." In an instant, a small, round-bottomed young woman scuttles in. She bows to him first, then to me, before being instructed to take me to my chamber.

I look over my shoulder as I start down the corridor with her. Roon stands at attention, his eyes closed and his expression misted with pleasure, as if he is listening to music.

THE SERVANT WOMAN holds open the drapery for me, and I step inside my new chamber. She bows and leaves without a word. Near the entrance, I find Salan asleep on a bed of soft furs and blankets, his feet sticking out and still dressed in his sandals. Next to him is a small window. That's covered by a square piece from a tiger's pelt, and I peek under it to view a courtyard below. One that's bustling with end of day business.

"Looks cheerful," I whisper, but perhaps a better word is oblivious.

Kneeling next to my brother, I nuzzle my face into the supple skin of his neck, then pull him tight and close. A yowl comes up from under his blanket and a tumbling little mass pokes its head out. It's a kitten. Calico, with a big brown spot over one eye. Can't be more than a few weeks old.

"Well, hello," I say.

The delicate thing sniffs my knuckles, its bitty pink nose like a spring bud. Satisfied that I'm not a mortal threat, it rubs its cheek against the pad of my thumb and curls up behind Salan's neck, in the cup between his shoulders and skull. After a face-splitting yawn, tongue curled like a shaving of wood, the kitten starts to purr.

I guess she—as I notice from gently lifting her leg—is hoping to stay.

"Fine by me," I whisper. "As long as you're a good mouser."

I cross my legs and sit up, finally taking a good look around. It's a simple chamber by the sultan's standards with two grand tapestries of peacock feathers covering the side walls and sturdy furniture crafted from Persian Juniper. The tapestries are brilliant even in torch light, and I wonder what they might look like under the glow of the sun. The stone floor is carved with poetry, words and images, all of them celebrating the palace and the desert region it rules over. A considerable step up from the tent I would have called home had I gone with the archer to the Waterless Sea. This austere palace chamber is far more luxurious than even my father's lovely home. Although not nearly as warm.

At that thought, my heart sinks.

There is a wind in the desert that will whisper of love and then blow it away. There is a wind that will take from you every-thing, then return it when you need it least, I sing to Salan as he sleeps. He barely stirs at the sound of my voice. The calico ignores me entirely. I'm lonesome, and all at once I feel like the only passenger on a sinking ship. One going down slowly but certainly. I didn't feel that way when I was with the archer and his men, and I don't know why the Palace City and Roon have not provided me with a sense of security.

In the corner of my chamber, on a small side table, lies a neatly folded cloth. The touch of linen is home to me, so I crawl over and take the cloth into my hands, running my fingers over its flawless thread—fine enough to have been made by my mother. It's deep purple—not quite a royal hue, more like something of the earth—an eggplant. At its waist is a red sash, and when I see it I know instantly what it is.

This is a mourning tunic. Roon must've had it brought to my chamber. From the moment I put it on, it will be my only costume for a year's time. Upon confirmation of the death of a spouse, or at least someone who would have been a spouse, a woman is to mourn for the four desert seasons of cold, tempest, fire, and rain. Not a day more.

The Waterless Sea would've handed me from one man to the next. They don't waste any time at all. Desert people lead a hard life and can't afford to.

There is a wind in the desert that hears the cries of a woman, a wife, a mother. He hears her but will not answer her grief.

Makes me wonder how often the archer thinks of his grief. The disjointed recollections of his family, his life as a boy. A time before the Vara swept his lands. Years ago now.

I saw a bare glimpse of that pain the first time I noticed the archer's eyes. One of meat gravy—the eye of hunger. His other, the tortoise shell with its golden flecks, the eye of wisdom, maybe. Just as mine are the eyes of life, at least according to my mother and her seer.

My eyes and his seem to jumble together in my dreams most nights, giving me a vague sense of longing when I awaken.

Then there's Roon. My new friend, if I can call him that. His eyes are a mystery to me. Too bright to see into or look past. Eyes afire with every possible aspiration. That of Soldier. Father. King.

And perhaps something else.

If I were in a body right now and Nif were with me, he'd take my face into his hands, kiss me with all his tenderness on my forehead, my eyelashes, my lips, and then my neck, where he would bury his face and whisper my name, much like I did to my sleeping brother on our first night in the palace. Only different.

Or perhaps he would sweep me up into his arms, crushing me to his chest. Our reunions have been varied, but there's a remarkable connection in them all. It's in that recognition— "Yes, it's you again. It can only ever be you."

Nif and I have traveled alone through an eternity of lives to touch one another again, feel our love's breath upon our skin, the brush of lips on sacred places. Or to merely tell each other about our day. The simplest pleasures are often the most precious.

"My eyes made their home with you from the first," Nif told me in that first life.

But first, I would have to make a home in the sultan's palace—for me and for Salan.

And so I did.

In my chamber filled with plump pillows and tapestries of peacock feathers. Furniture, strong and beautifully carved. Floors of stone, engraved with poetry from our language. About flowers, so fragile and precious, birds—the animals closest to the heavens, and the omniscient desert wind. About soldiers and sultans, wives and lovers. Ruling the world as it was known to us.

"Listen," Pete, the Australian, whispers.

His words startle me. I was too lost in Nif and forgot about the living world I've been eavesdropping on.

"Right there, do you hear it?"

They all stop, hardly breathing. Neville, Jordie, and the dozen or so students and assistants, along with a few Egyptian boys looking to make some coin out here. There's a light breeze and even that seems to still. Neville crouches to be close to the desert floor, and Jordie clicks on the digital recorder, holding it above the surface. Little red flags have been stuck into the sand, encompassing the general area where Nicho is thought to have disappeared. It's on the edge of the canvas village serving as their temporary home. Nicho had gone to his tent to fetch a PowerBar.

The rest of the crew are a full football field away, scattered about the dig, and working. They don't know about Nicho yet, and Neville's not keen on telling them. Dry quicksand has long been a myth among desert dwellers, though its existence has never been proven outside of a physics laboratory.

"There it is again."

Neville nods. The sound is so faint, like the distant caw of a buzzard. Ishaq, one of the Egyptian boys, hides behind a bright yellow backhoe, praying. Horus, his brother, tells him to shut up and quit being such a woman.

"Nicho," Neville calls. His voice is deep and resounding. If anyone's can penetrate the sand, it's his.

"Nicho, if you can hear me, yell *Crocodile Dundee*!"

It's Nicho's nickname because he's Australian, too, and looks like a young Paul Hogan. It's also a name with a lot of hard consonants that'll come through whatever lies between Nicho and the rest.

K-D-Dee

Not quite intelligible. Sounds more like a series of clicks than words.

"One more time, Nicho!"

There's a long pause, then it comes again. *K-D-Dee*

"It's him!" Pete says. "See, I told you."

Jordie rewinds the digital recorder, and puts it to Neville's ear. It's an excellent device, very sensitive and made to capture every nuance of sound. On the recording, the words are unmistakable, *Crocodile Dundee*. Nicho is in there somewhere.

"Play it again," Neville says, and Jordie rewinds the recording and puts it to Neville's ear.

"There."

"What?"

Neville listens one more time.

"He's not in an air pocket. Not unless it's a really big one."

"Maybe a crevasse," Jordie says.

"Maybe, but it sounds like an orderly space, geometric."

Jordie himself listens one more time. Very clear. Hollow. A slight echo when Nicho says *Crocodile Dundee*.

"A crevasse can be geometric in shape."

Neville shakes his head. "There's something about the way his voice echoes. Wherever he is, it's . . . square sounding."

Jordie squints at the area marked by the red flags. "I didn't know a sound could be square."

"Nicho!" Neville calls. "Can you see or feel anything?"

Jordie floats the digital recorder above the sand again, then plays it.

"I can hardly hear him this time," he says. "But I think he said, *dark*."

"Well, of course it's dark!"

Neville rubs the stubble on his cheek, a full two days growth. His eyes follow the lines of the dig, from the hole in the desert floor—looking like the scar a large meteor might make—to the ridge where they're standing.

"It's a helluva long march from where we found the palace gates, don't you think?" He turns to Pete and asks him for his flashlight, which the young man unclips from his belt. Neville tests the device and attaches it to his own belt. He swaps out his water bottle for Jordie's, which is full, and drops it into his backpack.

"Got any more of those PowerBars?"

Pete nods, running over to Nicho's tent. He emerges with several, which Neville stuffs into his pack.

"How about that?" He points to Jordie's digital recorder. "I've got another one in my tent. You should go get it after I'm gone." Neville drops Jordie's recorder in the pack, zipping it up and putting it on.

"Where are you going?" Jordie asks him.

Neville walks right up to the red flags, pauses, and then steps inside the circle.

"Dr. Neville, you can't!"

But Neville is gone. He's sunk into the sand before their very eyes, as if pulled by a spirit into the underworld. Ishaq, the Egyptian boy, screams and begins to flail. He says he told Horus the money wasn't worth it, but his brother wouldn't listen. He told him this Dr. Neville was a man Allah would be interested in teaching a lesson.

Chapter 14

Palace Life

"**M**ESUUU," Salan coos as we splash around.

The calico kitten—Salan calls her Mesu—watches us wearily. She hates bathing, standing in solidarity with her kind. Though I would swear she thinks Salan and I are her kind.

I grasp Salan's foot and blow through his toes until he squeals so loudly we're hushed by the harem guard. Mesu, in solidarity with us, hisses at the guard, letting him know what she thinks of him.

After walking so long in the empty mouth of the desert, the sultan's palace is like a wish granted. Its opulence makes me dizzy, and our every need is tended to. Salan is fed, napped, and changed all by a nurse. Although I won't allow her to bathe him. That will always be ours. The one piece from home we bring with us.

"Do you have to go see Toja?" Salan asks me, sulking. Mesu mimics his expression like I've done them wrong.

Since our arrival just over a moon ago, I've been tasked with being a maid to one of the sultan's lesser wives. Toja. She's a new wife, not much older than me. Haughty and distant, at times. Giggly and featherbrained at others.

"Toja sends you those candies." I stick out my tongue at both my brother and the cat.

"Best you go right away," Salan teases. I splash his face,

spraying Mesu on accident. She meows in objection, jumping back and lifting her paw as if she's royal or something.

It's a cushy job and easy work with Toja. A woman who was once a mala, like me, is only bound to convey messages, keep her company when she's lonely, and above all be discreet about her behavior. Palace life spawns many gossips, and I've found that even a foul mood is deliberated ad nauseum.

—◈◈—

"BE CAREFUL OF TOJA," Roon tells me. "She's a fool."

We've run into one another in a corridor only steps away from an outdoor courtyard where laundry is hung, meat is smoked, and information floats freely like pollen in the breeze.

"She's young," I say. "And being a fool isn't a crime."

"Fools die young these days."

His eyes flare.

"Do you know something about her?" I probably shouldn't have asked him. It isn't proper, and as a soldier he's bound not to tell me even if he does.

"I know nothing except that she's a fool, but I've lived here long enough to know when a woman is courting trouble."

And I've had enough trouble to last me a life time.

"Be very discreet," Roon says, gentler now. In a bedroom whisper. "Protecting her dignity secures your own. At least until you marry again."

While I'm new to the sultan's palace, I have some idea about palace life, passed to me from my father's observations in his dealings with the royal harems. He may have only been a fabric merchant, but he had a way of reading the series of tiny gestures that make up a culture. Even one as complicated as a royal court.

I know, for instance, that ministering to Toja is a double-edged sword. While a plum job of high status, it comes with dangers. For the time that I'm bound to Toja, both her triumphs and failings will fall on me as if I've committed them myself. If she's a fool, I can become a fool, too. And given that I'm in mourning and have no prospects for marriage, I best be careful.

"What are your days like here?" I ask Roon.

I glance at a troop of soldiers' wives fluttering by us. They nod to Roon, looking me up and down.

"My days?" Roon says. "My days will be very full again in a few weeks' time. But today I'll call on you to walk with me."

"When?"

"At a time of my choosing," he says.

"What if Toja needs me when you come?"

Roon's voice is steady, affirming, like a father's. "I'll call at a time when she doesn't."

He doesn't wait for me to ask another one of my questions. Instead, he turns and treads down the corridor toward the courtyard, where I'm headed as well. I let him get ahead of me before making my way, but when I arrive there, Roon is nowhere to be seen. Not by the bathing pool, where soldiers can often be found sitting on the large, polished stones that line it. Splashing their bald heads, cooling off. Nor in the center by the wine stalls.

I glide through the flocks of wives and throngs of soldiers, merchants, counselors and tutors—all doing their business, be it selling goods or simply dishing on the day's events. But he's gone. Just as well, I guess. I only had more questions, which he'll answer in his own time anyway, and not a moment before.

"Cradle fruit! Cradle fruit!" A merchant, black-skinned, calls out to me. He's selling young wine, bubbly and too sweet. The kind that gives me a terrible headache, but Toja loves. I jingle a pouch of tokens at him—one allotted to all harem attendants—and buy some for her lunch, along with resin wine that's said to come from the North. That's for me.

In the far corner of the courtyard, where meat cranks on a spit, there's raucous laughter from a group of royal butchers. Dressed in bloody robes, they gesture wildly to one another, telling stories. Behind them drips a fall of vines that grow from the rock wall and are studded with flowers the color of jasper, like the ones at my father's house.

The sight of it makes a hollow in my stomach.

Another laugh spurts up from within their midst. It's a confident laugh, the kind that comes from a man who moves freely from one band to the next with poise and assurance. I move toward them, and before I know it I'm running.

"Archer!"

The men round and look at me. Their hands are meaty and hang at their sides.

"There's no one here by that name," a stubby, broad-shouldered man tells me. They all burst out laughing again, like I'm a comedian. There are at least a dozen of them, bulbous and packed together, standing two deep.

"I thought the goat man was here, but I must be mistaken."

"No goat man," the stubby one says. "But there's a lamb boy." They all howl again.

My face burns.

"I'll have some lamb, then," I say. "For the sultan's wife."

They quit chortling at once, becoming all business, and cutting large chunks—ones with plenty of fat—from the spit. Even smiling. I pay them, returning none of their good humor.

"I gave two qabet more," Stubby says. It's true, I can feel it by weight.

"As you should," I say, in my snobbiest voice. I haven't used it in a while, but it's amazing how easily it's come back.

"The finest of days to you," Stubby bids, as I tuck the meat package into my bag.

I say nothing and spin on the heel of my slipper as they stutter their *sahjalohs*.

But the ghost of the archer's company follows me, the way it has since we parted ways in the desert. It's been as much a comfort to me as a disturbance, visiting me each night as I dream, where I see him standing beneath the desert moon with his hand out in *salan*. There are times in the day when I've caught his scent, or seen his eyes as I watched a brewmaster pour his amber ale into a pot the color of the richest earth. Now, I'm sure I heard his laugh. To be true, I've never actually heard his laugh before. Certainly not when I was in his presence. We had little reason to laugh then. And I can't figure out why I'm so sure I heard him among the butchers. A laugh I can't have identified in a place he can't possibly be. But I did. I swear I did. And somehow, it makes me ache for his company. For the loss of one who I believe would have become a true friend.

NEVILLE SINKS WITH ALARMING SPEED. He tumbles, being pushed by a rough current of sand. He's forgotten to breathe, but can't even if he wanted to. Finally, he slows, coming to a halt with his legs tucked up underneath him. He should be unable to move, packed in by a dense and heavy sea of desert floor, but the sand around him has an airiness to it, like the fine sand on the beach that his cousin used to bury him in up to his neck when they were kids. Neville hunches his back, and sure enough, with a little shouldering breaks the surface. Gradually, he goes up on all fours, then sits on his haunches, the sand rushing down over him like a landslide on a mountain.

He finds himself in a chilly space, as dark as Nicho said. Unhooking Aussie Pete's flashlight from his belt, he clicks it on. It's a good, bright camping light, an expensive piece, but it has its limits in a place so black.

"How much more black can it be? None. None more black," he says, quoting *This Is Spinal Tap*, the old comedy he pushed on his students the other night. They didn't think it was that funny.

He shines the light on the walls around him, on the floor ahead of him. Sandstone, smooth and beautifully chiseled. "Jesus," he says.

He looks over and sees the wave of sand that carried him in. It came through a doorway that looks like the entrance to a stairwell. One framed by engravings in the same language as the stone slab his father had found deep in a cave not too far from here. The same language on the colossal doors he and Jordie were studying when Pete came running into the tunnel.

Neville stands up, brushing the sand off his trousers, picking it out of the corners of his mouth and eyes. Blowing it out of his nose. Nasty stuff.

"Nicho?"

Nothing.

"Come on, man, you were awfully chatty when I was above ground."

The corridor is wide and clean. There are several doorways on each side of it, and he enters the first, where the beam from his flashlight lands upon a giant tapestry made of peacock feathers.

"Whoa," he whispers.

Neville fixes the flashlight between his teeth and slides off his backpack. He unzips it, taking out his digital recorder, clicking it on.

"The room is elegant, tidy, as if its inhabitant just left yesterday," he says. "A cabinet sits open. It's made of sturdy wood, smooth and polished to perfection. Whoever built it knew what he was doing. A bed of embroidered pillows and blankets lies in a corner, under what looks like a window covered with an animal pelt of some sort. Looks like it might belong to a tiger. And there are engravings in the floor."

He trains the light around his feet, where he sees several of the same symbols etched into the stone slab and the palace gate doors.

"Dr. Neville?" A voice calls out from behind him.

"Nicho, Jesus, where were you?" Neville spins around, his flashlight landing on the young Australian. The bloke stands there holding a single match that's nearly burned to his fingers.

"Dr. Neville, I found something. And you're not going to believe it."

Chapter 15

TOJA PREENS at her window, applying a generous smear of red ocher crayon across her lips. Dressed in a fine amber tunic, her hair is coiled with a gold ribbon curled around it. Her eyes are lined with kohl and wide with anticipation. I hand our lunch to her domestic, Sayib, who sniffs the contents with her tiny, beaked nose. She looks me up and down with a huff and pours Toja a cup of young wine, leaving me to dispense my own from the small cask of resin wine I bought for myself.

"Cradle fruit!" Toja cries, and promptly drinks too much of it, digging into her lunch only after the wine has made her giddy. I like Toja less when she's been drinking, but at least she's in good spirits. I take this opportunity to remind her of her coming appointment at the baths.

"I hate bathing," she whines.

Toja finds harem life boring much of the time and likes to sulk, making it my duty to entertain her. I don't have it in me today. Not after hearing the archer's laugh in the courtyard. I sit sideways—uncomfortably—on an over-stuffed cushion, pinching a bone needle between my teeth. There's a small fray at the foot of her tunic that needs mending.

"I have a secret!" Toja whirls around, and I almost stick her with the pin. That would've earned me a slap.

"I'm sure it's one of great value."

"Oh, it is," she says.

She cuts a chunk of fat from her roasted lamb and chews it, lips closed. Even drunk, she remembers her manners at least.

"I think you have a secret, too."

I shake my head, finishing up.

"I can see it in those eyes of yours," she says. "I know these things."

I offer her a napkin and she wipes her mouth, taking another sip of the cradle fruit.

"What can you see in my eyes?" I ask, batting my lashes.

Toja squeals with pleasure. "Love."

Sayib looks up. With the sides of her head plucked clean, and only one stripe of hair left in the middle, she has the look of a black-feathered bulbul. Incurious, but often startled by noises.

"I'm sorry?" I say.

"Love, love, love, love, love," Toja sings.

Clamping my lips together, I sit back, trying not to look haughty.

"I know it. I do!" She trills.

Roon is right. She is a fool. And an ass.

"You sound like our seer," I tell her.

I force a pleasant look onto my face. Better this time.

"And he's coming to see you!" She coos.

"What?"

Toja tosses her head and giggles. She picks up a nut shell and throws it at Sayib, who tries not to flinch as it bounces off her forehead.

"See, I knew it was true!" she crows. "He's calling on you in a few minutes."

"How could—?"

"And if you become a soldier's wife, we might even be friends!" She says, like she's delighted at the possibility.

I hear a sudden crash and look up to see that Sayib has dropped the now empty pot that had held Toja's cradle fruit. She sinks to her knees and begins picking up the broken pieces, swearing under her breath. Toja ignores her.

Roon, Toja mouths, licking her lips.

Soldier. Roon. Of course. I forgot he's coming by.

"He's my late fiancé's cousin," I explain. "And I'm in mourning."

Toja pulls up her knees, hugging them. "And I'm a married woman."

I fold my hands, sitting up straight like a nursery maid. "I don't follow."

"You're in mourning for someone you never even met, and I'm married to an old man I've only met once."

Toja flops onto her sleek, linen pillows. Soft as silk, all variations of blue, her favorite color. She stretches from finger to toe and turns her head, smiling sweetly. "I'm older than you, aren't I?"

"A little bit."

Toja reaches out and takes my thumb in her hand. "And you seem like a big sister to me. Funny, isn't it?"

I shrug my shoulders and cup my hand over hers. Fool or no fool, Toja does have a heart.

"Salan seems wiser than I am sometimes," I say. "He keeps his darkest thoughts to himself."

Toja sits up onto her elbow, studying me. She's clear-eyed all of a sudden.

"That must be it," she says. "Why you seem so grown up. You're practically a mother."

Toja should be a mother by now, but rumor has it the sultan favors his eldest wife and that's the reason the newest addition to his harem receives so little of his attention. Shame. She could use someone to focus her attention on. Other than herself.

"Can you be my mother, too?" she whispers.

A commotion sends Sayib into another tizzy—rushing about, grabbing a fan, and putting it to use. Roon's arrived. He stands at the door, taking up every bit of its space, and glowing with the faint sheen of a recent sweat. Sayib, drop-mouthed, takes Roon all in. She stops fanning altogether, just standing there, and I throw her a look.

"Oh," she bursts out and starts her fanning again, but Roon doesn't seem to pay her any mind.

The specter of an old joke paints his mouth, and I wonder if he's remembering my betrothment feast. I know I am, and all at once I find myself looking forward to Roon's company.

"SHE LIKES TO BREAK THE RULES, doesn't she?" I say.

Roon keeps a respectable distance. We walk down the dark stairwell leading away from the harem apartments. One of the torches is out.

"I don't want to talk about Toja," Roon says.

"What else would we talk about?"

We walk to the Palace Gardens, circling the exotic flowers, imported from the river regions up north. Some have petals as thick as a turtle's tongue, but brightly colored, long, as radiant as fire. Others are tiny, like insects. As varied as a change of seasons. I've been dying to get my hands on them.

We stroll the gardens three or four times, until a group-ing of clouds appears, threatening a much needed rain. Roon takes me back to Toja's apartment.

"Goodbye," he says. And that's it.

That's how it is for the next few weeks, too. Roon comes for me at Toja's apartment, we circle the gardens saying not one word to each other, and he drops me off.

It isn't a forced silence, exactly. Roon himself seems perfectly comfortable with it. He's the sort who only speaks if he has information to impart, something to arrange. I suppose it's his training. But despite our lack of conversation, I enjoy being with him, and not only because it's a break from Toja. I like that we have a past together, even if it's not much of one. He would have been kin to me, after all, and he's one of only two people alive who I've known for more than a few weeks.

"Do you like these flowers?" I ask, well into our ritual one day.

Roon contemplates what resembles torn violet flesh, bleeding a sunny yellow.

"They're hideous," he says, and I break up.

"What do you find so funny about that?"

"I planted them," I say, and a lightness seems to come upon him with this news.

"They're terribly difficult to grow," I explain. "And the palace gardener couldn't do a thing with them. Not even now, during the rain season. So I asked if I could give it a try. The mountain tribes think them sacred, you know."

"I didn't know," he says, looking all at once like the younger man I'd met at my betrothment feast. One who should have become handsome rather than hard.

"Who taught you to garden?" he asks me.

"No one. Things just seem to grow well when I tend to them. Don't see as I do anything much different than anyone else."

Roon lifts an eyebrow and shakes his head. He rounds a bush of small citrus fruit as I struggle to keep up. His shoulders settle and the weight of his burdens seems to revisit him.

"Are we back to silence again?"

"Don't you like silence?" Roon asks me.

"I like it fine. Just not all the time."

Now Roon stops.

"I only have one thing to say, and I was saving it for our last walk."

Roon is leaving. Going back out there. To war. To whatever is left. I knew that.

"Maybe you should tell me now," I say. "It doesn't seem like flower talk is going to take us anywhere."

This time it's Roon who smiles, though barely.

"You know what I have to say."

I look at my lilac slippers and cross my fingers. Flustered, toes wiggling, I nod.

Yes, I do know. But I can't say it and neither can he. Not officially, while I'm still in mourning. Roon is ready to take a wife, and for the third time I'm going to be claimed as a bride. My second time as a mala. Anyone who's seen us walking—which is everyone, given the grapevine of information that grows throughout the Palace City—knows it, too. I want to be pleased about his desire to have me as his wife. To feel some tingle of excitement. I know how fortunate I am and how many palace women want him. It's my losses that keep me from contentment, I'm sure of it. As my grief fades, my heart will open to him, I think. It opened to the archer, after all. As friend, I mean. And the archer was a stranger who came to pillage my home and take me to his prince. If I could grow fond of him in just a few short days, then I will surely come to care for Roon as a husband over time.

"Is there something else?" I ask him.

"Sherin." He closes his eyes and it's like blowing out a torch, leaving me in the darkness. Roon isn't himself. There's a cloud over him and a coldness to his movements. I don't like it at all.

"Sherin, I don't want to go."

I stop breathing for a moment, shocked he would dare to voice such a treason. War, for a soldier of the sultan, is religion. It has to be. And talk of war—all-out war in the region—has been escalating. Not just war with the Waterless Sea, but many small bands who are fighting for survival.

"You can't think you're going to lose me while you're gone," I say. "I'm in mourning for months yet and live on the edge of a desert. Where would I go?"

I try to sound light, but can't wring even the weakest smile from him this time.

"No," he says. "I'm afraid of losing myself."

He suffers the rest of his conflict in silence, saying only three words to me when he comes to say goodbye: "Think of me." Roon leaves me with a sense of unease that makes me restless at night. Makes me wonder if the man who will return to me after the desert is someone I could ever grow to love. I hope so, for Salan's sake at least.

⊢——•◅◈▻ ◅◈▻•——⊣

THEN THERE'S ADAMEN. A laborer at the palace, he's barely of a class that can make conversation with me. His conflict with Roon over my honor diminished his prospects, and I've watched his resentments simmer in these past weeks.

"Meet me behind the baths," he mumbles to me one day, when I'm doing Toja's usual business in the courtyard. Choosing her food and collecting gossip, mostly.

"No," I say.

The public baths are outside the Palace City walls, leading into a narrow gorge that opens out into the desert. There are many small caves and secluded areas. Places I have no intention of visiting with Adamen.

"But I have something for you. And your brother. A peace offering."

"Your liver, roasted with wine and saffron?"

"Don't be that way," he says. "You know what it was like out there. Right after the Vara had come, traveling with that caravan of traitors. Can hardly blame me for wanting to show my allegiance."

"I can blame you for whatever I want," I tell him. "And don't ever speak to me again. You know to whom I belong."

He snickers and a waft of his breath comes at me.

"Yes, of course. To the man you're mourning, right?" His eyes are black and all pupil. As small as cardamom pods. "What if I want to call on you the way your new soldier friend does?"

"Feel free to call on me if you've come to fetch my laundry," I say.

I make a conceited mask of my face, like Toja does when speaking to her slaves. "Do you really want to make an enemy of Roon?"

Adamen takes in a yawning, satisfied breath. "Assuming he ever returns. Or that he'll still want you if he does."

I laugh out loud at his unearned conceit, and he joins me as if we're in on a naughty joke together.

"Even if Roon rejected me a thousand times, along with every other man in the Palace City, I would live my life as a mistress to cats before receiving a call from you."

Adamen steps back and licks his lips.

"Then cats are what you shall have," he says.

Chapter 16

The Thief

I WISH it weren't just a dream.

I'm back in my father's house. The smell of mutton—which I love—is everywhere. Yina's mutton, with lots of garlic and thyme. I see the back of a young man's head. Dark, sinuous hair touching his neck. So familiar to me.

Can't see the young man's face, but I know I want to kiss it. So much.

But the smell of mutton grows stronger. Not Yina's anymore. Laced with pepper, it makes me want to sneeze.

"Oof."

That is not part of my dream.

A splash of something on the floor. A snicker, sneaky-like. "Shhh," I hear. I'm still groggy from sleep. The world is not yet real.

It can't be Salan. I'd come home from Toja's to find my poor boy vomiting into a big-bellied pot. He's with nurses, being fanned and tended to. Fragile and sleepy, with his eyes glazed. I remember now. Mesu's head, no bigger than a lemon, was resting on his aching belly as I tucked him in.

Creeping soundless as a spider, a man leans over me, sniffing at my neck and hair. His breath is sticky on my cheek and reeks of mutton and wine. I pray to the gods it's a mistake. That this man has wandered into the wrong chamber and will soon realize what he's done. He's drunk as a eunuch on the night before he's unmanned, that much is obvious, and the harem assistants' chambers all look the same from the outside.

The tip of a knife pricks my rib and I stiffen. No mistake then. I'm terrified that if he pricks me again I'll start, letting him know I'm awake. He does, drawing a pin-point of blood, I'm sure. But I don't start. Instead an icy electric current flows through me. I think it touches him, too. I hear him gasp.

"With those eyes like gemstones," Adamen pants. "It's no wonder the fancies want you to grow their tribes in your womb."

Adamen! I haven't seen him more than a handful of times in the full moon since Roon went into the desert, but I've felt his shadow around me. Have somehow known he would find me alone sooner or later.

I lie still, like the dead, as he picks up my hand, taking my middle finger into his mouth and sucking all the way to its tip. The wetness is sickly and makes my stomach lurch. Adamen snickers, and I hear him slide something from his pouch. He lowers whatever it is onto my chest. Light, warm, more still than I am. It's an animal. Tiny and dead.

I can feel her blood soaking my tunic—our Mesu! I bite the insides of my cheeks to keep from crying out and shaking like a tree in a storm.

Then a blind rage begins to boil inside me. I hold that in, too. There are no guards on my floor. No one but a few high-born girls who wait on harem wives. No fighters.

Except me.

And Adamen.

I take a couple of breaths and pinch my nightdress between my fingers. I know I have to act now, before he makes his move. Gently, as if I'm about to turn on my side and mumble into a dream—I open my mouth. I strike like a cobra, sinking my teeth into his nose. I pierce his flesh easily, and it almost feels as if I'll bite his nose clean off.

Adamen drops his knife and it scatters across the floor.

"Witch!"

He knocks me back down, swiping the dead kitten off me. I hear her land in a nest of pillows by our window, and it makes me shudder. Thank the gods Salan is with the nurses. Blood is oozing from Adamen's nose and he sniffs, smearing it into the crook of his elbow. I start to cry out, but he's fast and pushes his hand over my mouth.

"I want to talk," he hisses.

I try to wrestle out from under him.

"I could snap your neck," he says, pushing hard against me. "Or slit you down the middle like I did that little rat."

Adamen's clutching my ribs between his knees, and it's hard to catch a breath. He jams his hips into my stomach, crushing my soup and wine, making it travel up my throat so I can taste it again.

"I needed to talk to you. Alone!"

His face hovers right above mine and his lips quiver, almost like he's laughing to himself.

"Salan," I say into his cupped, dirty hand.

"He'll be fine by tomorrow. I gave him just a bit of raving ash to make his guts churn."

My arms flail and I try to grab at his hair, at anything, but he swats them away, bearing down on me further.

"I want to see him," I say.

"I told you he's fine, but he won't be for long if you don't—" Adamen huffs and grits his teeth. "Look, can we just talk?"

I don't want to talk. I don't want to smell him or look at him or listen to his slimy words! I want to scream is what I want to do. But more than anything, I want to know my brother will be safe. Slow and sure, I nod.

He eases up on me. Not much, but enough to allow a decent flow of air into my lungs. Confusion is plain on his face and he tips his head, taking me in.

"Do you know the first time I saw you?"

A droplet of blood dangles from his nose, but does not fall.

"No, you wouldn't," he says. "Doesn't matter. Not today. You know what does? Matter, I mean? What matters is this. You and me."

There is no you and me, I want to say. But I hold my tongue. He wants to talk, so I'll let him talk. Might buy me some time.

"I saw a girl today who looked like you."

He tells me this like it's very important.

"But not really. Long hair, though. Northern and straight, like yours. The kind that flows like water. Followed her. Couldn't stop myself. And she went to the baths," he continues. "Peeled her tunic off so leisurely before stepping in."

He looks through me like he's reliving the moment, and I feel a bit sick.

"At first I just wanted to touch her hair. While she floated in the bath, eyes closed to the world. Like everyone here in the Palace City. And I placed my hand on the top of her head, gentle—like so."

His other hand floats to my head like a feather. I never imagined he could be so tender. It rests on my hair like a mother bird on her nest.

"Don't know why I started pushing her under the water. It's like I was watching myself do it. Her arms flailed just like yours did now—skinny things—and I gripped her hair in my fist, pushing her lower, deeper into the bath. Wasn't hard. And wasn't long after that she stopped her flailing. All I could see was that hair of hers, floating about the surface of the bath, swaying like a tangle of sea vine."

"You killed her," I whisper. My skin grows so cold, and tears of sweat begin to pour from my underarms. I can't feel the presence of my heart at all, though it had been beating wild and hard only a moment ago.

"See what you made me do," he says. "She was the daughter of an old soldier. Once a commander, like your friend. I hear he's been dying from an axe wound that split his back."

Adamen's tunic has come loose in our struggle, revealing his torso. His bare skin looks buffed and oiled like the belly of a lamp. He glances down at himself and I see right then that his hatred of me is also born of something else. Keep talking, I want to say. Just keep talking. And he does.

"Thanks to you I'm going to have to leave here now. Back out into the sand and the Vara. At least I'll no longer be a slave for the good people of the Palace City," he sputters. "I can survive in the desert, I told you!"

His eyes are searching about him, as if he's looking for an answer. I swallow hard and take my chance, hoping to give him one.

"You'd get farther with a jewel or two from Toja," I offer.

"Shut up!" He smashes his palm over my lips again. "To think I was going to ask you to come with me. But no—I should've known you wouldn't. Never have been good enough for the likes of you."

I nod that yes, yes, of course I'll come, anything to keep him from another unhinged attack, either against me or Salan. It's not lost on me how easily he could enter the nurse's chamber after leaving me here, dead or ruined, and kill my brother just to spite me. But he ignores my offer and cinches my hair in his fist, like he did that girl. His lips all curled, he looks undone.

"Do you remember telling me I'm not as smart as I think?"

He says this almost like a gentleman.

"I can tell you this," he says, crushing my mouth. "I'm

smart enough to know that I disgust you, so keep your offers to yourself--"

Right then, I buck, jamming my knee into the soft peach hanging at his groin. Adamen's mouth tears open and he groans. I make a claw of my hand and scratch all the way down his cheek, my fingernails creaming with his flesh.

"Thief!" I shriek.

Adamen springs up, stumbling backward into my end table, shattering a pot. There are stirrings outside my door and voices. The palace hates a thief even more than a killer.

"There's a thief in my room!"

Adamen glares at me and I feel that cold current again. Coming right from me. As if every vein in my body could at any moment burst and become a lightning bolt. He feels it, I know it. His lips flush blue and his eyes tremble. Cinching them closed, he turns away, tripping over a small table, then pulling himself up by my tapestry. He shoves an attendant to the floor and leaps over her, bolting down the stairwell. I watch the torches flicker in his wake, and feel that current surge, then settle into my bones. A part of me now. As sure as a heartbeat.

Chapter 17

World of Thieves

"**H**E WANTED ME to take him to Toja's jewels," I say, stroking little Mesu's body.

The palace guards chased Adamen through a maze of rooms and into the gardens, but he lost them in a gorge behind the public baths, where he killed that girl.

"It must have been his escape route all along," I tell them. "He asked me to meet him there some days ago. To give me a gift of apology, he said, but I knew it was a lie and refused."

A breeze blows in from the small window above Salan's bed pillows. Feels like a visit from my father's spirit and lifts me up. Salan is feeling better, I've been told. Sleeping peacefully. But without his little cat.

"He was a spy, I think. He said he needed money to get out of here. And why else would he kill the daughter of a commander?"

A soldier enters my chamber and the palace guard stand at attention. I know him, a bit. He's one of the soldiers who was present when Adamen made his accusations against me to Roon.

"Sol," says my questioner, greeting him.

He's nursing a leg injury—that's why he's called sol, a soldier ineligible for war. I can't say whether his diminished status will help or hurt me, but I recount to him what happened.

He listens carefully, silently, the way Roon would. Finally, he tilts up his chin—smooth-shaven with a pitted scar under his bottom lip.

"Yes, a spy," he says to the guard. "He tried to have us kill her for treason, but I think now it was to send suspicion away from himself."

I close my eyes and nuzzle Mesu to my belly—into the blotch of her own blood. Even the whiff of a potential rape would not reflect well on Toja and could cause me to lose my job and, ultimately, Roon's proposed proposal. I'm glad there's no mention of it, even if Adamen did go running out of here with his tunic open and flapping behind him.

"It's those nomads from the Waterless Sea," the sol says. "I've had a feeling they're behind this."

"Behind what, exactly?" I say, though he wasn't talking to me.

"The Vara, the battles in the desert, all of it. The Sultan is convinced they're the root of our troubles."

This is not news to me. Adamen said as much back in the desert. This so-called prince that leads these men of the Waterless Sea could very well be the most savage of warlords. He's a man I would have ended up calling husband, and it's a truly despicable thought. Still, I can't help thinking of the archer and the men who follow him. Their decency and talent for enduring hardship. They were very good to me and Salan and didn't have to be. They could have attacked Roon and his men as we sheltered in the caves during the sandstorm.

He did that for you. This thought comes out of nowhere, and I all but stop breathing. Makes no sense at all. While it's true that a battle in a labyrinth of caves would be a deadly endeavor, it's one in which the archer and his men had the advantage, given their knowledge of the cave system and the fact that they essentially had us trapped. Heavy casualties, yes, and Salan and I would have been caught in the crossfire, probably killed. No, I'm thinking much too highly of myself. A new bride for a dwindling harem belonging to some desert warlord is hardly worth a victory against an enemy.

"Here's what's strange," I say, surprising myself again. "I don't think this Adamen's allegiance is to those men of the Waterless Sea. Now as I'm remembering our time in the desert, some of his words there are making sense to me."

The sol's eyes are all scrutiny, but he seems interested. He leans in close enough that he can surely detect the rosemary water that I'd run through my hair before bed. I know I can smell him. He wears a pleasant tonic of boiled reeds and cinnamon.

"He talked often of knowing the desert and how to survive in it," I explain. "And he told me of having watched the man who led that army of nomads in the market near our home before the Vara came. He didn't speak well of him, and it seemed to me the men of the Waterless Sea didn't trust Adamen either, and took him only because he was a healthy man who could load and unload stores."

My best defense, and the archer's, is the truth. As much of the truth as I can tell. Lies have a way of unraveling.

"It was the only reason we took him as well," the sol says. "Healthy men have become a rare commodity in the Rah'a."

Not so rare as healthy women. He doesn't say it outright, but it's true. I look at my night tunic and pull it tighter over my breast. At least it was still wrapped and tied about me when the palace guard came.

The sol heaves a sigh, dropping his shoulders and dismissing the witnesses brought to hear my story.

"Tell the sultan's wives they can go back to sleep," he says. "The palace is secured and no one can take their jewelry now."

I nod. Paranoia is high at the palace, especially among the military. With all the guerrilla tactics that the smaller nations have been employing against us, this looks like just one other act of terrorism, thank the night sky.

"In the meantime, I think you should take this." He removes a dagger from his belt.

It's curved, sharper than broken pottery, and has a simple but elegant handle that ends in a blunt round, like a hammer.

"Are there so many thieves in the Palace City these days?" I ask.

The sol shakes his head. "The world is fast becoming one of thieves."

"I TOLD YOU smoking isn't without its virtues."

Neville blows out Nicho's match and hands him the flashlight. "I wouldn't call matches a virtue. And they can exist independent of the cigarette, so they're hardly a virtue of smoking."

Nicho shrugs. "Maybe so, doc, but I wouldn't have had 'em with me if I didn't smoke." He tucks his half-empty pack of matches into his shirt pocket and aims the beam of the flashlight into a stairwell. "It's this way."

The stairwell is narrow, made for a smaller people. At the time it was built, it might have accommodated two individuals walking side by side, but Neville and the Australian bloke have to take the steps in single file.

"Look at these," Neville says. He points to a series of holes in the wall, still stuffed with the remnants of torches. Ones that look like they could have burned themselves out last week. Neville takes out the recorder again.

"At the bottom of the stairwell, there's a large chamber—the size of a cathedral hall. Christ, it's the size of Notre Dame. The ceilings are high, domed. And they sparkle. Probably with gems, but I can't tell from here."

Nicho shines the flashlight around the chamber, highlighting several doorways leading out of the hall itself. "Those go to some big rooms. Not as big as this one, though. I only saw a couple of them. My matches kept burning out. They're painted with murals, like it's the Sistine Chapel or something. One of 'em was pretty racy. Ancient porn. Another, a smaller one, was painted in a sunrise. It had these yellow stones in the ceiling that look like stars."

Neville commandeers the flashlight from Nicho, shining it into the communal bath chamber.

"Rooms in ancient structures are often decorated to reflect whatever use the room may have been made for," he says. "Not a whole lot different than modern times. Pictures of food in a kitchen and such."

They continue to the end of the great hall, which opens up to another of these rooms. One painted with rays of sun and volcanic eruptions, generations of sultans depicted standing with legs wide and arms folded. It is a room of judgment.

Nicho guides Neville to the center of the room, keeping the light beam trained to the floor. In the heart of the chamber is a large chair, a throne of sorts, but plain and with none of the usual pageantry carved into it. The many painted sultans fix their eyes on that chair.

"Come around front to get a look," Nicho says, and they do.

There, in the chair, are the remains of a man. His skin is pruned a bit, like an old hide, but he's no skeleton. More like a mummy. But fresher. Into each of his eyes have been shot three arrows. His mouth, horror-struck and open wide, is jammed with at least a dozen of the same arrows. Cast with precision and at a distance, the arrowheads peek out of the base of the corpse's neck and stick into the chair, effectively holding him up.

"Scared the shit out of me when I found him. That's when I hightailed it to where I fell in and found you."

Neville slips off his backpack and crouches next to the dead man, coming in close, but being careful not to breathe on him, or contaminate him in any way. His eyes search over every part of the body as he puts the recorder to his lips.

"Adult male. Muscular, given the way the tissue has calcified, and how the body is angled in the chair. Several broken bones—tibia, femur—but they look healed, like older injuries that gave him a crooked gait. I don't think they were broken by whoever killed him."

"Or whatever," Nicho whispers.

Neville glances up at him.

"I mean I've never seen a grouping like that before," Nicho says. "This guy was shot at some range, and each of these arrows couldn't have landed more than a half centimeter apart."

Neville examines the corpse's hands. He died clenching his fists.

"Well, if you're going to have a place like this, you better have warriors good enough to defend it."

"I guess," Nicho says. He unzips Neville's backpack and takes out the water bottle. "You mind?"

Neville shakes his head.

Nicho takes a deep swig, wiping his lips with his hand. A drop falls from his knuckle and lands on the dead man's shoulder. Neville rises up and spins around, making Nicho back up quick.

"Will you be careful, for Christ's sake," he hisses. "Do you have any idea what we've found here?"

As Neville berates the Australian over his negligence, I'm drawn to the body pinned into the Seat of Verdict. That's what it was called in my time. My first time.

I know the man. Recognized him instantly. And I do not mourn the way he died.

Adamen, in fact, deserved much worse than he got.

Chapter 18

The Insurgent

THERE'S A FUROR at the palace gates. Everyone's speaking of it and it's hard to get a clear story.

There is a man.

He's been left at the gates.

He's naked.

He's tied up like a pig.

He's covered in blood, but not his own. There's a circle of it drawn on his back.

It means he's a gift. Perhaps from a tribesman who'd like to make peace?

And he's alive.

But not for long.

My first thought is that it's Adamen. He's been gone for nearly six full moons—I've counted every one, but I keep expecting him to turn up. Whenever I hear of a thief or killer who's been captured, I can't help but think of him.

"He's a known enemy of the Rah'a," Toja says.

She tells me the man is leashed like an animal, and will be left in the courtyard for three days to incur the abuse of the palace population. On the fourth day, he'll be bound to a large spike at the palace gates and left first to die, and then to rot right down to his bones. A message to anyone else who might want to make trouble.

"I wonder how ferocious he'll be with a collar and chain?" Toja crows as we walk together to the courtyard.

"He'll look like any other condemned man, I imagine." I don't want to go. My only consolation is that we're running late and a curfew has been instituted in the Palace City due to the encroaching troubles on the outside. We won't be staying long.

"I was told he's handsome," she says.

So it can't be Adamen.

"The other wives are always saying someone somewhere is handsome," I whisper.

Toja giggles, fingering the rope of hair I braided for her.

"That's because they're married to the sultan."

"Toja!"

"It's true! He's old, but he still thinks of himself as young and believes we think of him that way, too."

"Be quiet!" I say.

"I am being quiet," she pouts. "And while he makes us bathe until our skin is raw, he doesn't require the same of himself. At least a dozen of the wives have told me he smells like yogurt that's sat for days in the sun."

"Toja," I say again, but this time it's hard to keep from cracking a smile.

We've entered the gardens, which are restricted from merchants, laborers, and slaves, so there's hardly anyone here, let alone within earshot.

"With so many well-made men at the palace, it's just depressing, that's all."

I can't argue that.

"But you do live very well," I remind her.

That perks her up a bit.

"And you want to keep it that way, so you best be careful around Sayib. You know how the servants love to talk."

Especially Sayib, but I don't say that.

"Sayib," Toja mimics. I think it's the first time I've heard her say the girl's name. "Sayib is a dunce. And besides, she has a wet loin for only one man and he belongs to you."

"Toja, don't be crass."

Toja leans in to me and smacks her lips. "I can be anything I want. I'm married to the Sultan of the Rah'a."

We run into a couple of the older wives with their attendants and walk the remainder of the way to the courtyard together. There's talk of nothing but the excitement of a captured insurgent and his forthcoming execution. Dresses are being made, parties planned, and the temples prepared for days long celebrations.

"Sherin, you look sullen," Patra, the most senior wife, says. She has a thin-lipped smile, elegant in shape and lovely in the way of clever women.

"She doesn't like the prospect of seeing blood," Toja explains.

"Not even the blood of an enemy?" Patra inquires.

Toja reminds them of my past. How I braved .the Vara, watching all those I love perish. The women nod and twitter with me about my captivity and rescue by the brave soldiers of the Rah'a, reliving my story as if it's the first time they've heard it. Death by Vara is the stuff of legend and life behind the palace walls is all fantasy.

As we near the entrance to the courtyard, we hear the ruckus. The courtyard is loud on any given day, but on this day, the first day of the prisoner's public internment, the place has turned virtually into a carnival. But I don't want to see a man naked and beaten—whoever he is and whatever he's done to deserve it. I'm too much my father's daughter that way. And I was on the outside long enough to know that in terms of a real threat to our kingdom, the torture and death of one man is meaningless.

"There he is!" Toja calls, but I close my eyes and turn away.

Taunts and insults flood the air. Words like *vermin* and *swine*. As we move closer, I begin to feel sick. I don't want to see him. I don't want to know his face. There are so many crowding around that the insurgent is totally obscured. And I'm glad. I watch a man pick up a jug of urine and heave it at the prisoner. The crowd jeers.

"I want to see!" Patra shoves the man in front of her. He spins with anger, but when he sees not one wife of the sultan, but three, he backs away, letting us move closer toward a prime spot. I hang my head.

First, I glimpse his feet. They're filthy, but unharmed. *Thank the gods*, I mouth. Then his calf muscles, also pretty good. His thighs are worse, bruised and scratched, and once I start, I can't take my eyes away. It's his torso that makes the blood start to rush from my head. Burns and whip lashes already and the people are only getting started. I can't imagine the torn mound of flesh this man will be at the end of three days.

Though he isn't worthy of it I'm sure, I feel pity for him. His suffering brings forth all of my memories of the Vara. Ones I've locked away. My mother's agony, Yina's begging, my name on my father's lips as he died. Then I think of after the Vara. Of the archer, the way he saved me from Kirin. The scent of his desert-worn tunic, the glint in his eyes, so deep in color. The brutal elegance with which he moved in battle.

"Mazal," I whisper to the god-wife. "Make it not so."

I want more than anything to run away from this place and never return.

But instead, I make myself look at his face.

Perfect. Unblemished. His back having taken most of the abuse. His man's beard and his boy's face. The curve of his cheek like a small pear. His skin flushed red as much from the ruthless desert sun as having to endure blow after blow.

"No," I cry, then cover my mouth. No one around me

hears. Not the sultan's wives, nor the palace citizens. There's too much noise and commotion.

But that's not true. One person heard me. *He* did. And our eyes meet. They seem to reach out to me. One like meat gravy with ribbons of blood, the other like a tortoise shell. The eyes that I've tried to shut out of my mind; the ones that have been watching me in my dreams.

"There you have him," calls one of the palace guards. He struts to the archer and bows, then turns to his audience. "The demon who brought the Vara to our kingdom. I give you the Prince of the Waterless Sea!"

Chapter 19

The Prince

"**No.**" It comes out as a whisper.

The archer swallows hard and takes another blow to his back—from a charred stick used to poke wood chips that smoke our fish stores. He hardly flinches, just stares into my eyes.

"No." I say it much louder this time.

"Please," he mouths.

No!" I wrench a jug of wine from a merchant's hands. Before a single thought can clear my mind, I throw the wine into the archer's face, then lift the empty pot high above my head. Now the thoughts come fast and ready. I'm going to smash it onto his skull—this man who brought the Vara to my home, killing everyone I love, and dragged me from my ruins to be his trophy. Who I'd prayed for on the battlefield, and believed had some nobility. *Idiot.*

The crowd around me cheers and heckles. He won't stop looking at me, his eyes like a shamed dog's. And I look right at him, too. My gaze travels the crimson rivers in his right eye and the golden rings in the other. They seem to go on endlessly.

"Murderer," I say, and with all of my might, I thrust the jug down, hearing it smash into pieces.

It lay in shards on the ground. A tiny piece has embedded in my toe, and a freckle of blood appears. My hands are shaking. I missed the archer's—nay, the Prince of the Waterless Sea's—head and I don't know how that could've happened. *You missed him on purpose*, a whisper inside me says, and I pick up my foot and bring it down, smashing one of the broken triangles nearly to dust.

"You can die on a spike!" I seethe at him.

Patra cackles and the entire crowd erupts into a disjointed choir of howls and guffaws.

"Whoops!" One of the merchants calls, slapping his thigh.

"Just as well," another says. "I want to see him bake on a spike, too."

A series of "yay"s and "here-here"s play like a chorus.

I can hardly stand it and lunge forward, slapping the archer as hard as I can. The crowd thunders and I hate them for it. Turning my back to him, to all of them, I push through the wives and guards and attendants—each one rushing in to catch a glimpse of the prisoner before the city closes for the night.

Plodding through the gardens, I climb up and up to my chamber, collapsing on my bed pillows. There, I heave bone-dry tears until my body shuts down and my thoughts become ink-black, empty and cold. I suppose it's in that state that I sleep.

MY EYES FLICKER OPEN. It's dark and silent, like on the night Adamen came. Must be very late. My throat is juiceless and sore.

Salan lies curled up next to me and I remember nothing of how he got here. I suppose his nurse brought him in. He's fresh and clean. It's the first time he's bathed without me, I realize.

Gradually, the events of the afternoon return. Going to the courtyard with Toja, seeing the archer chained and beaten, then learning that he was the man who destroyed my life. Mine and Salan's. That it's thanks to him I'll never again feel my mother's fingertips smooth a dress she's made for me. Making sure I look fine. I won't ever hear my father sing the "Songs of the Desert Wind".

There is a wind that divulges secrets and murmurs deceptions. It blows long hair wild, clawing skin from bone. There is a wind, there is a wind for everything.

They're gone. They'll always be gone. And it's all because the archer unleashed the Vara on our market.

I crane my neck, kissing Salan on his tea bud lips. He wrinkles and scratches his nose, then curls up on his side.

When I stand up, I find my legs are strong and willing, and I go to the cupboard and retrieve a dagger. The one the sol gave me the night Adamen fled the city. The one meant to protect me from thieves and killers and liars.

I creep from my chamber into the hallway, still low-lit by torches. The rosy, limestone walls blush in the tender light. It's empty here and deadly silent, like an unhappy marriage. I inch my way through the slumbering palace, past its temples and across its gardens, where I lurk behind some flowering thorn bushes. Then I slip onto the path that leads to the vacant courtyard. I've never dared to venture out after curfew and it's strange to see the Palace City so deserted. Stranger still to feel the heat in my veins—real heat that burns. Like a pepper on my tongue.

There, on the ground, still bound to the porous stone wall by a leather collar and chain, is the Prince of the Waterless Sea. I take a deep breath, and feel my stomach roil. His eyes are closed and he doesn't move. A torch is mounted behind him and casts a mellow light over his lean body—all bare skin and sinuous limbs. He's stretched out, his head cradled in the crook of his elbow. Sleeping just as he did when we traveled together in the desert. As I draw closer, I can see his back is strewn with welts and cuts, his skin all raw linen and cross-stitching like a coverlet sewn by a novice. Worse than before, but nothing so bad that it won't heal. It's only his first day, after all, and one that ended early due to curfew.

As I come to his person, I kneel down. He's been cleaned up by the palace guards, made ready for another round of torment. The public always wants a fresh canvas. His jaw is set, like my father's on any given day. Especially on the day the man with Vara limped into our sights.

Gripping the dagger tight, I think of my mother. How her hands made my comfortable lilac slippers, which I've mended over and over and intend to wear until I die, and the pillows and blankets that swaddled me at my father's house. And my tunics. The dress she made for my betrothment feast and our outings to the market. And the most glorious one. The one that made me look like a tulip . . . my wedding tunic. I clutch the dagger so hard my fingers tremble.

Then all at once my arms go limp and I slump to my heels. The dagger falls to my side, and hot, stinging tears come rushing fast down my face and neck. I'm conscious of nothing around me. Not the night air. Not the way the rough sand and pebbles poke into my flesh.

And as I sit there, drooping like a dying flower, I feel a warm hand come over mine. A calloused thumb strokes my knuckle.

"Sherin," he says.

I fall back and scuttle away from him, catching those damned eyes of his. They make me trip over my feet as I turn and break into a run. It's only when I reach the gardens that I catch a breath and collapse next to my blossom. It's the one Roon found so hideous. My heart is beating wild, and I'm shaking all over.

I can't reconcile the man who saved me from Kirin's derangement, and later protected me from his own men; a man who fought with skill and courage against a more powerful enemy, and then did not choose to slaughter them when they became trapped in the caves by a storm. All of this with a man who could kill an entire population for fleeting riches.

This same man who wanted to take me for his own. To bring me to his people and make me one of them.

The heat in my veins turns to fire at the sudden realization that I do not find that an unpleasant fate.

"I can't," I whisper.

My mind cannot stop its race from one horrible thought to the next. How in two days' time, after his flesh has been butchered by our population, he'll be tied to a spike. His arms and legs will be twisted into an agonizing configuration that will break his bones at the joint. He'll be left to die of thirst, of the burning sun, of the whip of blowing sand. The solar glare will blind him early on, and as he dies, he'll hear only the insults of watchers, the flapping wings from birds of prey, and the ever-present desert wind—hollow, mournful. Then, when he's gone, his body will roast and rot, the vultures will come, and he'll be the offering at his own funeral feast. It is a death suited to an enemy of the gods, being killed and consumed by all they have created.

And despite everything he's done, what confounds me the most is that I don't want him to die. Not in pieces or at all. Does that make me a fool or a monster?

I close my eyes and inhale the scent of the flora surrounding me. Fresh and fragrant in the night. Like a lady done up for a party. Some wafts are sweeter than honey, others bitter like weed, and they blend in the midnight air to make a rich perfume.

But among the wild grasses, figs, and flower buds, there's

another scent. One of blood and ash and fresh sweat. The smell grows stronger and I open up my eyes again, and wobble to my feet. There, in the path to the courtyard, he stands. Naked. There was nothing in the courtyard he could have used to cover himself. But it's as if that's of no consequence to him. It is to me. A naked prisoner is one thing—a creature chained and abused for his crimes, being prepared for death. A naked man is another. A free man who looks right at me, intent on living.

I can't move as he walks toward me. The dagger I'd left behind is gripped in his hand, reflecting a beam of silver off the light of the half moon. I pinch my eyes shut and when I open them again, I keep them trained above his waist.

As he approaches, I see the abrasions left from his collar and a fresh cut behind his ear. When he sliced the collar from his neck with my dagger, he must have nicked himself. In only the moon's glow, he doesn't look so bad. The bruises on his shoulders seem more like shadows, the cuts on his breast like simple lines drawn by a child. The ones Salan likes to make in soft clay.

And I see his lips, soft and sweet. Lips that deceived me, I remind myself.

He raises his hands to my face, and puts one on each of my cheeks. I can feel the cold blade of the dagger against my jaw, and his feverish skin. Makes me quiver. I should turn away, but I don't. His eyes take me in like the night sky, drowning me in the depth of their hue. I see a true blood integrity in their crimson threads—my father always said red was the color of virtue. There's a promise in their amber, but of what I don't know. Drawing in his breath, he leans in and kisses me. Tender and soft at first, but only at first. Then he brings me closer, crushing against me and curling his fingers around my hair.

And when we part—a day, a breath, a heartbeat later, I

don't know, the archer touches his forehead to mine. I can hear his breath—ragged, heavy. Strange and familiar all at once, like an instinct. He runs his fingertip over my lips, then my chin and neck. The skin of his finger is firm, like a wine grape. I want to taste it.

"Come with me," he whispers.

Chapter 20

I Came Here for You

HIS BREATH is in truth the only part of him that smells good. But still, I feel I could hold him close all night. This traitor and killer.

"What have you done? To me, to everyone," I whisper.

"I didn't . . . I'd never hurt you Sherin. Please believe me." His words are as clear as the coldest water. They taste of sincerity, but I want to spit them out. Ask him why he did what they say, as if there could possibly be a good enough reason.

But a cough echoes in the distance, along with a shuffle and a step. He hears it, too, but doesn't move. Waiting for me to say something, I guess. Maybe to answer him.

Come with me, he'd said.

Only to me, it's as if he spoke in another language. I might recognize the syllables and how they come together, yet they make no sense at all. None of this does.

Not who he is or isn't. Not what I'm doing here with him. This man who stands accused of trying to destroy us, and who may in the end succeed in that. Yet here I am aching to believe it's all a mistake. Wanting to kiss him again.

I touch a lesion on his collarbone, swollen and tender. The archer swallows and I watch his shoulders rise and fall. He's tired and must hurt all over. Ribs bruised or maybe broken, stinging cuts, hungry and parched. But his expression is soft and deliberate. And there are his eyes. Always those eyes of his. I can't get away from them.

"I came here for you," he whispers. "Only you."

The steps come closer. Clumsy steps from a drunken man. One who starts to sing to himself like a fool. Getting caught after curfew is no laughing matter, and the closer he comes, the more likely he draws attention to himself and to us.

But a drunk merely gets a beating. I, given that I'm with an enemy, would find myself joining the archer at the end of a chain come morning.

"You have to go," I say, but he takes my hand, putting it to his face and inhaling deeply. I stand there, my lips stinging, tasting of salt and blood, and him. My eyes wanting to take him in whole, but I don't dare.

The drunk trips and falls, cursing himself, and the archer glances behind us. He takes a step back, pulling me with him. I have no choice but to go, at least until I can find a place to hide.

We tramp over my flower and past the citrus grove, then through the colonnade that leads to the Temple of Pallah and her sister structures, all carved of alabaster with pillars made in the reptilian shapes of the demi-gods that rule our seasons. Our cult center, the temples are usually flooded with fire-light, but have been darkened in preparation for the archer's execution.

At the back of the temples, sandstone surrounds the Palace City—one of its natural walls. The archer brings me around, past the public baths and toward the gorge, where Adamen made his escape into the desert.

Adamen.

Salan.

The archer.

The Prince of the Waterless Sea.

My family.

I came here for you.

They're coming for you.

I stop suddenly and he squeezes my hand tight.

The man with the Vara, the first one. The one I saw in the market with my mother. His face visits me. "They're coming for you," he'd said on that day.

"Who's coming for me?" I ask him.

The archer turns around, his brow furrowed. A lone torch at the back of the baths illuminates his injuries and they no longer look benign, as they had when he kissed me. I run my eyes over the worst of them—inflamed, crusted with blood. Only a day ago, his skin had been unmarred, and now he stands before me as further evidence of how fragile life has become for us all. Especially the helpless, like Salan.

"Why did you do it?" I demand of him. "The Sultan says you brought the Vara."

"Sherin," he says, shaking his head.

"And you lied! You never told me who you were and pretended to be just another survivor!"

"No, I had every intention of telling you!"

"When? On our wedding day?"

I hear a thump and a loud curse. The drunk has fallen again. He cries out to the god Pallah, asking for another crock of wine, then laughs bitterly.

"Please, we don't have much time. You have to believe me . . . "

"I don't have to believe anything! And why should I?"

The archer takes my head in his hands, firm and hard. He kisses me once more. On my lips and my shoulder. I've forgotten to breathe. Without another word, and definitely without another damned kiss, I break away from him. My heels hit the ground like clubs.

And he comes after me, calling my name in a strained whisper, but I won't stop. His hand swipes at my back and I feel him clutch the sash at my waist. He pulls me to him.

"My men aren't far from here," he pants. "They're sheltered in the dunes—waiting for us. Please. Don't be afraid. I can tell you everything there."

"I'm not afraid," I tell him, but that's a lie.

Behind the temples come a march of footsteps. It's the palace guards on their watch.

"Let me go," I say.

My sash is still in his hands and I pull on it. He pulls back at first, but then releases it. I close my eyes tight, keeping away this garble of lies and truth that's pulling me every which way. With him, the Prince of the Waterless Sea—I can hardly say what they call him—there's only a confused series of events that wed survival, biological warfare, theft, and war . . . with a kiss.

I expect him to say my name again, but he doesn't. I want to say his, but I don't know it and I can't very well call him archer anymore.

A cool wind blows, lifting my hair, making me shiver. Catching my hair in the gust, he grips a handful of it and I gasp, my eyes bursting open. Raising my dagger, he swipes it down, slicing a lock of my hair clean off.

"Salan," he whispers, and kisses me quickly.

With my hair clenched in his fist, he sprints toward the gorge, wearing nothing but the cuts and welts the court inflicted on him. This time, I do look at all of him. If only because it might be the last time.

My senses return to me as I hear the guards rounding the corner toward the cult center. I can't be seen in the darkness, after curfew on the night the prisoner escaped. I sure as the damned can't answer questions or endeavor to tell lies—and poorly at that.

I duck into the temple of fire and of course the first thing I see is the goddess Kujuh, with her statue made of goat and fish bones. She stands there, her arms held wide, as if ready to take me into her cold embrace. She sat with me on the night of my engagement, after Yina fixed my hair and dressed me in a tunic the color of sand. Covered in a soft, blue blanket, I'd prayed she could inhabit my heart before my wedding, opening it to my husband, making me want to bear his children.

And tonight, I sit with her again, not knowing what to ask of her. As the guards go by, grumbling about the drunk, I find myself praying. I cannot say it is to Kujuh, as she's a single-minded goddess. It's a prayer to the earth, the night sky, the wind, the body. An entity that feels as if it encompasses all of those. I pray that I'll never again feel how I did when the archer kissed me.

Chapter 21

Parties and Parades

"**HOW COULD HE** have gotten away?" Toja asks me, looking from her apartment onto the courtyard where *he'd* been held captive.

I shrug, barely able to endure her. It's only a day and a night after his escape, and our kiss. I've gotten not one wink of sleep.

"He was chained," Toja says, holding up her palms. "And the guards!" She can't stop shaking her head.

"Toja," I say. "Nearly every able man has gone to war."

A secret smile passes Toja's face. "There are still plenty of able men at the palace."

I do feel like her mother sometimes.

"I mean the regiment at the palace gates. They're still here," she says.

Yes, that regiment is impressive, but they're all for show. And the guards in it are either too young, or sols like the one who gave me his dagger. Hardly better than an old woman wagging her finger.

"Didn't they say his collar had been cut?"

I swallow hard and feel my face flush.

"Perhaps he had a knife hidden," I say.

Toja tosses her head in frustration, as if I'm the child now. "He didn't have a single strip of linen on. Where in the world would he hide a weapon, unless he put it in his a--"

"Toja!"

"I'm trying to think this through, that's all," she says. "He couldn't have just disappeared."

Undoubtedly, the sultan and whatever soldiers are left in the Palace City are trying to think it through, too. I tidy Toja's braids, putting the finishing touches on her hairstyle. My hands tremble. No good at all.

"Maybe someone at the festivities will know something."

"Let's hope so," I say, unconvincing I'm sure.

Since hours before dawn on the night of *his* flight from the city, when the palace guard first discovered the big escape, there's been a mad scramble to put a festival together. Pigs and lambs have been slaughtered, flowers plaited together into sumptuous garlands, and bonfires lit into blazing fire-balls all over the Palace City. Dancers and acrobats have been thrown into hasty rehearsals. Songs and chants have begun to seep through our walls, ambling in and out of corridors and drifting above the temples and gardens—sending news of our revelry into the desert.

Salan danced with excitement all morning about it and didn't utter one word of complaint when a nurse brought him the hot porridge he hates and made him eat it before he could go to the festivities. He didn't even notice my poor humor.

While all of these amusements had been arranged before the insurgent's escape, it would have been some days away yet, as his torture was the prelude to the celebration. But since he appeared to vanish into thin air, the sultan had to come up with something fast, or else face a deeply unhappy citizenry. A tinderbox made up of anxious people who hear whispers about the desert from merchants and guards, but don't want to believe it.

"At the very least, it'll be exciting to learn what goes on in the desert. Ow!"

Toja yelps when I yank on her hair. I didn't meant to. Well, maybe a little.

"I'm sorry," I tell her. Toja turns, so girlish and moody. I stroke my fingers along her cheek. "It's just that I often wonder if the desert brings anything other than death and ruin these days."

I remember the archer running naked into that vast emptiness as I slide one last pin—jeweled and sparkling—into Toja's hair.

"How do I look?"

Her tunic is pale green, embroidered with blue and gold thread.

"Beautiful," I say, and it's true. This breaks the ice between us, finally. Toja loves to look pretty.

"It's nice to see you out of your mourning tunic," she says, smiling. "And to think, your first outing will be at a parade!"

It is, I suppose, an irony that my mourning ended on the night I was first kissed. And by whom.

"Lilac suits you." Toja appraises me.

My tunic is lilac, matching my slippers, which are still fine, though stained faintly with the archer's blood. And yes, my mother always told me lilac is my best color. But I can hardly get excited about fashion the way Toja does. Especially after I touched so intimately the man who brought woe upon us all, and the life I've stitched together for my brother and me can unravel any day.

This last part is something Toja doesn't at all seem to grasp.

As for the archer, or whatever I should call him, I try to chase him from my thoughts, which is no easy feat. I can still taste his mouth, imagine the soft wave of his hair.

"Ready," Toja says. Eager as always.

At the door, we're met by a palace guard, who'll be accompanying us to the parade. Not for protection, but pomposity. Every wife of the sultan gets an official escort. It makes the festivities all the more . . . more. Sayib is also there, trussed up in a formal yellow servant's tunic. She pitters behind us, fluffing the long, sheer train of Toja's dress, giving me the occasional eye. She cannot disguise her hatred of my company, though I know not what I've done to her, apart from being courted by a man who would never pay mind to a woman of her station anyway. I'm hardly keeping them apart.

——— ✦◈◈◈✦ ———

AT THE TEMPLE OF PALLAH, the wives are decked-out, posing like statuary, and finding artful opportunities to look good by praising their husband.

"There's going to be a great announcement," Patra says. She stands with her fist at her side, squeezing the fabric of her tunic. It's gold-threaded throughout and glitters in the sun, reflecting the gems on her headdress. She looks like a bright star, and if Salan was with us, he might mistake her for a goddess.

"An announcement!" Toja claps her hands. "Is it that prince or whatever they call him? Have they recaptured him?"

I pray to all the gods worshipped in the realm that they have not.

"Settle down, Toja," Patra chides. "If our husband wanted us to know, we would already know."

Patra adjusts her headdress, stroking the freshly shaved skin at the base of her skull. Most of the older wives shave their heads, having grown tired of years spent battling lice infestations. They wear turbans on regular days and fantastic coronets on special occasions.

"But *you* know, Patra, don't you?" Toja says.

Patra tips up her chin. Her patience with her husband's youngest wife has been eroding for some time.

"Oh, come on. He tells you things he doesn't tell any of us."

Patra smiles with great condescension and places her refined hand on Toja's shoulder.

"Because I don't divulge what he tells me."

Patra turns to me in a way she seldom does. As an attendant for a junior wife, I'm not much worth her attention.

"That man. The one sentenced to die. You knew him, didn't you?"

I close my eyes and nod.

"I didn't mean to bring unpleasant memories," she says. "I know he took you from your home."

"Yes," I whisper.

"You must feel a very personal injury at his escape."

I don't answer her. I can't. Silence is my best armor with a woman like Patra, who has heard every possible lie in her time as a sultan's wife. The moving plea for forgiveness. The vow of eternal loyalty by an enemy. The pretense of burning desire that a young wife performs for an old and ugly husband. Not to mention all the little smarmy lies about the fit of a dress, the curve of a figure, the ageless beauty of a face. If I answer her in the only way I can, she'll know I'm lying, too.

"Today's events might not bring you the outcome you'd expected," Patra goes on to tell me. "But I do think they'll bring you some satisfaction."

On the temple steps, music swells from the palace band. It's a clap of hands and stomping, clicks from tongues, whistles and animal calls, all of which create a symphony that explodes with the raucous sounds of a river at night.

As the song fades, the clatter of a chariot makes its way from the garden doors. Gold, gem-lined, painted, and carved, its sumptuous linens drip from its windows. The Sultan of Rah'a, of course, lies inside. He's draped in white, the costume of a hero, with his head wrapped in a turban. He seems to glow like snow on a mountain top.

The band begins to sing now. In something between a wail and a chant, they voice the call I've come to know well. "Kaji. Kajiiiii. Kajiiiiiiiiii." The call of war. They're welcoming a battalion of the army home.

Roon, Toja mouths.

All at once I feel a bit too cold. I'm glad that he's safe, of course, and hopefully unharmed, but I'm not ready to see him now that I'm officially out of mourning. It means our marriage, if he still wants me, will come soon. Perhaps even in a matter of days.

"There they are!" Toja calls out.

From both sides of the temple, the soldiers come in formation, flanking the sultan's carriage.

I don't see Roon, but I hear his voice. He gives a "ha" and his men fall in line, standing in defiance against the strong, midday sun. One limb at a time, the sultan emerges from his carriage. He's sheltered by palm fronds, fanned to keep him from breaking a sweat. The rest of us aren't so lucky. My own dress clings to me like a swimming frock.

The sultan's throne is carried to the temple steps by two guards who are unremarkable in stature so as not to make our monarch look small. They march reverently to the sultan, pick him up, and place him on his seat of gold. That's embellished with plum-sized gems and mythical taxidermy. Invented creatures of prey—catbirds, clawed snakes with spotted fur, crocodile jackals.

A pitcher, also of gold, is put at the sultan's feet, while a matching bowl is placed in his lap. A soldier—young and unscarred, a symbol of hope—lifts the pitcher, kneels, and pours a deeply red wine from the pitcher into the bowl.

So, that's what this is all about. A hero is being honored in our realm today. A man who will, for a time, become the most important citizen in the Rah'a. It's a grand distraction, and a good one at that, I have to admit. Everybody loves a hero.

Toja grips my hand and trills. I can sense the whole crowd's anticipation. Panting, teeth clenched, throats dry. There's an almost sexual need for good news in the Palace City.

The sun beats down hard, and my tongue is stiff and thirsty already. I sip my own wine as a chain of palace guards emerges from the gardens—they're the big ones used for pomp. The ones who will never stand next to the sultan.

Then I see him for the first time in nearly a year. Roon.

I put my cup down and step up onto a footrest for a better view.

He looks much like he did when we used to walk in the gardens. With no serious battle wounds, he walks straight and high, as always. A light sheen of sweat covers his shoulders and arms, the back of his neck, his thighs. His breastplate shimmers in the late-morning light. I'd forgotten what an impressive sight he is, and part of my heart is so happy to see him.

Roon meets the palace guard at the base of the temple steps. And while they're big in stature, he looks even bigger. The guards are holding someone, but I can't see him. It's only once they fall back, unraveling like a braid, that the new hero of our realm is visible.

His legs are crooked, as if they've been broken and set more than once, but he holds himself erect, like a soldier, and in a soldier's stance.

But he's not one.

His skin is deep in color—burned by the sun, then healed many times over. His scars are numerous, although they're not scars of battle, but survival. The cut of a knife from a thief in a stripe across his neck. Whipping lesions all over his body—undoubtedly from being caught as a thief himself.

His expression, though proud, is hard. As hard as I have ever seen. It's callous, evil, and undaunted.

It's Adamen.

Chapter 22

The Hero

ADAMEN MARCHES with Roon to the sultan's throne, and I can hardly keep from screaming out for everyone to hear! Roon's face is fixed in a dutiful mask, but his opinion of Adamen is not improved, that much is obvious. I can tell by the way he moves. There's no pride in Roon's step.

At the throne, Adamen drops to his knees—all theatrical, as if worshiping a god. He drinks down every drop in the golden bowl, then gazes up at the Sultan of Rah'a. Drunk off his good fortune, he falls prostrate to the ground, chanting a prayer of submission to Pallah, not that he's ever been the praying type. Pallah, the god of the sun's light who is believed to inhabit the Sultan of Rah'a's heart. Pallah, the god of a soldier's courage. Right.

And our monarch laps it all up. From his throne, he catalogs Adamen's alleged feats of bravery.

"He, who like the serpent to the spiny mouse, wandered the Rah'a to find our enemies and fight them. He, who like the olive baboon found the Prince of the Waterless Sea, conquered him, and left him at our gates."

So, Adamen now claims to be the one who left *him* at our palace gates. Tied like a pig and covered with someone or something's blood.

"Like the wasp, he is small. But his sting causes men to shriek. To run away, flailing, waving their hands."

Cringey attempts at poetry.

"And one more thing," our monarch proclaims.

He holds out his hands to Adamen, who rolls his shoulders back as if on cue. His broken, twisted form has cut half a head from his stature. Thrusting his hand into his tunic, Adamen digs in, then pulls out a dagger. He holds it up over his head, letting its blade wink in the sunlight.

I know it. I would know it anywhere. That dagger is mine. The one the sol gave me after Adamen's attack, and I dropped next to the archer. The one he worked to cut off his collar, and then held at my cheek as he kissed me. The one he used to take a lock of my hair.

I've come for you.

Adamen bears down, as if he's going to plunge the dagger into the heart of a bitter foe.

"That is how I killed him," he snarls, and the crowd goes silent. Even the drunkest of us hold still.

"He crawled out near the public baths, where one of his men waited. And where I waited—knowing he would try to escape."

Adamen scans the palace population, meeting as many eyes as he can. I pinch mine closed.

"He got on a camel and started away, but I had a beast, too. A mule. And while not as fast, it was strong, and I tracked him to the dunes, where all the scum gathers sooner or later."

Adamen lowers the knife and flips it over, admiring it, hungering for it as if it were a leg of lamb.

"And at the dunes, I did see him," Adamen tells us. "They camped there, his tribe, and I watched them. Biding my time while he dressed and tended to his wounds, eating and drinking with his men. Beastly men. No manners. And this knife—this knife was with him. Tucked into the tie at his waist. He wore the robe of nomad, a nothing. Then, as they went to sleep—one by one—I took my chance. I jumped onto his back and pushed him down, holding him. This dagger pressed into my thigh, cutting it deep."

Adamen holds aside his tunic to show a fresh wound. Not bleeding anymore, but raw and inflamed.

"So I took the dagger from his hip and I thrust it into him, twisting it, letting him squeal like a swine. I slit his throat to shut him up. He deserved no last words."

My throat goes sticky with bile and I cup my hand over my mouth. Black spots appear before my eyes until there are so many they blend into one.

"DRINK!" Sayib splashes my lips with wine.

I sputter and cough.

The sultan's wives and attendants are bent over me. Their brows knitted in concern. Toja is actually holding my hand.

Sayib refills my goblet and I feel sick.

"Wine is medicine," Patra says.

She takes the goblet from Sayib and tips it gently to my lips. The wine is cool, barely sweet, and takes my head like a pillow after a long day. She pours me another.

"I must have stumbled," I whisper.

"No, you fainted. Are you feeling better?"

I think I nod, but I'm not sure.

"It's hot," I say.

"I have something that'll help you feel better," Toja trills. "And much better than wine at that."

The crowd parts, forming a crescent around me. Sayib bites her lip and bows.

Because there he is. Roon. He seems bigger, with a few more scars. His eyes burn like the sun gems on the sultan's chariot. They're one of the only things left from my old life, and they seem somehow in danger of leaving me, too.

Chapter 23

The Hideous Flower

ROON CROUCHES at my side, his eyes sweeping over my face. He's sad, I can see that much. His time in the desert hasn't done him any good.

He scoops me up and carries me away from the more spirited parts of the celebration. Where Toja and the other wives are getting drunk and teasing the jugglers.

I know Roon is taking me to the gardens, our place before he left. Only now, it's the place where the archer—all skin and bruises—kissed me.

Next to his hideous flower, my lula, Roon sets me down. The plant is crooked and one of its petals torn from my having stomped on it as I ran in the dark that night.

"Is it true what he said?" I ask. "About killing the man from the Waterless Sea?"

Roon sits beside me, never taking his eyes away. "Adamen won't hurt you, Sherin, despite the honors bestowed on him. Not now."

Roon thinks I was asking out of fear for myself, a fear of Adamen, and I'm glad. My first question to him should have been one of concern for his welfare while he was at war.

"Adamen weaves lies with the truth," I say. "He's very skillful at it."

I think of the things Adamen boasted about when he described his kill. That the archer had crawled from the Palace

City, which was not at all true. He ran upright and quick. That one of his men had been waiting for him. Probably true. The archer had said as much. That the men of the Waterless Sea had camped near the dunes. Maybe. But Adamen must have ridden his mule like hellfire if he was to make it there and back in so little time.

What is undeniable is that Adamen has my dagger, and the last time I saw it, it was in the hands of the archer. At some point, their paths crossed.

"Adamen claims to have left the insurgent at the palace gates a few nights ago," Roon says. "According to his account, he camped outside the Palace City to watch the execution. It's how he saw him escape."

"Adamen says so many things," I tell him. "Like that Salan isn't my brother, but my child with an enemy I'd only just met."

"He's been in the desert on his own for a long time, Sherin, and the desert makes desperate men."

"That's right. Long enough to say anything to ingratiate himself. And it worked, didn't it? He came back not just forgiven, but as a celebrity." I shake my head, pounding my fist into the soft flesh of my thigh. "And why? Why would he wait until the arch—the insurgent's—execution? Why not offer him up and take the credit right away? Makes no sense at all."

The power of the liar is that they always hide truths in their fiction. They make you doubt yourself and cast suspicion on others, and I'm not going to let Adamen do that to me again.

"It doesn't matter what's true and isn't," Roon insists. "Fame of his sort comes and goes. It'll be forgotten about when another hero comes along. Or a greater problem. And those are plenty these days."

"The way it was forgotten that he murdered the daughter of a dying commander? Is there no price for life anymore?"

Roon shrugs. "Her mother now claims she drowned by accident."

"Of course she does! And what was she given in return? Or threatened with?"

I lean in to Roon in a way that's probably inappropriate—certainly ill mannered—so close that I can smell the infusion of incense that seeps not only from his scant soldier's wardrobe, but his very skin. Damask rose—as common a masculine scent in our realm as sweat.

Instead of slanting to put space between us, Roon angles toward me. If we were anywhere else, under any other circumstances, I think he might kiss me.

"I have to know," I whisper. "I have to know if it's true. Is he really dead?"

Roon shakes his head.

"You don't have to know. You have to trust that once you're the wife of a commander in the Sultan's army, your standing will be permanent. Adamen's is fleeting."

"As fleeting as the memory of his crimes, apparently."

"Yes," Roon acknowledges.

In another brazen act, I put my hands on Roon's shoulders. Upon his flesh, my fingers look tiny, the way Salan's hands look when he puts them over mine.

"Please," I say. "You can tell me."

Roon's eyes are glassy and guarded. He doesn't want to talk about what goes on outside the Palace City.

"Roon, I've been there, too," I say. "It's been a long time since I've set foot outside the palace gates, but I know about the desert."

"A lot happens in a year, Sherin."

"You tell me this like I don't know? My life was destroyed in three days' time. I poisoned my own father to end his suffering!"

I've thought of it a million times over, but I've never said it out loud.

"I did it so easily," I say.

Roon's eyes come alive again, even if only for a glance. He reaches out to me with them, and I feel almost as much heartbreak for the pain I see there as I do at the thought of the archer's death at Adamen's hands. The thought of my father's death at mine.

And then, like the draw of a curtain, his eyes are closed to me again. My whole body shivers and Roon sees it. He lowers his gaze and begins to speak.

"He said he slayed the insurgent as he claimed. He couldn't carry his body, not with the weakness in his legs—they'd been broken and healed badly. So he left him to be eaten by vultures, but returned with the knife you saw. It was bloody when I met him, and so was he."

I shut my eyes tight.

"You saw him right after?"

"Yes," he says. "Our regiment was on the march home and he approached us carrying a pouch containing a heart."

"A heart," I whisper. "And you believed him just like that?"

Roon touches my cheek with his thumb and I blink my eyes, but close them again. I can't look, not yet.

"Not just like that," he tells me. "I took him into custody and brought him here to face justice in the Hall of Judgement."

"Some justice!"

Tears streaming down my face.

"The sultan's verdict is not mine, Sherin, but . . ."

"But what?"

"But he claims to have killed an enemy of the Rah'a. Our greatest enemy, according to the sultan."

I hate every word coming out of his mouth.

"He could've found the knife, or stolen it. That could have been anyone's heart!"

I feel Roon look at me and open my eyes to him again. They're not near what they were before. I want to shake him and tell him never to go into the desert again. Whatever is there, it isn't for a man like Roon.

"He'd clearly been in a scuffle—beaten and fatigued," Roon continues. "He led us to the camp not far from the dunes where the men of the Waterless Sea had been, but they'd already packed up and moved on, as their kind does. They must have taken the body with them, but there was blood at the mouth of a small cave. More than enough to empty a man."

My shoulders droop. I feel as drained as Roon's eyes. The savage storm of the archer and his execution, our kiss . . . his murder. It's all too much.

Could've been thieves or migrants, I tell myself. Ones who took my knife or traded for it, maybe found it. The archer had no place to put it, after all. No clothes. He could've dropped it as he went to rejoin his men, and Adamen could've picked it up.

I could've gone with the archer when he'd asked me.

Should have, but couldn't.

Life changes in the flick of a finger, the crease of a brow.

As surely as a man with plague in a crowded market.

I take Roon's face in my hands and rub his ears between my fingers. They're the only delicate thing on his body.

"What's happened to you?" I whisper. He's the one trembling now.

"Sherin, what's in the desert now isn't for a woman."

I slide my palms over the sides of his face, so closely shaven. It gives pleasure to my hands and reminds me so much of the first time we met, even if I didn't touch him then. I imagined how his skin might feel, though, and I'd been right. Like suede over marble.

But Roon tilts away from me and stands up. His eyebrows knit together—dark and groomed to severity. The hideous flower between us sags, nearly collapsing. Roon's knee jammed it down as he rose.

"I'm sorry," he says. "I've stayed too long already."

Distant as a ghost, Roon bows and leaves me.

Whatever happened in the garden is fading way . . . Roon and our silent walks, the kisses from a dead man.

I pluck the hideous flower from the ground and cradle her in my arms. The flower I grew and nurtured and that Roon hates so much. Near death, her scent is almost putrid. I'll take her to my chamber and give her some water, maybe a few more days of life. Salan should be playing with his nurse. Spry, real, growing like a palm under my care. I can do anything if it's for Salan. Even marry a man as torn as this flower.

IN THE TEMPLE ARENA the wives and their attendants are well on their way to total inebriation.

"Sherin, go dance!" Patra notices my reappearance immediately, and I notice that she isn't drunk at all. She has a chalice in her hand, yes, but she wears it like a piece of jewelry. Moving toward me, neck straight, headdress erect, she seems to float.

"I'm not much of a dancer," I lie.

There's no sign of Toja. She's probably at another part of the Temple grounds, entertaining herself with contortionists and sword-swallowers.

"Toja has no need for me, apparently," I say, shrugging.

Patra takes an imperceptible sip of her wine, tipping her head yet keeping her coronet in place. A deep scarlet gemstone is set in its epicenter—easily the size of a kidney.

"Oh, I think she has a great need for you."

Patra glances at the flower I'm holding.

"It got trampled," I explain. "I want to put it in water and grow another from its seed."

"And I have just the vase for it—one I left in Toja's apartment. Go fill it, then leave the flower in my bed chamber." Patra touches one of the lippy purple petals. "I've always liked this flower. It has a terrible beauty."

"And a worse fragrance," I say. Pungent, perfumy, like a ripe pear wrapped in a rotting animal pelt.

"I can do that, Most Honorable Wife," Sayib breaks in. She licks her lips and sniffs at me, the plume of her hairstyle casting a shadow like a claw.

"Do hurry on, Sherin," Patra says, ignoring the girl.

Bowing to her order, I move past a sullen Sayib and push my way through the crowd with a splitting headache. One made of the archer, Roon, and Adamen.

The aromas—spiced meat, sickly sweet purees of date, musk oil, smoke, and lust are as strong as a latrine's. I hurry on into the cool air of the palace and up the stairs to the harem apartments. At Toja's door, I slip past the tapestry.

Patra's vase sits at the center of Toja's foyer like a temple offering, but I take little notice of it. Because from Toja's bed chamber come sounds I've only ever heard when I tiptoed past my parents' bed late at night. Or as I ran by the comfort houses doing Toja's bidding.

There, on Toja's mat, lie Toja and a soldier guard, naked and entwined, weeping with sweat.

And they are my undoing.

IT'S SAID A BIRD IS BORN TWICE. Once as an egg and again as a bird. This is why birds are the messengers of the gods, at least according to the oldest human civilizations. As I've been born so many times, I wonder what that makes me. A messenger of some sort, I imagine. Someone who can offer bits and pieces of history for others—those with only one life, one chance.

But in my first life, I was winging it like everybody else. I had no phantom memories of experiences in different eras to bolster my intuition.

And I couldn't see what was plainly in front of me.

Not the feelings that had taken hold of me. Not a genuine appreciation for the danger I was in.

Neville can't fully see what's in front of him either. The Rah'a is as distant as an old movie to him. It's a movie he loves and can watch over and over, but it's still a movie, a myth; a family legacy that he's been carrying with him like an amulet.

"Jordie!"

Neville and Nicho are still underground and have returned to the harem apartments, where I lived with Salan. The muffled sounds of a working backhoe grumble above them on the surface. Neville waits for the machine to still and calls out to Jordie again.

"Smart flashlights. As many as we have. Lots of batteries. Enough water for two to three days."

"Smart flashlights?" Nicho says.

"They're like the Swiss Army Knife of flashlights."

"Hmm, we didn't get any of those," Nicho grumbles.

Neville shrugs. "That's because they cost a small fortune."

"PowerBars," Nicho says.

"PowerBars. Got that? And five sleeping bags."

Nicho mouths his name, Neville's, Jordie's and Pete's.

"Five?"

Neville bites on his lip. His face a distorted mask of light and shadow in the beam of their dimming, un-smart flashlight.

"And call my wife and tell her to take the first plane out of Virginia!"

Chapter 24

The Visitor

TOJA STICKS out her tongue, coated red from rose jam and currant wine. I throw her tunic at her.

"Wait," she calls to the guard, who's sprung from her bed like a baboon. He fumbles, shamefaced at least, wrapping his belt around his waist and tying up his laces.

"The back way," I say, and he nods. His back is still glistening with sweat, but of the nervous variety now. He leaves without even a nod towards his idiot lover.

"What are you doing?" Squeaky-voiced, she stands up, making no attempt at getting dressed.

"You know very well what I'm doing."

Toja's tunic hangs open and her hair looks exactly as expected after what she's been up to. I start tucking her pleats and sniffing her breath. I'm *this close* to strangling her.

Toja huffs and swats at me.

"It's not your business what I do. You belong to me."

"And you belong to your husband!"

Toja wrinkles her nose like a pissy lap-dog. "How dare you speak to me like that!"

Oh, I dare all right. I seize her chin and squish her cheeks, until her eyes pop wide and furious.

"Patra saw you with your guard!"

I let her go, and she claps her hand to her cheek as if I'd slapped her.

"She sent me to your chamber under the ruse of fetching a vase for her." I glance over at the hideous flower lying next to said vase. "That's a message for both you and me!"

Toja crosses her arms staunchly under her breasts—lifting them up in grudging presentation.

"That doesn't mean anything."

"It means everything! Why do you suppose she'd send your attendant to your chamber in the middle of a party?"

Toja doesn't want to stop sulking, but I can see that some of the realities of the situation are starting to dawn on her. She puts her breasts down and meets my eyes.

"He takes no notice of me and never even visits! And I've had no knowledge of him since after our wedding. Not that I care."

"Toja, you are the sultan's wife whether he visits you or not." I clutch her shoulders and shake her—something I should have done months ago. "As a royal wife, you may be spared your three days at the public's mercy, but you'll still be locked into your tomb to waste away and die."

And I'll be locked in with her. The two of us, losing air and dying of thirst. Better than the Vara, I suppose, but not by much.

"I know what it's like to watch someone die slowly," I tell her.

The sultan's youngest wife chews her bottom lip and bunches up the linen of her tunic, wringing her hands.

"Surely, if Patra meant to tell anyone she wouldn't have sent you, who's bound to me in eternal loyalty."

I roll my eyes, wishing I had slapped her.

"Patra sent me as warning!"

"Well, I'm not the only wife who has lovers."

I take her hand and intertwine my fingers with hers. I can smell her fear mingling with her perfume—an oud of botanicals with sweet, balsamic notes given to all the sultan's wives.

"Maybe you're the only one who's been careless."

Toja puckers her lips, but at least she's still listening. I am, in a strange way, the closest thing she has to a mother and she's definitely still in need of one of those.

"Don't disregard her, Toja. She's the most senior wife and it's in her best interest to keep you in line and respectable. But not if you're stupid."

Toja nods.

"Well?" I say.

"Fine."

"Fine what?"

"Fine, I'll be good."

I CLING TO TOJA like wet linen for the remaining events, ones mostly consisting of drink and out-of-tune chanting.

"Toja, you look tired," I say. "Forgive me for not taking you to your apartment earlier, the way you'd asked."

My part of our rehearsed exchange. I nudge her, earning Patra's approval when I escort her most junior wife away from the festivities. And away from the men. She gives nothing but the most casual acknowledgement, but brushes her hand over my elbow as I pass. Lightly, as if thanking me for plaiting her hair.

It feels like days since I've seen Salan, and I wish I could hold him tonight. I'll have to wait until the festival is over, and life has returned to normal, whatever that means. The children have their own parties and are kept largely away from the drink and other adult amusements. It'll just be me and a lone glass of much-needed wine tonight in our chamber.

"What a day!" I hear immediately as I enter my room.

As if today could possibly get any worse.

Spread over the mat Salan and I sleep on, Adamen
stretches, pointing his toes. The slash on his thigh looks
deeper up close. More like a stab wound. He swings a thin
chain around his finger, winding and unwinding it.

"Aren't you going to offer a hero some refreshments?"

I open my mouth to call for the guard, scream, I don't
know.

"Ah-ah-ah. You wouldn't want to be caught with a man
in your room, would you? Wouldn't reflect well on yourself
or, uh . . ." He points his thumb in the direction of Toja's
apartment. "Don't worry. I've only come to talk."

"Like last time?"

Adamen shrugs a bit sheepishly. "I think you'll want to
hear what I have to say. If you don't, well, I'll leave it to you
to explain how the hero of the realm ended up lying on your
bed mat."

He hikes up his tunic and spreads his legs, offering me a
view I'll be hard pressed to forget. On the end of the chain
is an amulet of some kind and he lowers it into his mouth,
sucking on it.

"What now?" I say.

Adamen spits the amulet out and grins. Two of his teeth
are missing. One above, up front, and one below, a canine.
The rest are gray, with deep, dark stains between them.

Despite what I know he's capable of—Adamen has a pro-
found instinct for self-preservation—his time in the desert
seems not to have been easy for him. In less than a year, he's
aged ten.

"I'd love a cup of wine," he says.

"As if you haven't had enough already."

"Mmmm, how about some red?" He puts his hands
behind his head and stares at my breasts. "You've grown up."

I watch him as I retrieve my carafe from the cupboard,
making sure never to give him my back.

"You're welcome," I say, and crouch down to place the cup on the ground near him, but not too close.

Adamen reaches out, trying to touch my finger, but I snap my hand away. He jerks, splashing the wine over his chest, and cackling like an old, witchy woman.

"You haven't changed a bit."

"And you're even worse than before."

"You have no idea," he says.

"I'm sure you'll tell me all about it."

"Oh, I will," he says. "But first, I want to talk about you."

I back up towards the cupboard and lean against the bold, peacock feather tapestry.

"Me?"

"Well, your unstable position here in the Palace City." Adamen sets his elbows onto his knees, and flaunts his whole, heinous smile. An appalling wedge that looks like a string of tiny button mushrooms, all rotted and withering.

"What do you know about my position or anyone else's here? You've been back for what? A couple of days?"

He sucks on a tooth and smacks his lips. "Got anything to eat?"

I ignore his request and he shrugs. Lifting his head, he hangs the amulet around his neck, holding his eyes on me the whole time, like he's dressing for me.

"Brothels are wonderful places, you know. For so many reasons." He sticks his hand into his tunic and rubs his chest, grunting. "Apart from the obvious, they're places of great conversation. It's true. Ask anyone who visits them." Adamen cups his hand into a duck's bill. "Yap-yap-yap-yap-yap."

He stretches forward and tries to grab the hem of my tunic and I kick at his hand. He laughs, planting a wet kiss on the tips of his fingers.

"The girls love to talk," he crows. "About which little servant girls offer special comforts to the soldiers, for instance.

But especially about bad girls who pretend to be good girls. Levels things out, makes them feel better about what they do."

"So?" I say.

So, he grimaces, mouthing the word.

"So—You're barely hanging on thanks to the easy virtue of the sultan's most esteemed youngest wife. And if I know it—having only been back for two days, as you say—then it's only a matter of time before someone gets up the courage to let it slip to the sultan."

He licks his lips and fingers the little amulet around his neck. "And I have to say, the Palace City just isn't going to be the same without you."

Chapter 25

Geet

"**YOU THINK YOU** can come in here and slander a sultan's wife?" I ask him. "Treason offers a leisurely death."

Adamen glugs the wine in four throat-bulgers. He wipes his chin and holds his cup out for more. I set the bottle down and nudge it toward him. He's dragged the stink of sweat and alcohol, reeking breath and luxury oils into my place, making it smell like the palace brothels he likes so much.

"It's only treason if it isn't true," he says.

"It's always treason if the sultan says it is!"

Adamen reclines again, nestling into my bed like a maggot in the folds of a deep gash.

"Now you listen to me," he rasps. "And I don't want to hear a single word come out of that conceited little mouth of yours until I'm finished."

I have the urge to scream for the palace guard, but I know it would do me no good. Instead, I lean back against the tapestry again, settling my breath.

"Good girl," he says. "I would've hated to have to rip your tongue out of your throat. Even if it would make you better company in the long run."

Such a charmer. He bids me to sit next to him, but I remain where I am, staring him down. He thinks it's funny.

"That idiot mistress of yours has been very naughty. And

not because of the young hulk you caught her with a few hours ago. She's had three you know, and that's just today. But hey, it's a party. Who am I to judge?"

Toja didn't have time for three—at least I hope. But the trouble with Adamen's lies is that they often see past a mere fact and hit on a much greater truth. Toja might not have had three today, but she has most certainly had three. The sultan would hardly make the distinction.

"See, time in the desert makes a man sharp-eyed. You have to be to stay alive." Adamen scratches at a blotch of dry, scaly skin spilling out from under his hairline.

"My eyes are open, and wide," he says. "Watched your lady come and go with an acrobat, a singer, and that guard you got a chance to meet so close up. I watched you all day. The way you dropped like an apple at the mention of me killing that nomad you like so much."

"It was sweltering."

"Shhhh. I'm not finished."

Adamen drums his fingers along his ribs, eying me with intention. He takes the amulet between his fingers and rubs it like a charm.

"The Palace City is the only livable place left in all the lands," he tells me, like this is news. "If it falls, and I pray to every god I've never believed in that it doesn't, the survivors will have to go into the desert and try to make it."

"Like you did."

He stops rubbing and rests his hands on his heart. His nostrils twitch like a dog's, sniffing my scents.

"You have no idea what it's like out there," he says. "If you thought it was bad after the Vara, well, I tell you I'd take the Vara ten times over what I've seen."

Adamen shifts his gaze toward my window, where the setting sun has left only a feeble light in the sky, the way a lone candle glows in an empty chamber.

"You want to stay in the Palace City, Sherin. It's the only way to live. Treason makes for a bad death, no matter which way you look at it. Leisurely, like you say. And your Toja? Well, I wouldn't count on her getting the gentle, quiet darkness that other faithless harem wives might've got before. She'll get the whole bounty. The torture, the defiling of her body, the public spectacle. And so will you."

"What are you talking about?"

Adamen drives his hand into his waist cloth and slides my dagger out from a sheath of mole rat hide.

"Expensive to make. Bronze. Rare outside of the Palace City." He holds the blade upright, looking at it fondly. "Maybe your friend stole it when he fled the Palace City? Or maybe your Toja gave it to him so he could set himself free. One of her many lovers. Or one of yours. I haven't decided yet." He kisses the dagger's tip.

"I've never even seen that dagger, and what would I be doing with a soldier's dagger anyway?"

"A soldier's dagger? I never said it was a soldier's dagger. Although, funny you should mention it, this fine weapon comes from a blade-maker who caters to the sultan's army."

I grit my teeth and press my heels hard into the floor. "I do live here, Adamen. And I do know a few soldiers. I'm marrying one as a matter of fact."

"So you are," he says. "And I know soldiers' weapons. One of my jobs, you know, the last time I was here, was taking care of the personal armory. For the soldiers who live here—sols and the like. I know those weapons very well. I know who this belonged to, for instance. I bet he'd be happy to have it back, and might wonder how it got into the hands of an escaped insurgent."

Adamen springs up from my bed, standing up fully, and I gasp. Can't help it.

"And don't bother crying to me about Roon! The way he'll

believe you no matter what I say. They need men like me, who live on the outside. You think I haven't been walking the desert floor with him and his regiment for months?"

"Liar! I've talked to Roon and he only saw you after the arch—the insurgent—escaped. After you supposedly slayed him."

"I'm the liar, am I? Not Roon? Not you?" He points his finger into my face. "You know that insurgent, as you call him, better than you say. Or at least, he knows you."

Adamen shakes in a silent chuckle. "The desert might be vast, but I've been in it a long time. I've scrummed with everyone who's left standing."

"So what?"

"So what, you say? Someone's had his eye on you. That's so what."

"And you killed him," I whisper.

"I did what I had to do! There was no other way your Roon would have taken me behind these walls!"

He steps toward me and clutches my arms, almost lifting me up off the floor. I try to wriggle away from him, but it does no good.

"Roon and I will be married," I warn him. "I'll call him here right now!"

"Heh," he grunts. "Most esteemed Mala."

Swaying, Adamen lets go of me and takes a drowsy breath. He's drunk, yes, but he's also in pain, and getting to his feet so quickly winded him.

"You know what I've had to do? Hmm? I've had to live like a jackal."

His voice raises the hair on my neck. He isn't mocking this time as he looks me over. It's almost like he's admiring my tunic.

"Roon," he says. "You want to be waiting for him in his bed night after night? Is that how you see your life?"

Adamen turns from me and limps past my bed and over to the window, where he looks out. His head is swallowed up by an inky-black sky, the stars floating about his ears like insects.

"I make you sick, do I? Even more than when we first came here with Roon's regiment." He nods, as if talking to himself. "Yeah, I do, I know I do. But at least I know what I am. I know what he is, too."

"You don't know anything," I say.

Adamen's shoulders spread out and he rests his chin on my windowsill as if star-gazing. "Roon is a killer like me."

He says it into the night air, like it's his confessor.

"Why don't you ask Roon about the girl from the Ayashi? You know it? It's a region on the outer edge of the Rah'a. We came through it a while back. Maybe five or six full moons have since passed."

"Yes, I know it," I say. It's part of the Rah'a, but barely. A lot of plains and dry grasses. A small river. Not much, but enough. More than the Waterless Sea has going for it.

"She was younger than you," he continues. "Only by a couple of years. Bitty teats. Eyes a little like yours. Well, nobody has eyes like yours. But they did have something other than the soil to them. Like a marsh, maybe. Tiny flecks of green when you looked really close. And I did. Look close, I mean."

Adamen turns, falling right into my eyes. I don't like it. He seems vulnerable—a rabid dog covered in lumps and gashes. Empathy for such a creature can kill you.

"Roon was at war. He doesn't owe me any explanations," I say.

"Geet." He nearly chokes on the word.

"Geet?"

"It was her name. Geet. I know because I heard her father screaming it until they shoved a sword down his gullet. There were maybe fifty of them—hard to tell. And they tied her to a post. Roon and the valiant men of the Rah'a."

The blood runs from my face and pools all the way in my heels. I think of the archer's men. How easily things could have gone a very different way if they'd seen the red stain at my seat. The one that marked my journey from girl to woman.

"I'm not going to listen to your lies."

"Her people—Geet's—there weren't that many of them, but they had stores, and knew how to survive. Not really fighters, though. A bit timid. It was after we killed them— that's when I knew I had to get back here. I'd go mad if I stayed out there." His voice is soft and grating, like the muffled chirp of a cricket.

"Ask him," Adamen says. "See what Roon's face tells you."

He cranes his neck, coming closer, until I can see the whites of his eyes are streaked red. He wants me to look into them.

"I, for instance, could tell you that I wasn't one of them," he rasps. "That even a man like me was revolted by her cries and the bloody mess she became as they took their turns. Or that I got in line like they did. That her wailing turned into any other noise after a while, and I didn't have to look at her to do what I had to do. In what the desert has become, you can get used to anything. Only I did look at her. Just that one time. The flecks of green in her eyes."

I squeeze my eyes shut. I hear Adamen teeter to my door, his gait like an old man's.

"This part is true," he whispers. "She was raped to death, that girl. And she wasn't the only one. But she was the first. And the hardest. Your Roon wanted to kill himself after. Kill all of us. But he didn't. We had to move on. Fight more bands. Take more stores. Keep the Palace City going or we all die with it."

"Roon would never do that."

Adamen takes a deep breath, like it's his last one. "Maybe not the Roon of your youth. Or the one you knew before he went away. Today's Roon is a different man. He changes by the day. We all do. And one day the Roon I know will show himself to you, and you'll regret the day you ever met him."

He lifts the amulet and chain off his neck and hangs it delicately over mine. I can hardly move.

"A gift from your Roon?" I can feel the cool circle of the amulet between my breasts.

"I've never seen it before."

"No?" He says, staring down at it. "Well I found it on your pillow. It's gold. Do you know what it's got on the back?"

I shake my head. "How would I know that?"

"Two interlinked circles with a real bloodstone in the center."

Ah'kwarah'a. It's a hieroglyph that means *I was born for you*.

"How romantic," he sighs. "A gift of Nahoor for a bride. And then there's the stone. Isn't a bloodstone meant to signify everlasting love? You should wear it for a while. See how it feels."

Adamen caresses the bloodstone with his finger, then pushes past me. He leaves just like that, the flap of the tapestry slapping the edges of my door frame. My hand goes to the amulet, touching it as he did. The gold is pounded thin and shaped into a sun. I stroke the cool bubble of bloodstone at its heart, then flip it over to see the symbol—*Ah'kwarah'a*. Delicate and personal, it seems like nothing Roon would ever give me.

Adamen is a liar, I say out loud. But maybe in his own way he's right, and I don't know Roon after all.

Chapter 26

Roon

"**WE CAN ANNOUNCE** that we're going to marry now," Roon tells me.

No longer at the sultan's call, he's come as my escort on the last day of the festival. An almost official declaration of our intentions.

"Good," I say. Though the word almost gets stuck in my mouth. I touch the bloodstone at the center of the amulet and meet his eyes, but Roon makes no remark about his gift.

We're walking in silence as we did before his last tour in the desert. The way we used to in the gardens, only it doesn't feel the same. The quiet between us is deliberate now, whereas before it had been our way of being together in peace.

"Will our marriage be this wordless, too?" I try to say it with good humor, not sarcasm.

Roon takes my hand and walks faster, pulling me along. Down the same path the archer and I ran on the night he escaped. The one that leads to the public baths where Adamen fled the city. Where the archer asked me to leave with him. A path that seems to say something about my future.

The rock corridor narrows, until finally we slip through a slit of an opening that lets golden light burst through like it's a door to another universe. We find ourselves standing in a gusty wind that picks up the sand and throws it like an angry child.

Otherwise, the horizon is empty—not at all the fearsome carnival of dangers that's been whispered about, and that Roon and Adamen have warned me of. The desert looks no different than it did when I was traveling through it with the archer and his men.

But somehow, it is different. Like Roon and I. Like Adamen. Like the gardens without our hideous flower.

"Look," Roon says.

Stark, empty. Only the wind.

"There is a wind that speaks of ghosts and memories; there is a wind that sings your funeral song and beckons you to the next world," I sing.

"The Songs of the Desert Wind."

"You know it?"

"Of course I know it," Roon says. "I think of little else when I'm out here."

Roon strides ahead of me into the sea of sand. He looks lonely here, untethered. Like it's the last place he belongs. The archer had always seemed at home. I can imagine him nowhere else, and feel his spirit in the sand and sun.

"It must have been written by a nomad," Roon says. "Because I could never see the angel winds that live here. Only the demons who take everything away."

I go to stand next to him, the sun glowing blood-orange on the horizon. Just moments from beginning its final decent.

"Roon, the desert wind can't take you away."

"It already has," he says.

"Don't even say that."

Roon turns to me, his eyes blazing like that sun.

He takes me very suddenly into his arms and holds me, rocking gently.

"I wish I could take you away," he says. "If there was a place to go."

"There will be a place. Our home."

In this moment, I can't for the life of me imagine Roon and I sharing a home.

Yet his arms feel as strong as anything I've ever known.

"I knew you belonged to me, Sherin. I knew it the moment we met." He says my name as if it's all he has left. That much we have in common. We're all the other has left.

There's such an intimacy in that, and for a moment I'm tempted to mention what Adamen told me about Geet. But not because I believe it. Not all of it anyway. I believe there was a Geet. I believe she succumbed to a horrible end, as he said. I believe that Adamen was a part of it. But I don't believe Roon could do anything remotely like that.

"Roon," I say, my lips so close to his heart that I can almost feel it beating. "Our army will prevail against our enemies in the desert. We have to. This unrest can only last for so long."

Now I sound like a palace wife, but there is some reason to what I'm saying. My father's reason about the way of the Rah'a. Why we're strong and the other regions are not.

"Sherin," Roon says, his voice as low as I've ever heard it. "There are no warring tribes."

"What are you talking about?"

Roon lets go of me. He shakes his head and cinches his eyes shut.

"We thought the same as you, my men and I, when we were first sent out into the desert to defend our realm. But then we saw what it was."

Now I'm the one shaking my head.

"Sherin," he says. "We're the only ones at war. At war with ourselves and the tribes around us. The sultan squandered most of his treasury. He needed the riches of our best settle-ments. And then whatever settlements lay beyond those."

"Roon, you're not making any sense."

He rests his hand on my neck. His fingers are grit-rough and hard, his palm pressing the amulet into my flesh.

"I couldn't stop it, Sherin," he says. "I don't think I can ever stop it."

It sounds impossible, what Roon is saying. That the Sultan of Rah'a sent the Vara to rob his own kingdom, and then went to war with the smaller kingdoms that surround us. To save his finances and keep the Palace City afloat. That it's he who killed my parents and Yina. Who turned the desert and the fertile islands within it into a wasteland of savage violence. It's not the archer, the prince of nothing, the dead man. And it's Roon who was sent to clean up the sultan's mess and win a war against ourselves.

We could talk more of it. We should talk, but we don't.

Roon opens his arms again, and I walk into them.

We watch the desert sun set with Roon wrapped around me, all hot skin and scars. Feeling lost. The desert is a feast of color. Blood and citrus. Beautiful. The only thing in our lives a thief like the sultan can't strip away from us.

"Sherin," he finally says. "We may be seeing the end of the world."

Chapter 27

A Second Proposal

"**H**AVE YOU EVER seen such a drunken mess?" It's one of the butchers who asks.

I tell him I can't say as I have.

Salan and I are walking among the merchants and their customers, bidding hello to friends and listening to gossip about the festival.

"That's the last time I'll dance with a contortionist!" That's from a woman in the crowd.

"No doubt," I whisper to Salan.

"What's a contortionist?" Salan asks me, butchering the word.

"It's someone who can twist themselves up into very uncomfortable positions."

"Like you did, trying to fit in the cupboard."

Salan and I were playing our game of trying to fit into small or peculiar spaces this morning—the way we used to in our family home. Except that it's gotten harder of late. I barely managed to squeeze into that cupboard and, once I did, had to crawl out right away. I could hardly breathe.

"I wouldn't say I fit into that cupboard," I tell him.

"That Roon couldn't fit his left foot in there," Salan says.

I laugh. Salan always calls Roon *that Roon*. "No, he probably couldn't."

I've yet to tell Salan about me and Roon. I'm not sure

why. Until days ago I wasn't sure Roon would return from the desert and didn't want to set up an expectation, but that's not it. The words have simply been reluctant to leave my mouth.

"About Roon," I start.

⊢————+⟨◈⟩ ⟨◈⟩+————⊣

BUT SALAN HAS LOST INTEREST in Roon and runs off to play tag by the rock garden. Fast and nimble, he ducks in and out of the crowd, easily outrunning the other children. I try to pretend that mornings like this will go on forever.

Pa, the cheese man, comes over to me. When I first came to the Palace City he was portly, but no more. Although he himself must be living on scraps, he gives me a little extra goat cheese and a patty of bread, like always, then winks. Things almost seem normal again.

"You're divine," I say.

"And you are by far the sweetest of all the harem attendants. I'm delighted it's you who's come and not pipsqueak."

"Flattery will get you an extra qabat." Which I press right in the center of his palm. Pipsqueak is Sayib, who none of the merchants can stand. Can't say as I blame them. She's rude and a notorious gossip.

Near the cheese vendor is a gathering of other attendants. Patra's girl, Ri, is there, and three or four others. They stand in a tight coil and murmur to one another, and while I know I should say hello, the way they stand makes any intrusion— even a lighthearted one from another attendant—seem unwelcome.

Ri notices me. All hair and eyes, both of them black. Ri's eyes settle on me in a way that I don't like at all.

"*Sahjaloh,* Mala," says another voice out of the crowd, and

this time I jump. Adamen is surrounded by a circle of admir-
ers and moves through them, excusing himself.

"Well, not quite yet a mala." Adamen lifts the flap of my
satchel and tries to inspect its contents, but I jerk it away
from him.

"You seem rather anxious this morning," he says.

Adamen looks exactly as he should after how hard he's
been hitting it. His skin is pale and pasty, with dark circles
under his eyes. Hair stringy with oils.

"What do you want?"

"I want to talk to you."

I huff and shake my head. "Is that all you ever say?"

"Things have grown worse," he rasps.

As if they can possibly be worse.

"You must be joking."

"Do I look like I joke?"

"Why don't you just go back to your new friends? They
seem ready for a good time."

He steps closer, just short of dishonor.

"Oh, but I told them I had urgent business with you.
Wouldn't want to make it look like you have a distaste for the
hero of the realm, would you?"

"I'm already set to marry a hero. Ten times the hero you
claim to be."

"That's funny," he says. "How about a new leader of the
Rah'a. Can you spare a precious moment for him?"

"What?" I say.

"That got your attention."

Against my better judgment, I ask Lada, one of the spice
vendors, to keep an eye on Salan. I won't allow Adamen to
take me outside the crowds entirely—that would be utter
stupidity. Instead, we hover near the entryway, where there
are plenty of people around—smiling, tipping their heads
at him.

"The soldiers," he says. "They love me, you know. They're well aware of the losing proposition on that throne."

"No one is looking to replace a sultan with a thug."

He grits his teeth.

"Thug? How about survivor? Deal maker? They've been out there. They know what's been and what's coming."

"And I know everything, too. Roon told me."

Adamen blinks hard and shrugs as if his tunic irks him.

"When I say worse, I mean worse for you."

"Why don't you leave me alone?" I say. "What have I ever done to you?"

Adamen's mouth drifts open. It's the only truly tender movement I've ever seen from him. His eyes flit down. When he's speaking his evil to me, he has no problem meeting my eyes, but right now he can't.

"Answer me!"

His throat rises and falls in a hard swallow.

"You looked at me," Adamen whispers. "In the desert, the day the nomads from the Waterless Sea took me into their caravan. You looked at me."

"I don't understand."

Now he tips his head up, locking his eyes onto mine. They're ravaged by the desert sun, bloodshot. "You can't," he says. "The gods cursed you when they gave you your eyes. They make a man want you, or want to kill you."

If that's what he means by things being worse for me, he's wrong. I know he wants to kill me. And that he wants me. He wants everything that's out of his reach. My eyes are his excuse for being a pig, just as Roon is his excuse for being a murderer.

"I have to go," I say.

"Don't."

"If you have something to say, say it."

A wind blows in from the gardens on the other side of the

market entrance. It's unpleasant, like the hot breath of a stray dog, and seems to remind Adamen of who he is and where he is. His face hardens again.

"See, I think there are two ways it could go for you, for us. It could go fast. Your mistress will be taken into royal custody, and then you can die with her. Or you can become the chosen bride of the greatest hero the Rah'a has ever seen. Perhaps even my queen one day, if the desert winds keep blowing in my favor. Not so bad an offer now, is it? I'm not hauling reed bundles anymore while you look down on me."

"I'm engaged to a high commander in the army, which is more protection than you could ever give me. And Roon would never let your lies hold up."

"Oh, he'd let them all right. You think he'd want you if you came with even a whiff of scandal, a whisper about your good times with your harem mistress while he's off fighting our so-called enemies in the desert? No man of his stature wants a wife others will look at through squinted eyes. I, myself, don't mind that part in the least. People can look at you however they want, as long as I get the last look every night."

He glances down at my amulet and I reach up, covering it with my palm.

"No one would believe a —"

"What? A hero of the realm? The entire city is ready to give me anything I want."

"Well, short of the throne."

He cranes his neck, an ugly blue vein throbbing at his throat.

"For now. But in a few months' time, who knows? These days fortunes change with the wind, if you haven't noticed. And you saw them, hanging on my every word about the battles I've fought side by side with the brave men in our army. I bet I could get you a better jewel than the one at the center of that necklace your Roon gave you. At the very least, I could get some third-rate harem wife and her attendant their day of reckoning."

"You couldn't get either."

"Haven't you heard the whispers? They say I've been traveling with Roon and his men since I left the Palace City. Unfairly accused by a certain wife and her attendant, yet risking everything to fight for my realm. They say whatever victories our armies have accrued are because of my counsel to your Roon."

"You say, you mean."

"I say, they say. Certain words have a way of becoming truths. After all, I did travel with Roon's men; I told you that. Out there no one's picky about the company they keep. In the desert, everyone's a murderer at some time or another."

"What is it you want?"

"I want a life!" he hisses. "I want a wife. A prize. I deserve it as much as anyone else. More. Because I'm willing to do what it takes. And people are starting to realize that."

"I'm not your prize."

"Whose then? Roon's? The man who helped spread the Vara, then blamed it on some stupid tribes who can barely build a hut."

"I'm so sick of you and your delusions of grandeur."

Adamen looks around, then lowers his voice.

"A greedy, harebrained sultan thought he could contain a plague he spread because he had a few battalions immune from that hateful death. One that turned his kingdom into nothing! Did you know he made his soldiers try to clean up his mess, after he'd killed most of their families? Is that delusional enough for you?"

Adamen's words become thicker and slurred as he continues. Like he's drifting into memories that are best locked away.

"That he thought his army could come back after what's out there, after the things they had to do."

His shoulders fall, his neck relaxing into a smooth, wet stump of a thing.

"It's not the Rah'a anymore, Sherin. I don't know what it is. I just want to live a few good years before the Palace City falls and we go with it. I want to forget—even if for a while."

"I thought you wanted to rule the kingdom."

Adamen starts to laugh—a laugh that comes from deep within his belly. The whole market seems to be looking at him now. He puts his face right up to mine. I can smell his breath of minted lamb.

"I've watched infants get boiled in oil, cut from their mother's breast," he whispers, ever-clear this time. "The men who were made to watch. I've watched. I've watched it all. It'll come here, too, one day. People acting like animals. Doesn't take much, believe me. This is paradise. Maybe not for long, but for now. That's enough."

Adamen leans on an empty table. One that would've belonged to a sweets merchant, were there any sweets left to sell. He waves at a group of young women and they giggle, if a bit nervously. Then he turns back to me.

"So, here is my offer. Me. As simple as cake. The best offer you've ever had. Either that or end up chained like your friend. Not even a stitch of clothing. Beaten with sticks, burned with torches. In the end, you'll get sealed in a tomb with that stupid Toja. And there's not a thing you or anyone else will be able to do about it. Especially not Roon."

Chapter 28

"I'M SORRY," I say, as Roon approaches me in the foyer. I'm out of breath, having rushed past the guard with hardly a pleasantry. "Can we talk here?"

Roon nods.

The entry to the military offices is as mannered as ever—correct and diligent with perfect postures and strict diction.

"It's Adamen. I think his new role as hero has given him fantasies," I tell him. "He came to the market and threatened me. He said things were about to get worse for me if I didn't marry him. "

Roon furrows his brow, biting down.

"Sherin, I told you not to concern yourself with Adamen. He's famous for his stories, and we have greater things to worry about."

I step closer to Roon. Part of me wants to take his hand, but I don't think it's a gesture he'd appreciate right here.

"Adamen paid me a visit a few nights ago," I whisper. "When I came home from the festival, he was waiting. He said filthy things about Toja and her behavior at the festival. At least some of them are true."

Roon stiffens. "Why didn't you tell me?"

Adamen has accused him of the vilest act of all. How can I have told him any of it?

"It's been hard for us to talk lately," I say. "But I should've told you last night."

Roon nods. He's thoughtful, not angry with me.

"And he's spreading terrible rumors," I say. "Not just about me, but about you and his purported role as your counselor. He even talks about ruling in place of the sultan, but then gets all maudlin and says we'll all be dead in a few seasons anyway."

Roon tenses up and his lip curls a bit, but he seems not at all surprised by my revelations. This troubles me.

"Go to your chamber and dress in your finest. Don't stop anywhere on the way," he tells me. "I'll notify the sultan's emissary of our engagement and we'll marry this afternoon."

I can feel my face pale, though I know full well that I shouldn't dread marrying Roon—especially after everything he's done for me. And when my alternative is Adamen or death.

If the Palace City does fall, who but Roon can protect me and Salan?

"It'll all be all right," Roon says. "I'll meet you in your chamber before midday. Wait for me there and nowhere else."

I'M IMPATIENT WITH THE BOY who washes my feet before I enter the palace apartments, and push my toes into my slippers while they're still wet.

"Sherin!"

Sayib chases me, wiggle-wagging her hands.

"Toja's looking for you. She's demanding her lunch."

I look at my satchel, then at Sayib. I'd completely forgotten about it. "The market was crowded today," I say. "There weren't many good things."

"You must bring it to her now!"

Just behind her, I see the boy who washed my feet—his head peeking out from behind an arrangement of blood lilies. He's shadowed us into the corridor, listening, and it makes me wonder what else he might have heard today.

"Can you bring it to her, Sayib? Tell her I'm ill." I hold the satchel out to the girl, but she purses her lips.

"I will not," she says, much too loudly. "I was given my commands, and that was to make sure you came with Toja's lunch!"

More curious heads poke out from other chambers, not even bothering to be casual about it.

"No," I say. "I can't!"

Sayib's voice, high and grating under normal circumstances, rises to an outright squeal when she becomes excited. She carps about how difficult we attendants make her work. How this is not part of her job and that she was told explicitly what was expected of her, and unlike me she isn't going to let the harem down.

"All right! I'll bring Toja her lunch." I turn from Sayib, but she follows me.

"Alone," I say. "I'm Toja's attendant. Not you."

Sayib "hmmf's." "Wouldn't do to fail your Most Esteemed Harem Wife! And you, supposedly about to marry a great soldier no less."

"That's right, I am. I'm the one marrying Roon. Not you, and not supposedly!"

Sayib narrows her eyes. Her nose twitches like a gerbil's.

"I'll make sure to check in with Toja that you did as you said. And let the commander know if you did not."

"Go right ahead," I tell her, making my way without looking back.

The stairwell leading to the harem apartments is empty, unusual for this time of day. But a relief. No more curious onlookers and no more Sayib. My footsteps click in a solitary rhythm on the stepping stones until I reach the top.

"I bet whatever it was, Tani did it!"

Toja's voice, ringing with panic, trills from her apartment. I hear the hard step of two men, most certainly palace guard, clamoring about as they search her rooms.

"I'm the most faithful and loving of all the sultan's wives! Unlike *some* of them. That Tani has blown her kisses all over the palace! And much worse, I can tell you that."

Shut up, Toja! I want to scream it, but instead I crouch at the top of the stairs, with my fingers in my mouth.

"Kera," she cries. "Who among the palace guard hasn't had a taste of her candy?"

She keeps babbling like an imbecile! Everyone knows arrest is only the first stage in the palace judiciary process! It's executed with a sense of mystery and meant to elicit revealing information from a frightened, presumed guilty individual. Like her.

"My touch is only for my husband! As handsome and firm in his body as his guard."

That guard slaps her so hard she comes tumbling out of her apartment. I gasp, cupping my hand over my mouth. It's her guard that struck her, the lover she took during the festival. He stomps over and pulls her up by the elbow, pushing her back in to her suite of rooms. I hear her start to sniffle.

As for me, my stomach feels as if it has dropped all the way to the catacombs where promiscuous wives and traitors find themselves. Where I could be entombed in a few days' time. The youngest harem wife and I, together in eternity.

"I waited every night for my husband! It's he who never came to me."

While Toja bursts into heaving sobs, I turn, running down the stairs, jumping two at a time. There, I slip unnoticed into my chamber.

"Salan," I call out. Quiet about it. It's a small space and I'm sure he can hear me. "We have to go."

Nothing.

From the hallway I hear the clang and rustle of men who wear blades at their waists. And the patter of a small woman's feet as she scuttles to keep up with them.

"She promised she would bring Toja her lunch right away, and I should've known she wouldn't."

Sayib.

Whatever luck has stuck around with me this long appears to be gone.

Chapter 29

Help

I'VE GOT SWEAT beading all over me, scarcely any air, and my torso is crushed up. My legs are crossed, with my knees pinned all the way to my ears. This morning, I'd barely lasted a few moments in this cupboard, and now I have no way of knowing how long I'll have to stand it. I pray they don't find me, and pray even harder that if they do, they won't be long about it.

"Late coming from the market. Not unusual for her, I can tell you that!"

I hear the whoosh and thud of the tapestry at my entryway as it's lifted and falls to its place. The steps of the palace guard are like they always are, while Sayib's have a jolly sprightliness to them that's downright infuriating.

"You know, I was always having to prod her. And it's not like I could go to the market in her place every time she shirked her responsibilities, and went off to the gardens. Going for strolls or planting flowers. Not at my station. The market is for *attendants* only, unless otherwise arranged."

And it's not like I'm at all surprised at the note of gratification in Sayib's voice. Or the way she speaks the word "attendants" like it is a curse. Sayib and I have always had thorns between us. Especially when her gaze practically strokes every last bit of Roon when he comes by to see me.

"And look here," she says. "This is the lunch I was talking about. She left it sitting on the floor."

The palace guard asks about where I might have gone. One of them kicks my pillows, and an over-stuffed one—ruby red with golden studs—strikes the door of the cupboard. I jerk at the noise, making the cupboard creak and my heart nearly come to a stop.

"Probably went back to the market, I'd say. She'd complained how the food she got wasn't fit for a harem."

A guard asks about which vendors it's my habit to visit. I can't remember his name, but he's a familiar face around the palace, with a voice at once deep and nearly always thick with mucus. I hear him march to my wall tapestry—the brilliant one made of peacock feathers—and lift it up. There aren't many places to hide in my chamber.

In the one place there is to hide—a place no one in their right mind would think a woman of my size could possibly fit into—I'm perilously close to giving myself away. My joints are burning, my feet are asleep, and I can hardly take in enough air not to go mad.

The guard clears his throat—a wet and gross endeavor—and there are footsteps again. The other guard, the one whose voice I don't know, mumbles something, but I can't quite make out what it is. Then without another word, not even from Sayib, who never runs out of needless conversation, they leave.

As desperate as I am to push my way out of the cupboard, I wait. Wait until I'm sure they're gone. That they aren't questioning my neighbors, or other attendants. My most paranoid thoughts have them outside my door, fooling me, seeing if I'm not hiding after all.

My eyes tear and it takes everything in me to keep from emitting a deep groan that could be heard from here to Toja's apartment no doubt. *Just a few more moments*, I tell myself. But I can't anymore. Forcing my shoulder against the cupboard door, I fling it open, freeing my body piece by piece from a place that could barely hold me when I was a half head smaller and had no breasts to speak of.

I lay on the floor, outstretched and gulping air. The pins and needles start in my arms and that's good. There's no time to waste, so I wobble to a stand, testing my legs. Those are alright, coming back to life with a bout of sharp little pains that stab at me as I dress in my best, like Roon told me. In a tunic I've chosen to match my eyes and flatter the amulet he gave me. Proof of our engagement. I raise up the tapestry and peek my head out into the hallway. It's empty, but won't be for long. If I can get back to Roon before he leaves to meet me here, we may be able to register our marriage before Toja is brought up on any formal charges, releasing me from my legal bonds to the harem wife I serve.

I sprint down the hallway to the stairwell. At the top I stop to listen and look down the hall passage that opens to the many harem apartments. Including Toja's empty one. The smell of clay pots filled with rosewater infuses the air, a wifely smell.

No doubt the other wives are holed up in their rooms. Afraid to come out after one of them was taken. Afraid that they could be next. The sultan could be cleaning house, after all. Wives are expensive.

Stealing a glance at my slippers, the lilac ones my mother made for me, that I've mended over and over to fit my growing feet, I force myself to move. I've worn them through every possible misfortune so far, and they've always seemed to bring me luck.

But no sooner do I have this thought than my skin explodes into goose pimples. Voices. Everywhere it seems, and they're coming closer. From the stairwell I came from and the one I'm going to. With me in the middle. I inch past a tapestry, one hanging over the entry to a chamber. I can't think of whose.

"*Shhhh.*"

A warm hand grips my bicep. Tight and meaning business. Pulling me under the tapestry, all chilled fingers and long nails.

"Not a word out of you, Sherin."

It's Patra.

I nod tersely, forgetting to breathe.

Patra turns me around and puts her face right up to mine. Her lips form a thin, fixed line.

"If you want a chance to live, you'll do exactly as I say."

Chapter 30

Patra

WIVES AND GUARDS pass each other in silence outside of Patra's apartment. They smell of sweat and oranges. We can hear the shuffle of their feet, deliberately casual; the men going on with business as usual. I can't figure what in the world they're doing here, simply parading through the halls. They don't appear to be looking for me or questioning other wives. More theater, perhaps. The sultan putting his wives on notice. *One of you was taken today. Tomorrow, maybe another.*

"He must hate you terribly," Patra says.

"Who?"

"The hero of our realm."

Yes, of course, Adamen. The last person I want to think about.

"What did you do to him?"

I shrug, having asked myself that question countless times. I asked Adamen little more than an hour ago.

"He says I looked at him."

Patra's eyes narrow in understanding. I wish I understood, but now isn't the time to question the sultan's most senior wife about her theories on Adamen's motives.

"We have to move quickly." Patra's hands tremble as she goes to her wardrobe, removing a tunic. It's plain by her standards, but beautiful nonetheless. The gentle hue of cantaloupe.

"Take this," she says. "You'll need it. I'll get you some water, some food. A new pair of shoes."

"What?"

Patra stops her busy actions. She folds her hands decisively and points her gaze at me like an arrow. "You have to leave the Palace City immediately."

"Leave? Salan and I can't just leave! And I've done nothing wrong. Adamen is the thief and liar!"

Patra shuts her eyes. I can see her pulse throbbing in her neck, her prominent jugular vein streaming like a fat tear down her delicate skin.

"And Roon and I will be married today. In minutes, in fact. He even asked me to dress. A mala can't marry in an attendant's tunic." I reach down, smoothing my garment; its green as brilliant as fresh spring leaves.

Patra's eyes sweep over me as I fix and fidget. She rubs her lips together, then starts to speak in a tone I've heard a hundred times. The one she uses on the sultan's junior wives when they're acting up.

"It's too late for that, Sherin. You and Roon will not be marrying and Toja's sentence is all but a formality now. So is yours."

I think a dagger plunging into my heart might possibly feel worse, but I'm not so sure.

"Adamen played his hand well, appealing to the fear and vanity of a fragile monarch. And Toja? Well, Toja wasn't smart enough to know a game was being played at all."

I must look stricken at her candor. A habit of never mincing words is a quality I've always appreciated about her. Until now.

"Toja is finished, and you . . . "

"Yes, I know," I snap. "I'll be put on a chain then locked with Toja in her tomb."

I still have sense enough to feel shame for the way I'm speaking to the one person who's offering support.

Patra takes my hand. Something she would never do, not as a woman of her station. Not even if I became the esteemed wife of her husband's best soldier. It's a gesture reserved for the dying, and I wish she'd kept it to herself.

"If that were so, it would be a mercy," she says. "The sultan is already arranging a dissolution of his marriage to Toja. On the grounds of his distaste for her person."

A cold, sickly pearl of sweat moves down my cheek. A dissolution of this type is rarely employed. It means the husband is disgusted physically by his bride and has no intention of consummating the marriage.

According to Toja, who is not disgusting in the least, the marriage had been consummated, although only a time or two. This is hardly uncommon in such a large harem. The sultan has his favorites, and can exhaust his taste for them before moving on to his new wife. It isn't like she's going anywhere.

No, dissolutions of this type happen only when the bride comes from afar and her people have clearly lied about her appearance. And this, too, is rare given the customs of our kingdom. Even if her proposed husband had not seen her, his emissaries had, reporting on her person to an excruciating degree. I can't imagine what the sultan hopes to accomplish with an annulment.

Patra seems to read my thoughts.

"Sherin, if Toja is no longer by law a harem wife, she is eligible for the death of a traitor to the realm. And so are you."

At that, I really do need to sit, and Patra helps me to her chair. One carved like a panther, shiny black with eyes of opal and sapphire. I sit there for a moment, my throat as tight and dry as a gecko's.

As a legal strategy, it's bizarre to say the least. A wife, who's not really a wife is accused of infidelity and thus branded a traitor? Makes little sense, unless . . .

"Adamen has also accused Toja of freeing the insurgent, who he claims is her lover," Patra tells me.

"It's a lie," I whisper, but it hardly matters now.

The execution of a woman traitor differs in what a man can expect under the same circumstances. It differs in only one, but very crucial way.

After her public ordeal, a traitorous woman is sentenced by her accuser to die in any manner that pleases him. Sadistic or plain. An added amusement for Adamen.

I've never seen such a death in my time at the palace, but the stories of these rare and horrific occasions are legend. Treason is not taken lightly, and the barbaric executions of traitors are intentionally graphic and vicious. It sends a message, making treason a most unappealing crime. Especially when committed by a woman—a mother to our citizens, a wife to our most honored. Women are the moral centers of our lives, and when one betrays her monarch, her people, she's offered little sympathy.

Thoughts of Adamen infuse my senses like a poison. His mawkish breath, his marred skin. Then there's the wicked glint in his eyes—in truth, the only thing that brings them to life. The way he leers at the thought of another's pain. I've seen that, too. Close up on the night he attacked me, and from a distance as we walked with Roon's men in the desert. Patra is right. The desert is a better option. At least there, Salan and I can fight for our survival or die on our own terms.

"Sherin," Patra whispers.

She puts her finger to her lips and steps into her bedchamber. I'm numb. All I can do is stare out her window at the sky. Cloudless. Like nothing is wrong. I vaguely hear Patra's footsteps. When I look away from the sky, and back to my surroundings, we're no longer alone. Ri is there, and holding her finger is my Salan.

———— ♦♦ ♦♦ ————

"**THERE YOU ARE!**" I say, kissing his face all over and tussling his hair.

He squirms and pushes me away, but not too hard. He knows the relief I feel at his appearance.

"You were supposed to wait for me in our chamber."

Salan leans in to me like a conspirator. "That Roon came by," he tells me. "He looked angry."

"He always looks angry," I tell him. "That's his job."

"Say your goodbyes quickly," Patra interrupts us with a strained lightness to her voice.

"What do you mean goodbyes?"

Salan comes into my arms and I stroke his hair. It's standing up all over the place like he's just gotten out of bed.

"Sherin, you'll be back tomorrow," Salan says. "And with candies."

It seems Patra's already been feeding him stories.

"This boy cannot go where you're going," she says.

Yes, yes, he can. Salan and I survived the Vara. Salan and I lived alone at our parent's house. Salan and I rode with the men of the Waterless Sea. Salan and I walked with Roon to the palace. Now, Salan and I will go to the desert. Together.

"Leaving the Palace City is not for a child. But your sister will be fine, won't she Salan? Ri can get you out of the palace and from there you'll be taken by cart. We can get you close to a settlement."

"He can't stay here without me!"

That was much too loud and close to panic. Patra grasps my hand, but not in comfort this time. She speaks to Ri, but does not take her eyes off of me.

"There's a honey chew in my chamber. Why don't you and Salan get it to give to his sister. For her little journey."

"I'll be fine here while you're gone," Salan says. "I'm big." I do my best at a smile for him as Ri shuttles my brother under the tapestry, leaving Patra and I alone again. Salan hesitates once, throwing a glance at me over his shoulder, but then goes when faced with our canvas of smiles—even mine, tense and unnatural.

"He has to come with me," I beg her. "What will they do to him once I've left?"

Patra gnaws at her bottom lip. The reek of fear has nearly overcome the more pleasant scents of luxury that float in her apartment. She's risking her life.

"I think nothing," she says. "He's a boy, and he'll be a strong man one day and useful. While no one of any birth could raise him after your disgrace, there are many good servants who would welcome a smart boy into their homes. And people's memories are short these days."

"What if they don't welcome him?"

Patra's gaze becomes sure.

"They will, Sherin. Even if they don't, his prospects are better here than out in the desert. I suspect you know it better than anyone."

"The Palace City itself will fall eventually," I say. "You know that, don't you?"

I can see by Patra's grave expression that she does.

I don't know why it surprises me. I suppose because day to day, Patra behaves as if the most important matters at hand are to dress appropriately and see to her own household. When she isn't minding the sultan and keeping the other wives in line. These are important administrative duties for the most senior wife, certainly, but hardly the sorts of responsibilities that compare with the knowledge of imminent destruction.

"I can protect him out there. It wouldn't be the first time."

"You can't."

"I won't leave him here to go down with the Palace City! Not without me to hold him."

Patra raises an olive-skinned finger and smooths a stray hair at my ear.

"He's a child," she says. "Better that he has a chance in the future."

"I can make it to a settlement," I say.

Patra gives the tiniest of smiles. One born of an ache that I've never seen before.

"Perhaps," she acknowledges. "But settlements are full of people. And in these days, people will burn you as surely as the desert sun."

Now it's not just Adamen's person that comes back to me, but his words. It's terrible to think of my brother's throat parched and his skin blistered from exposure. Famished, tired, bewildered as to why we had to leave safety, and crying out for a mother he barely remembers anymore. But the fact is, what is more terrible is that I don't know if I can protect him in the desert anymore. From thieves or slavers. Those starved enough to imagine a child turning on a spit.

"Roon will take him," I say, my voice so small I don't know if she can hear me.

"Could we get word to him? Maybe he could escort me to a settlement as well. The guard wouldn't think twice if they saw him leaving the palace."

"Sherin," she says. For the first time she lacks the courage to look at me. "You heard what Salan said. Roon is the one who came first to your chamber."

"He'd told me to go there. To meet him. He wanted to marry me today."

"No," Patra says. "To arrest you. You heard Salan. He went there alone even before Toja's apartment was searched and she was taken into custody. That's why Salan came looking for me. He saw Roon coming up the steps and he hid, thinking it a game at first. But then he heard him summon the palace guard, ordering them to get Toja and find that servant girl of hers."

"Sayib."

Patra nods. Just behind her is a small table displaying the vase she'd asked me to retrieve from Toja's apartment on the day I walked in on her tryst with that damned guard. Seems so long ago. The hideous flower, mine and Roon's, sits in the vase, thriving again. Its gold and violet flesh as radiant as if it had just bloomed. I have an insane urge to push past Patra and rip it to shreds, leaving its reeking petals all over the floor, but all I do is put my hand to my throat. The way some of the shoppers had done on the day the man with Vara stumbled into our market.

"I'm sure he didn't wish to," Patra says. "But he's sworn his life to the sultan."

Patra's shoulders curl in defeat. She holds the cantaloupe tunic to her breast like a baby. "I'll do well by him, Sherin. I promise you. I will not let harm fall to your brother."

Small, hot tears come to her eyes now and she steps closer to me. Two slender fingers trace my cheeks, then run tenderly over my chin. Patra lets the tunic drop and takes me into her embrace.

"May the gods protect you," she whispers.

GOODBYES HAVE BECOME an art form for me in my lives. I mostly say goodbye to Nif, of course. And it's something I've never gotten used to.

But saying goodbye to my brother, though it wasn't the first time I had to let go of someone I loved, was the worst of all. He was my first child, and the only thing I would have given my life for then.

I can feel his presence here and there, I think. Like a word on the tip of my tongue. He's always childlike and fresh when I sense him, and I call out to him in the way I used to. Baby talk to a forever child. Salan, my little man. All as I drift bodiless, awaiting the spark of conception.

And God gave us light.

That part is true, you know. Those words from the Old Testament. There is light at the moment of conception. It is my beacon and it is dazzling. A trillion stars are nothing compared to it.

That cosmic match will be struck soon.

A guiding light that makes Neville's flashlight seem quaint, even if it is illuminating a rather extraordinary discovery within the palace walls. He holds his high-tech torch for his wife, who stands with her mouth agape. She shakes her head, her corkscrew curls brushing Neville's nose. She hates them, but I think they're beautiful. I wish I had a hand with which I could reach out and touch them.

Neville clicks on his digital recorder once again and starts to speak.

"We found the first body in what we're calling the judicial chamber. Several more were strewn about a pathway leading out of that hall. Those were all men, and had been killed with a single arrow through the right eye. What we assume was a harem chamber of some sort—given the exclusively feminine imagery on the walls—was empty. But here, in a palace waiting room adjacent to the sultan's apartments, there are another thirty bodies."

Neville's flashlight vibrates, emitting a twangy jingle.

"Damn Jordie and his bluegrass."

He presses the walkie-talkie button in the handle of the smart flashlight. "What's up?"

"Dr. Abramov has been trying to reach Dr. Neville," Jordie pipes in.

Neville presses the button again and barks into the handle. "Tell him I'm busy."

"The other Dr. Neville, Dr. Neville. Calliope Neville, sir."

Calliope Neville finally speaks. Her voice is as high and pretty as that of a young girl. One who can sing the most beautiful arias. "Tell him I'm not giving any lectures on this visit," she says.

Neville tells this to Jordie, and Calliope takes the flashlight from his hands, shining it all over the chamber. Her eyes—so much like the eyes of the people of the Rah'a—are wide and wet, dark. Glittering above the light beam. They're the eyes of an old soul, and peer undistracted into the details of her surroundings, despite Jordie's voice honking from the handle.

"Dr. Abramov is quite an insistent man, I'm afraid. He says if you're going to be in the neighborhood, so to speak, it would be unthinkable for you not to give a lecture at the Society for Biblical Scholarship . . ."

Calliope hangs up on Jordie, walking further into the chamber. She's small of stature, but her limbs are strong and lithe. Her walk is as sure and graceful as a dancer's. Neville follows, talking into the recorder.

"All of them are soldiers, given their dress. Men like this

are depicted all over the palace in murals and sculpture. Each of them has been shot in the right eye, like the men in the pathway."

Calliope trains the light on the ancient corpse of a soldier, once thick and stocky. I'd seen him with Roon a few times, but I don't know his name. She looks upon him with deep sympathy, as if she had been there when he died. Held his hand.

"His skin looks tough, hard, but not withered like a mummy's," Neville continues. "No hair. A skirt of animal hide at his waist, embroidered with metal studs and thin, bronze strips. A breastplate pressed with the image of a snake—mouth wide open, like it's about to strike."

The long dead man's expression is one of surprise . . . and awe. They all look that way, the sultan's soldiers. Men I'd known in passing millennia ago.

"Have you ever seen anything like this?" Neville asks his wife.

Calliope leans in, almost nose-to-nose with the ancient corpse. "Not on your life."

"But you think it was a ritual of some sort."

"Hell if I know," she says. "It doesn't look like any ritual I've ever come across."

Neville puts his arm around her slender shoulders. He's much happier in her company. She has that way with people, but especially with him.

"Can you venture a guess?"

"About a civilization we didn't even know existed—not for sure anyway—until a few months ago?"

Neville looks at her with a mixture of pride and humor. "Well, more than any living person, you do know a helluva lot about ancient religions. It's why I dragged you away from your precious summer research initiatives."

Calliope Neville raises a thick, well-groomed eyebrow.

"And here I thought it was because you missed my sense of humor."

Neville kisses the top of his wife's head and mimes a rim shot. "Badum-pum! Ching!"

Calliope squats, taking a closer look at the soldier's face. She's careful not to aim the LED light directly at him. It's strong enough that it could burn his delicate tissues. "You know, babe, I'm not sure this was a ritual at all."

"All of the bodies we've found have been shot pretty much the same way," Neville says as he kneels beside her. "Except for the first guy, who got it in the mouth and heart. And you saw how many arrows were crammed into his gullet. He would've had to have had his mouth held open by something to achieve that."

Calliope Neville nods her head. I can see how badly she wants to touch the soldier's face. She takes a deep breath and closes her eyes, as if envisioning his life.

"The manner of death would certainly indicate some ritualistic component," she concedes. "But I don't know, Neil. There's an element of surprise to this that I find . . . weird. It's not just evident in the looks on their faces, but the way the bodies are scattered about. They weren't grouped; they seem to have been shot where they stood."

"And where are the women?"

"Damn good question," she says. "If it was a death ritual, they might have been burned or buried somewhere else, I suppose. None of this makes any sense."

Neville rests his chin on Calliope's shoulder. She reaches up, scratching lightly on his five o'clock shadow.

"Could it have been a mass suicide?" he asks. "Jonestown style?"

Calliope shakes her head, narrowing her eyes at the soldier's single, mortal wound.

"An entire civilization committing suicide? And a rich one

with a family monarchy and stately architecture built over generations? That's crazytown."

The flashlight blinks, as Jordie's bluegrass alert begins its refrain. Calliope hands it to Neville.

"Yup."

"Dr. Neville . . . and Dr. Neville. You best come here."

"What is it?"

Jordie's deep, dry swallow comes through loud and clear.

"Well, to be honest, we're not really sure. The radar has picked up something terribly strange. In an unexplored part of the site, near the palace structure."

"Maybe we should try to check it out from here."

"No! You see, Dr. Neville . . . and Dr. Neville, it appears to be outside the palace structure. In a part, we assume, that is utterly consumed by sand."

Neville takes a deep breath and stands, helping Calliope up from the floor. "Give us another hour," he says. "We've got one more thing we need to look at."

Chapter 31

A Return to the Desert

PATRA'S SERVANT, Alal, throws a dun-colored cloak over my head. Under its hood my hair is pulled back, boy-like, and stuffed under the collar. My face is rubbed with ash. Alal has tied my hands as if I'm an untrustworthy slave. One who might make a run for it given the chance. He can't know how close I am to breaking away from him and running back to Salan—all be damned. Taking my brother in my arms, smelling his boy's breath.

"I'll see you in a few days," I told him, as we were parting. I could feel my lip trembling and watched his eyes narrow.

"Do you really have to go?" Salan asked. "I don't care much about the candies."

"You'll care once you see them," I said. "They've been a rare treat around here lately."

I could hardly bear his expression as I turned from him, trying to make light of my departure. The glint of doubt and fear in his eyes, while he struggled to believe Patra's story.

I shake this memory away and look down at my bound hands, folding them tightly at my waist. Digging my nails into my palms. Alal tugs at the length of rope that connects us and I stumble.

Like this, the servant smuggles me out of the city, past palace guard after palace guard. They greet my companion, but pay no heed to me. All the while Roon becomes an unwelcome visitor in my thoughts.

I wonder if he felt any sting over his betrayal when he told me to change into a suitable tunic for our wedding. Is that how he would have taken me into custody? In the tunic I would have worn to become his wife? The one I might have saved for one of our daughters? I try to see into his heart and imagine how he might have felt watching Adamen abuse me before the whole palace population. As the highest ranking of the sultan's soldiers he would be an honored guest at the spectacle. Could he have looked into Salan's eyes after such a thing? The boy he'd once promised to raise to manhood?

It's only as we approach the Palace City gates that these thoughts fade and I become truly afraid for my immediate fate. I suffer a shrill ringing in my head and ears; a fiery churning in the pit of my stomach. But Patra has done well. Alal is known and my presence isn't questioned. One like me, tied to him with twine, is a common enough sight. A slave is a slave and hardly worth paying attention to.

Alal's cart lies outside the gates, and I crawl into the back, under a tarp. With me are bags of grain, small pottery, and not nearly enough cheese and dried fruit for the effort. I settle in, using one of the bags as a pillow—the smell of starch and jasmine is a comfort.

"Aloooo, the desert," I hear him croon.

We drive for a long time, our camel marching at a tedious pace. Sleeping for only part of the night, we get up when it's still hours before dawn, make some tea and begin our move again. The gentle rocking of the camel's gait makes me drowsy throughout the day, and I find myself drifting in and out of short, otherworldly dreams that take me to people and places I've lost, leaving me grasping to remember them after

I've been jostled awake by an awkward step, or one of Alal's out of tune chants.

Finally, the second day into our journey, we slow, then stop altogether. My back hurts in the way I've heard old men complain about and my mouth is full of sores. Peeking out from under the tarp, I see the sun is still high. It can't be later than mid-afternoon. Patra's servant ushers me out of the cart, my tunic pasted to me like a wet leaf. I peel the fabric away from my legs and fan it in the hot, desert air.

All the time, I think of Salan. His tousled hair, sticking up like straw. His flushed cheeks and big front teeth. Patra never explained what she was going to tell him about my longer absence. That story hasn't been written yet. Open as the desert himself.

The desert.

Not even the specks of a potential settlement on the horizon. We feel much farther away than yesterday, when there were still tall waves of sand undulating all around us.

"Are we stopping to drink?" The sun is at its peak strength, and I'm thirsty beyond words.

Patra's servant digs into a bag strapped to his camel's side, pulling out a pouch of water. He gives it to me and I start to gulp it.

"No," he scolds. "This will have to last you."

I'm sure I look at him as if he's fallen from the sky.

"This can't be where you're leaving me, Alal! There's nothing here!"

Nothing is being generous. Not a distant dune on the horizon. Not even a breeze. The desert floor is as flat as Salan's chest.

Alal points east. "They'll come from there."

"Who?"

A temporary settlement has sprung up some days in that

direction. There's a stretch of savanna there. The people seem all right, he assures me, though he can't say what tribe they came from. In all likelihood just a disparate clan assembled out of survivors of Vara.

"The ones I met didn't seem like natural criminals."

I look out to the east, to nothingness, then over my shoulder. At least there's the promise of a sunset. I turn to the servant, who's scratching the insides of his thighs with some relief. I can feel his skepticism. Of me, of the hot sand, and my prospects. He wants to have his rest and take his leave, putting me far behind him.

"Can you take me farther?" I ask him. "Another day or so."

The servant ignores me, groping into a small purse. Carefully, he plucks out some thorny weeds he's collected along the way, placing them flat on his palm. His camel, all leather-lipped, has no problem ingesting the dried, prickly greens.

"Please," I say. "The dunes can't be too far from here. I've been to them before. And they're sort of back in the direction of the Palace City, only to the north a ways."

"The dunes?" The servant shakes his head, petting his beast. "That's no place for a woman. Besides, they're far from here. At least three days."

"Three days," I say. "That's not so much."

"Not so much! I don't have enough stores for three days let alone that and more days to get back." He begins grumbling that I can walk it alone if I want to and there's no way he's going. That's not what Patra told him to do and he does as he's told. "There's nothing but thieves and killers there, you know!"

"And you're so sure they're better than these *not* criminals you're giving me to?"

The servant shakes his head and won't meet my eyes.

"I'm not giving you to them. You're waiting for them. Should be here by tomorrow. I'll leave you some food and drink. Bit of canvas. You'll be fine."

"Fine, yes, I'm sure," I say.

I take another drink from the water pouch, paying no mind to the look he gives me. My business if I want to run out of water. The servant leans against his camel, his eyes drowsy. He catnaps, while I chew on a piece of jerky.

"Hey," I say.

From the north, a couple of dots appear on the horizon.

"Get up!"

Alal snorts awake and shakes like a dog. He squints, his mouth curling downward. Two men. Swaddled in rags. That I can tell even from this far. Good fabric moves with a man. Gives him grace. The linen on these men flings around like a bad hairstyle.

Patra's servant sits up tall, watching their approach. Seems to take forever. He reaches into his tunic and slips a small dagger out from under his waist pouch, palming it to me in secret.

"I thought you said they didn't seem like criminals," I whisper, though they're at a distance of ten carts at least.

"Doesn't hurt to be careful."

"Ayah," one of them calls, and I slip the dagger up my sleeve. The man is sturdily built, with a fleshy face; it looks as if he's been eating well at least.

The other man says nothing. He's short, shorter than me, and there's a deep fresh cut on his face that starts at his temple, slicing just under his eye, and across the bridge of his nose. Sand has crusted into it.

"Ayah," the servant says.

The bigger one looks us over, then turns his attention to the camel.

"Strong," he says, admiring the beast. "Fetch a good price."

"Not for sale," Alal tells him. He untethers the camel from the cart and strokes his face.

The man sniffs and casts a glance at his little companion. He opens his mouth as if to say something, but thinks better of it.

"What do we have here?" he finally says, pointing to me.

Alal changes. He bares his teeth, settling into a crouch.

"Move along," Alal tells him. "She's not for sale either."

"Don't be that way," the taller man says. "We've been traveling a while."

Alal eyes him mean and cold. Well done.

"Caravan coming soon. You don't want to be here when they arrive," he says.

The little man cracks a smile, bursting open one of his scabs. His tall friend takes a loud, deep sniff in through his nose and chuckles.

"A caravan?" He elbows his little friend. "We met a caravan."

He flashes his teeth, and I wince. He's filed his two front teeth, as well as his canines into sharp points. They appear to be the only teeth he has left, so I suppose he had to make the best of them.

"And, uh," he says, hardly able to contain his amusement. "They weren't much of a caravan. Just a man and his wife and their sorry mule. Tasted good enough, though. The mule, I mean." This, he finds, very, very funny. "That's right—the mule!"

Alal leaps up and slices at the fanged man's throat. He misses, catching the frayed sleeve of his tunic as the man's arm goes up to defend himself. Little good it does him. Determined not to miss again, Alal plunges his dagger into the man's side, pushing him down.

The little man with the slashed face wastes no time. He hurls himself onto Alal, grabbing him by the hair. Shrieking, he pulls a blade no bigger than his pinky finger and thrusts it into Alal's face.

I scream, fumbling up my sleeve, shaking it, until the dagger Alal gave me falls onto the sand. I pluck it off the desert floor and get a good grip on its handle as the small fiend rolls off poor Alal and lunges at me nimble and quick.

He rushes me, knocking the water pouch down, spilling its contents into the sand. As I fall to the camel's feet, the animal groans and shuffles. Ambling a few feet away, he canters off the way the two thieves came.

The little man lands on top of me and cries out. A feral, hideous sound. He wriggles, laboring in his breath. I try to extract my dagger from under him and realize I can't do it because it's stuck. Stuck inside him! His breath is wheezing and I feel the wetness between us. More by the moment. Flowing out of him as his breath slows. Moving sluggishly, writhing like a worm, his eyes bulge out. A gurgle, one final whistling breath, and he stills. His soul, if he had one, is gone.

Slowly, I push him off me. My tunic is soaked with his blood and my hands are shaking. Yes, he's dead. So is Patra's servant, I think. The taller man is crawling away, an effort in vain. His face is a pale gray, and his movements are at once slogged and jerky. The futile actions of a failing body. I watch him die, knowing he's gone when a biting fly lands on the white of his eyeball and he doesn't even flinch.

It's only then I dare to look away and make an assessment of my situation. A dreaded thing. I'm alone in the desert and I don't much care to meet these people from the eastern settlement. The ones Alal alleged were coming for me, but could be as dead as the corpses surrounding me. Or as dangerous as they were in life. And I can't go back to the Palace City.

I have a cart. Some food. Whatever water Alal stowed away for his journey home. Our trusty camel is but a smear on the horizon. The thieves have nothing much worth taking.

The dunes may well be a dangerous place, "where the scum gather," as Adamen put it. But the archer's men gather there, too. It is, according to Adamen, the place where he found and murdered the archer, taking my dagger as a trophy.

I don't know how much of Adamen's story is true, but it is likely that, at some point, the men of the Waterless Sea have been there. And even if the archer is dead for certain, maybe one of the men will remember me and allow me to tag along. If only for a few days. That makes everything bearable. Planning for short bits of time. Nothing more.

Unwrapping my pouch of supplies, I stuff them with what Alal had, which isn't much. No wonder he didn't want to take me to the dunes. He had barely enough water to get to the Palace City. Only some dried nuts and jerky for sustenance. It appears he gave me all the good food on the way here. Decent man. He didn't deserve what he got. My eyes start to fill with tears, but I can't have that. Not now.

I face toward the east and count fourteen steps to where the tall thief has died. That's fourteen down. Short bits, I tell myself again. Yanking Alal's blade from between the man's ribs, I assess its virtues. A good weapon. Nothing fancy, not curved or carved like the one the sol gave me, but sturdy. Its knife-edge is especially sharp and will pierce any number of surfaces—skin, hide, cloth, bone. The handle is plain, and fashioned from polished ivory. Yes, it will do.

I take more steps toward the dunes. As my feet sink into the sand, I become surer of myself. For the next few days, I'll be alone and exposed to the elements. The spirits of the desert air will either comfort me or conspire against me. I don't know. And I will have to pray I encounter no one on my way.

Chapter 32

The Dunes

There is a wind in the desert as commanding as the tide, its story is told to one in only a thousand hearts.

THE EARTH MOVES like a side-winder, the sand hovering in a mist of tiny grains just above the surface of the desert floor. I carry my empty water pouch like a last hope. Two days on my own. Not long at all for the nomadic people who make their home in this bleak environment, but for me it feels like forever. My fever is so high now that each step is a heroic effort. I've never had sun-sickness before, and it's every bit as brutal as my father once warned me. The vomiting and sharp pains in my head. The weakness. The burning.

I drop to one knee, then the next, too weak to get up again this time. I look back over my shoulder, pinching my eyes open and shut. It's still there. Something. Maybe a man. Maybe our camel. Or nothing at all. I don't know what's real or delirium. But I can't summon the will to care anymore. So, I collapse into the sand, letting my face rest on my hands. The soft sand is hot, like porridge fresh from a cauldron, and my palms sting.

The dreams come again, but these are more vivid than the ones on the way here with poor Alal. They don't dissolve when I jerk awake at a noise, or the scamper of a spiny tailed lizard across my back. It makes me wonder if I'm dying, and if this isn't part of the curious passage to the afterworld.

I seem to float in the air at times. At others I'm nestled into linens, leaning back onto a firm and warm berth. Like this, I advance towards a chasm with an oval mouth and deep throat. It's a cave, and the desert comes with me in a short gust of wind, and then promptly leaves, purged by a backdraft.

The air is quiet and cool, at odds with my fever. I have a tongue of leather, and there's a bare aftertaste of bile in my mouth. And then nothing. Only a fierce headache rousing me from sleep time to time.

A torch snuffs out, but is lit again. I can smell its smoke. But I haven't lit a torch, as far as I know. Hard to say. Seems to me, the dead don't need a torch, but the gods may have other ideas.

Under the torchlight, my battered tunic is loosened and unwound carefully like gift wrap. My mother used to wrap my presents in cloth. As a child I wanted to cut and tear at them to see what was inside, but I knew better than to destroy her handiwork. Now, my tunic falls away like my mother's wrapping, leaving me naked on the ground. A pair of hands removes the amulet Roon gave me from my neck. Damn thing. I'd forgotten I was still wearing it.

My father is speaking to me.

"The desert is so like a beautiful woman," he says. Only it isn't his voice. This one is deeper, with a rough melody to it. "Sandstone and echoes," he whispers. "The sand hills are like the curve of her hip and breast."

My father always thought the desert was like a man and described it so. Thick and muscular, he'd said. Domineering. It's how the people of the Rah'a understand the desert.

My skin is still hot. A damp rag blots around my face, softly, as if trying not to wake me.

"A fever needs sleep," the whisperer tells me.

"Papa? What are you doing here?"

Cool water pours through my hair, soaking it, and I hear a sweet sound come from my throat. A woman's sound, like when she samples something delicious. The whisperer tells me my voice has changed. It's more wine than juice now.

"Yes," I say. "I've grown up."

The water dribbles over my shoulder. It runs down my breasts, washing away a dense film of desert grime.

"I never did get married." I touch my hand to my wet hair, unwound from its coil and flowing down the length of my body.

"No?" says the whisperer. "I'm so glad."

I SLEEP FOR A LONG TIME, I think. Maybe as long as a whole day and night. As I stretch awake, I open my eyes to clusters of cottony brown ovals grouped all along the curve of a cave ceiling dripping intermittently with stalactites.

"Bats," I say. My voice is low and scratchy.

Blinking, I turn towards the mouth of the cave, and find the sun starting to set. Indigo, flaming orange, gold. No clouds. I'm most certain this is neither a dream nor the afterworld, and it starts to dawn on me that my luck hasn't completely run out. I've made it. Somehow, I've made it to the caves. After a most satisfying yawn, I realize my head no longer hurts. My fever is nearly gone and my mouth is pleasantly wet.

Dizzy at first, I stand barefooted, swaying like a hanging rope. My slippers! I spin around—too quickly, nearly falling to the ground—and spot them behind me. They're perched on a rock, heels delicately put together with the toes spread apart. Next to them is my tunic, dirty and stained with that thief's blood. I'm dressed in the cantaloupe tunic Patra packed for me. I must have changed clothes at some point.

Patra's tunic is even lovelier on—much softer to the touch than the other one had ever been, more pliant. This one has been trundled and pounded for days and blushed with only the finest dyes. It's one my mother would have been proud of.

The concave formation of the dune is visible from the mouth of my cave. *My cave,* I think. Hardly. But there is more than a trace of the familiar here, which in my circumstances is as close to home as I will get. To my right, I spot the wide and deep cavern where Roon's men and I waited out the sand storm. Where I glimpsed the archer in the shadows. To my left, only the unfruitful spread of the landscape.

Makes me feel lonely all of a sudden. I've been on my own for days. Now, here I am at the much warned about dunes—full of thieves and killers, I've been told—and they're as empty as most promises. The wind howls through them like a sad old song. I miss Salan, so much.

But I don't have the luxury to dwell on that. Night will come soon and I have to build a fire. The crude elements of one are present throughout the cave—rocks for the frame, brush and some stick piles that must have been left behind by some former inhabitants. And recently at that.

After assembling a good fire bed, I set to work getting it going. I've always been good at this part, tedious as it is, and find a certain calm in the repetitive motion of rubbing the sticks together to generate a spark. It's like playing a crude musical instrument, and I sing along to the chafing, making things seem almost normal.

After a time, the fire catches, starting as a tiny lick and growing all wild-haired. I snuggle in, enjoying the warmth of it, trying to pay no mind to my empty belly. Can't remember when I last ate or drank anything, and find it strange I don't feel the unbearable thirst of my last hours out in the desert.

Humming quietly, I'm hypnotized by the flickering blaze.

As far as company, it will have to do. Dozing, I see a face in the flames. Not exactly in the flames but beyond them. Hair so dark it blends into the night. The fire illuminates one eye of tortoise shell, the other of meat gravy. Another mirage.

"Don't go," I say.

"Never."

Chapter 33

Another Old Acquaintance

IT MUST BE the middle of the night. The crackling of the fire, the stillness of the cold, dry air, a strand of my hair getting trapped under my shoulder. I want more than anything to be pulled into sleep, but a smacking noise—sloppy, mucky—won't let me.

A face dawns in the flames, seeming to float in the darkness.

"Archer?" I whisper, and my spirits lift like a curl of smoke.

But then my eyes adjust to a thin face. Too thin, and attached to a neck too thick for the slender lines of his cheeks and jaw. He has a loose black tunic that does little to hide a series of pitted scars across his collarbone. As if a cook used a paring knife to gouge unsightly growths from his skin.

I watch him lift a cut of meat to his lips; a hare he's been roasting on my fire. In that moment I realize I know him! He's one of the archer's men, the one I called antelope man, but who's name was . . .

"Taran," he says, as if reading my mind.

I clutch the small dagger Alal gave me, and hold it at my side just in case. While Taran was never a threat to me when I traveled the desert with him before, I don't know what all this time has done to him, or how badly he needs the civilizing effects of a man like the archer.

"How long have you been here, Taran?"

Taran glances at me, and continues to eat. His scent, as

pungent and bitter as ale and piss, is carried by the warm air of the fire.

"My cave," he says.

I see. So, that's how it's going to be.

"Your cave? This isn't anyone's cave. It belongs to the dunes and the dunes belong to themselves. At least that's what your leader once told me."

He gives me a cold eye and licks his fingers, then sips a drink from his pouch. Placing his hands on the handle of a long knife that's somewhere between a dagger and a sword, he turns the blade so that it twinkles in the firelight.

"My cave," he repeats.

I hold my hard-won dagger up, so that its pointed tip stares into his face. His thin mug has a witless expression. He sinks his teeth into a fistful of hare, pulling a long string of meat off the bone, shaking his head as he sucks it up past his lips. He tears a leg off the creature and holds it out to me. Without a thought, I take it from his hand and dig into it with no manners at all.

It occurs to me that I should be more scared. Here, an armed man has claimed my fire, my space. No matter if it's a man I've met before, he could now be one of the boogey-men Roon and Adamen warned me about. A murderer, rapist, or outlaw banished to a dying land, and one who will do anything to stay alive. Yet he doesn't seem eager to slit my throat. He just seems hungry. And he did share his hare with me.

"Are you with your tribe?" I ask.

"Hmm." He sniffs.

"Is he with you?"

Taran burps and hiccups, throwing his stripped bone into my fire. He leans back, wiggling his toes. "You're alone."

"I'm not alone. My friends will return any time now." I wrap my arms around my knees, pulling my tunic tight.

"That so?" He says, taking another swig from his water pouch.

I'm about to embark on a long, fishy explanation of my circumstances, only my old acquaintance seems not at all interested—neither in hearing my stories or answering my questions. In fact, he pretty much ignores me, resting his head in the crook of his elbow and closing his eyes. In a few moments, a light snore wells up from his throat, and whatever vain hope I had of the archer being alive close to vanishes. If he had survived Adamen's attack, he would be here with me. Surely Taran would speak news of his welfare.

———— ⊰◈⊱ ⊰◈⊱ ————

JUST AT DAWN, I wake up after a deep and dreamless night of sleep. No visits from the past, or the dead to comfort me.

"Taran?"

His space on the other end of our dying fire is empty, and he's left behind only the gnawed bones of the hare he'd roasted the night before. But worse than that: It appears he's taken my stores as well! Alal's jerky and nuts, my old tunic—even my empty water pouch! The only thing he's left me is the clothes on my back and the slippers on my feet.

"Taran!"

I dash out of the cave, shivering. It's after first light, but there's still a chill in the air and I'm woozy. I scan the configuration of caves and spot Taran climbing up a rock face, the pelt of his hare hanging from the back of his belt like a fluffy tail and my stores dangling from a rope wrapped around his ankle!

Before I can call out to him, he pulls himself up to the mouth of a much bigger cave than the one we shared and disappears inside. This one has an entrance shaped like hands pressed in prayer, which seems an ominous sign.

"Oh, I'll get you, you mangy goat!"

I race back and light a torch from the remaining embers of our fire. With several fine sticks tucked into my tunic, and my torch gritted between my teeth, I follow Taran up the way he went.

Scaling the rock face as he did, I wedge my torch between some stones when I arrive up top. I can smell how deep a cave he entered. It has that dank, hollow scent tinged with too many small notes of sand, dust, water, reptile, and mineral.

It is fitting how the mouth of this cave points to the heavens. Inside, it looks like a house for gods, putting the Temple of Pallah in the Palace City to shame. The floor and ceiling shimmer with rock and mineral, crystal and gem. In some parts they look a bit like a pastry painted and baked with egg wash.

While most of the cave wall is smooth, there are points where great masses of rock jut out in strong-boned formations that look like the faces of alien warriors. Fierce, organic jumbles of stone that watch as protectors over this place, the way sculptures of ancestors line the entrance to the sultan's palace—a place that feels more distant with every beat of my heart.

Deeper in, stalactites and stalagmites twist into fantastic serpent shapes. Rocky creatures of beauty and savage sensuality. Sharp as glass in some places, smooth as water in others. It must have been a very wet place once long, long ago.

The cavern offers a number of alleyways branching along the passage. Some tiny, like mouse holes, others made for giants. Men like Roon. In only a few steps, I manage to stub my toe. It's cold in here, suddenly and decidedly so. Raking my fingers through my hair, I rub my scalp the way Yina used to. A simple motion that offers companionship.

"Yina," I say. I wish she was here.

When I turn onto a wider path, my same damned toe encounters another obstacle—a bigger rock this time and I bash into it with both my foot and knee, pitching over it. I hit the floor hard, my hip bone and elbow taking the brunt of my fall, searing with pain. My torch flies from my grasp, landing in a puddle with a threatening hiss, before leaving me in complete and utter darkness.

"Damned goat's ass," I swear. "A mangy, dying goat with a filthy ass!"

I punch my fist into the ground and that hurts, too.

Right now, I want the pleasure of murdering Toja myself. For being such an idiot and getting us into this mess! For knowing only what pleases her. I sniff back my anger, then take a deep breath, letting it melt away like honey in tea. Toja, for all of her faults, is collared and chained in the palace courtyard, paying a terrible price for immaturity.

I'll settle for murdering Taran. Or at least getting my things back.

Sitting up, I rub my hip and elbow. At least nothing's broken. Damn me for not sticking closer to the walls!

"Not the end of the world," I say. "Or maybe it is."

I creep along, moving in a direction I hope is the way I came. But the air is so thick and black that I can't see my hand in front of my face.

Inching like a snail, I run my hands delicately over the bulging stones. Cool and silky in places, craggy and wild in others. One has holes and I dread what might live in them. Another is grooved and prickly, like an instrument of torture.

And still another isn't made of rock at all. It's flesh and blood under a worn pleat of linen. The curve of a muscular calf beneath my fingertips.

Chapter 34

The Dark

AT FIRST I TURN to stone and think I might never feel the courage to move again. Above me, I hear a rich, full breath as it's taken in and let out. Somehow, the tips of my fingers begin to move, and I find myself strumming the hairs on the man's calves, as I might new blades of grass. Making my way up his leg just a little. And he is a man, of that I'm sure. It's evident by the shape of his muscle, thick from long days of walking in sand, of staying gripped in the saddle of a camel. I can feel him looking down on me, though I don't know how he could possibly see me or anything else in this darkness. Or how I could sense his gaze. But there it is. Maybe it's that antelope-looking robber again, except that his feet had been clad in sandals, I'm sure. I watched them wedge into the rock wall as he climbed. This man's feet are naked.

Maybe it's . . . *don't be a fool,* Sherin, I say to myself.

From behind me, there's a sound; a soft brush on the cavern floor. The rope of calf muscle tenses beneath my fingertips, and the man's hand skims my ear as he bends over me. I freeze at his touch, paralyzed again. But he doesn't linger—instead, he reaches behind me, his hand hovering above my shoulder blades.

His palm sweeps through the pitch-black air, taking a strand of my hair with it. I feel the pluck from my skull, then the stroke of a cool and slender body swipe across my shoulder. Wicked in its caress.

It isn't a finger or any human part, and I fear I know exactly what it is. The tail of a snake. I can hear the whisper of its writhing figure above my head, where the man holds it for a moment, before flinging it against the rock wall. It lands in a thud on the cave floor, quite dead.

Only now do I realize I haven't been breathing.

Reaching down, he takes my fingers and guides me to my feet. While he's close—so close I feel the heat of his skin—I still can't see him. Not at all. But I can tell he's a good bit taller than I and has eaten something seasoned with mint paste for lunch. A fresh, luxurious scent that I know well from my father's house. Yina had been an artist of a cook and this reminds me of one of her chutneys.

I heave a deep sigh full of homesickness and hate myself for it. This is no time for indulgences.

"Is it you?" I whisper.

Without a word, he bends and scoops me up, holding me to his chest. His skin is bare and dry, as smooth as a plum. As warm as Salan's belly. He smells of bitter herbs and with a lingering ghost of well-worn linen. I can't help but rest my head against him, even if reason tells me I should put up at least some kind of fight. This man might be bringing me to his people as a sacrifice for all I know. Just my luck, too.

But I stay snug in his arms, as we turn and sway through a labyrinth of rocks. It's as if he's born to this cave, knows its every landmark. He carries me to a place where the air is different. Less biting, laced with calcite. Here, he lays me on a sheet of rock. A comfortable slab of stone as far as slabs of stones go. One that's drawing me into sleep—I'm still weak from journeying in the desert.

If it wasn't for his palm beneath my head, I would think he's disappeared. Like a spirit. Can a spirit have a warm palm? So warm and plush. I wish he'd hold my whole body the way he's holding my head, so I can curl up and sleep until the world is better again. But instead of floating off into my dreams, I feel a cool stroke from the tip of his finger.

He touches me between my breasts, at the lowest point where my tunic lies open. It's only a light tap, barely a chip off the crag of a raw gem, but I feel it as surely as the lash of a whip.

My breath hitches and I rise off the stone, settling like a linen sheet.

"You must be a ghost," I say.

His finger moves under my collarbone, tracing a vein. I make a faint sound—the beginnings of a word I can't finish. Then, his finger dips into the hollow of my throat and follows the terrain of my Adam's apple. I hear him lick his lips.

My breath is coming fast and sharp now, and I smell the undertones of the desert on his skin. Unmistakable, like a faint aroma of toasted nuts. And I hear his breath, too. Deep and low, awestruck.

He swallows. Such a succulent sound. I want to hear it again.

More breath. His and mine. Heavier. More urgent.

I should say something. But my words are stuck in my throat. And if you want to know the truth? If I can find my voice, even a single word, it will not be *stop*.

His finger travels up and over the curve of my ear, like he's handling the wings of a butterfly. He takes his time. Stroking my earlobe, he settles his fingertip in the divot behind it, pressing gently.

Can ghosts touch the living, I wonder? I thought only gods could do that.

The backs of his fingers caress my cheeks, and his breath draws in, almost a laugh. I laugh, too. I can't help it. That same single finger pets my eyes, playing softly with my lashes.

More. Please more.

Four of his fingers—two calloused, two as supple as moss—drum over my brow. Light, wispy. Like the sweet and silly kisses of a tiny fish. The fish Yina used to keep for my father. Those would nibble at the skin of my toes when I dangled my feet in their pond.

Gliding down the slope of my nose, he lands at its tip before moving lower. My lips tremble as he touches them, caressing every bend and bow. Wetting the pad of his fingertip with my juices, I hear him bring it to his mouth and taste me.

Before I can let the air from my lungs, he lifts my head off the stone. He expels his breath in a slow hiss, letting it linger over the skin of my face. Warm and damp. So unlike the desert. So unlike a ghost.

Gently, he nestles his free fingers in my hair, letting them ride a long lock all the way to my waist. He leans in—I can feel every inch of him drawing toward me—and puts his lips to mine. As tender as a ripe berry. His beard supple, as if he's oiled it for me.

Our lips barely touching, he finally speaks, kissing me lightly as he does so.

"I still have your hair," he says. "I've carried it with me until I could kiss you again."

I GULP A FULL BREATH, and take his face in my hands, letting my fingers roam over his features. The pear shapes of his cheekbones feel tender and swollen beneath my touch. His eyes are deep-set and slanted. He feels softer and younger than the man I'd known in the light of the desert sun, and a happiness I haven't known since I was a child rushes me.

"Are you cold?" the archer whispers.

"Yes."

I'm not, but I know if I say so he'll hold me. And he does. The archer lays next to me on the slab of rock, taking me into his arms. It's a decadent thing to be held by someone I can't see. Strange, intimate. And beautiful. This time, I let my tears fall.

"I kept hoping you weren't dead, and then lost all hope entirely." I stroke his hair. He has soft waves, like ripples in the sand. His hair is exactly as I remember it. "Adamen. He said he'd followed you from the Palace City and killed you."

"He says a lot of things."

He turns toward me, our lips nearly close enough to kiss again.

"Sherin, Adamen did follow me." His voice becomes terribly grave, full of regret and apology. "Only it wasn't me he killed, but Taran's young son."

"Taran," I say.

I can feel the archer's smile. A warm smile full of affection for a friend.

"The man who fed you last night, while I was securing the dunes."

This makes me smile, too. "It was your face I saw in the fire."

The archer shifts his weight and his hair brushes my hand.

"Did you not notice being followed in the desert?"

I coil a lock of his hair around my finger. Softer than the hardest-beaten linen.

"I had my own problems to think of at the time." Basic survival, mainly, I want to say.

"Well, whatever problems you have, always remember that a man following you in the desert is your greatest concern."

I think of the dead thieves and poor Alal.

"Not this time, though."

"No," the archer whispers. His fingers pinch my tunic and pull it down from my shoulder. He leans over and kisses me there. "I'd arranged to retrieve you from that harem wife's servant. But you were early and trouble, it seems, has a way of finding you."

"That was you? The people from the eastern settlement?"

The archer nods. "The rest of the tribe moved to the dunes only last night as you slept so deeply. I didn't wish to wake you."

My first hours at the dunes come to mind. Sick from the sun, feverish, all the time dreaming of my father. Of being cared for and washed. Only it wasn't my father. I sit up with a start and pull my tunic back over my shoulder and tightly over my breast.

"Did Taran change my clothes?"

The archer lay still on the stone slab beside me. I feel his chest rise and fall.

"No," he says. "That was me."

"Don't you have any women with you who could have done that bit?"

"Yes," he says.

"And you didn't think to bring one to me?"

He waits an eternity to answer.

"I did think of it, but our women were busy packing and moving camp." I can hear his hand slide along the cave wall. "Besides, I didn't want to."

"Why not?"

"Why didn't you protest when I kissed you in the Palace Gardens? I was the naked one then. It's only fair."

Though I can't see his face, I know exactly the expression he's wearing. It's the same one from when we sat at my father's house and he teased me by pushing his unwashed underarm in my face.

"Fair," I sputter. "Fair to be undressing me without asking permission?"

"You were delirious and in no state to give permission. Rambling on about all sorts of things."

He grazes me as if he's just shifting his weight, but I know he did it on purpose. And I know he felt me quiver, damn him.

"Like what?"

That amused laugh of his again. "Like me."

"And what were you doing sneaking around me anyway? You could have announced yourself!"

I hate how he's smirking at me. And yes, even in the dark I'm quite positive he's smirking. Like he's the only one in on a secret.

"I wasn't sneaking around, I brought you here and cared for you! Did you think you crawled here on your own?"

I hear him run his fingers through his hair. Lush as a garden.

"Well, I didn't see you here when I finally woke up, did I? Only that Taran fellow. And please don't tell me that he helped wash me, too."

"Of course not," he whispers. "That was my pleasure alone."

The way he says that, I'm very glad we're in the dark.

"Does it matter?" He asks.

"What?"

"That I bathed you for my pleasure. You were preparing to marry me once."

That is a sobering reminder.

"I don't even know your name!"

The archer sits up beside me, his breath in my ear. It no longer smells only of mint chutney. It smells of me, too. Cold meat and colder water.

"My name? Do ghosts even have names?"

"Yes."

"Ghosts have names?"

"You have a name."

"You don't know it?"

"You never told me. I've always called you archer in my head."

He snickers.

"Because of that man I killed with my bow? In your father's house?"

"That's right."

"I'm a good swordsman, too. Why not swordsman? Archer seems rather weak."

I give him a look—not that he can see it. I'm certain he feels it, though. "Archer, swordsman, snake-killer, cave-walker."

"Lover."

My blood becomes iron.

"The Prince of the Waterless Sea," I hiss from between my gritted teeth. "At least that's what they call you."

The archer settles next to me again, touching my arm lightly. I let him.

"And you didn't know I was the man I'd planned on marrying you to until we saw each other in the palace courtyard?"

I'm feeling stupid right now. And cruel. On top of all of the abuse that had been heaped on him that day, I'd slapped him, believing he'd brought the Vara to my home.

"No, I didn't."

"Not even suspected?"

"No," I say curtly.

He places his chin on my shoulder and I almost push it off. Almost.

"So what is it?"

"My name?"

"I have to call you something other than archer, and I'll

definitely not call you swordsman or that ridiculous title of yours."

He nestles closer and feigns indignation. "It's not my title. Not one I gave myself anyway. People love titles. They think them up all the time."

So they do.

"What?" He asks.

"I'm waiting."

"The name."

The archer—whatever his name is—lifts his hand to my cheek and brushes his thumb over my lips. I bite at it and he laughs. Leaning in, he kisses me again. It's a brief kiss, anything but chaste.

"My name is Nif."

NIF. A NAME WRITTEN INTO MY EVERY DESTINY.

That sounds very flowery, I know. Like the words in a romance novel. But my words are true to how I feel, and love has been everything in my short lives. The times I've lived without it have been empty, just as, after I've died, the years Nif has had to struggle through have been half-hearted and lonely. Even when he's been busy and successful, displaying all the outward signs of a good life.

"My name is Nif." Funny. Of all the things he's said to me throughout time, that one simple sentence still stops my heart. Just as following the Nevilles through the Rah'a palace would make it pound, if I had a beating heart right now.

"It's like Pompeii," Calliope Neville remarks. "Why do you suppose they're so well preserved?"

They're passing the body of the sol who'd given me his dagger on the night Adamen attacked me. He was a decent man, I think. Calliope closes her eyes ever so briefly and says a little prayer.

"We've taken samples of stone, air, you name it. We should be able to figure out whatever environmental brew turned this place into an ancient version of Madame Tussaud's Wax Museum."

Calliope walks around the sol, her eyes fixed on his hand. It's starred, as if he was reaching up and out to something before he was slain. Seems to me he should have been reaching for his sword.

"I think it's beautiful," she says. "The most beautiful thing I've ever seen."

Neville takes her hand and kisses it. "Yes, it is."

They march slowly up the steps leading to the sultan's apartments, and enter another bathing chamber. There to scrub down anyone the sultan might deign to receive. There's a sweetness to the room, both in its style and simplicity. Even in the taste the air leaves on your tongue. A light current seems to flow through the air, too. Calliope shivers and puts her hand into the air as if to touch it. Her husband doesn't seem to notice it, but she most certainly does.

"Look at this," Neville whispers.

The bathing pool, round and lined with rubies sits at the center of the chamber.

"The water is crystal clear," Neville says to both the digital recorder and his wife. "Like it was poured yesterday. You could probably drink it."

Calliope sits at its edge, half reclining, and Neil Neville smiles at her reflection. He loves the wrinkle in her brow, and the way her curls tumble over, dangling above the surface of the pool. He's been known to say how much he hopes that one day, if they're blessed with a child, he'll get her hair. I hope so, too.

"Neil," she says. "I don't feel the presence of their souls, the way I thought I would."

He pockets the recorder and sits behind her, fitting his body to hers like a puzzle piece. Lifting some of that hair off her shoulder, he nuzzles the crook of her neck.

"Their souls are long gone, don't you think?"

Calliope takes his hand, intertwining their fingers and pulling it around her waist.

"I guess I don't mean it literally. It's just that, in a cemetery people come and go. They visit the people they love, and that keeps them alive somehow. Their souls close. When I visit my mother's grave . . . oh, I'm talking nonsense, I guess. I never even knew my mother. It's just that these people had no one to keep them alive in any way. To give their existence, their end, any meaning."

Neil Neville lays his wife down, kissing her nose and her lips. "They have us," he whispers.

"Yes," she says. "These people are ours somehow, aren't they? It's like they've been waiting for us."

Chapter 35

The Tribe

"WHERE are we going, Nif?"

He's carrying me again, weaving around unseen obstacles. Nif wears his tunic tied around his waist. His bare skin is warm, even in the chill of the cave.

"We're going to my people," he says.

His words are like warm bread. I met some of his people when he took me from my father's house. That was many a days' journey across a desert region in the early stages of its collapse. All of them had been men—soldiers. Coarse and uncultivated, but loyal. Nif was never once disrespected by them, as far as I saw. I hope seeing them will feel like a homecoming somehow.

"And you say there are women with your tribe?"

"Some," he says. "None like you."

He finds that amusing. I'm not sure I do. If the women are anything like his men, I can't imagine fitting in very well.

We round a rock wall that scrapes my back, leaving it stinging and wet. My eyes have adjusted to the dark, and I can see Nif's profile and the outline of his shoulders. The way his mouth is set in determination. I have a reckless urge to kiss that mouth again.

"Did you know I was set to marry one of the sultan's soldiers?"

Nif stops. He leans in and kisses me again, but not tenderly this time. He crushes his lips to mine, opening them, taking my mouth suddenly and quickly before breaking from me. "Not while I still draw a breath."

"Oh, really?" I stroke my teeth over his clavicle and kiss the bone. "And what did you think you could do about it?"

Nif snorts, but then goes quiet and serious.

"Sherin, I would have cut him down where he stood. Even if you'd wanted to marry Roon."

"You know his name. Do you know him?"

I feel Nif's grip tighten around me.

"Know of him," he says. "Just as he knows of me. There are fewer people every day in the desert."

Part of me wants to ask him what he knows of Roon, but I don't want to hear any more rumors. Those have a way of sticking lies to them like pollen to a bee. Of obscuring a greater truth.

And I need to figure out the greater truth about Roon, I just do. While part of me can understand why Roon would give me up to his monarch, I can't reconcile that young man with the one who would execute a girl by rape, as Adamen contended. Geet. That was her name. I wonder what Roon's reaction would have been if I'd said her name to him on the evening we'd watched the sun set over the desert horizon—less than a week ago. Part of me is sorry I missed the opportunity, while a greater part is glad not to know. Because truth be told, even now, I can't forget the young man who rescued me at my engagement party. That was a selfless act committed by someone who knows the human heart. Or did at one point.

"But you weren't there," I say. I shouldn't have. None of this is Nif's fault. I was just thinking out loud.

Nif stops and for a moment I think he might kiss me again. Even harder this time.

"I knew your every move," he says. "And I promise you would have never married Roon."

It's a promise that rings of certainty and I don't know what else to say.

We remain quiet until we come upon another cavern. Enormous, but simple, like my cave. It's lit by several fires, all with people clustered around them in rings. People in over-worn tunics who are covered in that thin layer of sand dust that settles on desert dwellers like finely ground pepper.

Nif enters the cavern with me still cradled in his arms, and everyone looks up. Setting me down all careful like I could shatter, he puts his hand on the small of my back, where it feels like it belongs. He positions me in front of him, present-ing me like an effigy of a goddess. Although of what I can't imagine. The goddess of bad luck, maybe.

"This is my wife," he says simply.

Nif takes my hand and leads me to the central fire—the largest one. No one seems surprised by his pronouncement, save me, and I look around in a stunned silence. While there are most certainly curious stares thrown in my direction, especially by the few—the very few—women in the group, I feel more like an expected guest.

"Are you hungry?" Nif asks me.

Starving, actually. Nif gestures toward a man I recognize. His name is Karat and he's one of the men who was with Nif when he took me from my father's house. He has a laugh like a hyena as I recall, although he isn't laughing now. He's selecting the best cuts of meat from an unidentifiable animal—a rather sturdy lizard by the looks of it. One that's been roasted and charred over the fire into a hunk resembling a small meteor. He arranges the pulled meat on a clean cloth and lays it at my feet.

"It's good to see you again," I say, and he grunts as respect-fully as a grunt can allow.

Next comes a man who tells me his name is Duman. Rough featured, skeptical eyes. He shoves a cup of wine into my hand, and it splashes all over. On purpose, I think.

"Thank you," I tell him, and he ignores me. Bowing to Nif, he calls him *sam*, like they all do. Nif wastes not a moment and takes my hand, holding it out, making Duman honor me. The man changes his expression, almost smiling. Just like that. He bows deeply to me before turning on his heel and returning to his fire pit.

"Duman didn't like me much when I first came to the tribe either," Nif whispers.

I sit cross-legged and take the cloth onto my lap, beginning to eat. In the Palace City it was said that the desert people eat raw meat and I'm pleased to see this isn't the case.

"It's delicious," I say, and Karat's eyes flash.

I'm feeling shy and awkward, perhaps because of Nif's false representation of me as his wife. I can understand why he did it. For the same reason why he had me change my bloodstained tunic. Or maybe it's to grant me immediate acceptance as a new member of the tribe. I'm not sure. What I do know is that I'd feel much better with the truth. Even if taking me as his wife is Nif's intention at some point—it certainly was when we met—the fact remains that I'm not his wife.

I place a chunk of charred meat on my cloth and lick my fingers. Eyes closed, I taste a faint ghost of spice—cumin, I think—that must have been hard to come by. Expensive spices for a new bride, I guess. The wife of their chief.

Marriages, as I've experienced them, are a complicated negotiation. One usually involving a fair share of both family and tribal politics. Yet from the moment Nif told me his name, it's felt as if the world is just he and I.

Of course, it's not. There's Nif's tribe, my tribe now, too. Long hair, grizzled faces, whispers, laughter here and

there . . . always the furtive glances at me. Fewer of them
than I expected. Many have fallen since the last time I saw
them at these very dunes. The women, no more than thirty
out of the hundred or so who huddle around the fires, wear
the same tunics as the men. Only with sashes of earthy, un-
dyed cloth at their waists and the same tied around their
heads in neat turbans. They're pretty. Much prettier than the
men. Except for Nif.

Nif is the prettiest of them all, which I imagine is why he
hides behind a beard.

At the rear of the cavern, three men stand up and press
their shoulders to a large rock, rounded like a wheel.
Groaning as they push and roll it a few steps, they let a long
blade of the late afternoon sun cut the dim firelight inside.
Dry, desert air, like a warm puff of breath, seeps into the cave,
feeling sweet and balmy. Through the crack laid open by this
makeshift door, I can see a high ledge that supports a sea of
tents, not at all visible from the desert floor beneath it. Some
are open, others closed. Inside one, a woman is feeding a
baby at her breast. A baby! Squirming bundle of hope. From
where I sit, the mother looks about my age. When she smiles
at her infant, she reveals a tooth-poor mouth and a pale set
of gums.

"Is this where your tribe lives?" I turn to Nif and see he's
been watching me.

"Most of the time," he answers. "Few soldiers would dare
come this far into the cave. It's too dangerous and they'd have
to bring a lot of torches to make it through with any success,
as you found out." Nif laughs, giving a playful kick to my
foot.

"Over there, on the other side, we're up a good ways." He
inclines his head toward the ledge. "We'd see anyone coming
and could pick them off one by one if they tried to climb the
dune and attack us."

"A clever perch," I say.

"But sometimes, we have to move. Especially when the dunes become over-crowded. The worst sort comes here. Ones who prey on our women and children."

"You don't defend your place? You just go?"

Nif shakes his head.

"There are already enough battles to fight. For food, weapons, and other resources. We're a mobile people, used to moving. It's easier to split into smaller groups and leave for a time. Come back here when the others have gone."

I finish my meat and Nif leans over, digging his hand into a sack that rests between Karat and a carrot-nosed man I don't know. He produces three fresh figs, peeling the first and opening its body to my lips. Honeyed and delicious. He plucks a seed off my bottom lip and eats it, smiling.

"No one stays here for longer than they have to, Sherin."

Nif peels another fig.

"No one stays anywhere longer than they have to anymore."

Nif gives me a meaningful look. Like the one he gave me when he first told me of his tribe of tent-dwellers with no permanent settlement. It had been before the battle with Roon and he'd said it with shame, embarrassed that he was offering me so little, and believing I couldn't be happy to be marrying so far down. The Prince of Nothing, I'd called my proposed husband then. Nif is anything but that.

"This is a fine settlement," I tell him. "Much nobler than a failing Palace City. It is salan." *To be.*

Nif smiles.

"Salan," he says. "Yes, it is salan. As salan as anything can be these days."

THROUGHOUT THE EVENING, there's fire-cooking. Eating and drinking. Enough meat, a bit of cheese. Flatbread. Only I get the figs. And there's wine. Plenty of wine for everyone. Nif is providing for his people. No small feat in these times.

Long after dark, when the desert settles and stills, the rock is rolled all the way open, so we can look out at the stars. Smoke meanders across the high ceiling of the cavern in a slow creep, like fog. The moon is nearly full and the air grows cool, but not yet cold. It still clings, however barely, to the heat of the day.

An older woman with long gray hair—no turban—walks, almost drifting, to the center of the cavern. With her hands floating delicately at the sides of her slight frame, she starts to sing. It's a subtle and fragile melody at first, but rises to a haunting wail that shivers throughout the grotto. I ride every note on a magic carpet. And when she finishes, my body slumps, as if a spirit has left it. Nif places his hand on my shoulder.

"That was exquisite," I tell him.

"She has a gift," Nif says. "Her name is Saru and you'll come to know her well."

The fire is warm and I'm drowsy. I wish I could lean against Nif, but it doesn't seem proper, despite our encounter in the cave and his introduction of me as his wife. Maybe because of it.

"Come with me," he says, taking my hand, leading me through the throng of seated tribesmen and women.

Out on the ledge it's cool and the sky is clear and twinkling. Thousands of winks by the goddesses, my father used to say. It'll be my first night in relative safety out here. I've made it this far, against all odds. And now, all I want to do is sleep.

Nif guides me to a tent that's much like the other tents. Some bigger, some smaller. They're constructed of heavy linen canvas and oryx pelts, held up by poles that allow a breeze when there is one. In cold, excessive heat, or blowing sand, the flaps can be rolled down, creating a protected shelter.

Nif holds open a flap for me, and I crawl in, nestling into a soft pile of linens. I welcome the prospect of sleep as soon as my body lies still. I can feel Nif taking off my slippers. Nice of him. The callous on his index finger skims the arch of my foot, tickling me as I curl onto my side, snuggling the linens as I used to in my father's house.

Vaguely, I hear rustling inside the tent, and in the next moment Nif lies down, fitting his body to mine, and putting his arms around me.

"What are you doing?" I ask. Ask is the polite way to put it. My tone is anything but polite. Tired and irritated is more like it. I'd been on the brink of sleep. And I'm most definitely offended.

"I'm going to sleep."

"With me?"

"You are my wife."

While the crisp desert air couldn't wake me, this revelation does.

"I'm not your wife because you say so! You need to find yourself another place to sleep."

Nif sits up, shushing me. He speaks low, through gnashed teeth. "You are my wife exactly because I say so. And I'm sleeping right here in my—*our*—tent."

Now I sit up. As awake as I've ever been.

"No vow. No ceremony. And you think you can just lie with me?"

I voice this in a tight whisper for his sake, but I want to yell.

"I'm not imposing myself on you. Not tonight. I want to sleep."

"Not in here."

Nif huffs, pulling at the short hairs on his chin, shaking his head. "Is not my saying that you're my wife a vow? Does it not bind me to you and make me responsible for your welfare?"

"No!"

Leaning in, Nif grabs me by my shoulders, speaking right into my face.

"I realize that you're used to some pageantry. The Rah'a has an elaborate party, it seems, for every occasion. But that's not the way of our people. We have more immediate needs."

He releases me, like I'm a hot stone or something.

"So, what? A man says to a woman—you're my wife—and that's it?"

"Not exactly, but, well, yes."

"Even the simplest tribes have ceremonies. I've seen them."

"Well, I suppose we're the simplest of the simple then, and you'd best get used to it."

I wind up my hand to slap him and he catches it. He's dumbfounded for a second, and then lunges, pushing me down. I'm afraid he might slap me, but he doesn't.

Instead, he points at the canvas wall, in the direction that leads off the ledge. "You wouldn't last a week in the desert."

I push him and he lets up.

"Don't you patronize me like I'm some spoiled harem wife," I hiss. "I walked here alone, and the woman I served is on a spike right now!"

Nif climbs off his haunches. He looks at the linens, his breath slight and uneven. "I know."

"I didn't mean you're to blame for that," I tell him, and I really didn't. "What I meant was that we have so little left of what we were, of how we used to live. We can't lose everything just for the sake of survival. Especially not a vow. Sometimes I think a vow will be all we'll have left when this is over."

We sit in silence for some time, listening to bare footsteps, mumbles from the cavern, a loud fart from a nearby tent. I try not to laugh, but can't help it and neither can Nif.

"So, you would like some words spoken," he says, softly. "In the presence of the tribe. A vow."

"Yes," I say, staring at my hands, pretending to smooth a jagged fingernail.

It isn't lost on me that, less than a week ago, I would have been making my vow to Roon, had things gone a different way.

I tip my head up and notice Nif is looking at me again. He isn't angry anymore, but I can't say as to what he's feeling either.

"You're not unhappy about becoming my wife?" he asks.

I take my first breath in what seems like a day. "No, I'm not unhappy about it. I don't want to live like an animal. Or mate like one, though."

Nif appears very young for the first time since I've made his acquaintance. Vulnerable. Although it's too dark to see the intricate colors in his eyes, I can tell by the way he holds them that he, too, is making a record of his losses. Not just his, but his people's. All that has fallen away since the region that had held our civilization in its embrace suddenly let go.

"Sherin, I can't leave our tent tonight," he says. "I told everyone you're my wife."

I do realize that.

"Well," I say. "I suppose we can sleep next to one another."

I roll one of the linens, placing it between us. Then, as a true peace offering, lie down. Nif follows on his portion of our bed.

My heart is beating hard and I'm no longer in the least bit sleepy. All I can do is stare up at the point in the tent ceiling, trying to discern whether it's wood or bone that holds it up . . . trying to understand where my life has led me, and what I will do from this day forward. Nif and I finding each other has changed everything.

Salan's face comes to me and it's both a gift and a heartache. Right about this time of night, I would be wrapping him in his linens and telling him a story. Kissing his forehead and each of his eyelids. Smoothing his cowlick with my fingers. Singing a song of his choice.

"Can't you sleep?"

"No," I say.

"Me either."

Nif turns onto his side and is quiet for a little while.

"In my culture there are words that bind a marriage and there are actions." He seems to hesitate, pulling the linen higher up on his collarbone. "When I kissed you in the Palace City . . . and the way we touched one another in the darkness. That was an action, a ceremony for me."

He starts to reach for me, reconsiders, resting his hand on the roll of linen I've placed between us.

"That's not enough," I say.

Nif moves a bit closer, nudging the roll of linen, resting his knee on it.

"Sherin, can I touch you?"

I stop breathing altogether. "Where?"

"Just your arm. The way I did your face in the dark. Nothing more."

I suppose that's fine under the circumstances, and push the sleeve of my tunic nearly all the way to my shoulder. "Go ahead."

Nif props himself up on his elbow and slides closer to me. He cranes his neck to smell my hair as his index finger lands on mine. He toys with it, squeezing its tip, then makes his way up and over my knuckle. Exploring between my fingers, he flips my hand over and places his thumb in the middle, tracing the lines of my palm.

"Did you know there are seers who believe the lines of our palms tell the stories of our fates?"

"No," I say. "What do you suppose my lines say of me?"

Nif intertwines his fingers with mine, squeezing tight. "That you were made to be loved by me."

Chapter 36

My Body Tells a Story

I **WAKE UP** with the first light, having slept heavily. The linens are tangled around me and I fight them, rolling over to Nif's side of our bed in a bundle of mint, royal indigo and amber. He's gone. Outside, I hear the rumblings of the morning. Throats clearing, the shuffle of early chores, a baby crying. The pleasing sounds of civility. I want to follow Nif's example and be up and about before most of the others— being of use, learning my role. But as soon as I crawl out of our tent, there are hands upon me. It's Saru, the woman who sang for us.

"Back to sleep," she chides.

"There's work to be done."

"Not this morning."

I have to admit that going back to bed sounds glorious. And Saru is standing there, wild gray hair and arms folded, like someone who is used to getting her way. Her eyes are wet and black, and in complete command of her whole face. In complete command of me, too, it appears.

I shrug, yielding to her judgment. Saru releases her arms to her sides, where they sway like palm fronds in a gentle breeze. There's something verdant and otherworldly about her.

"Wake me in a little while," I say. Her eyes, youthful except for two tiny crinkles at their corners twitch in agreement.

Back in my tent, I sink into the bed linens, running my hands over their supple fabric. It's flawless, downy as skin, and has a scent of . . . I shoot up, stretching the linen over my legs. Marital linens, meant for two—I examine its every grain and groove. I recognize the weave and the dye. A tight twill the color of hibiscus. Moreover, I remember my mother making it.

I remember the sky on the day she'd woven it. It had been under a cover of clouds that spread like a thick, woolen shawl over a pale blue sky. Yina made fresh bread and we ate it with honey and pistachio nuts. My father bent to kiss my mother on the tip of her nose, before going out to help a neighbor birth his goat.

I nearly forgot that Nif still had the many fine things he'd taken from my father's house. Our linens and pottery, oils and perfumes, bowls and baskets. Perhaps even a few of Yina's chutneys are left, saved for special occasions. I fall back into my dreams nestled in the sweet serenity of home.

"SHERIN, TIME TO RISE."

It's hot in the tent, as if the entire day's heat is trapped inside. The linens about me are damp with sweat and my cheeks are red-hot, like a child's. Like Salan's.

I force my eyes open, squinting at Saru, who's at my side. She has with her a pot of water and square linens for washing. I assume they're for me, as I'm the only one of us in desperate need of a bath.

She asks me to unwrap my tunic and I do. The water she's brought for dipping the linens is cool, oiled, and herbed. Heaven on my parched skin. I can't imagine this is going to be the treatment I'll get every day in this tribe, but if it is my welcome—I'll take it. Fluttering my eyes open, I glance up at Saru, whose tiny mouth opens to a dreamy song. When she finishes, she asks me to sit up.

Saru stands, untying several thick, canvas ribbons at the far end of our tent. She rolls up each flap, pinning one at a time, exposing the doorway to another room—a sitting room filled with bright carpets and pillows, patterned with swirls and geometric shapes that have a look of insanity. Some are woolen, and some canvas, and shouldn't match in either grade or design, yet do. None of these have come from my father's house, but they are nonetheless fine and free in their style.

There's a hearth, just lit and roaring, and a polished square of copper that was my father's looking glass. I remember the last time I watched him shave, his rosy reflection staring back at him in earnest concentration.

Dried flowers and thistles are tied in posies and dangle from the ceiling in subdued hues of lavender, periwinkle, and gold—quite pretty. I reach up and stroke the crisp petals of a yellow chamomile lightly, so that it doesn't crumble at my touch.

"What is your tent like?" I ask.

Saru grins in that way of hers. "A bed of linens. A place to put a few things."

So, it appears there is a distinction between tents—one I couldn't see last night when everything blended together in the darkness. Our tent, mine and Nif's, has this sitting room next to where we sleep. A place where the leader of the tribe can receive visitors, settle skirmishes. Where his wife can dress and invite in other women.

"What is that?" I ask, pointing to a palette of colorful pastes. I'm hoping to change the subject, gracefully. In the Palace City I didn't mind receiving preferential treatment as a woman of station, but here it feels vulgar somehow. Unearned.

"They're for you."

"I'm afraid I'm not much of a painter," I say, and Saru laughs.

"Not for you to paint. For you to be painted with."

Saru plaits and twists my damp tresses, easing me onto a pillow. She places a bone hairpin into my hair and picks up a tiny brush. "I'll paint your story onto your person as you tell it to me."

I stand there open-mouthed for a moment. "Whatever for?"

"So that your story will be ours, too."

Saru looks me over, her great black eyes moving slowly along the lines of my figure.

"You are luminous," she says. Unprepared for the compliment, I wrap my arms over my breasts.

"I didn't say you were beautiful, although you are. I said you are luminous. Like the moon. Or deep water." She tips her head and exhales fully through her nose. "Your eyes," she begins, but then stops, as if thinking better of it. She reaches behind her and sets the palette of colors on a small wooden stool. Kneeling, she adjusts a worn piece of linen on her lap and lifts my foot, placing it there.

"Tell me everything of your life."

I feel awkward—terribly. Unsure of what to say. I mean obviously I must tell her about my life, but I want to make sure that whatever I say is honest but can also withstand my being paraded naked through the tribe with only the story of my life dressing me. If that's the case, though, so be it. I mean, if everyone else had to do it at some point, then I should do it, too.

"My mother's hands," I whisper.

It's my first memory. Saru mixes a pinkish-brown color with the pastes and dips the very tip of the brush into it. She begins to paint at the top of my foot—the brush so soft it tickles.

It must be near evening as Saru finishes the last touch of my story. The light under canvas is dimmed, like a sheaf of muslin that's been thrown over the sun. She's done painting Nif's hands, palms open just under my collarbone, as if holding the whole of my head up to the heavens. The rest of my body is a wild storm of hues. It is an intricate mural displaying the night sky above my father's house, the flora of my garden at home and in the Palace City—even the hideous flower, which Saru chose to put at the center. There are the tiny fish Yina used to farm for my father, Salan's delicate profile on my hip, a view of the sunset from the roof of our house on my belly and breasts. The moon gushing over my neck, leading to Nif's arrows, which stand along my spine. Fire licking up and down my arms—the funeral pyre I'd built for my loved ones after the Vara.

"You'll need to dress," she says, handing me a bundle of fabric rippled with colors of blood and pearl with touches of cinnamon. I know it at once. It belonged to my mother and is one of the many linens we took with us when we left my home. I thought I'd never see it again.

"I can't," I tell her.

When I was a girl, I used to sneak into my mother's chamber and take this very tunic out of its basket, laying it on her bed linens, running the pads of my fingertips over it. It was the softest linen I'd ever touched. Softer than spider's silk.

A few times, I'd put this tunic on, letting the fabric swallow me. My mother herself had only worn this tunic the one time, and I was told she'd looked magnificent. It was on the day of her wedding to my father.

"Your husband is waiting for you," Saru says, casually. "And so are your people." She places my mother's tunic in my hands, leaving me to dress alone. I can either put on my mother's wedding dress, or face my new tribe naked, but for Saru's paints.

It's nearly dark by the time I summon the courage to actually dress in the tunic. And it fits so perfectly, as if my mother herself is wearing it. A far cry from when I tried it on as a girl and it bunched and gapped all over. Falling long past my toes, and dragging behind me as I attempted a strut.

I run my hands over it. The way it binds my shoulders and drapes around my breasts, giving me form. How it falls in a graceful swoon to my ankles.

With a deep breath, I face my tent's entrance, splitting open its flaps. I emerge into a brilliant desert sunset of fire and blood. And to Nif standing not a few steps away from me.

Chapter 37

A Vow

NIF LOOKS NOT at all like himself. A strange thing to say; of course he looks like himself. It's only he's clean and wears a tunic like one I've never seen on anyone in his tribe or anywhere else. It's crimson and impeccable, tightly swathed across his chest and shoulders, but open nearly to his belly with the rest loosely tumbling to the ground. At his waist is a belt woven with the most extraordinary beads— wooden and carved with intricate designs that come together to form a moving picture, cat-like, that crouches or springs, depending upon his movements. Long strands of beaded leather hang from his belt all the way to his ankles.

Knowing something of form and dress, I can imagine how those strands will whip and swing when he endeavors to move with any spirit. He'll look like a tempest. It's as dramatic a design as I've ever seen on a man, though not at all like the costumes of splendor and theater that the sultan wears. Nif's is a masculine attire that conveys honor and influence, not pomp. And it's very effective.

Nif's person has also been tended to. His hair, dark as soil and wavy, strips of it almost blue, touches his shoulders. His beard is trimmed so close he's nearly shaven. Both his skin and his hair have been oiled in defense against the desert's bone-dry air.

It is not the first time I've noticed that Nif is beautiful.

Anyone can see that, even if he's only ever disheveled and gritty or downright filthy—at least in my experience of him. But to witness him dressed in red and arranged like a man of civility and command is a sight to behold.

Nif opens his arms to me and I go, but I can't help but take the skirt of his tunic into my hands. Habit I suppose. I rub the thread between my fingers and Nif laughs.

"Is it up to your standards?"

"Oh, it's very fine," I say. "Where did you get it?"

"It was my father's."

His father, who died in an outbreak of the Vara when Nif was a boy. Leaving him alone and with the knowledge he was immune to the contagion. He told me this at my father's house on the day we met, after he shot the arrow through Kirin. I remember every word.

Nif runs his fingertips along the edging of his garment. It strikes me that we're dressed to complement one another, as well as in tribute to the twilight playing out behind us. I imagine we look like part of the sky. Our bodies, our pasts— in unity with the world the gods have made for us.

"Did you choose my tunic to match yours, or did Saru?"

Nif shakes his head. "I chose it, but only because I thought you would love it. This," he says, running his hand over the soft twist of fabric at my waist. "This looks as if it was made for you."

"It wasn't," I whisper. "It was my mother's."

"She would want you to wear it."

It's hard to meet his gaze when he says that. I turn my head as if to enjoy the sunset, and take in my surroundings for the first time. Nif's very presence, his striking transformation, blinded me to everything around us. And that everything . . . is nothing. Except for my own tent, *ours* Nif would remind me, the herd of canvas on the dune ledge is packed up and put away. Back into caves, I imagine, from where I can hear the muffled drone of quiet conversations. All that remains are standing torches at the far sides of the drop-off, interspersed with a scattering of crystalline rocks that absorb and reflect whatever radiance is around them—the eruption of the sunset and the blaze of torchlight. Us.

"There are words told only between a husband and a wife, Sherin." Nif says quietly. He takes my hands, grazing his thumbs over my knuckles as if he's memorizing their every feature.

"These words are given as a gift to the person who will share your life. Of hopes and truths and secrets. It's what my people have always done. The people I was born to."

I nod in understanding, although in truth, I'm not sure where he's headed with this.

"You said you wanted a vow and a ceremony."

Nif smiles, raising his hands to my face.

"Are you all right?" He asks, pulling me closer.

"It's just . . . we only spoke of it last night."

A piece of my hair tumbles out of my loose braid and Nif tucks it behind my ear. My whole body stiffens. Nerves. I hope he knows that. Because truly, I want more than anything for him to touch me. I don't know how to accept his caress outside of the dark.

"Since we're expected to live together, I figured you'd want to do this as soon as possible."

"I do," I say. My insides feel like at any moment they'll grow wings, burst out of my belly and fly away. "It's that I know so little about you."

Stupid thing to say. What wife knows anything about her husband before they marry?

"You will." Nif again takes my face in his hands and kisses my forehead.

"My tribe was the Beih. A dead tribe now with only a few of us littered about on the outskirts of the Rah'a." He releases me, letting his hands rest at his sides.

I've heard of the Beih. My father spoke of them. Cultured, by desert standards, with a great tradition of storytelling. It's said that, in generations past, the sultan had taken many of his soldiers from the Beih. Resilient men known as philosopher warriors. Intelligent. Strategic.

"In my tribe," he continues. "We did have a ceremony for taking a wife. I hadn't thought much of it until we spoke last night. The last wedding I attended of this sort was my cousin's, when I was eight."

My thoughts are racing. I try to recall every piece of news I've ever heard of the Beih from my father and others. One, in particular, springs to mind. The men are known to bind themselves to one woman, unless she's barren. That in itself is unusual among the desert tribes, and a relief. I can't, under any circumstances, imagine sharing Nif.

"Is that what we're doing right now?" I say. "Making our wedding vows?"

Nif nods.

"I don't know your rituals, what to say . . . " I'm stuttering and my hands are starting to sweat. I blot them gently on the sides of my tunic, trying not to be obvious about it.

"You don't have to," Nif says. "I'm the one who does the talking. See, it's very easy for you. You just have to decide if my vows are worthy of you."

"Don't you have a say?"

Nif raises his eyebrows at me. "Well, since I'm the one making my case, I think my intentions are pretty clear."

"Are they so different from other vows?" I whisper. I know the common vows of fidelity, unity, and child-making. The trading of honor, position, and goods negotiated in most marriages.

"Our vows are more than promises, Sherin. They're of the past, present, and future. We tell them within a story. The story of how fate delivered us to each other. I'll tell you how our story began, and I'll tell you how it will end."

My vision blurs a bit and I bat my eyes, taking him in. His skin is the color of juniper wood with an undertone of olive. A work of perfection between every line and scar. Its creases—at the mouth, a trident from the corners of each of his eyes—are deep and sinuous, like the rings in a gorge of sandstone.

"You know that? How it will end?"

"I do."

"How do you know?"

He gives me his smile again. A gift on our wedding day.

"Because my people have always believed in destiny. It's one of the few things I carried away with me when I left my home."

Nif inhales deeply. I watch his whole body rise and fall with his breath as if a gust of wind has taken possession of him. He peers out at the sun, now dipping the dome of her belly into the horizon. Our sun is a feminine god. All fire, big and pregnant, watching over her children.

"And destiny," he says, "is like a written language. You just have to know its symbols."

Nif steps back, and I startle. He sweeps his arms about the desert vista.

"I've lived all my life here, Sherin. And I'll die here. It is, for most cultivated people, a place of scarcity. Little food. Water, rarer still. Even fewer people. But for me, for mine—the Beih, the Waterless Sea—it has always been a land of abundance. A habitat rich with sun, wealthy with a lavish treasure of freedoms. And bonds. Bonds of courage and determination that bring generations as close as the petals that flank the pistil of a flower."

Nif's lips are set by a swell of pride. He tips his head, the last beams of the sun stroking his neck. His hands press together, as if in prayer, and his eyes close to everything but his story.

"My father was the chief of the Beih. Erid, was his name. It means *he who lives the truth*. You see, we—the people I was born to—the meanings of our names are a part of us. They are as sure an inheritance as the color of our hair."

His voice is low, reverential, as if he's talking to his unborn child.

"My mother was Piri, and she died just within the reach of my memory. My parents had known each other all their lives, and been promised since infancy. But it's the desert, my father told me, that gave life to their love."

Nif closes and opens his eyes. *Mismatched in color, yet as inclined to one another as pieces in a mosaic.*

"The desert, Sherin, holds lovers dearest of all. In the palm of her hand. In every shadow where they stop to kiss. And every grain of sand that lashes their shins. In the cavern where I lay you down and touched your face."

He brushes his fingers along his brow, just as he did mine in that cavern. I can't help but mirror the gesture, feeling almost as if we're there again. In the dark. As alone together as we might ever be.

"At night, when I think of you," he says, "you sit on the corner of my brow. Talking to me. Just as you used to sit with your father on the smooth stones that lined the roasting pit of the market near your home. Sharing meat and bread. His laugh betraying the pleasure he took in your company." He smiles at me, and I recall the many times I sat with my father as Nif describes. Unconscious and unaware that some-one—Nif—was watching me. It's a startling thought, but the gentleness with which he retells what he saw makes me wish I could have watched him, too.

"Perhaps you were no more than a girl of seven when I first saw you there," he goes on. "I wasn't much older, and hadn't been with these people very long."

He gestures toward the cavern and I look that way. From here I can see its back wall, splayed with the shadows of its inhabitants. "Do you believe in soul sight, Sherin?"

Soul sight. I shrug, unsure. I know our seer had been right about my father, had made claims about me. But I'm uncertain about the ability to spin a tale of prophecy, as someone with soul sight does—or claims to. One which promises to unfold with startling intricacy and accuracy, to a most definite conclusion.

Nif studies me as if he can see my thoughts running in script across my face.

"Do *you*?" I ask. "Is that why you've been watching me?"

"From the first time I saw you, I could see taking your hand and leading you from your father's house. As young as I was, I could imagine the feel of your lips. Yesterday, in the dark, I knew every part of you."

I swallow. My throat dry and tender. I feel a fool. "Was I familiar to you when you washed me in my cave?"

Nif looks at his feet, smiling. "No. That was new."

I'm glad he doesn't look at me, only to see me flush to the color of his tunic. It isn't shyness, really. It's the way he speaks of it, bringing to light the fear and excitement of breaking beyond the barriers of tribe and custom, walking onto a completely unmarked path with him. That's what makes me feel naked.

"There was one day," he tells me. "When I saw you with a servant woman. I only knew she was a slave by her dress, pale blue. Because you held her hand and walked with her as if she was your sister. She poked at your rib and fixed the collar of your tunic, whispering something into your ear as you tried not to laugh. I envied her."

"Yina," I say.

Nif turns away from me, and repeats her name. It sounds nice coming from him. I wish he'd known her.

"My father told me all the things we learn about others can be found in their littlest behaviors. We don't need to wait for a war to find out whether a man is brave in battle, whether he'll be a faithful friend. You can see all of this from the way a person walks through his day, and in the looks others cast upon him."

It's as if Nif is talking to his father, honoring him for his wisdom. I know conversations like this very well. The ones between me and a spirit world. A place where those I've loved can hear me, maybe answer in some way.

"This is how I knew I loved you," he says. "By watching you walk through the small rituals of your life."

Nif looks at me, our faces like two sides of the moon. It feels good to be known by him.

"I knew you were competent when I saw that your father depended upon your eye and its judgments whenever he took you on his business. I could see you laughed easily and could do so at your own expense. And your movements were buoyant, even once you were bound to wear the formal tunic of a mala."

I bite my lip, suppressing a giggle.

"And you are imperfect," Nif says, eyes all narrow now. "As imperfect a woman as I've ever met."

I cross my arms, and he winks at me. I admit I like his flattery more than his rational assessments of my virtues.

"Prideful and stubborn, at times. But inclined to joy. I could see it in the way you kicked stones with the other children. Most girls of your age stood to the side, trying too hard to look like women. But you wanted to play."

Nif walks all around me, looking me up and down. As he

moves, the beads that hang from his belt swing to and fro, giving his words an added drama.

"Not all of them saw you as a friend," he says. "And for good reason. You never hesitated to lash out when you were paid a slight."

Not quite the vow I'd been expecting, but I hold my chin high and hang on to my dignity.

"You played fair, though," he acknowledges. "Only giving as good as you got. This was how I knew you understood love."

"Because I lashed out at the boys who played with me?"

Nif moves even closer. "You played as a girl who was loved by her father. And who had watched her father love her mother."

His breath skims my mouth as if he might kiss me. "That, I think, is a girl who can truly love a man."

I pretend something has scampered by my feet, casting my eyes down and taking shelter from Nif's gaze. He will have none of it. He takes my right hand, the hand of truth, according to the gods, and lifts it to his lips, but doesn't kiss it. He waits until my eyes meet his again to do that.

"Even before the Vara came, I dreamed of it and knew that the gods would spare you for me. Then I set out for you, to bring you home to this tribe. Taking your things with us to comfort you. And giving you what I had in return—the protection of my arms and my weapons, the solace of my heart. Hands that will never strike you in anger. Children to worship you as I will."

"Why didn't you tell me that when you came to my house?" I whisper.

Nif's eyes search the air as if the right words might be floating around us.

"I meant to," he says. "But it was so soon after your family died. And you didn't seem to enjoy my company right then. I wanted to warm your heart to me first."

My hand falls away from his fingers. It's not in my nature to bare myself the way he has. My people are not born storytellers, who can fix their emotions to words like gemstones to gold. While he's right that I do understand love, I haven't practiced it in a very long time. Except with Salan. And now I feel clumsy and self-conscious about it.

Nif's eyes shimmer in the lowlight. They're brighter than I've ever seen them, with the streams of blood in his right eye even more vivid than the royal hue of his garment. And the fiery amber of his other, the one like the tortoise shell, glowing with the dying gasp of sunset.

"Then came the battle—the one in these dunes—and you slipped away from me," he continues. "Not just one battle, but many. One after another."

His eyes fix to my gaze. "And so I fought, and I fought more. Until the desert took its victims. Then I came for you again."

I think of him battered and insulted at the end of a chain and feel shamed. He takes my hand again, lifting it from my breast and pressing it against his own heart.

"I was the one who bathed in pig's blood and had myself tied up and left at the city gates," he says. "It wasn't Adamen. I wanted you to know what I would do for you, since it was all I could offer. Not the influence of a soldier or the walls of a city. Even if those will be short-lived luxuries, they are difficult to leave behind."

That night I had turned him down, but not for luxuries. It had been for Salan. For what everyone said about the Prince of the Waterless Sea, even if deep in my heart I felt it couldn't be true. "You could've been killed."

"A day of bruises. Maybe two."

"A day of bruises? They wanted blood! And how could

you know that I would come after I saw you in the courtyard and I--"

"Well, I didn't know you believed I'd brought the Vara to your home at that time. That's true. I might have said something in that case. But I did know, by soul sight perhaps, I can't say. I did know you would come to me. And you did."

My legs feel as fragile as honeycomb. And my breath . . . well. My breath is quaking and shallow, as unruly as my fingers, which I twist in damp knots.

"So, I ask you, Sherin of the Rah'a," Nif says. "By what you have seen of my character and what you have heard of my love for you. Do you know I will not let you thirst or starve? That I will offer you a life with the people here? And will never leave you to cry alone? Do you know that I will die in your arms and search for you throughout eternity?"

Chapter 38

A Feast

IT'S A WALL of words Nif has given me. Tall and well-built. And a good thing that the burden is upon the bridegroom to do all the talking. All I can do is stand here, counting the beats of my pulse.

"Sherin," he says. His hand is still on my cheek, holding my face like a piece of fragile pottery. "Do you accept my vow?"

I try to say something, but it's as if I've set with the sun. I can feel my lips moving, but I'm not sure what words they're forming. Thank the gods Nif knows.

"I can manage that," he whispers. Then he bends toward me and presses his lips to mine.

I must have said, *kiss me.*

And he does as he did in the courtyard, and the cave, only more so. He kisses me with his tongue and his breath, his hands caressing my neck. He kisses me deeply and hard, as if he will never stop.

"Am I your wife now?" I gasp, as we break from each other. He touches his nose softly to mine.

"You were my wife from the first day I saw you." Then he brings me close to him, holding me, my head resting at his throat.

FROM INSIDE THE CAVERN, we can hear laughter. Dinner is cooking, and the night is settling in. The tribe is so close, but it's as if we're an entire region removed from them. Nif takes in the scent of my hair before letting me go. He offers his elbow to lead me inside, and I take it, nearly bursting into laughter. It feels like we've done something both sacred and wicked, and we haven't even gotten to our wedding night yet. I lift up onto my toes and kiss his cheek.

"Nahoor," I say.

The Rah'a word of promise that joins the meaning of eternity and today. I've never, until now, been able to voice it. But there it is. My official answer to his vow. Nif smiles and glances at my fingers; they're peeking out from the crook of his elbow like crab legs from a shell.

"I almost forgot," he says.

Nif reaches into a fold of his garment and pulls out the necklace that Roon gave me. I start to protest, but stop as I watch Nif kiss the bloodstone at the center of the amulet, as if it's his intimate possession.

"I was glad to see you wearing it when I found you."

I say nothing, but I'm sure my face does my talking for me.

"I had a merchant smuggle it into the Palace City for me. I wanted you to know you were under my protection. Today and always. That I was born for you."

"Ah'kwarah'a."

"I knew you'd know the symbol."

"Nif," I say. "I didn't know it was from you! I didn't . . . think."

"You wore it here."

"Not on purpose."

Nif reaches over my head and places his amulet around my neck.

"Everything is on purpose," he tells me. "That's the very meaning of destiny."

We start to walk.

Near the entrance, where the stone has been rolled away, my heart starts beating faster. I hear not the sounds of the evening ritual I'd been part of last night—chants, songs and the like—but raucous ones of laughter, playful banter and too much wine. A celebration.

When we enter the cavern, chatter tapers off to a quiet rustle and many look up at us. I can see Saru standing in the midst of a group of women. Her eyes meet mine and her tiny lips turn up into a crescent moon smile. Under the firelight, the walls of the cavern have a distinctive sparkle to them, like the way the sea glistens when the sun shines upon it. Points of light everywhere, blinking like lightning within a dark cloud. Feels almost like magic.

"There is a wind in the desert that speaks of lineage," I start.

The last stanza in the "Songs of the Desert Wind" is always improvised, honoring the occasion in which the song is evoked. My father had been a master at this part. I remember how he'd sung when he and my mother had lost my younger brother, the unnamed one who came before Salan. His voice full of their love, he sang how for all their grief, a dozen sons could never make one of her.

I want my own words to carry such weight. But I won't sing them. I'll speak them, as if talking to a dear friend.

"The desert has given our people strong families since the beginning of time, until we grew even where all the crops and flowers would not."

The tribe is rapt. Karat scratches his beard and Taran, my antelope friend, stands slowly. The young woman who I noticed breast-feeding her baby the night before, holds the child over her shoulder and rocks, soothing him.

"There is a wind in the desert that speaks of children. The ones here tonight and the ones we will make. One day, the desert will again be filled with our numbers. We will be as many as the tiny crystals that lie in these sands. I promise you. We will build structures as great as the Palace City and go beyond the borders of our kingdoms. Our region will give birth to a world again."

The survivors of the Waterless Sea are deadly quiet for a moment. Then Taran holds up his hands and falls to his knees, kissing the sandy floor of the cavern, clutching crystals in his palm. Others follow, some of the women crying as they sink down. The men beseech the gods. I had meant my words to be hopeful and inspiring, but I can't have guessed the emotion they would stir within these men and women. In all of their losses, their wandering and battles, faith remains.

I glance up to see what Nif thinks of all this, but he isn't there. Or rather, he is, but he isn't standing anymore. He's fallen to his knees like the others, both thanking the gods and begging them for mercy. So, I join him.

I FIGURE OUR VOWS are over and done with. We made them privately, sharing our hopes and truths and secrets. Nif, after all, had already introduced me as his wife when I first arrived.

But I'm wrong.

There's another part to the ritual. A public part.

A man named Buri, older than Nif by at least ten years, has also come from the Beih. He has the same fullness of cheekbone and wide bridge across his nose that Nif has, although his features don't come together with quite so much elegance. He's a handsome man, though, and learned, too. He speaks with natural eloquence as he takes my hand, welcoming me.

"May the moon quench your heart's thirst," he tells me. His hair has ruddy streaks, and shades his face like a palm.

That is, Nif whispers, a most honored blessing among the Beih. The moon, a symbol of love eternal, both carnal and ancestral, is also the natural emblem of a leader. It casts the blue light of wisdom.

Without another word, Buri takes both of our hands and guides us to the central hearth. He holds each of our left hands, positioning them palms up, side by side. With a small pair of pincers he crouches, plucking an ember from the fire. Small, no bigger than a wine grape, but glowing ferociously.

His face is pinched in concentration, watching the fireball, careful to keep it from dropping. I'm mesmerized by his absorption in the task, until he clutches my hand.

"A love that doesn't burn is for acquaintances," he says.

I try to twist out of his grasp, hot breath flaring out of my nostrils. Hardly a dignified pose for a bride, but hardly something I have any inclination to dwell on either, given what I think he wants to do to me.

In the flash of a second, Nif lifts his palm over mine and Buri drops the burning ember into it. Nif grits his teeth, breaking into an instant sweat. He meets my eyes. Before I can strike the fiery thing from his hand, Buri jerks my arm and fuses our palms together. Crying out, nay, screaming, I struggle with all of my might, all the while Buri crushes our hands, one on top of the other, with the cinder scorching our flesh in between.

"Let go!" I shriek, and Buri does, letting me fall to the ground.

The pong of burning flesh weaves together with the stares of everyone around us. I look at Nif, and want to die right there.

But cheers and hooting laughter erupt all around us with a *better you than me* quality that I find more than a little irritating. The men stomp their feet as the women trill a piercing, desert wail. Nif is breathing hard, watching me, sweat rushing down his temples. He bends to me, taking my blistered hand into his, kissing my wrist.

"You did well," he says, and I finally exhale. My hands are shaking. Before I can think of what to say, we're surrounded by the medicine women.

As the young ones chant, an older woman, nearly bald, with a deeply lined face, steps forward and bows. Her eyes mere slits, she sprinkles a black powder onto our palms, providing relief. A boy, no older than five, runs up to us carrying several strips of un-dyed linen, and the woman kisses the child.

"Mama," he says. Apparently, she's not nearly as old as I thought.

The medicine woman wraps linen strips around our hands, tying them loosely then holding them up to the ovations of all those around. Nif kisses my temple.

"I'm sorry," he says. "I should have warned you about that part of the ritual. I was going to, but Buri insisted that it's best to get it over with."

"Wise on Buri's part," I say, blotting my tears with the edge of the bandage. "Otherwise most brides and bridegrooms would run screaming."

Nif shrugs.

I'm angry and Nif knows it, but I don't want the tribe to know. He holds my hand gingerly, massaging the pillow beneath my thumb, while I do my best to make an agreeable face of it. My hand hurts, that's for sure, but whatever the medicine woman put into the pit of my palm is working.

We sit around the big fire again after a promenade around the cavern. Meeting and greeting, learning names, and receiving well-wishes and small tokens. Mole rat hides, a bracelet of bone fragments—all smoothed and polished, a poem, a prayer, a small pot of scented oil for later. An old man has given us that, leering over a single front tooth as he dutifully explains its purpose. Like we have no idea.

People fuss around us, placing cushions beneath our seats and offering goblets of wine, which I most happily take into my good hand. I'll be needing several of those to get through the night.

"Sherin," Nif whispers. "The ritual is called a haaza and is meant as a tribute to the fortitude it takes to join with another." He holds his bandaged palm to mine, his lips caressing every syllable. "The way the pain of birth is a reminder to a mother of her undertaking. That of guiding a soul into the world, and building a being who lives his life for the glory of the gods."

Lovely words, but I'm not quite convinced.

"A funeral is quite a tribute, too," I sneer.

Nif thinks that's funny.

"As far as I know, no one has ever died from the haaza, regardless of how unpleasant it is."

"No? Not of infection?" I've seen burns cause some nasty infections. Plenty of people die from burns.

"Not of infection, or even bad temper."

I *ha* at that. "You would actually deny me a bad temper for this brutal ritual you've subjected me to?"

Nif places his palm against mine again and squeezes, making me wince. "I suppose if we were more cultured, we would have exchanged gold pieces instead. Held that between our palms, like we were buying a trinket in the market."

He releases my hand and places it on my lap, taking his wine and drinking. His eyes not letting go of me.

"Maybe a thorn," I offer. "Draws blood, makes the point, but without permanent damage."

Nif leans closer, dangling his bandaged hand over his knee and staring at it with a certain fondness. "A thorn is only one prick." He holds up his palm in salan. "This will always be with us, and is meant to leave us changed."

I almost giggle at that. Almost.

While I hate being branded, for however noble a reason, my anger dwindles as I soak in the air of the occasion. The cavern is warm and filled with the smells of meat, wine and ale, bread baking in crocks over the fires, sweat, smoke, dry skin, and long-unwashed hair. Sounds of gentle conversation and forgotten hardships. Flirting, joking, deep sighs. It's good. Even Duman is laughing and throws me a quick smile, a first for him.

Taran crawls up to us, settling on his haunches. He cracks a nutshell between his molars, then spits it out onto his palm, fishing the meat out from between the cracked shell pieces.

"The dunes are secure, *sam*," he says, smacking his lips.

Tonight, he's on alert. His tone is clear as cold water.

Nif nods, placing his hand on Taran's shoulder.

"Is there something wrong?" I ask.

Taran turns to me, expressionless, and Nif shakes his head. "Nothing that we don't contend with every night."

Nif's manner is light, but Taran looks in no mood for a good time. His eyes tell me everything Nif's will not. That, wedding or no wedding, every dusk brings with it a potential danger.

I excuse myself and saunter around the party, studying Nif's people—our people. They're all songs and stories tonight. People telling tales of eternal love between men and animals and gods. Legends of heroes and sagas of suffering and romance. The kind of lore that fortifies a culture, breeding resilience, courage and hope. This is Nif's doing. I know it. Nif, a natural storyteller from a tribe of bards and warriors. A mighty fusion that's drawn these people to him, made them embrace the leadership of someone who has only just become a man.

"*Sahjaloh*, Sah-Mala."

An impish fellow with big round eyes, much too far apart, addresses me by the title given a new bride—a Rah'a bride—on her wedding day. He brings me two roasted legs to gnaw on, probably belonging to the mole-rats whose hides were gifted to us. I bite into them and hum with pleasure. They're tender and sweet, with a glaze that tastes of honey and olives.

"I am Rin," he tells me.

Rin, the masculine form of my name. I smile and give a short bow.

"Of the Rah'a?"

"My mother," he says, nodding excitedly. "But she married into the desert, where I was born."

I know what that means. His mother was either deformed, orphaned into extreme poverty, or shamed by rape or promiscuity, which are viewed in much the same vein. Whatever the case, it doesn't seem to bother Rin.

"We're all born of the desert now," I say.

Rin stands on his tiptoes, coming nose-to-nose with me in a most intrusive way.

"Your eyes," he says. "They're very . . ."

"Green."

"Yes, yes, green. I can see that even in this light." Rin, still on his toes, grips my shoulders lightly and tips his head, getting a better look. "They are like nothing in the desert."

I can't help but laugh.

"I wouldn't think so," I say. "There's little green in the sand is there?"

Rin opens his mouth wide in what should be a guffaw worthy of a donkey. His laugh, however, is purely silent. Lips parted, teeth bared, shoulders quaking, belly in spasms. It's a most unusual laugh and suits him to perfection.

I go to lift a cup of wine from the grasp of a passing helper, but Rin beats me to it, presenting the drink to me.

"Did you get them from your parents?"

"My eyes?"

Rin nods.

"No. Not even my grandparents." I've never thought about it, but it's true. "I don't know where I got them from."

"I should say there's nothing like them in the world." He's quite serious, his head cocked and his hands folded, thumbs twiddling. "Though the desert is my only world and there isn't much here."

I shrug and offer him a sip of my wine, which he declines.

"Your husband. He has peculiar eyes, too. Though more subtle."

"I think to most everyone here, there's little about me that's subtle."

Rin laughs again and I join in. My laugh is nothing near a quiet affair and never has been, so people notice, including Nif. Taran is gone and he's talking to an older man, middle-aged, with thick, fleshy lips and a strong, broad chest that must have been impressive before hunger and age worried away at it. Nif nods at the man, excusing himself, crossing the chamber to me and Rin.

"*Sahjaloh.*" Rin gives salutation and bows deeply.

"I've come to take my wife back," Nif says.

Rin puts his hand to his heart, as if he's in great pain at the thought. "It is your privilege."

He blows me a kiss, slobbery, leaving a string of spit hanging from his bottom lip. Plopping down next to the fire, a cryptic smile pressed onto his mouth, Rin begins to forage through a pile of pulled meat.

"Quite a comedian," I say.

Nif casts a side-glance at Rin. "He only plays the fool."

It occurs to me how well Nif must know his people. They've struggled together, gathered, worked to eat and mend and move. Children have been born along the way, each babe held at least once by every member of the tribe. I wonder how many of them there were in the beginning, and how many have died in battles, or of the diseases and afflictions that curse a troubled region during times of plague and all-out war.

"Nif."

I squeeze his arm. We stop in the middle of the cavern, surrounded by the jolly and curious, all with wet, dancing eyes.

"What is it?"

I shake my head. There will be time, later, to ask for my wedding present.

Chapter 39

The Night

A HISSING SOUND swells up from the crowded cavern. Savage and spitty, it spreads from one person to another until it reaches the outside ledge, where there's a play of crude instruments—reed flutes, sticks, scratchboards, drums. A rambling symphony of poor musicians, but joyful as anything I've ever heard. All at once, the music tapers off, replaced by more hissing.

Soon, the entire cavern is susurrating like a thousand feral cats. The ledge empties, everyone trickling inside. All of them staring at us, hisses fizzing through teeth framed by lusty smiles. Nif is the only one not making the noise. The only one besides me. And he wears an embarrassed grin that he's doing his best to conceal.

"What is this?" I whisper.

"They want us to go."

"Go where?"

Nif raises an eyebrow. "To our tent."

Our tent.

I look out onto the ledge, but it's empty. "We don't have a tent."

"We do have a tent," Nif says. "It's been moved."

This being my third time as a potential bride, I should be quite ready. But instead, it's like I've swallowed a beehive, and the little creatures are whirring in my stomach.

Nif leads me around, in a bit of a parade. He doesn't look at me, and it's all a bit awkward. As we make each pass, the hissing grows louder, and I feel sprinkles of spittle land on my cheeks. My face burns hot. So hot that even the fried flesh on my palm seems cool by comparison.

Near the ledge, a young man with a skinny, concave belly scampers up to us. He's shaking his head, saliva running down the corners of his mouth. I haven't seen him before and I step back. Nif puts his arm around me.

"Hello," I say, trying to appear sociable. Nif bites his bottom lip. Yes, very funny, I want to tell him.

"It's all right, Yaz," Nif says.

Yaz's mouth is nearly lipless, and his teeth are tiny, like freshwater pearls. His grin is almost all gum. Yaz wipes his nose on the bottom of my tunic before critter-crawling away, and I gape at the smear of sandy snot he's left on my wedding dress.

"He's simple," Nif says. "But harmless."

Nif steers me out onto the ledge, where it's cold. Typical of a desert night, and refreshing after the warm, smoke-filled cavern. The torches are burning bright, the stones glowing with the blue tones of a large moon. One that seems so close that I could hit it with a chucked stone. In the middle of the ledge is a circular tarp made of pale linen. Not a single crease in its spread. Nif guides me to it, stepping out of his sandals and urging me to do the same.

We tread lightly onto the tarp and Nif kneels, pulling me with him. The tribe is circling around us, still hissing, each face blending into the next. I start to breathe hard and heavy, gnawing on the insides of my cheeks. Nif is flushed, holding my hands, but not meeting my eyes.

"Nif," I call out, but as soon as I say it, the tribespeople stop circling. They crowd around us, no longer hissing in one note, but in staccato—their chests bouncing and heaving like wild animals.

"Nif!"

Then all at once the hisses stop. One by one, the tribe falls away, and Rin, my namesake, bows his head as he goes. Saru hums a languorous melody, overly sensual, as she returns to the cavern.

We're alone again.

I close my eyes, letting out a breath I didn't realize I'd been holding.

In the open cavern, I can see all the shadows moving to and fro as if nothing at all happened. They're swaying, lifting skin pouches to their lips, enjoying the night. Ignoring us entirely now.

"I've heard that some tribes, that they—I know in the Palace City even, there were some people who didn't mind doing this with other people around."

"Ah," Nif says, clearing his throat. He stares down at our hands. "Our tent has been made, it's . . . I'll show you where it is. This—the song, all of it—is a blessing. That's all."

I sit for a moment, my palms growing wet. "I thought . . . well. I mean." I look at the pale tarp, which looks suspiciously like bedding. "And you call that a song?"

Nif lifts a shoulder. "A love song of sorts. In hopes that you'll take with child soon."

"Ah, that kind of love song."

"I mean in light of what you said earlier. That meant a lot to everyone."

I swallow, all quiver and nervous grin. "I'm glad."

Our hands come loose from each other's. We're tentative, like strangers. The torchlight casts shadows over Nif's face, making his close-cropped beard seem to glint like pebbles of onyx.

"We can stay here as long as you like," he says. "Talking, admiring the heavens."

The moon is too bright for the full confetti of twinkling stars that usually cover the night sky. But the pale, perfect yolk of her face more than makes up for it. She looks over us, illuminating our bodies. I want to see Nif's bare skin in that light again, as I did on that night in the Palace Gardens. Only this time he'll be healed and clean, with only the faint remnants of the scars he incurred for my sake.

"We can go to our tent now, too, if you want," he whispers.

IT'S A STEEP PATH to our canvas, which has been moved to the top of the dunes—the top of the world as far as we're concerned. It's up on another ledge, much smaller, more like a balcony, and illuminated with a single torch. No stones at all. Nif helps me along, making sure I don't tear my dress.

The canvas flaps of our tent are open, facing the desert as if presenting our future. Despite the crisp air, a trickle of sweat runs from my neck to between my shoulder blades. Nif is cool and dry, just as when I first saw him standing there in his father's tunic. Looking as near a god as I've ever seen anyone look.

"Quite a view," I say.

The moon is at our right, gushing over waves of sand that look like an ocean stopped in time. Its swells and ripples as fixed as marble.

Nif has seen this view a thousand times, but he seems no less awed by it. All power and stillness; the dead silence of eternity. As if at any moment, a spark of life will begin, igniting the growth of a dense jungle.

Nif pulls me closer—my teeth begin chattering. The night air is biting through my tunic.

"I had our best linens brought up. The ones from your father's house that were so carefully wrapped."

Under our canvas, sure enough, our bed is dressed in its best. I can see it from here. Linens as light as clouds, snug as pelts. I think they're a shade of periwinkle, but it's hard to tell. Whatever the case, their tight weave will trap the heat of our bodies and keep us warm throughout the night.

I crawl inside, beckoning Nif to follow. We lay on our sides, facing one another, but not touching. Not yet. I cuddle our linens to my breast.

We have satchels of fragrant herbs and the scented oils that had been gifted to us earlier in the evening; they line the rear of our tent. I dip my finger into one of the tiny, clay jugs and rub a bit of the oil onto my hand, its musky aroma blending with the herbals meant to freshen our bed. The two scents are both at odds and in perfect harmony—blending through the thin, dry air.

"You're very beautiful," Nif says, but so softly I'm not sure if I haven't imagined it.

"Nif, I assume you've done this before?"

He shakes his head.

"Really? Why not?"

"I've been busy."

I laugh out loud and Nif lies there smiling at me. He gets a bit more earnest as he leans in.

"Wouldn't be right taking a woman in the tribe if I didn't mean to marry her," he tells me. "As for women we've come across in the desert? They have their own problems. And a child given to them by a nomad would only add to their burden."

Nif knits his brow together and looks down at his hand,

which strums at the leather strands flowing from his belt. "Have you?"

"Yes, every day and all the time."

I say it with a deadly sincerity and we both burst out laughing. It's oddly sensual to share a few moments of humor, given what we're about to do.

"I've seen animals do it, of course," he says, quite seriously now. "I especially love to watch snakes." Nif's eyes light in interest and he props himself onto his elbow. "Have you ever seen them?"

I shake my head no. At least I don't think so.

"They wrap around each other in a splice and move balanced on their tails as if in a slow dance." Nif sits up further and pushes the sleeves of his tunic to his biceps. He raises his arms to demonstrate, twisting them together and forming the two heads with his hands.

"They tangle around one another. Smooth. Skin on skin, like bodies." His arms move to his description—perfect except for a fresh scar running nearly the length of one of his forearms.

"It's quite extraordinary," he says, unwinding. "I've always hoped people do it that way."

There's an eagerness in his tone that strikes me deep in my belly.

"People kiss," I say softly, feeling shy.

"Yes," he whispers, his lips intent on mine.

"I've seen people," I say.

He stops, but stays close.

"At the palace," I whisper. "The comfort women and others. They don't make much of an attempt to hide what they're doing." I think of Toja and her soldier, who had looked nothing like snakes. More like a tiger and a housecat.

"I've seen people, too," Nif says. "Although usually under the cover of a blanket. There's not a lot of privacy in our ranks."

The thought reminds me of the tarp on the ledge and my stomach sinks. We won't always have the comfort of a secluded canvas.

"Nif," I say. "You told me your father's name meant 'he who lives in truth'."

Nif nods.

"What, then, does your name mean?"

Nif moves his leg, a bare foot covering mine. His feet are softer than his hands, sloughed smooth by daily trudges through a pumice of desert rock and sand. Sublime.

"It means, he who lives with honor." Nif scoots closer to me, resting his hand on my hip. While the stroke of his foot is suggestive, the lay of his hand feels solid and protective on my body. As if I'm something precious to hold.

"You see, all of our names—the men of the Beih—signify how we are to live," he continues. "With truth or honor or dignity or courage. Our names are a key to our legacy, of how we're to distinguish ourselves."

The feel of Nif's hand is so warm, passing easily through the fabric of my wedding tunic. His toes play up the arch of my foot.

"What about the women of your tribe? What are their names like?"

Nif thinks for a moment, his eyes drifting.

"Their names are florid. Like poetry."

His hand caresses the curve of my hip, settling into the valley under my ribcage. Like it's always belonged there.

"They're to signify the mystery of women. Much harder to decipher and meant to be revealed over time. Interpreted and re-interpreted."

"I like that," I say. "What was your mother's name again?"

Nif makes a sad, sweet smile.

"Piri," he tells me. "I think it meant 'the heartbeat of the storm' or something." He nuzzles his face next to mine. "I don't know. I've forgotten so much of my native language. It comes back, though, from time to time. Like tonight. I think tonight I could have said anything without having to reach for single word."

I lift my fingers to his mouth, resting a digit on his bottom lip. I do love his lips—the most feminine of his features. Soft and full. Always wanting something—a word, a taste, a kiss.

"If you were to name me, then, as a woman of your tribe—what name would you give me?" I ask him.

Nif contemplates me for a few moments. Cradling my head, he lifts me up close to his face.

"I would call you Sherin."

"Sherin? You wouldn't give me another name? A more poetic one?"

He shakes his head. "Did you know that in Beih your name means breath?"

Unconsciously, I take a very deep breath at his words. Nif closes his eyes, inhaling.

"Its sweet scent, its warmth, the way it nourishes your body. How it feels on mine. What could have more poetry than your breath?"

He kisses me softly, then starts to trace the lines of my face with his hands. This time, his fingers work down my neck and over my collarbone—then lower, all the way to the tie that binds my tunic around me. Pushing onto my elbows, I watch him labor over the tight knot I made.

"Wait," I whisper.

I peel his fingers one by one from the slackened bulb at my middle and put his hand to my lips, kissing his palm before setting it between us.

My eyes meet his as I sit all the way up, appraising the construct of his garment. It's a neat and clever ensemble that's tied and woven at the waist, like an elaborate hair-style. It's designed never to come undone—not in dance or battle—only at the hands of someone who knows its secrets. Someone with knowledge of dress—like me.

"I want to go first," I say.

Nif smiles. "You're supposed to show me your story. Take me through every part of it."

I'd forgotten about Saru and her paints. That my whole body is a mural. All of a sudden, I feel like a secret garden.

"It's our custom," he says.

"I'd like to change custom and see your story first."

Nif shakes his head. "I have no story painted on me. My story, a husband's story, is told. A wife's story is to be seen and discovered. Like her name."

I take his hand, kissing his fingers. "Perhaps yours is a story only I can see?"

His lips part, his eyes appraising me. Nif stretches across the linens, putting one hand behind his head. The other remains free—maybe to help me if I need it. But I won't.

I unravel his belt strings and pull the leather fringe through a series of embroidered slits until his tunic begins to loosen. Nif's eyes never leave me. I can feel him watching my every move with interest. As the last belt string comes undone, I hold it closed, counting silently to three. Then, inhaling deeply, I meet Nif's eyes again and let it fall away from my hands. I hear the linen of his tunic brush his skin, relaxing at his sides. Swallowing, I make my eyes leave his and travel slowly over the length of his body, never stopping, nor averting my gaze from his most intimate features.

At his feet, my fingers ride the curves of his toes and the divots between them, the elegant arch of his foot, the solid, and determined bow of his heel. My mouth follows in their wake, and I hear Nif gasp. It's a sound I like very much. I pet the veins of his feet, charting the strong bones of his ankles.

"I think right here, I see the dunes where you used to play as a child," I tell him.

His shins are firm and graceful and my lips tickle as I brush the fine, curly hairs that grow over his muscles. Strong, straight knees and the thighs of a wild horse.

"This is the path you traveled to find me," I say, kissing just under the bone of his hip.

At his stomach, I kiss into the hollow of his bellybutton. "I should think this is the Palace Garden where you first kissed me. And here," I say, biting at the skin that covers his heart. "Under here is the cave you carried me to. Where we touched one another in the dark."

"Sherin," Nif rasps, scarcely more than mouthing my name. "Show me your story."

THE LIGHT IS ONLY BEGINNING TO BREAK, its blush seeping into the canvas. It's still dark and cold, with only the twitter of a warbler cutting the silence.

Far below us, a murmur of conversation begins. It has a solemn tone.

"Is it Taran?" I whisper.

Nif shakes his head. "It's nothing. Only the usual."

Our magic circle is broken.

"Stop."

"What?"

"Your head if full of thorns."

I open my mouth, but somehow find it impossible to say what's really on my mind.

"You're thinking about your brother," he says.

From the day we met in my father's house, Nif has displayed an uncanny ability to know my heart. And in the span of a few minutes, I've gone from feeling drenched by love to shriveled up like a worm in the high heat of the sun. Salan's absence burns. Even more than the weeping blisters on my palm.

"Could Taran sneak in to get him?"

Nif swallows.

"No. Not anymore."

The Palace City, Nif explains, has been closed to outsiders since a few days ago. They're living on stores and plunder, not even the merchants are allowed in anymore—a significant hardship for the remaining pockets of tribespeople in the desert. Ones who are still trying to forge a living, not resorting to thievery and aimlessness.

"You did right in leaving him there, Sherin," he whispers. "He wouldn't have survived your trek into the desert, and the sultan and his circle will be the last to fall." Nif's features harden and he grips my shoulders as if I might fall away. "When the time is right, I'll get him for you. I swear it."

Maybe it's the influence of a pleasure-rich body, or my full heart. Maybe the break of another day. But I can see Nif's thoughts as clearly as my own. And they're not just on the Palace City's problems and Salan. He's reached far back into his life. The one he told me he rarely visits, but came into relief with the Beih wedding ceremony we performed together. The burning reminder of which is branded onto his palm. And mine.

I know little about his people—just the bits and pieces I tried to recall as he made his vows to me. More are coming to mind. Memories, facts that seemed unimportant at the time, but I'd stored away regardless. As if part of me knew a Beih would one day come to hold me.

There had been a falling out with our monarch—of that much I'm sure. The Beih were all at once no longer a source for the most privileged roles in the military. Odd. The Beih built the Rah'a with previous sultans. Their loss would have been a blow, one of many that would make the more recent events seem inevitable.

I have a sudden and horrific vision. One made up of my recent experience, a more cynical view of power and human nature, and the distressed look on Nif's face. I see our sultan sending the Vara to wipe out the Beih when Nif was a boy. They were thriving without the Rah'a's protection and that can't have suited him. Rule by genocide, a first attempt, and it seemed to work. The Beih were gone, the Rah'a retained its power, and the sultan was emboldened to try this plan again . . . the next time to rob its most prosperous citizens.

I hear myself gasp.

"Nif, will you . . . ?"

"Yes," he says.

Nif doesn't try to hide his purposes from me. He leaves his face plain, as honest as his smile, but touched with a ruthless intensity. He isn't just trying to survive, stealing into the Palace City for trade, for information. His attempts to get me out of the city confines, to keep me close to him, make all the more sense now.

Once again, Adamen, in his twisted way was right. Nif is every bit the insurgent he was accused of being. A provoked one, certainly. One whose world was decimated not once, but twice by a vain and incompetent ruler. Nif is at war and has been from the day he watched the Beih die by Vara. He's been waiting, biding his time.

And Nif means to take the Palace City down.

"THE DESERT WIND," Calliope Neville whispers. "It's so hollow tonight."

Neville peels off his pants and undergarments. Naked, he shakes out his clothes, grains of sand hopping from them like fleas.

"The wind is hollow every night," he says.

After separating his laundry, distinguishing filthy from merely dirty, he lies down next to his wife on their cot, digging under the covers and wrapping himself around her small, thin frame.

The canvas roof of their tent ripples like water, causing their lantern to sway. That wind, hooting with an owl's shrewd intonation, sounds as if it's passing judgement. Nif always believed it was a vessel for communicating with the spirit world, the dead's only way of giving tidings to the living.

But to me, the wind was only ever music.

"Sounds like she's asking us to stay," Calliope says.

"She?"

"Of course the wind is a she. Show me a he who could make a tornado."

Neville chuckles low and deep into her hair.

"I'm glad she's welcomed us," she says in all seriousness. "Seems a good omen."

Calliope may not be fluent in the languages of Mother Nature—the chatter of water and bellows of thunder, the laments of the wind—but she can pick up a word or two, recognize intent. She's always been that way.

"What is it?"

Neville tips his head, studying her eyes. "There's just the

prettiest violet undertone to those charcoal eyes of yours. I've never noticed it until now."

Neville shrugs.

"I can see it even in this light."

Calliope reaches up and tweaks his nose. "Maybe you just want to see it."

The outer flaps of the tent seem to clap like hands and the wind turns from hoot to whistle.

"What's she saying now, your friend the wind?"

Calliope breathes deeply and nuzzles into her husband's chest.

"We're not alone."

"We're most certainly not alone. There are a dozen archaeology students out there, not to mention Jordie and all the kids he brought from Cairo to work."

They lie quietly together until Neville begins a light snore.

"I meant we're not alone in this tent."

Calliope looks all around her; the light of the dim lantern above them casting inky blots of shadow all around. Her eyes of charcoal and violet flitter about until they land upon a lambent twinkle spread across the ceiling of their canvas. She stares at it for a long time, wondering if what she's seeing is a prism of moonlight.

I want to reach out to her, but I don't know how. I can only ever talk to her when she's dreaming, but I haven't got up the nerve to do that. Not in all these years. I've showed her things, yes, of course. But I've never properly introduced myself.

Chapter 40

New Bride

HER NAME IS AYLA, the young mother in the tribe. She's got these ferrety eyes squinted practically into nonexistence, and drags an enormous pile of sun-beaten linens to the cavern entry, where I sit. She collapses into the mound, huffing and puffing. Ayla's lips are plump as a succulent and spread across her face like a slice of muskmelon. In the tuft of linens lies her infant son, and she coos at him. He's sprawled on top of the crumpled fabrics and his tiny penis bobs and wiggles as he kicks his spindly legs.

She hasn't named him yet, but she calls her son *Bibi,* which means raisin, and he does rather look like one. Skinny, wrinkled, with eyes as tiny as his mother's. Unlike hers, his mouth is a mere slit.

"Good morning," I say, tickling his toes. And it is a good morning. My first full day as Nif's wife.

Ayla lifts him to her breast, easing down cross-legged on the opposite side of the heap of linens. She "aahs." Nif, watching the spectacle from the main hearth fire, catches my glance, and we share a brief flicker of a personal moment.

Newly wed or not, there's water to be gathered, food to be caught and prepared, fires to be built and nurtured, canvases beaten, linens made wearable again. The stuff of living, I hope, not merely staying alive.

My role is decided, falling into place for no other reason

than my skills. I am, quite simply, the woman of all things linen now. Clothing is as vital as water in the desert. Without proper dress, death can come within a matter of hours—whether in day or night. I know how to make linen, protect it and repair it—a skill as elite as literacy, but much more critical in the efforts of day to day survival.

I'm happy I have something of real value to offer, other than being Nif's wife and a hoped-for vessel of childbearing—not that either of those are small things. So, in my first official day as first wife of our tribe, I sit to a long day of careful mending. Yaz the simpleton is at my side, staring at me in wonder as I pull tiny threads from a large, fringed hole in a tunic. I knot them delicately using a crude weaving needle, looped at the end at least, but having seen better days. It's an arduous process Yaz finds fascinating.

"We can fashion new ones if we find some nice, long bones," I say, handing Yaz a second needle.

Yaz, his fingers slim and nimble, goes to work on a small hole in the tunic I'm wearing. An indigo—not one of my mother's—that's rough in places, but good for wear during tedious work. It gives plenty of protection from the sun and soaks up a good deal of sweat. Yaz gives a rousing *"Hopah!"* each time he manages to merge one thread with the other. I follow suit, and within a scant hour, everyone around us is giving a proud *hopah* for their every meager accomplishment. It passes the time.

At mid-morning, when a particularly ear-piercing *hopah* bursts my concentration, I glance up, annoyed. It's Ayla, who now has her little *Bibi* secured to her breast in a clumsy tangle of rags. I smile and make a mental note to myself to show her how to bind a child properly. Ayla turns and whispers something to a leggy, hawk-faced man, whose name I can't remember. I know he raised work horses before the Vara came this time around. The horseman snickers at whatever

Ayla has told him, averting his eyes from me, as if he's seen me naked.

"What?"

Ayla starts digging through the linens I took out from Nif's and my tent. I want to air them out and dry-wash some portions with white root powder and a pumice stone, once I have the time. She laughs and begins pulling one of our linen blankets from the pile.

"Stop it," I say.

She puffs the pale sheet of fabric into the air, and to my abject horror exposes an oval stain of blood. Mine, I assume. Yaz wheezes. He paws at me, thinking the blood must have come from my burned hand.

Shaking him off, I shoot up and try to snatch the linen away from Ayla, but she's quick and takes off between the rows of canvas, calling out in a shrill squeal and waving my bloodied linens like a flag.

"Get back here this instant!" I yell, but she continues her run through the camp, damned proud of herself. Cat-calls, whoops and whistles come at me from every direction. I grit my teeth together, crunching on the ever-present layer of sand and dust that collects everywhere—especially, and most unpleasantly, inside the mouth.

"Ayla!" I scream.

Not only am I ignored, but my rage becomes a source of great amusement. Insinuations about Nif's and my most private deeds—what sorts of noises I might have made and in what positions—make me the butt of a big joke.

"Well enough," I say, trying to be a good sport. "We can all return to work now."

Nobody gets back to work. I have to wonder what good it is being the wife of their so-called prince if no one feels any inclination to listen to me. In fact, Ayla's little show is taking on a life of its own, with our stained linen being passed from man to man, each one in turn touching it, kissing it, and sniffing it. Even Nif—*traitor*—stands smiling at the edge of camp with Taran who, in a rare moment of good humor, is nudging him.

Nif sees me and adjusts his expression, but it's too late. I straighten up to my full height, throw down the linens, and storm into the cavern as Yaz shouts my name in confusion, poor thing.

I stomp into the dark pathway that leads into the bowels of the dunes. Torchless and tripping my way through the passage, I reach our smaller cavern—Nif's and mine.

Feeling along, I sit on the smooth slab. Ours.

It isn't that I don't understand what Ayla's done and why. We have a similar custom in the Rah'a, although ours is far, far more discreet. If my marriage to either of my other fiancés had gone through, it would only have been a matter of quietly passing the bloodied slip to persons who needed to see it. Family, people of distinction who could vouch for my virtue and the like. If for some reason there had been no blood, which certainly happens even with a chaste bride on occasion, a woman in the household would make sure some appeared. Through the prick of a finger, let's say.

But this is a vulgar and dangerous display, in my mind. What if, for instance, I hadn't bled? Besides that, Ayla's spectacle is a gross invasion of intimacy and Nif should know that!

I breathe in, suddenly hit by the cool-air smells of the grotto. Damp sand and rodent droppings. A blend of assorted minerals. What had been perfume to me as Nif and I lay on the stone slab two days before.

The tribe can laugh and make lurid gestures at me. They don't know me. But Nif does. Or so I thought. And in one wave of a bloody sheet, I feel dragged into a life of lovelessness again.

"Sherin?"

I can smell him before I register his voice. Resin, fire, and sweat. The faint scent of me all over him.

"You're here," he says softly. He's brought a torch and tucks it into a split in the craggy rock that flowers from the cave wall.

"What of it?"

"You can't be that angry if you're willing to come to this place."

Our place, he means. Right.

"Well, you're wrong."

He doesn't ask if he can sit, but does, closely, so that our sides come together in a seam. I would scoot away if it wasn't for how his touch makes me feel. Warm, nay, more than that. It makes the burn on my palm come to life again.

"You think Ayla's display was disrespectful."

"And you don't?"

Nif expels a breath and tries to take my fingers in his, but I'll have none of it. Sitting close to him is weakening my resolve as it is, and a tender touch will put me under his control.

"You're an oddity to most of them."

"An oddity? I thought I was your wife!"

Nif's eyes steal over me as if he's searching for the right thing to say.

"You're an outsider."

That is not the right thing to say.

"We're all outsiders! Look at where we are, what we're doing, how we got to be here!"

Nif leans in to me and goes to touch my face, but then stops himself. "Some are outsiders more than others."

That is definitely not the right thing to say.

"And what is that supposed to mean?"

Nif shrugs one shoulder, then treads carefully into his next blunder.

"That under the circumstances, you've been allotted great courtesy."

I slap my hand on the stone and the "splat" sound echoes in the chamber, sounding sickly and raw. Exactly how I feel. "Courtesy? You call flaunting the loss of my virginity a courtesy?"

"We are married, Sherin. It's hardly a loss."

"That's right. We are married, and I would expect greater *courtesy* from my husband. Or was it that you felt rather pleased with yourself at my expense?"

Nif gets up. The one side of his mouth curls up and his eyes bore directly into mine.

"When I told them that I meant to take a wife from the Rah'a, one who'd lived in the Palace City, no one challenged me," he began. "But it could have been a source of uproar. Don't you see? They trusted me and accepted a good deal of risk in my quest to bring you here."

His words stop any inclination I have to breathe. It takes a hard swallow for me to regain my composure.

"Because I was brought—in the custody of an army and not by my choice—to the Palace City? This is a source of controversy?"

Nif crouches to the ground, looking up at me, his face illuminated in the torchlight. He puts his hands on my knees and parts them slightly, bringing himself closer, resting his chin on my thigh.

"Do you think anyone else here would have been found after a battle and brought to live in the Palace City? These people know that they would have been left in the desert to die or been killed. Certainly not fed and clothed and given a prestigious role. Under the protection of the man who murdered their families."

I feel a huge injury at his words. It's never occurred to me that Nif could see me as someone who comes from the people who have brought so much misery upon all of us. I feel a part of that misery. A victim of it. Just like them.

"Who murdered my family, too." My voice is as weak as a feather. "And you knew that when you first came to me at my father's house. Didn't they know?"

"They did," Nif says. "But you're rich and they see you differently because of it. They're at once proud to have you among us and . . . resentful. And this was all further complicated by your time in the Palace City." He reaches up and holds my cheek in his palm. The burned palm, which he unwrapped early in the morning. I can feel its pulpy, enflamed center.

"Sherin, as embarrassing as it was, Ayla did you a kindness. She must like you. And I suspect if she had found no stains on our linens, she would have bled for you herself. I don't remember seeing any, but then I wasn't looking for them."

I snort at that, and Nif allows himself a smile, hopeful that I'm no longer on the verge of striking him.

"It's no small vindication for you—and for their sacrifices—to have them know that you aren't what they think the other palace women to be."

"And what do they know of other palace women?" I ask. "Who, besides Taran, has ever been to the Palace City?"

Nif raises his eyebrows and his smile leaves him. "They do know that the wife you served was a known adulteress."

This is a barely healing wound, and he's ripped it wide open. It's true that in the Palace City I would have died along with Toja. Legally, I'm tainted with her behavior. But it's a sophisticated place, and there's an understanding that her moral character doesn't automatically reflect mine. Her morals were my responsibility, and that's why I would have paid for them with my life, but my own morals were never under suspicion. Only my competence as her assistant.

332 VICTORIA DOUGHERTY

"When I explained that a woman of your particular breeding needed an official ceremony before the consummation of a marriage, some in the tribe expressed a bit of skepticism."

By some, I know exactly who he means. Duman and his cohorts.

"They needed proof I wasn't some jade you'd brought home."

Nif nods. "They want to see I've chosen well. Someone who'll honor me. Honor them."

I sit tall again, extricating my cheek from his palm. "And what about you? Did you not say our linens seemed clean to you after our first night?"

Nif slides his hand over my neck and collar, stopping between my breasts, and holding it there, over my heart. My breath hitches audibly.

"I didn't need any proof. Not from the first time I saw you."

Nif takes my burned hand. He uncurls my fingers and kisses the tender center.

"The night of our wedding, I wasn't entirely truthful with you," he says. He kisses each of my knees, pulling up my tunic and rubbing his bristly cheeks on my thighs. He kisses my shoulders next, then the hollow at my throat, and last, my lips. "When I told you why I had been chaste. It wasn't because I didn't want to give false hope to women in our tribe. It was because I was waiting for you."

Lying me down onto the stone, loving all of my body this time. Kissing every part of my fading story. My past that led me to him.

I HALF EXPECT more taunts and leering when Nif and I emerge from the dune. No, fully expect it, especially given how long we've been gone and my own guilty knowledge of what we've been doing. Surely, it shows on our faces. Smoothing my hair and tunic, I brace myself against anger and pride, which I'm rarely good at disguising. Nif puts his arm around me, holding me tight, and we walk onto the ledge with a fake casual air.

The ledge has the quiet drone of a hive about it, a graceful current of industry. Karat, who employed his full hyena laugh during the flaunting of our bed linens, is sober-minded now, and whispering something to Saru. Her eyes meet mine, as gentle as my mother's, and I want to run to her.

A few people do look up at us, and there are some knowing smiles cast in our direction—from Duman, for instance—but otherwise a peace has settled upon the tribe. Part of me still hates to concede that Nif is right. Our bloodied sheets are at least some bit of reassurance that their leader hasn't been misled by infatuation. Virginity, precisely because it is so easy to lose to rape or need, has a price above water. It represents the hope of a return to civilization, of family, and I can hardly deny them that.

I brush Nif's thigh and he bends to kiss my cheek. Taran is waiting and they need to prepare for the next day's hunt. The tribe is low on meat after the extravagance of our wedding feast, and our water supply is so low as to be almost nonexistent. It's a good thing we have plenty of ale. Nif has told me of his plans to gather several of the men for an expedition to the river beds. I feel guilty about it, since I'm the one who insisted on some kind of formal observance of our vows, but Nif told me not to trouble myself. The feast had been his idea and an event long overdue. My husband, more than anyone, understands the value of breaking tensions, and a few extra days at a hunt is worth morale.

"Sherin!" Yaz calls. He's happy at my return, eager to show me his progress, which is considerable, if clumsy. I smile and compliment his efforts and Yaz nuzzles his face to my sleeve in appreciation. Sweet, like a puppy. Guileless. I lay my hand on his matted hair.

Ayla is at the linens, too, having hung several of them for airing. I notice our linens are among them, and that the oval stain, shaped and hued like a piece of calf's liver, is hardly visible at all anymore. She's taken to it with salt and a rolling pin. I sit next to her, making sweet faces at her baby, and don't have the heart to tell her that salt isn't the best choice for a fine cloth. That teaching moment will be saved for another time, though. As it is, I'm glad simply for things to seem normal.

"*Sahjaloh*, Sah-Mala." Rin, my namesake, squats next to me, balancing on his haunches. "Can I borrow your attentions for a moment?"

There's a brightness to Rin. He scuttles closer, his breath scented of anise seed and vinegar, then digs under his tunic.

"Do you want to see?"

I tilt my head in question.

"It was painted once. Beautifully, my mother told me. And her mother told her."

Slowly, he raises his hands up, cupping one over the other like a clam shell. He opens them up revealing a statue lying flat on the length of his palm.

A bird's head.

A lion's mouth.

Once-red wings, still flecked with paint in some areas, but mostly worn to clay.

A strong, thin body.

Clawed feet.

"My only toy," he says. "Besides a jumping rope."

"This was yours?"

Rin nods.

"Passed down. My only heirloom."

I pick it up delicately, turning it about. The little sculpture is baked of mud clay, but seems smoother, sturdier than the mud bricks that had made up my father's house. Those had something of a porous quality, while this toy is silky and level, almost like copper.

"Well made, don't you think?"

"I would say so if it's lasted as long as it has, and traveled with you throughout a war in the desert."

Rin laughs, staring proudly at his possession.

"What is it supposed to be?"

"Ah," he says. "A Lady."

I examine the sculpture's anatomy and shake my head. "Hardly looks like a Lady."

"What it looks like and what it is are not the same." Scratching his nose, Rin appraises me. I feel strangely like a piece of candy he'd pop right into his mouth if he could.

"She's for you," he crows.

I look at the bird-like face, pointed, intense. The face of an intelligent predator.

"I can't." I try to give the statue back to him, but he shoos her away.

"You must."

"Why?"

"Because I wish to give her to you."

Rin's toy is buoyant in my hand. I think it should feel much heavier. "But this is an heirloom. A part of your family. Don't you want to give it to someone who belongs to you?"

It occurs to me right then how few in the tribe have someone who belongs to them. I don't know if that makes an heirloom more precious or utterly insignificant.

"Doubtless I will have no children," Rin says, rather off-handedly. The way we have all come to accept what is lost to us. "As poor and ugly a man as I had few prospects before, let alone now. But a Lady could be of use to you. She can bring many children to your union."

"Is that what she does? She's a token of fertility?"

Rin shrugs. "I have no notion of what she does. Only what I told you. Couldn't hurt, though. And she does look awfully serious about her business, doesn't she?"

I can't deny him that.

"Thank you," I say, rolling the figurine into the sash at my waist. "I'll treasure her."

Rin has concluded his business with me, but sticks around nonetheless. Too close as always, giving me little elbow room to do my mending. He looks from my hands to my face as I try to concentrate on my work, which he himself feels no need to participate in. Rin, come to think of it, is the only tribesman I've never seen engage in labor of any sort.

A MOTHER'S PURPOSE is to give to the world a being. One she loves with a rare passion, but can't keep for herself. As a mother, I've raised none of my babies. But their existence is, at least, a legacy.

Together, Nif and I have brought hundreds of children into the world. Kings, farmers, scientists, presidents, slaves, poets, gladiators, peasants, philosophers, and priests. We've also spawned one prolific murderer, an art thief, a dictator, three vindictive wives, a handful of utter fools, a drug dealer or two, a pimp, a prig, and a sanctimonious rock star. No legacy is perfect.

But if I could, I would take at least one of these babes by the hand, even if just the one. I would teach her to walk, to write, to play music, how to love. And I would give her to the world with my imprint. As my parents did for me. My child would remember the sound of my voice, the shelter of my breast, my assurances. My reproach, my advice.

If only there was ever time.

Calliope Neville, I hope, will have what has not been my destiny. I felt the spark of life in her womb the moment it flared. Something between a lightning bolt and an atomic bomb, her child's creation burst through me, creating a ripple in the universe. I'd felt Calliope's presence once, too, in my own womb, but it was nothing like that. A limitation of being human, maybe, not being quite so sensitive to the cosmic forces around us. But being human has its own bene-dictions. I could feel the way she tumbled and kicked inside me. The way my belly shook when she had the hiccups. I could love her, even if I never got to hold her when she was born. Bleeding and feverish, all I could do was die to the lullaby of her birth cries.

But when I see her now, she is as close to me as my own heartbeat—if I were in a body, of course. I felt her child coming from the moment she and Neville made love at the bathing pool in the sultan's apartments, to the millisecond of a millisecond of a millisecond before conception occurred. Such a rush I almost thought it was time for my own conception. Close, but not yet. I still have a little time to spend with my daughter.

"Six points. Like a star. With the palace exactly in its center." Jordie runs his finger over the map he's drawn of the Palace City. One made mostly by radar, but also by the Nevilles' careful explorations of the palace over the past eight weeks.

"Extraordinary," Calliope Neville says.

Unconsciously, my daughter puts her hand on her belly. They haven't told anyone yet. The wind picks up outside and the canvas above them heaves eerily. Like the ghost of the storm that buried the Rah'a has come to pay a visit all these years later.

"As the sand storm took hold, they might have endeavored to erect some sort of shelter for the city—maybe that's it," Calliope says, her voice nearly drowned out by a wailing gust that makes the whole tent shudder. When it finishes, a dead stillness takes its place. "Perhaps the six-pointed star was a religious symbol for them, and they hoped employing it would help protect them somehow."

Neville leans back and crosses his arms.

"If that's the case, you think we would have seen this symbol somewhere in the palace structure. Plenty of religious symbols there, but nothing resembling the Star of David."

Calliope tips her head, taking a deep breath. The three of them stand like an inquisition around the poor map.

"Celestial bodies have been subjects of worship since the Stone and Bronze ages," Calliope says. "That's going back maybe forty thousand years. The Star of David came to use somewhere around the eleventh century. By then any trace of this culture, even in oral traditions, was long gone. I'll bet you any last references to the Rah'a were destroyed when the Library of Alexandria burned down."

Jordie nods, but Neville narrows his eyes at the map, concentrating—almost meditating.

"It's awfully precise, this star shape that appears to surround the palace itself," Neville finally tells them. "Like it was built of something a helluva lot sturdier than canvas and animal pelts—which would have never withstood a sandstorm that lasted at least a couple of years. And if it was built of, say, wood or stone, how could they have possibly erected something like that during the storm? And why would they even try when they could just hole up in the palace? The interior was completely untouched by the storm."

Jordie rises up onto his toes, bouncing like an excited kid.

"What?" Neville asks him.

Jordie smirks a bit, crinkling his eyes. They've started calling him the Sultan of Superstition and Crazy Ideas, but more often than not, even his most far-out assertions have merit.

"Well, maybe they had some sort of warning—like from one of their gods or an oracle—and built this protective structure pre-emptively?"

"Kind of like an ancient Noah's Ark?" Neville shakes his head. "Well, uh, that doesn't explain the fact that the inhabitants of the city were either shot by arrow—the men, at least—or simply vanished. You'd think one of their oracles might've predicted that."

Neville opens a folding chair for his wife and urges her to sit. He doesn't need to ask twice.

"In any case," Calliope says, stretching her legs. "Given

that we don't know what it is, we're going to have one helluva time excavating it."

Neville kisses the top of her head. "Assuming we can secure enough funding and keep competing governments from kicking us out of here."

"And the extremists from trying to blow us up again." Jordie sits on the floor in a huff.

"Well, look at it this way," Calliope says. "As far as we know, there hasn't been a curse placed on us. The Egyptians are still convinced Carter's team got hexed by King Tut's priests. Here we are, healthier than ever." She pats her belly and winks at Neville. Jordie perks up, his eyes darting between them.

"Hungry," Calliope says, all innocence.

Jordie lifts an eyebrow. "Again? How on earth do you stay so thin?"

Calliope shrugs. "Super human genes I guess."

Neville puts his fingers to his temples. "My wife has a way of willing things to be so. As if by magic, they--"

"Magic," Calliope says. "And don't look at me that way."

The one and only point of contention in the Neville's marriage centers around her ardent belief in God and the mysteries of the universe and Neville's ardent belief in the facts in front of him, which inevitably lead to reasonable explanations.

"You're not about to say that the star structure could have been made by magic are you?"

She smirks.

"That's exactly what I was going to say."

Chapter 41

Rin of the Rah'a

EVEN WITH so much to do every day, and our plight growing more precarious by the week, Nif and I often steal away to the darkness of our cave. There, we can love without the tribe hearing our every rustle and whisper, the shuffling rhythm of our bodies.

"I hate to be away from you," Nif whispers as we lie in the dark, after.

I squeeze him tighter, kissing the scratch that rakes across his chest at the tip of his sternum. The result of an encounter with an ill-tempered lizard who ended up as our dinner.

His arms coil around me and Nif nuzzles his face into my hair. I lick the briny dampness of his neck, pinching his taut skin between my teeth.

"I wish I could be like the wind and follow you." I say.

Nif is taking a group with him to the foot of the mountains for a few days on a raid for sheep. He hates leaving me without his protection, and is troubled by the clouds of change that loom over our future. In the near-on year I've been with the tribe, we've seen the dunes become even more violent as loose bands of thieves have become tightknit gangs. Nif is sure that any time now we'll be faced with the choice of having to fight for dominion over all the caves or move on for good. He dribbles his fingertips along my spine, and I close my eyes, absorbing the shiver that runs through me. This, at least, won't change.

"It'll be nice to have wool," I say. "I can weave some fine cloaks and blankets."

Nif hums absently. He doesn't seem much interested in talking about the sheep. He starts to glide his fingers through my hair, untangling the tiny knots that form at its ends. He likes to do that.

I slip my hand across Nif's chest. He no longer feels different to me in the dark, and I could draw him with only the sight of my fingertips. As I've become familiar with the curve of his every limb and muscle, where each hair grows, and with each bouquet that comes from his mouth, his hair, his belly and groin, his palms, he's become even more vivid to me than Salan.

"And you'll be home in a few days," I say more to comfort myself than him.

While Nif often has pleasant dreams of me when he's away, I have nothing but nightmares. Ones that depict any number of terrible fates for him. An attack by cheetahs, venomous snake bites, and of course, the roaming troops of the sultan's forsaken army.

The stories about them support every single wicked tale Adamen told me at the Palace City. The vicious rapes of girls—even infants—are being used as a method of warfare, the defiled corpses left to rot where they lie. Arranged for spearing practice. Half-eaten sometimes. Boys, prepubescent, are also fair game, abused until they bleed to death from the inside. It's an effective means of warning. The very sight of a single soldier—one with a body plucked free of hair and a Rah'a breastplate—is enough. Often, no swords are even drawn. People flee, leaving behind their few possessions. Plunder for the warriors, if there's anything good. The useless bits—single shoes, broken pottery, even a dying child—are left to litter the desert floor. Evidence of a people no more, these traces of despair always make me shudder.

But so far, the soldiers haven't dared to invade the dunes. Too many hidden passages, unknown to the sultan's men. Too many opportunities for surprise attack. Too many of the worst sorts of undesirables who dare to camp for the night. Men every bit as broken as the army and even less disciplined.

While the dunes can be empty for days, they can also fill up in the span of a few hours, forcing even our tribe to flee. The crowding gives rise to ferocious brawls that leave a sprawl of human debris for us to clean up when we return. Severed fingers, chunks of flesh, a head now and then.

"Has he spoken to you today?" Nif breaks my train of thought. He rolls me onto my back and looms over my torso, placing his hands on my swollen belly.

"Not yet," I whisper.

Our baby doesn't actually speak to me, not when I'm awake. I've heard his voice in my dreams. Not a child's voice, but a man's, and most definitely our son. He tells me I must give him a name of his own and not my father's, and that he'll be born on the night of a crescent moon. But they are only dreams. Nif, however, takes them more seriously than I. The Beih put great stock in dreams. They consider the night a prophet who never lies.

"He's awake."

When thrashing around, our baby feels like a drum roll beneath Nif's palms. He thumps right back at him, bringing his lips to my belly button and kissing all the way around the bump, as if he doesn't want to miss a single part of his body.

"Use care when I'm gone," he says. "The dunes have been crowding more often."

Every sojourn into the desert comes with its own set of dangers. In the dunes, we can become trapped and overcome if there are too many thieves who band together against us. Hoping to take our stores and divide them up among themselves. Steal our women.

But out on the open sand and especially on a coveted and lush island of savanna, we're easy prey. The only advantage of decamping in the desert for a time is its vastness, and that we can see—at least during the daylight hours—if anyone approaches.

"Stay close to Buri," he tells me.

I open my hand and touch the numb scar in its center. Buri's work. Unnaturally smooth, it feels at once a part of me and a separate entity, like a cloud in the sky.

"It's a large party you're taking to the base of those mountains," I say.

Nif lays his head onto my full breasts and strokes the arc of my middle.

"I'll need a decent number of men to take as many sheep as we need." Nif lifts his head up and kisses me. "But I'll leave some of the strongest and most able with you."

"I'm strong and able, you know."

"But you carry someone else with you, too."

I place his hand firmly on my belly, where a hard kick thrums his palm. "How do you know he's not stronger than the both of us put together?"

———◈◈———

"Uuuh," Rin moans, curled up like a scorpion's tail. A loud and wet sound trumpets from his backside and he winces. "Gravest apologies," he rasps, before passing out.

"Might he have eaten something?"

Ayla's mashing together some asafetida root and dill, her elixir for stomach and bowel ailments. Precious, given our dwindling medical supplies. She sits outside of Rin's canvas, mortar and pestle in hand, grinding them down with hard, angry movements.

"No one else seems to have taken ill," she says. "At least not yet."

A potentially poisoned food supply is no laughing matter. A contagious stomach sickness is even worse given the general state of dehydration that plagues any desert people. Vomiting and diarrhea can be as dangerous as Vara when there isn't enough water, and whatever little there is can't be kept down.

Ayla sniffs. The sister of our one remaining medicine woman, she's in poor humor about having to take care of a man who's lost control of his bowels. And she hates medicine. Hates it. She'd rather work the hearths or the linens with me.

I turn to face Nif, who's standing behind us, his eyes intent on Rin. I know what he's thinking.

"You can't cancel the raid," I tell him. "We need the animals desperately."

Nif inhales through his nose and grunts.

"I'll be fine," I assure him.

It's true. In the year I've lived with the tribe, we've come and gone from the dunes more than a dozen times when trouble has brewed. And this is certainly not our first experience of illness.

"If you become sick . . ."

"If I become sick, Ayla will take care of me and your presence will do little to change the outcome."

Another long-winded, pungent fart rips from the tent, but Rin, a slight grin on his face, sleeps through it this time. I poke Nif, hoping he'll laugh at least a little, but he'll have none of it.

"I want you kept away from him. In case he's contagious."

To this, I reluctantly agree. At least until he's on the mend.

"You know," I say. "When you leave here, you're in far more danger than I am."

"But you're the one with child, which is a danger in and of itself."

Nif gives me one of his looks and pulls me close, nestling my head beneath the frame of his jaw.

"Taran could go in my place."

I lean away and give him a look. One of my best. Taran is a fine man, but a loner. Awkward and unhappy as a leader. Prickly at his best. None of the men like him, and fights always seem to break out when Nif's presence isn't there to settle things. Besides that, Nif knows the outskirts of those mountains, while the other men are afraid of them. Actively volcanic, they give rise to a number of stories and superstitions, not to mention very real dangers.

"It's only a few days. And you might find fruit, too."

I hate that I'm essentially talking him out of staying, but there's no choice in the matter. We all know life in the desert is only getting harder, and it's clear I'm having a difficult time putting on weight. My arms and legs are thin as worms, and my facial bones jut out in relief.

"In the past months, there has been a foul humor to the desert air," Nif says. I don't think he meant to say it out loud and catches himself.

I finish the rest for him. "One as old as time, isn't it? Reeks like the breath of a dying man."

┝━━━━━━ ┥◈》◈◈》┝━━━━┥

RIN, IT APPEARS, is in no threat of dying. He's still sick, even days after Nif and his party have gone to claim the sheep, but his coloring is better and he's able to hold down water. No food yet. His bowels continue to be loose, but he's regained some control over them, putting Ayla in a better mood. No one else has fallen ill, so I've decided Rin is safe enough for company.

I have to say, I've missed him terribly. He's the only one besides Nif I can really talk to. We reminisce about the grasses that grow where I grew up, and how we both loved the taste of them when we were young—sucking on their white, milky roots, chewing their young, emerald stalks. Plant matter, which is always scarce in the desert environment, has become a true rarity. Only now and then do we come across some form of edible vegetation that hasn't already been plucked away. Our older tribesmen are losing teeth at an alarming rate, and scurvy is becoming more common.

We also speak of philosophy. Rin has serious doubts about the Rah'a's understanding of gods, and loves to speculate as to the origins of the world. Once he even told me that he believes it's possible that all of life has come from some grand explosion. A divine burst that breathed life into the natural world that we see around us.

It's so good to have him back.

I help him into the cavern, making sure we stay near the door lest he should have to run out and empty his bowels all of a sudden. Evenings are the highlight of most everyone's day, and Rin doesn't want to miss a single one of Saru's songs—even in his delicate condition.

"You must be sorry not to have gone with Nif and the others. Getting away, spending time in the mountains. I know *you're* not afraid of them. Didn't you say you lived at an oasis there for a time when you were a boy?"

Rin makes a grunt, shifting his weight. "They left me with a lifelong revulsion to the smell of sulfur, I'm afraid. So, no. I'm quite happy here despite my overall misery."

"Really?" I inquire. "You haven't one fond memory?"

Rin scratches behind his ear like a hound. "Perhaps one."

He sits up a bit taller and scratches at the uneven stubble on his chin. Rin's a great storyteller and I feel one of his yarns coming on.

"My mother had found herself a new husband, you see," He folds his hands in front of him, as he tends to do, and leans in. "A decent provider, but heartless. I kept out of his way. But my aunt had found a stray kitten—black-furred and green-eyed—and gave her to me as a gift. I was auntie's favorite since, like me, she was homely. Terrible warts all over her face, large buck teeth. Even uglier than I am."

I have to look away not to laugh. Rin has neither warts nor buck teeth, but is wall-eyed and cursed with an enormous, sharply hooked nose and a grossly protruding upper lip. I've grown used to his face, liking it from the beginning, but I have to admit, the first time I saw him in daylight it was difficult not to stare.

"But so, this kitten—much prettier than either of us— grew to love me better than any puppy ever could. Quite unusual. Cats are godly creatures. Solitary. But she followed me everywhere—nibbling at my ankles, clawing up my tunic to nestle in my arms. She was the first and only woman to ever pay me any attention."

"I'm sure that's not true," I say, although I suspect it is. Rin had been married briefly, but his wife up and died only days after their nuptials. Karat likes to say it was from having to lie with him.

"On one very pleasant afternoon, I was sitting by the hearth with my kitten when my mother's husband came round and picked her up by the scruff. 'Come on,' he said. And I followed him, thinking we were going to one of the drainage canals for water. But he didn't take me to the canals. We went instead up higher, past the hot springs to where the molten lava bubbles under the earth and flows in rivers that look like the veins on my hand." He holds up a very veiny hand and runs his index finger along one especially prominent blue ribbon. Then he gazes up at me with a sweet expression that softens his features so much that he's almost lovely.

"He dropped my kitten into one of those rivers and made me watch her hiss and flail until she boiled to death."

I wrap my arms around my belly and swallow hard, my throat tacky as resin. I think of Adamen and Mesu. How Salan had cried and cried. "That's terrible."

"Yes, it is," he says. "But then here you are, so much like my kitten. But I won't let you burn into nothing. Never."

Chapter 42

Justice

A T FIRST, I think it's just a jittery, whistling wind. But it's a cry. A twisted one that howls like a wolf pup slowly being wrung to death. I think of Rin's kitten and our Mesu; one burned, the other sliced to ribbons, and sit up with a jolt. With Nif gone, Saru has been sleeping with me in our tent. But her place next to me is cold. It's still smelling of her—almond oil and frankincense, so she can't have been gone long.

Pushing the linens aside, I press up onto all fours, making my way to the front flaps.

Outside it's breezy and chilly, a half moon peeking out from behind a thin, lacy trim of cloud. I wrap my bed linens around my shoulders, listening for the noise again. I walk at first to the brink of the ledge, where I watch the sand blow in a low mist over the desert floor. My feet are growing icy and I shift, rubbing them on each other.

Over my shoulder, I catch sight of the cavern entrance. The stone is normally rolled closed at night—in case of unwanted visitors—and it appears so at first. But as I turn and walk closer, treading lightly on the balls of my feet, I notice it's open just enough for a man to slip through. Though I'm not huge yet by any stretch, I'm not quite able to pass, so I nudge my head and shoulders inside to have a look around.

A fire is lit. A healthy one, not the burning embers usually

kept agitated until the morning. And behind its dancing
flames are two shadows, stretched long and slender up the
rock wall.

"Hello! Saru, is that you?"

She steps out from behind the hearth fire, floating toward
me, her face slumped like a thirsty lily.

"You should go to sleep," she murmurs.

"What's happening?"

Saru shakes her head, glancing toward the fire.

"Nothing that won't wait until morning."

She blinks at me, scarcely seeming to draw breath, then
lifts a hand and waves Duman forward. He steps toward
us, clearly put out, and drenched in a sweat I can catch at a
distance.

Duman isn't an easy man to warm to. Scrunch-faced
and quick to anger, he's the type who nurtures his grudges.
Dangerous in the wrong context, but a great fighter. For his
part, he feared I'd be a useless addition to our band, but I've
fixed him up a fine tunic that makes him feel like a man
of importance, and demonstrated a knowledge of plant life,
however little we've come across. Over time, I think we've
developed a cautious respect for the other.

He puts his back into rolling the stone, placing his hands
on either side. I notice his knuckles are raw and bleeding,
swollen at the joints. I wiggle in.

"What happened to you?" I ask.

Duman glances over to Saru and she takes a deep,
exhausted breath.

"Come with me," she says.

Duman retrieves a torch for Saru and she leads me in a
wide orbit around the hearth, her tunic seeming to flutter
in the firelight like butterfly wings. Her movements are hyp-
notic. Deliberate as a dance.

At the back of the cavern is a supply cove. One of several,

as it would be stupid to hoard our reserves in one place. The one Saru leads me to is filled with a few days of fresh stores, and easy to access. Unlike the ones buried beneath the ledge, or tucked away in the labyrinth of the dunes. Of course things of real value, portable ones, are most often stitched roughly into our clothes. Small weapons, spare footwear, bronze and copper objects—needles and the like—things that can be melted down, repurposed, sold or traded if the need arises. Or used to fight off an enemy.

The supply cove entrance is made of dark, shiny stone and looks wet in the darkness. As we come closer, the torchlight faintly illuminates the lumps and bumps of grain, dried plums, and salted heron. There's an ale pot balanced on top of a barrel that contains some young wine. Our newly-made arrows are stacked, rolled in old, unwearable linen. And there are other rolls—large and uneven. Wrapped in rough fabric that's filthy from old animal blood, I can smell it from where I stand. They're bound tightly all the way around, and as I step closer I can see these aren't sacks of provisions at all. They're men.

"Who are they?" I demand.

Duman goes to the smallest one and kicks it. A throaty squeal cranks out from under the material.

"The other two are dead," he says. "I killed them."

He unties the hood of the first man and pulls it off. His eyes have been gouged out by Duman's thumbs, I imagine, and his open mouth is filled with a pool of blood. As I lean over him, I can see that his hair is short for a man of the desert, like his scalp was kept clean until recent months. I crouch down at his side and loosen the linen at his neck. Just beneath his collar, I find the start of a breastplate.

"This man's a soldier," I say.

Duman nods. "One of the sultan's men. Or was."

"And the other dead man?"

Duman shrugs.

"A vagrant, a robber—I've seen him around. He comes to the dunes here and there. We even fed him a few days back, when he came begging."

He means *I* fed him when he came begging, which Duman had warned me not to do. But the man looked like he was on the verge of starving and I couldn't imagine he could harm us in any way. Except to lead a soldier into our midst, it turns out.

"And the last one. The one you didn't kill."

That one is definitely not a soldier. Too small. The pitch of his moaning has a feminine edge to it. The bound man is squirming like a maggot, and Saru lifts her tunic and squats next to him, placing her hand daintily on the top of his head. He writhes some more, but not in avoidance of her touch. Like he enjoys being petted by her. As if it's a familiar pleasure.

"It can't be," I say.

I crawl to Saru's side, fumbling with the rope and fabric, peeling it back and exposing his face. My hand flies to my mouth, stifling a gasp. Grimy, streaked with tears, his lips swollen with bruises and eyes pinched in distress. It's Yaz.

"He poisoned the grasses Rin made into wine," Duman snarls. "Fool that he is, he tainted the wrong barrel."

The one Rin was still tasting for strength and readiness, poor man. Only a finger dip was apparently enough to lay him out for days.

"This makes no sense," I say. "Yaz doesn't sneak around doing anything."

Duman summons a foaming gob of mucus from his throat and spits it at Yaz's head, missing it by two fingers. He leans against the cave wall.

"Well, he was sneaking around tonight. I found him trying to slip some of that juice he fouled into our ale pot—the one we drink from, me and the men who stand guard at night."

Yaz starts to whimper again, and I reach down to squeeze his foot, wanting to reassure him somehow.

"Did he tell you why?"

"Why? He's an imbecile! He'd a done it for a honey chew."

Duman removes a small hand-knife from his belt and begins sharpening it. He won't meet my eyes.

"Sherin," Saru starts.

"Don't tell me you think he could have come up with this on his own," I tell her. "Who among us is easier to trick?"

Saru looks down at the simpleton. She gathers a deep, wispy breath and touches Yaz's brow. "Hardly a thought in his head."

I'm relieved she says it, so that I'm not the only one defending him. Saru has always been a part of this tribe and has not a single enemy among us. We rely on her songs for a sense of well-being, a nightly respite from our misfortunes. While I've grown in esteem over the past year, especially due to my pregnancy, the dangerous prospect of childbirth looms in my future, threatening to take me away as suddenly as I've appeared.

"We should keep this to ourselves," I say. "Yaz has a story to tell us, and if the whole tribe is up in arms, calling for his blood, he won't be inclined to share it."

Duman wrinkles his nose, as he does whenever he endeavors to think, which isn't often. He prefers doing to thinking, which has its uses . . . although not in a situation like this. Knotting his arms over his chest, he emits a growl of deep and habitual skepticism.

"The bottom of what? He tried to kill me and anyone who drank from that pot." Duman points to the poisoned ale pot, which stands center of the room like an eyewitness. "He was going to let this soldier and that thief with him get a good look around in here. Steal our stores, take a woman. Or maybe just learn the ways of the cavern so they can come back and kill us all."

He kicks the dead soldier's head, breaking his neck with a sickly crack.

"Yaz told you all this?"

Duman shrugs.

"He told me the soldier wanted to be shown the way in after we'd drank up the ale. And I beat Yaz but good and made him tell me where these curs were hiding. Out in one of the bitty caves when you first come up on the dunes, that's what he said. The ones only big enough for a goat or two."

Duman flips the tarp back over Yaz's face. The look of contempt on his own is troubling, but it's hard to blame him considering what poor Yaz has done.

"Did he tell you anything else? How he met them in the first place or what they said they wanted?"

Duman gives me a look like I'm truly the most ignorant creature.

"What they wanted was to get in here. It's what they've always wanted."

An unholy moan comes up from under the tarp. It's not the sort that sounds of aching bruises, but deep and terrible agony. I look up at Duman, who's gnawing on his lip.

"Duman, what have you done?"

Saru begins unraveling the tarp and, as she does so, I can already smell a potent mix of feces and blood. Yaz's insides are emptying from him at a shocking pace, the ooze spreading out from under his backside.

"I gave him a nice, big cup of ale," Duman says. "So witless he even thanked me for it."

Saru takes Yaz's hand, already limp with fate, and I shuffle around to the other side of him. He's breathing heavily through his nose, crimson snot oozing from each nostril, thick as jelly.

"Why, Yaz?" I ask him. "What made you do it?"

He starts to say something, one part murmur and the other part gurgle. His throat bulges from the strain.

"What is it?" I lean over, placing my ear right above his lips. "You must tell me."

He starts to speak again, even lower this time. I listen, breathing deeply, rubbing his shoulder as he struggles to get the words out. But with each word my skin grows colder, and I struggle to keep my composure. The blood drains from my face and my belly feels thick and bilious. Even our son stills.

"What's he saying?" Saru asks me.

There's a note of panic in her voice and I reach out to her. Just as I do, Yaz's hand slips from hers. I put my palm on his chest and can feel his heart pittering out as a last, lone breath escapes his lips.

"What did he tell you?" Saru puts her fingers to my cheek. I know she can see the disturbance within me.

I pet Yaz's head, rubbing his filthy mess of hair.

"He was confused," I say. The last thing I want is to tell her what he said in front of Duman—if I tell her anything at all.

Duman grips the old linen wrap that's bound around the dead soldier and begins to drag him to the far back of the cave. There's a crevasse there where we toss the worst sort of our refuse.

"Confused," he mumbles. "When wasn't he confused?"

Saru looks down at poor Yaz and flicks a few over-eager ants off his cheek. Sweet and damnable Yaz, always trying so hard to get things right.

"Duman," I say. "I don't care what you do with that soldier or the vagrant. But Yaz was part of us, no matter what he's done. Only we can send him off to his home in the next world."

Duman lets go of the man he's dragging and stretches his

back. He gives a big sniff and winds up his leg, kicking the dead soldier, then shoots me a look of grudging agreement.

"Don't expect me to get all weepy about your friend here. I told the *sam* we should've left him to shrivel up in the sand long ago."

"Nif would never do such a thing," I tell him. "That's why you call him *sam*."

Duman actually comes something close to a smile. "Maybe you're right," he says. "But the time for sentiments is long past. And when it comes to it, you cut out your kidney to save your heart."

Saru takes my hand and we walk back to the warmth of the fire. My steps are unsteady, and I put a hand to my middle, rubbing it. She's made tea and pours me some. We stand there taking sips, watching the blaze surge and leap, as if dancing to appease the gods.

"What Yaz said," she whispers. "I won't tell anyone."

"Not even Nif?"

She stares into the fire a long moment.

"If you tell him, he'll go after them. Now is not the time and you know it." The sultan's army is weakening, but it's still too strong, too many. We can outrun them, outwit them, but we can't outfight them yet.

Saru folds her hands in front of her, kneading them like a worried mother watching a storm. "Not even Nif," she says.

I step behind her, pressing my belly against the small of her back. Her silken hair, white and fragile as the head of a dandelion, drifts across her shoulders. I lean in close.

"He said they were looking for me."

Chapter 43

What the Mountains Give Us

SARU TRILLS a song of mourning, just as the sun begins its roost, settling on the horizon like a fat old hen. Her voice is aquiver, like a bird's, and Buri joins in. The others sway in a terrible, discordant dance. I can't bring myself to move or sing.

A funeral must conclude before the sun sets, so, as the last notes of Saru's lament fade into the evening air, I take some rags I plucked from our kitchen stores and go to Yaz. Saru helps me clean him, removing his tunic, mopping up the residual blood and ordure from his pimpled, hairy skin. A black tunic, fine, one of my father's, wraps easily around his whole body, leaving only his face exposed.

"A man must always allow death to see his face, or risk not being let in to the afterworld," Buri chants.

It's Duman who lays Yaz at the top of the dunes. There, the birds of prey can better carry Yaz off in pieces to the next life. We bow to the last glint of light in the sky, but only I raise my hand in salan.

And when it's over, it's simply over.

Fires are lit and stoked. Bread is set to bake, ale passed around. A bad batch, sour as stale breath, but it does the job. No dried fruit or nuts—these are meted out only every third day in our rations, so everyone is cranky already, which I seek to soften with an extra pass of ale. Ale, regardless of its quality, is something we have plenty of, relatively speaking. Buried in the sand, it stays cool and hidden, and can be kept from greedy hands.

"Boney women lose the devotion of their husbands," Duman says, handing me some jerky from our stores, along with a portion of his bread.

"Boney warriors lose their heads." I offer him back his bread, but he won't have it. The dunes are being secured, he tells me. An easy feat with so few squatters in the outer caves. The desert is all a hush. Quite a relief, for now.

Normally, when there's trouble in the dunes, we decamp for some days into the desert until things settle down and the worst sorts of incendiaries are either killed in some act of savagery, driven off, or simply leave on their own. Inconvenience is worth the price of keeping our women safe. But with the prospect of a regiment being close by, I've made the decision we're going to stay. At least until Nif's return. Even Duman sees the wisdom in this.

Despite the ominous events of the previous night, it has been a day of our usual chores. Yaz's absence was noted only as much as he usually floats around, a minor buzz in the ear. But it was impossible for me to stop thinking of him. I took to mastering the new weaving needles I'd whittled, just to settle my mind. Months of uncertainty and frequent moves between the dunes and the desert have taken a toll on our linens, and we would soon have been dressed in little more than rags. A dangerous state in a land of deadly sun and sandstorms.

It takes a long while, the day. I watch the sun drift across the sky like a nutshell floating on a gentle current. My baby tosses and tumbles nearly the whole time, as if he's having bad dreams. I try not to think about what a new night could bring.

"You haven't slept," Saru tells me. She blots a cool and

damp swatch of linen on my neck. "Go. The day is done. Duman's men will be up tonight making the watch."

I drink up my ale to the last drop, making the small, necessary conversations that end the day. The state of provisions and condition of weapons, tools, linens. The state of our animals. Saru minds me the whole time, until I do finally take my leave. I'm not at all convinced I'll be able to catch a wink of sleep, but the demands of pregnancy wrest away the ramblings of my troubled mind, letting me drift off until well into the night. It's then, when all is as quiet as a nursery, that I stir, rousing to a blur of color-wild shapes.

A hand is stroking my hair and I startle at first, until a tender pair of lips presses against my forehead. It's very dark and I'm groggy. Saru's place is empty again.

"A firefinch landed at my feet the other day," Nif says. "Don't know how it got so far from home."

I sit up and wrap myself around him, tighter than a damned tunic. He rubs my back and kisses my earlobe, his skin soft and dry as if it's been dusted with flour.

"He tweeted at me and I wondered if he might be bringing a message from you."

"Yaz," I say.

Curling up in Nif's arms, I collapse around my middle like a clam shell around a pearl. There's a jolt inside me, as if our little son is kicking and stretching. I feel a sudden wash of relief. With so much death, there's always fear of more, and I've seen my share of still births since the Vara.

"Duman told me about what happened last night," he says.

I nuzzle up to his neck, kissing a patch of three little hairs sprouting beneath his collar.

"I was so afraid you'd run into more soldiers. Like the one who came here."

Nif shakes his head.

"We saw traces of a regiment, what they left behind, but

they seemed long gone. Taran left us a few days ago and went scouting, to see if there's any other trouble out there."

Nif takes a wick from his pouch and leans outside of our canvas to light it off one of the tiny torches we keep going throughout the night. Once back inside, he lights the small, clay lantern I brought from my father's house and settles in to our linens. He takes my foot in his hands and presses his thumbs into my arches, which is about the best thing that's happened to me in weeks.

"Duman said the soldier was with one of the vagrants who come here, so perhaps he was a deserter."

I think of the bloody hollows on his face. The man's eyeballs must be long gone from the floor of the little cave where Duman found and killed him. Already made their way into the belly of a snake.

"Did you recognize him?"

"No," I say. "But in truth he was hardly recognizable after what Duman had done to him. And he'd grown hair, which always changes a man."

Nif touches his own full head of hair, running his fingers through it. "That used to be the mark of a deserter, but hardly any of the Sultan's men pluck their scalps anymore."

There's a rustle outside and Nif parts one of our flaps to have a look. Taran is entering camp, greeting the men on lookout with a grumble and a slap on the back. He shambles over to our tent, bear-crawling in on hand and toe, then sits cross-legged between us. Even in our weak light, I can see the sand crusted at the base of his eyelashes, and peppered throughout his brows. He leans forward, elbows on knees and folds his hands, resigned as he always is to delivering bad news.

"The army," he says. "Plenty of them, and armed to the teeth. At least they're slow-going, given all they're carrying. Like it's everything they've ever owned."

"More like everything the desert people have ever owned," I say, and Taran grunts in agreement.

"At least three, maybe four days from here," he says in consolation.

"They can't be the same regiment we found traces of on the way back," Nif says. "Those were only a dozen strong, if that, and were moving in the direction of the Palace City."

Taran is of the same mind.

"Did you get a good look at them?" I ask.

Taran shakes his head, moving a thin bone pick he's sucking on from one side of his mouth to the other. "It was dark and the moon wasn't much help. Only reason I found them was I'd been hunting their tracks all day. They leave a lot in their wake."

"Odd they were moving at night," I note.

Nif rubs his hand over the heavy stubble that's grown on his cheeks.

"We could wait for them," Taran says. "We know the darkest hollows of this place and could pick them off one by one."

"How many, you said?"

Taran pulls on his ear, a habit of his when he's twitchy. "More than a garan, but not two."

"That's near three times our size."

Taran winces. "Wouldn't be the first time."

Nif picks up the little statue Rin gave me, stroking her face with his thumb. "No, but if it's come to this, it won't be just a garan or two who makes their way here." He bites at his lip, eyeing the Lady. "Enough of them and they could surround the dunes and wait us out until another garan arrives. Maybe another after that."

"They're not as organized as they were," Taran counters. "A lot of infighting between them."

Nif leans back, staring up at our ceiling. He waves away

the tiny bugs that flutter up there. "But still well-armed and well-trained."

Squeezing the Lady, he looks my way. Giving birth on the move presents all sorts of potential problems—dehydration, raids, premature labor. Death for mother and child. But we do have some time yet.

"We should go to the oasis Rin told us about," I say. "It's far and secluded. If we start tomorrow and the weather stays good, we may make it before the baby's born."

The mountains, though lush by desert standards, are a dubious proposition. They rise murky-black and craggy from the golden desert floor and are believed to harbor all sorts of wickedness. Creatures, fire-breathing, are thought to dwell in caves and crevasses. Their volcanic nature makes the mountains themselves seem to breathe and grumble, as if alive. Rivers of ash and fire and water, hissing, steaming, coughing dust. Anger incarnate, they warn you not to come closer. And in spots, surprising and hidden, oases grow like thick patches of hair. Even if evil spirits are thought to inhabit them, the Vara has made them a treasure too valuable for us to ignore. That, and they're just far enough away from the Palace City as to not be workable for the army. It takes a good four phases of the moon just to get near them, and another half dozen to get to the verdant parts inside the range.

"Our people prefer the straightforward toils of the desert," Nif says. I know he prefers them as well. While he's hunted near their base, he's never actually gone into the mountains and doesn't care for places that are unfamiliar to him.

"Rin knows them well," I say. "Well enough to know they're made only of his own demons and not the cruel spirits of an underworld."

Nif snorts at that.

"The army is coming here and we have to move to a place where they won't follow," I tell him. "And not just decamp into the desert where they can find us. If we go now, they won't even know where we've gone. We leave no litter when we travel and in two day's time the desert will have swallowed our footprints."

He runs his fingers into my hair and brings me closer again. His warm breath, sweet from anise seed, floats between us.

"The desert is vast and we know it far better than they do, but we know nothing about the mountains."

While Nif is not easily spooked, there are plenty in the tribe who put great stock in curses, and the mountains are thought to be nothing if not cursed.

The mountains. They have no other name. To have chosen one and then spoken the name out loud would have given the mountains power in the human domain, or so the common logic goes. Desert people are a superstitious people, but you can hardly blame us. You need only to hear the hollow note of the desert wind once to believe in a shadow world.

"Once our people see the bounty there, and how much easier life will be, they'll forget all about their fears," I tell them.

Nif's eyes meet Taran's and they speak to one another without a word. It's not the first time I've seen them do this.

"Forgetting a fear doesn't make it go away," Nif says.

"Nor does submitting to it." I open Nif's hand and place it at the growing dome of my middle.

"The fears of the mountains are all legend. Not a single one can be told of experience. But the Sultan's soldiers are real and just as cursed. You've fought them, and seen the carnage they leave behind everywhere they go. Are you honestly more afraid of a tall tale than men of flesh and blood?"

Nif takes a deep breath and closes his eyes.

"It's a foreign territory where we'll be marooned far away from anywhere we've ever known," he says. "Far from your brother."

That is a stake of iron in my heart, but not one I haven't considered. "Better to lose time than lose him forever," I tell them. "If the army takes us, he'll be left without any hope of our protection when the Palace City falls."

Taran spits out his pick and takes it between his fingers, rolling it like a worry stone.

I lay my leg over Nif's.

"We'll be far away from what we know, but even farther from the men who leave the sand soaked with the blood of women and children. The men who hate you and would have us die like animals. Rip our child from my womb and eat him in front of us, if the stories are true."

Nif turns to me, his eyes kindling. The fiery amber in the one glows like an ember, while the ruby in the other seems to rush like a river.

"Please," I whisper.

———

THAT NIGHT, we go into the cave—our cave—and bring with us several torches to light our slab as we do our work. We have paints with us, and Saru's brushes. In truth, neither one of us is very good at making pictures, but Nif and I, as chief and his wife, set to the task of chronicling the plight of our people. We paint what has been—the Vara and the death of the desert, and we paint what we're about to do. Journey away from the bands of the desperate and unworthy, to the mountains . . . a place forsaken and cursed, they say, but the only place we have left to go.

———

WHEN WE FIRST CATCH SIGHT of the mountains, I think they can't possibly belong to the desert. Thin and rough featured, at a glance they could be a band of misshapen giants wearily making their way across the sand. Only a few peaks are high enough to harbor snow, further giving the range a forbidden quality that speaks to the darker nature of the universe.

According to Rin, there's an active volcano at the center of the range. At its foot lies a valley pitted with craters, and many have speculated that when seen from above they make the face of a grinning skull. It's why the local nomads—the only ones who dare name them—call them the Slay Mountains. They're thought to inspire men to murder.

"From the dunes of earthly criminals to the mountains of devils," Rin says, as we enter the pass. The reek of sulfur hits us like a blow to the nose.

Nif's face is etched with worry, his lips are parched and cracked. He's been giving me the lion's share of his water.

"It's nothing much you know—this first oasis," Rin tell us. "There are much bigger and better ones here—beautiful, in fact—but it's a place to start."

My odd little countryman is trying to appear happy about returning to this place, but doing a rather lousy job.

"Look," Rin says, pointing to a stringy patch of grass sprouting up from under one of the volcanic formations. It has the look of a haggard blonde felled by big, black rock. But it's a sign of life, greenery. An hour of walking through a chasm, and we arrive at a more hardy place, a crescent moon smiling down on us.

While this is a damned poor oasis, it does have the remnants of a stream. It trickles down the middle of our camp like a rolling bead of sweat through a scattering of chest hair. The mountains surround us—high priests of another dimension. It looks as if, at any moment, they'll begin to chant.

———— ┼◈》 ◈┼ ————

THE LADY OF LIFE, the small statue Rin gave me, grows hot in my hand. I squeeze her during my contractions.

"Damned witch!" I cry out, dropping the Lady. She's grown too hot to hold. Or maybe it's me.

Rin picks her up, wrapping her shape in a densely woven piece of linen—handing her to me, closing my fingers around her.

"Hold her tight," he says, and I nod. Rin has lost another tooth, a canine, I notice. I've been lucky to keep all of mine, especially with a baby growing in me.

Saru massages oil onto my thighs and belly as Ayla prepares water and clean linen. They have the help of a prickly crone we picked up in the dunes some time back. All iron-haired with deep-set eyes, she lights a fresh torch and begins praying, so I know I'm very close.

"There is a wind that speaks of life," Nif sings to me in a whisper, but then stops, not remembering the rest.

He's behind me, his legs enfolding my body, applying a cool cloth to my forehead. For the first time in so long my mind is free, and all I can think about is the fire of birth.

A ring of fire. I can see it as our son passes from my body. And through its center, I see the brightening sky, at the cusp of dawn. It must be a dream, because I see the strangest birds, stiff and gray. They don't even flap their wings and look enormous, like dragons. Older children all around me and Nif. We look different, he and I. Not at all like ourselves, yet the same. Then the dream bursts and I hear our baby's cry.

THEY WERE PLANES, the birds I saw. I know that now. I've always been able to glimpse a future life when I'm giving birth. The planes were British or Turkish, I don't know. I also saw Nif, who looked nothing like the Nif I loved in the desert of the Rah'a, but he was unmistakably him. His eyes were following me—the same eyes I've always known, with their rivers of blood and amber enveloped in sweet darkness, like chocolate. But he had ginger hair this time. Fair skin. Lips remarkably similar, though—tender and honest in the way they're set.

And Neville's great-grandfather—also named Cornelius. He was there, too. Holding my hand. Rin's Lady of Life tucked into his belt.

He calls me Nadia and Nif Alexei.

Cornelius was worried, telling us we have to go. He was tugging at my hand. Nif and I continued to stare into one another's eyes, the ghost memory of our past life burning in them.

Nif and Cornelius. I loved them both.

This knowledge came to me in an instant, a match lit, then blown out as soon as I heard our little boy's first cries. But I saw the knowledge once more, reflected on Rin's face as he watched me turn my gaze from the heavens.

"It's not a dream," Rin whispered. "It's real, and you will know it one day."

Nif heard him, too. I'm sure of it.

AND HERE STANDS Cornelius Rodin Neville, thousands of years later. A steely, low-flying plane, military by the looks of it, glides over the Nile. Neville's father and grandfather each spent parts of a world war in this city and he feels a strange and nostalgic sense of déjà vu—I can see it on his face. Like his own war is coming.

"I hope you got some sleep, babe." Calliope Neville rolls onto her side, grunting. She blinks hard and sits up part way, leaning her elbow on a big, fluffy Ritz Carlton pillow. Her hair is a mess of sweet, ringlets, and she rubs her eyes like a child. Dawn is creeping up and Neville, draped in a white, hotel robe, stands at the picture window. He rubs the coarse shadow of his emerging beard and huffs like a bull.

"Are you talking to me or *the* babe?"

"Both," Calliope says, patting her mostly-flat stomach. "First couple of nights in a real bed are a killer. So's the first night after some bum luck."

Neville turns slowly to face his wife, too tired to do what he really wants to do—which is stomp and scream. Maybe throw a heavy glass and watch it shatter against the wall.

Rising up from bed, Calliope goes to her husband, wrapping her arms around him. They stand together, breathing slow and deep. Watching the sky brighten. All is better when they're like this.

"We'll get back to the Rah'a," she whispers. "You've got plenty of funding, we just have to wait it out as a wicked trio of governments fight over who has to pay what, when and to whom."

Neville snuggles her into his arms, her wild hair twisting all over his neck, looking almost like part of his new beard.

"I know."

"Those people," she says. "Their beautiful things. I feel like they were waiting for us all this time. And they'll wait a little longer. Jordie says things should get sorted out even before the baby's born, and his dad is an ambassador for the love of God. He ought to know something about the way things work over there."

Calliope slides open the glass door and leads Neville out onto the balcony. It's lovely there, but hardly a place for fresh air. Pollution wafts up from Cairo, smelling of metal and oil, fire and spices. In an odd way, it's a smell the Nevilles have grown to love. I want to breathe it in with them. Trace over their cheeks and feel the curious differences in their skins. Her's supple like a leaf, and his like raw silk, I'm sure of it.

"It's such a damned heartbreaker," he tells her. "Everything felt ready to break open, you know?"

Calliope cups Neville's neck and scratches at a cluster of bug bites at his hairline.

"That feels good," he says.

She brings him close.

"Have some faith, okay? I know that's a hard one for you. This delay—and that's all it is—couldn't be better in terms of timing," she whispers. "In a few months, the baby will be here and you've got a book to write about all of this don't forget."

She buries her head in Neville's chest and he holds her.

"Been tossing and turning," she says. "I can't get it out of my mind. That room. The body."

It had been a horrible sight. Even for me. A hidden room of luxuries. Gold. Precious gems. And the sultan, dressed in his finest. Jewels of every sort shoved down his throat, filling his stomach and intestines. Ruby chips dribbling from his mouth. His eyes wide open, but not in fear. It was recognition I saw in his eyes, though of whom I can't say.

"I haven't stopped thinking about it either," Neville tells her. He puts his hand over Calliope's womb. "In a few months, he—or she—will be tossing and turning. The doctor said you'll be able to feel it at about the middle of the second trimester, right?"

Calliope nods, breathing in her husband's scent—nut shells, a faint musk of sweat, and a ghost of the La Nuit De L'Homme cologne she got him for his birthday. "Sometimes I already think I can feel him."

Neville sinks to his knees and lifts up Calliope's night shirt. "I hate that this is keeping you up, too," he says, planting light kisses on her belly. "Part of me wishes we'd never found the antechamber. That man with the gems in his throat."

"That's not the only thing keeping me up. I've been up every night since he—or she—was conceived. Pregnancy-induced insomnia, I guess." She takes his face in her hands.

"Neil, the Palace City of the Rah'a is arguably the most significant archaeological discovery of all time. And it's yours. You found it. Your name will go down in the annals of archaeology, not some bureaucrat's."

"That's not what I mean." Neville stands up, kissing her hand, squeezing it. "It's more like I feel that man—the sultan—like we were led to him."

"What? To avenge his murder?"

Neville shakes his head.

"Whoever killed him and everyone else in the city for that matter, came for a reason and it sure as hell wasn't to rob the place." Neville lets go of Calliope's hand and grasps the balcony railing, gazing out onto the rising sun. "I think there's something there waiting for us, too, and it's not just the people. It's . . . I don't know what it is. Maybe you've got it right. It's just as well that we have some time to be together and have our baby while everything else gets sorted out."

He cracks his neck and knuckles, submitting to a deep breath that delivers on its promise to make him feel better. Turning back to Calliope, he takes her pinky and shakes it.

"Besides," he says. "My mother is dying for us to visit her. To pamper you and take you shopping for you know who."

Calliope nods, looking away. Tears well up in her eyes and she sniffs them back. "I'm sorry."

"Come here," he says.

She walks right back into his arms, her most favorite place in the world.

"I'd love that, I really would. It's just, oh, God," Calliope wipes her face in Neville's robe. "They say orphans always think about their mothers when they're about to become one themselves. Whoever they are, I guess they're right."

"Totally natural," he says.

"Yeah." She loosens his robe and puts her ear right on his bare chest, listening to his heart. "I swear sometimes I feel like my mother's in the room with me."

"After what we've seen the past few months, I might actually be willing to consider that possibility."

She laughs right into a curly cluster of hair splattered across his sternum like a constellation of stars. "I'll make a believer out of you yet."

Chapter 44

What the Mountains Take Away

"**H**E'S JUST LIKE YOU," Nif whispers, kissing my temple.

Saru washes our baby and wraps him in a fine swathe of linen. She hands him to Nif, and his eyes flit over our tiny son. He mouths a silent something—not a prayer, a welcome.

"A poet, a priest, and a king," I say softly. It's a Rah'a mother's greeting for a newly born boy.

The ring of fire has gone out, but the Lady is still burning in my hands—even through the linen. My feet are cold and my legs tremble. Saru is kneading my belly, helping to expel the placenta, and Rin is fixing an herbal elixir to bathe it in before we eat it. Saru will prepare this small fruit of birth with vinegar and the yolk of an egg. An unborn bird is a messenger to our next child, bidding him or her to come, so finding an egg was vital. Buri spotted a thrush's nest in a crag several feet above us while we were setting up camp and climbed for it, cradling the fragile oval in his palm as he made his way down one-handed.

"What will you name him?" Rin asks us.

To say it's improper to name a child before birth is an understatement. Most children of our lands don't get a name until at least their fifth birthday. But I insist. Naming Salan had felt right and good. I can't imagine not having a real name to call our son.

"Oah," Nif says, caressing the slope of our baby's tiny nose.

Oah's got little more than ebony fuzz for hair, but dark eyebrows, well defined, like mine. Eyes set wide upon a skull of blue-veined marble. Mouth like Nif's. Despite our poor diet, he's born looking almost plump. His fingers long and refined, like his father's. Made for crafting intricate things. Feet, strong and straight for walking great distances. Oah, which means lifelong friend, since we sensed him from the moment of his conception.

"Oah," Rin repeats, as if he's taken the name for himself.

OAH'S BIRTH BRINGS JOY and even more bustle to our lives. He gives us hope for the future and makes us feel connected to the gods. Like we have uncovered our purpose. But he also brings a strange dream to my nights. One I'm too afraid to tell Nif about because of what stock his people put in the truth of dreams. And more than anything, I don't want this dream to be true.

It always starts with Saru.

Saru is covered in blood and holding Oah. She looks at him so tenderly, then at me.

"Sherin," she says. Her voice is like a love song.

She turns to Rin, who takes our baby from her arms. He walks away with him, fading into the desert horizon, stopping only once to hold his hand out in salan.

It's then I awaken, out of breath with my heart pounding. Terrified I'll never see my son again.

It's a dream I have for several nights in a row, till I think it's the only dream I'll ever have. I'm afraid to go to sleep for fear of having it again.

But then out of nowhere I start to sleep like the dead.

No dreams or nightmares. I should be glad, but I can only feel that somehow the mountains have taken something from me.

I feel a bit uneasy when we start our move deeper into the range, further into the embrace of these mountains. But whatever trepidations I have quickly fade when Rin guides us to a far more verdant oasis. One with palms, cool, plentiful water, and an actual spring. Animals to hunt and lots of grasses for foraging. No smell of sulfur or burning at all—only the fresh perfume of globularia and ficus.

It's on a day with a mountain wind as tender as a sigh, and a sky dotted with popcorn clouds, that Nif and I sneak away to the guelta near our new oasis. We take some of our camels, so they can drink in the cool waters of the drainage canals.

We swaddle Oah in a soft piece of linen, one of my mother's, and lay him to sleep in a bed of puzzlegrass. Wading through the spring-fed water, we make our way to a cove ringed with a beach of moss. There we undress, taking a sun bath. Talking little, tracing our fingers over each other's bodies, breathing deeply. If I could, I would live this single hour forever.

A chorus of *burrs* make Nif spring to his feet. He hands me my tunic and wraps himself swiftly in his. The camels only sound distressed for one of two reasons—a large animal, or the sight of an unfamiliar human being. Both of which they've learned to view as a menace.

We retrieve Oah from the grass and I bind him tightly to my breast. Like this, we slink silently through the water, until we can see around the cove. There, we find a lone tribesman, dressed in an indigo wraparound like a native cave-dweller. He sits at the water's edge, filling up his pouch and splashing his face. Nif slides the dagger from his belt and I close my arms around our son, standing back a few steps.

"What brings you here, brother?"

The tribesman squints up at him, breathing through a dry, swollen nose.

"Nothing," he says.

I come up behind Nif, tentatively, and can smell the tribesman from where we stand. Sweat, sunburn, and the unmistakable bitter draft of long desert walking.

"Something drew you to the mountains," Nif persists. "Food, water. We have both and will share with you."

The man raises a brow, and leans back on his haunches.

"How kind," he says.

"Are you alone?" Nif asks him.

"Alone?" The man runs his hand through the water, a look of sudden bliss on his face.

"Yes," he says, his eyes flitting between my face and Nif's. "I'm alone."

———— ⟨⟨⟩⟩ ⟨⟨⟩⟩ ————

WE TAKE THE TRIBESMAN back to camp, Nif having him walk a few steps in front of us, his knife ready. The man seems to stroll about as if in a dream, stopping to caress a leaf from a bush, or kick a stone. When we arrive at our hearth, he settles down onto a tuft of grass and Ayla brings him food.

His name is Ness, he tells us between mouthfuls of hyrax. Even as we pepper him with questions and he attacks his food with gusto, the faraway look on his face remains.

"I'm a Folouk," he finally says.

A cave-dweller, as we thought. Driven out of the dunes shortly after the Vara, they've been picked off by the sultan's army, until only a core group of their strongest remain.

It was a year ago, Ness tells us, that his tribe—what was left of them—came to the mountains to shore up their supplies. But soon after, they decided to travel all the way back to the Palace City. The mere mention of that place makes my hair rise, both in hope for my brother and with a terrible fear of the unmentionable; that the city is on the brink of falling, and we may never be able to get Salan back.

"The Palace City is closed," Nif tells him. It seems a madness for them to have undertaken such a journey just for the sake of it.

"It's what we thought, too," the man says. "We found a soldier wandering near the mountain pass. Deserter. They're all deserters now you know. Only a few groups of soldiers are still traveling together. The poor bastard said the sultan needed hunters and was willing to take them in."

"So you went?" Nif persists.

Ness takes a deep glug of wine and closes his eyes. His head drifts slowly to his shoulder, giving him the look of a broken-necked chicken. He inhales a gasping breath and this seems to revive him.

"What did we have to lose?" He says. "But when we got there, it didn't seem right."

"What didn't seem right?" I ask.

"The guards. They wanted us to come in back, like they were sneaking us in."

Nif nudges my thigh, warning me not to panic. He knows I'm thinking about Salan.

"And your soldier, the one who told you about the sultan needing hunters?"

Ness shakes his head. "Oh, we killed him before we went. Ate him raw."

A quiet comes over us and even Duman keeps his mouth shut.

"You didn't sneak in?" Nif says, barely in a whisper.

"We pretended we would, just like they wanted us to. But no." Ness leans in conspiratorially, as if we'd been there with him. "The way we figured, they were trying to lure us in."

"Why?" I rasp.

Ness shrugs. "Who knows? Maybe cook us into something tasty the palace fancies wouldn't recognize. Like soup. Maybe sacrifice us to the gods."

His talk of sacrifices is an odd comfort to me, as it at least seems to indicate that there's a level of ritual left at the Palace City. But the thought of food being scarce enough that they would lure in wanderers to eat them gives a terrible trouble to my thoughts. Nif sees my distress and takes me aside. He reminds me how a man like Ness, who himself has resorted to cannibalism, would surely assume others would do the same. It doesn't make it true.

"Doesn't make it false either," I say.

Ness makes no attempt to resist when Nif and Taran tie him up. He's tethered to a post, but comfortable enough so that he can at least fall into something resembling sleep. I know I'll get none. My fear for Salan has burned a hole in me.

But all of our attempts to accommodate our unfortunate guest are for nothing. By morning, Ness is dead. He'd wriggled a bone pin from a hidden pocket in his tunic and punctured himself dozens of times—anywhere he could reach within the confines of the rope that bound him. He bled to death at leisure throughout the night, wearing the same remote expression in death that we saw in the last hours of his life.

Dry-tongued. White-lipped. Blood-soaked. Covered in a funeral sheath of black flies.

Ness, we fear, is an omen. A glimpse of what awaits us all. The strongest men carry his body to the top of the volcano and throw him in—a measly bid to quiet the dark gods of this place.

———｜◄◊►〉 〈◄◊►｜———

"MY WAY-MAKER," Nif says, kissing my earlobe. His kisses are so soft sometimes that they feel like no more than the brush of a feather. Especially in the dark. And it is dark, with the dawn hours away and sleep still clawing at me.

"I'm coming with you," I tell him.

Nif lights a thumb torch, propping it in a pot of sand, then turns his attention to me. He plaits his fingers through my hair and brings my face close, putting his eyes right up to mine. I follow the rivers of blood and golden honey that run through his irises, memorizing every variation of color. I've taken to doing this as often as I can, mindful of how every day could be our last.

"Duman is a beast of a man," he rasps. "He can take three men without a weapon in his hand."

"I'm not afraid to stay," I tell him. Except for the man at the guelta, we've met not a soul since coming here. And I refuse to let the mountains torment me. "I just don't think we should be apart."

"I won't be gone more than a couple of months." He lifts my chin with the pad of his thumb and throws me a sly smile. "And when I return, the Palace City will belong to us and your brother will be home."

"Might as well be years. We're coming with you!"

"You and Oah?"

I take his hands and bring them to my face. They smell of our son—a cologne of fresh dough, milky linens, and warm urine. It's a smell that I love above all others.

"It might be his first venture into the desert, but you and I both know it won't be his last."

Nif shakes his head.

"He's still small and helpless," he says. "And you'll both slow us down."

I bring our hands to my lap, rubbing his fingers between mine. It's good to see them together.

"Sherin," he says. "The Palace City is weak and now is our only chance. You heard what Ness said. They couldn't even force a band of Folouks inside. Had to lure them in with stories. And you heard what else he told us. The army has all but fallen apart. There's but a skeleton crew protecting the Palace City, and we must strike before others do. Others who care none for the welfare of little boys."

"Assuming what Ness said is true."

It's our first real chance to bring back my brother and here I am trying to talk Nif out of it. But there's more to my life today than there was when it was just me and Salan. I have a husband and child to think of now.

"I know there's truth in what you're saying, and there would come a time to take the Palace City, but what if . . . ?"

"What if?"

Nif shakes his head again, more forcefully this time. He squeezes my fingers.

"As long as there is a sun and moon, I'll return to you. I swear it."

Chapter 45

Why the Skull Grins

MY TOES are all the way at the very edge of the plateau, as my eyes sweep the landscape. I've been doing this for more than a fortnight, knowing Nif could arrive any time now. I want to catch him on his approach, but all I can see from up high are the small craters that drip across the ground like ink spots.

Our camp is obscured by a high shelf of volcanic rock, but I can see a sliver of the doum palms that mark its entry point from the north. Other than that, it's palm groves, canyons, and basalt spires. Lava fields are everywhere, both fresh and cold, along with fumaroles, mud pools, and hot springs, all spread out among the rocky terrain and random oases. Beyond that, it's the golden pelt of the desert. Nothing else for weeks. The vastness that separates me from Nif seems infinite, and all I can do to console myself is to look up and see that there is still a sun in our sky. And, I presume, a moon.

I sit on the plateau for hours, and it's wrong of me. There's always so much to do, but Rin and Ayla are minding Oah and I can't bear to go back without catching some glimpse of Nif. I'll settle for a sign as simple as a change in weather. A southern wind can shorten a journey by more than a day.

Finally, breasts swelling with milk, I move to head back, placing all of my hope in what the next day will bring. I'm ravenous—supper can't be more than a couple of hours away—still, I move slowly, careful not to twist an ankle.

But as I enter the passage leading to our camp, I'm startled by the presence of a vulture perched on a shiny, black hump of a rock. Orange-faced, curved beak the shape of a claw, feathers that puff around his head like a lion's mane. He sits low and heavy, just gorged from his fill, and eyes me with scrutiny. As if I don't belong here.

Several more of his kind fly over me, landing in a tamarix tree. Its cottony leaves, fuzzy at a distance, obscure them in part, but even from my vantage point I can see that they've all recently been scavenging.

"Maybe a hippo, bitten by a horn viper," I say aloud.

Hippos often fall victim to what we call the sleepy-eyed menace—wide-faced and the color of sand. Blending in. Nif was nearly bitten by one. I try to comfort myself with that theory, but it's no good. The sultry glow of the setting sun makes it feel as though the mountains are closing in on me.

I start to run. Tripping over the stump of an old palm, I fall face-first, and it knocks the air clean out of me. I sit up, gasping, crawling to the black rock wall, helping myself up and moving as quickly as I can through the path.

My hand grazes over a slick patch on the rough façade of the rock and I think for a moment that I've cut myself. Even the smoother rock faces have sharp bits that can slice like a blade. Trembling, I turn my hand over to see that it is painted with blood. Still wet, but not warm. A tackiness to it. The rock wall is glossy, viscous in parts, giving me gooseflesh. Stepping back, I spot streams of blood coming from above, and make my eyes trail upward.

There, I find Duman.

His hands are tied at the wrist, hanging over a spike pounded into the volcanic slab. Eyes wide, his mouth is slack. No fewer than a half dozen spears piercing his neck, shoulders, chest and legs.

Oah. I can feel my mouth form his name.

"Oah!"

It's a cry that screams from every cell in my body—from the blood in my veins, to the balls of my feet as they strike the sandy ground. My skin beads with a cold sweat as I race over the grasses and sandy soil, grinding old volcanic rocks to dust.

When I enter our camp, it all seems to stop. My body, my screaming, time.

It's the silence. An unearthly quiet haunted by the labored flapping of vulture's wings, then the *thunk* of such a bird landing a few steps away from me. A beastly scent—of musk, gluttony, blood, and need wafts at me as he spreads his wings lazily, like a fat, rich oligarch stretching after a heavy meal. He turns his head, looking right into my face, then tucks his wings and waddles to a severed arm lying next to a laundry cauldron. The hand is still clutching a piece of flatbread, as if taken unawares during breakfast and flung far from its owner.

Wide-eyed, I stagger around boulders, my feet splashing in puddles of blood and waste. Many of the tents have been cut down, and I wrench open the ones that are still intact. Most of those are empty, with only some jugs and dirty linens left behind. Then I come upon her.

Splayed on the ground, her tunic open, a dagger is thrust into her neck.

"Ayla," I whisper.

I go to her, running my hands over her bruised skin—still warm. Covering her with her torn tunic, I give back a small part of her dignity.

All of it is like a fevered dream. Mutilated bodies are strewn about our camp. Fires are burning, water is boiling. Half-finished chores lie about. Ayla had been mending from a pile of linens we'd been working on together only this morning before I left. The smell of fresh meat, hot stones, warm bread, urine, feces, too many violent men. I say the names of my dead tribesmen out loud, when I can recognize them. Ipollo, Adiv. No Saru, no Rin, no Oah. Not that I can see. Not yet.

Their absence is my only spark of hope. Barely the wink of a distant star, but enough to keep me standing. They could have been away when the savages came—like I was.

A shifting breeze brings with it an awful smell. One familiar only to those who have lit funeral pyres. Sickly sweet, like a too young lamb braised in pomegranate juice and sumac. At the far end of our camp, away from the palms and fluffs of grasses, is our spit for roasting large kills—gazelles, addax, and the like. The spear is empty, but the embers are burning—crudely lit. Someone has fired them in a hurry.

A few paces from that, dragged from the pit, lies Buri.

Buri, the one-time Beih priest who'd joined Nif and me by placing an ember in each of our palms. Marking us forever as belonging only to the other.

Cawing, waving my arms like a wild woman, I chase two vultures away from him and kneel at his side, stroking a small square of unburned skin on his arm. He's been roasted sloppily with his legs well done, but the rest of him charred in patches. His hair is fried off on the right, but his face recognizable, twisted into a terrible grimace. His thighs have been partly eaten, but not just by the birds. His flesh has been sliced off with a knife, neatly, the meat pulled from bone.

Tears rush over my cheeks, washing the death away—at least there's that. I can do nothing but breathe, letting the foul air in and out of me. Tasting it.

Then somewhere in the lonesome hush of this foul graveyard, I hear my name.

Chapter 46

Voices

OAH'S VOICE. Not wishful thinking. Not the mountains trying to trick me.

I say his name, touching my belly as if I'm still pregnant.

He doesn't answer, but I no longer feel alone among the dead.

Shutting my eyes, I touch Buri for the last time and stand up. I'm oddly graceful, no longer shaking with fear. I know only that Oah is here somewhere and it gives me strength.

A toddler's foot—perfect, unmarred, but unmistakably lifeless, sticks out from behind a martaya bush. It's Ayla's son. Bibi, the little raisin. I can tell by his birthmark, a raised spot nearly the same violet color as the tiny flowers that dot the spindly branches of the bush that's hiding him. And I can smell a hint of the mint leaves he likes to chew. Treading closer, his body comes into view piece by piece. Naked and flawless, as if he's died only of grief. If it weren't for the blood seeping out from under him, I would think he was sleeping.

Breaking a branch off the hedge, I sprinkle the petals over his body.

"Night," I say.

At the end of our camp, I edge around a cauldron of simmering fatty oils that we use for everything from tanning to cooking. A human head bobs clumsily in it—I can tell by the hair. Black and swaying in the boil like seaweed. *Clunk,*

clunk. The skull bumps the sides of the pot, and I feel a mad need to run. But I don't. I keep my pace.

As I near the guelta, evidence of the massacre fades away. No more bodies, no more body fluids, except for the bloody footprints I leave in my wake. Only an occasional whiff of the horror comes to me on a cat's paw of mountain breeze, along with fresh water smells of minerals, soil, and vegetation. A sweet bouquet of desert wildflowers floating daintily above it all.

At the shore of the guelta, I hear the lapping of water as it kisses the moss. Old camel prints fleck the crust of shoreline, but none of our beasts are anywhere to be seen. They must have been led away before the attack.

Orderly. An orderly assault. That's what it was. One with promises made.

Keep calm, we'll just take your animals.

I think of the hand with flatbread gripped in its fist. Sliced from its owner.

It's all right, you can continue your chores. We'll be off soon.

I can hear the voices, how they must have sounded. Good at this. Disciplined. Just the right tone.

Then, with one signal, a torrent of death unleashed. Reward for a brotherhood of broken men.

Not just men. Not thieves. Not bands of survivors like us. Soldiers. The men who did this belonged to the sultan.

"Sherin."

I jerk, biting my tongue. My whole mouth swamps with the taste of iron.

It's a voice that's spoken my name a hundred times at least, and speaks it again with a grave familiarity. And I hate it.

The water licks the tips of my slippers. The lilac ones my mother made for me so long ago. Scuffed, bloodstained, shaped to my feet, pointed at the big toe, soft from wear and repair. Such a fine pair to last all this time. Made by such a fine woman. Taking strength from my mother, I square my shoulders and unclench my fists. Spitting the blood from my mouth, I say a prayer to my father, asking him to put Oah and Nif under his protection.

"Roon," I say.

Chapter 47

A Dreaded Reunion

HE HAS HAIR. That's the first thing I notice. Black and glossy like polished ebony, and reaching nearly to his shoulders. I wish that with his hair had come back at least some of who he'd been. That young man I'd met at my engagement feast years ago. But I catch not a glimpse of that person. In his eyes, I see a pool of turbulent emotions that range from wrath to lust.

Not the lust of a husband for his wife. Or even a common man for a whore. It's lust for blood, lust denied, lust for what was lost, and lust for what he will take.

"I've wondered a thousand times how you would look," he says. "Whether your hair would be pinned up or flowing to your waist. What your eyes would think of me."

This might be the most he's ever said to me at one go.

"You knew I would be here." I don't phrase it as a question.

"Oh, yes."

His breath is barely noticeable and his chest is hairless, except for a trail of fine dark hairs that trickle from his bellybutton into the cloth that covers his groin. His legs are covered in the same fine hairs and look as if they've been scribbled onto his skin with a thin, charcoal pencil. He's barefoot. Feet hard and leathered. It's odd to find him stripped of the fashions of a sultan's soldier. To see him look like a man.

A large man. A strong one. But just a man. And not a good one—not anymore.

"What do my eyes tell you?" I ask him.

Roon blinks and licks the dry corners of his lips, crusted with the salty sediment that plagues every desert wanderer. His jaw tenses as if he's considering me.

"You've grown up," is all he says.

"Did you expect that I'd remain the same?"

He takes a deep breath and exhales through his nose. "No."

Roon's gaze brushes me all over, landing on my slippers, which he well recognizes even in their shabby state. Splattered with the blood he and men like him have spilled. Seeing my slippers almost makes him smile, I think.

"You're so much like you were," he says. "I didn't expect that."

And in this moment he's the same, too. The same man who called upon me to walk silently with him in the Palace Gardens. Who left and always came back with missing pieces. Doesn't last long, this bit of recognition. Roon isn't changed as much as gone.

"You did this," I whisper.

I'd do anything to demand what he's done with my child. Rake my nails across his chest. But I can't. A child is a weakness, and there's a chance he has no idea about Oah.

"That flower in the garden. It never grew back," he says, as if recalling an old song that once meant something to him.

"What?"

"The flower—the ugly one in the Palace Gardens."

I swallow hard, stepping closer. I'm afraid of what else he might tell me.

"Salan," I say, my voice hardly a scratch on a soft swatch of linen.

Roon raises an eyebrow, indicating at least that he does

remember my brother. Even if not quite as strongly as his hideous flower.

"I haven't seen him since the Feast of Pallah."

The Feast of Pallah. We honored it not long after our wedding feast, eating a stew of tomb bats harvested from one of the deeper caves.

"And?" I'm hoping for anything—whether my brother is content, cared for, the length of his hair, how much he's grown.

But Roon has lost interest in this conversation.

"I came to get you and you were gone." He raises his arm and runs his fingers through his hair, slowly, as if he's not quite used to having it yet. He's as well-built as ever, his biceps bulging with work, his hands thick from holding heavy weapons, carrying stores. And other things.

"You came to arrest me."

"I told you to get dressed and wait for me at your apartment."

I cross my arms over my chest—for strength, for warmth. All of me is chilled, though the air about us is still warm.

"So you could drag me away to my death?"

Roon's eyes fix upon mine. They soften, becoming intimate, like on the night we stood in the desert together. Intimate, but not benign. Their hue is different, I notice. Made of sunsets and apricots and much bolder than the last time I saw him. It doesn't flatter him. His eyes, once a bewitching feature, now rule his face with an iron determination. The way a scorpion's tail rules its body.

"So we could marry," he says, turning his back to me. "I'd come to take you. To kill the men with me and steal you away from the Palace City." He shakes his head. "But you'd gone. To be with a wanderer with no brick home, who eats raw meat, and doesn't bury his dead."

I have an urge to put my hands on his shoulders and make

him face me. To see what he's done—to me, to countless others. But I don't.

"As opposed to going with a man who butchers entire
tribes of innocents?" I tell him. "People whose families had
already been killed by the Vara, so our sultan could enrich
himself. Your family. Mine. They're gone, too."

This, he ignores.

"Toja did not die well," he says, as if in answer to my
accusation.

"I can't imagine anyone would under such conditions."

Roon shrugs.

"Some die better than others. Not Toja. She died exactly
as I expected. Begging, hurling accusations, crying till the
very end, like a child."

"She was a child," I say.

Roon reaches for his belt and unties his purse. Fine leather
from one of the Palace City tanners. Casually, he flings it at
my feet.

I don't want to open it. What I want is to fell Roon with
a stone and search for my son. Shout his name all over the
hot, black highlands and run to every place I've ever taken
him—the springs where we bathe, the grottos, the struggling
olive orchard Rin's people had planted years ago in their time
at the oasis. I want to call for Nif and search him out, join
with what is left of our tribe and flee these lands for good.

But my needs have little to do with anything today.

Crouching low, I stick out my hand. It trembles as I
retrieve the leather pouch from the ground, opening its flap
and removing what appears to be a wadded-up assortment
of leather thongs wrapped around a hard strip of hide. Roon
makes no move to face me, but cocks his head slightly, listening. He hears me unwrap the bundle and begin to make sense
of it.

I hold in my hands a pair of sandals. Small and familiar.

He'd never liked to take them off. I bring them up to my nose and inhale the faded scents of sandy dirt and soap. The one scented with herbals, that the sultan insists everyone in his palace use to wash.

"He died well," Roon says.

Chapter 48

I Say Her Name

A BLINDING PAIN strikes me below the belly, and I fold over the last of my brother—his shoes—curling up like a burning wisp of brush. Roon takes his time explaining to me the terrible particulars of Salan's death sentence. How he took my place at Toja's side, naked and chained in the palace courtyard. Beaten and burned. Whipped. Spat and urinated upon. Unconventional, yes, but it had been Adamen's idea. The Hero of the Realm. An idea embraced by the sultan and the good citizens of the Palace City. A new law and ultimate deterrent for anyone else thinking they might make a run for it like I had.

Patra had pled for him, begging on her knees, and this, too, had displeased our monarch. Such a public display against his wishes, and by an esteemed wife no less, was tantamount to treason, he decided. So she, too, joined them in the courtyard. But only for a day, not the required three. She was then closed in her tomb to die of wasting.

"Because of you," Roon says.

The sultan had closed the city, and they had not been spiked outside its walls as was the custom. Rather, they were fixed high on the inner wall, mounted like game, salted and set to roast in the daytime sun. Salan, the most weakened by the abuse, took only an hour to die of exposure. Healthy and grown, Toja lingered, taking all of a day. Mocked by the many who stayed to witness her long and tortured demise.

Even the children had chimed in. Salan's playmates. Throwing sand in Toja's face and calling her a traitor and whore. Fear and foot-dragging on her part curried no respect from onlookers, though it made a better show.

"Because of you," he says again.

Roon spares me no detail of their suffering. He recites their fate in an even voice, as if reading from a tablet. The flayed skin of Salan's back and legs. Toja's face—burned with hot irons. Patra beaten with sticks. Adamen, as accuser, was given the honor of Toja, and my brother. He chose their manner of torment in tribute to me. Dishonor by rape. Death by the sun. As long and cruel an end as possible.

I lie on the ground like a stone. So heavy I can't move. I want only to sink into the earth.

"What was that?" Roon asks.

So, he did hear me.

Rousing all I have left, I lick my lips, swallow, and say it again. Louder this time. Well above a whisper.

"Geet."

Chapter 49

Lost

THE CHANGE in Roon is as decisive as a clap of thunder. He clutches a fistful of my hair, and drags me to the water, plunging my face into its shallows, holding me by the neck. His grip is impossibly strong, and my lungs feel as if they'll burst. I think of inhaling the water, getting it over with, but Oah comes back to mind—his sweet toothless smile. Just then, Roon pulls me up, and I gasp for breath, sandy water flushing my eyes.

"Do you know what you did to me?" he demands.

With three quick rushes, he thrusts my head underwater again. In and up, over and over, until he tires of it, and throws me to the side, leaving me flat on the moss, breathless and wheezing.

Roon leans over me like a lion, his great paw swiping hard at my face. I hear the crackle of my cheekbone as it splits, and a searing pain spiders through every inch of my skull.

He dives onto me, bracing my chin with his hand, making me look at him. All I see is his mouth. Lips gently parted, as if he's about to tell me a secret. His hair wet with water and sweat, sticking in clumps to his high, broad cheeks. With an odd sort of tenderness, one reserved for an ancient enemy with whom you've tangled many times before, he takes my face in his hands and kisses me. Like love itself.

His last act of tenderness, if you can call it that.

My spirit floats above us. I can't smell the bitter tang of his sweat, but it has to be there. I feel almost nothing. Only the heaviness of him. His face as he pants.

And when it's done, he rolls off me and I take a deep gulp of air. We lay there for some time, quiet and numb, until his temper starts to rise again, built of confusion, indignation, and loathing. Of me, himself, I don't know.

I hear steps. Many of them. Hard and hurried. A group of a dozen or so men. Killers. All of them. The ones who made a feast of Buri, and an unwilling whore of Ayla. Who ripped and sliced and speared their way through my people.

Roon gets up.

"Justice, Sherin."

After that, I know nothing. See nothing. All I feel is electricity. As if I have become a bolt of lightning. I feel myself rise up into the clouds and spread across the sky. My body below, my spirit above. I am invincible.

Chapter 50

Sacrifice

I WAKE UP to a burning smell. Not burning flesh, just a regular fire—thank the gods. Inhaling, I detect damp and minerals. A cave then. And the unmistakable musk of a living being, with a lingering trace of frankincense.

I try opening my eyes, but can't do it. It's as if they've been sealed shut. Parting my lips sends a dull but impressive pain through my jaw, and lifting my hand makes every part of my body hurt like the sting of a thousand wasps.

My finger lands at the top of my forehead, a soft thump the way Nif would have done. From my hairline, I let my fingertip roam gently over my face—what has become a foreign terrain. My skin is hot with fever. Moist and clammy. As for my eyes, they're caked with dried blood and tears. My cheekbones have been crushed and the skin covering them is raw and riven. My lips are cut up from the inside and out. I push softly on a few of my teeth. Those are generally loose, with only one canine gone—a too soft, mushy hole in its place. My nose, incredibly, is perfectly intact. No wonder I can smell so easily. Breathe. It hasn't been broken.

"I was afraid you'd never wake up."

"Saru," I whisper, starting to shake. Damn, it hurts.

"I'm right here."

What memories I have are disjointed and frightening. From the plateau—I'd come to feed Oah, and there were beetles and birds . . . a massacre. I was punched and whipped. I know that. But I'm not sure by whom. Then I remember Rin. Or rather, don't remember him. He wasn't there, and he was last with Oah, watching him.

I try to say my son's name, but damn it all, I can hardly speak.

Saru crawls over to me on hands and knees. Her hair is unwashed and her breath smells of hunger. Sips of spoiled milk and tree resin.

"Oah," she says, low and tight lipped.

A cool, wet cloth blots around my most tender injuries. I take a careful breath.

"You were lucky," Saru says. "He stopped them after a while. Otherwise you'd be dead. We both would be."

She reaches across me to a jug of water, the wet linen dripping onto my breasts and stomach. I force open my eyes and see a faint glow of light enshrining Saru's hair. It's long, but matted. She's not at all like her usual tidy self.

"We haven't much time," she whispers. "You leave tomorrow."

She smoothes her tunic, and I notice its taupe linen is flecked with a menagerie of ill-boding stains.

"Where have I been today?"

Saru picks up a small pitcher and pours its contents—cool water laced with a bit of moss—over my hair. The pleasure of it nearly makes me cry.

"I don't know," she says. "But they're taking you to the barren lands come morning. They move on to the coastal plains after. Or so they say." She runs her fingers gently through my hair, unraveling some of the knots. "Reminds me of your wedding day," she says, gently squeezing the water from my ends.

Saru hums as she continues washing me, digging the dried

blood out of the curves of my ears, dabbing at the dirt on my fingers. "It'll be a long way."

The barren lands are simply the most desolate and remote place known to us. They're part of no kingdom, not even a poor one. And not a soul lives there. Even the nomads stay away. There's only one reason you bring a person to the barren lands. To leave them there to die. If that's the case, I don't understand why they don't just kill me here.

"It's the one they call Roon." Saru says. "He's insistent about it. Says you must die there. I think he's mad."

Saru leans close, her lips wet and poised. "We hid when we started to hear the commotion. Terrible. I still hear every sound."

I touch Saru's hand. Seeing it in the aftermath was a horror, but hearing would have been worse.

"They came closer. I knew they were going to find us. So, I sent Rin away with your child. I let them see me, chase me to the guelta."

Saru pulls her tunic closed, but not before I see a dark, hand-print bruise over her breast. A deep scratch under her collarbone.

"You were there with them ... and that Roon. Your face. I'd never seen such a look on your face. Like it wasn't you. Like you were but a doll and your spirit was elsewhere. He stood watching. Tearing at his hair, beating himself. And when he saw me, he began to shout. He slayed two of them—the ones abusing you. The rest fell away then. They fear him, you know."

And turned their attention from me to Saru. I could see it.

"Sherin," Saru murmurs. Her tiny Adam's apple bobbles as she swallows, and her finger taps lightly on my shoulder. "You're too frail to escape and you'll die on the way to the barren lands. A slow death. With them. Would you like me to?" She shakes her head. "It's a dreadful thing to offer, but I know Nif would want me to ask."

I sit up all the way, and much too fast. Damn the hurt. Sweat streaming from every pore, my hands cold and quaking like a hungry dog.

"Nif! Did he come?"

"Lie down," Saru's voice is buttery, like my mother's. "You can't be making noise or they'll know you're awake."

Saru lays her hands on me. Temples, shoulders. It's calming.

"Nif hasn't come, Sherin," she says. "Not yet. If he had, he would have killed them all."

Saru's eyes fill with tears as she flits them over me.

"I hate what they've done to you."

She tucks her head into her knees, her arms seeming bony and frail. Her hair falls like an old sheet of linen, touching the floor. I touch my hand to hers, gliding my thumb over her knuckles.

"Help me," I whisper. "We have to find Oah."

Saru looks up, her eyes wet and startled. The whites of them sparkling like opals.

"You can't."

Her finger lands on my brow, tracing around my eyes. Even now, she moves with a grace as delicate as a speck of dust suspended in a ray of sun. "These always seemed to me to be the color of life itself."

She lifts the wad of wet linen from the ground—the one she used to tend my wounds. For a second, she stops, seeming confused. She's in great pain. I can see it.

"You are like a daughter to me," she whispers.

Then she places the linen delicately over my mouth and nose. Slowly, pushing down, she holds it there. Her eyes absorbing mine as if she's sure she's saving me. I try to fight her, but my body is so broken that I can't summon the strength. I try to call her name.

From Saru's eyes drip a procession of tears, one after the other. She flinches, then her eyes widen again, this time draining of her essence. Gradually, she lets go her grip on the linen, and it slips away from my face.

"Sherin," she says.

I watch her fall to her side, her eyes still open. She blinks once and, a moment later, whatever life she has left fades like a puff of smoke into the night air. Behind her, Rin straightens up. The dagger he holds is dripping with Saru's blood and his face is fixed with a deadly purpose.

"I have your kitten," he says.

Chapter 51

A Kitten Saved

WE HEAR FOOTSTEPS and I go limp, pretending to sleep. Rin scuttles into a dark recess of the cave, the dagger he used to kill Saru held tightly in his fist.

A man enters the cave and scratches the hairy skin of his groin. I smell a pungent hash of elements, heavily fecal, exuding from his feet. He swears with little feeling, then turns and leaves.

"He'll come back," Rin whispers.

Sure enough he does. This time with another one of them. I won't call them soldiers. They're not that anymore.

"I didn't do it," he says. "I found her like that."

"What, you think *she* killed her?"

He must mean me. The soldier snickers, gruff and annoyed. His voice is rough, like he's been shouting all day. I think I recognize it and my stomach lurches.

"I'm not dragging the old woman out there—you are," he says. "Now we're going to have to build another fire, too."

"Why? We're leaving come morning."

His friend grunts. "It's bad luck."

"To leave a dead woman out for the vultures?"

"You don't leave one like her. She's a sorceress."

"How do you know?"

"It's what Roon said. They both are, these two."

I hear their feet shifting. They stop talking and I can feel them looking at me and Saru. Their boredom with it all—with death and rape and living—is as plain as the smell of garlic.

"What about her?" the new one says, lightly kicking my shin.

"He wants her alive."

This, apparently, is very funny until it isn't. The new man gets all serious.

"We're moving on, and not coming back. That's what Roon said. And we're taking her with us. He wants her to make it to the barren lands."

Silence again. A long one, as if contemplating the doubtfulness of my survival.

"She used to be beautiful," he says. It takes everything I have not to scream.

"They all did."

There's a rustle and some labored steps. I can hear them dragging Saru out of the cave, the heels of her feet bumping over the toothy shards of rock near the entrance.

"Rin," I say, as soon as I'm sure they've gone.

"Here." Rin scampers over to me. "Oah's alive. I fed him the goat's milk you wanted and left him nestled in the arms of an olive tree. He won't wake for hours."

Rin cups my face, thumbs stroking my temples. "I'll take you to him and we'll hide in one of the grottos. After they go, we can pack up some stores. Nif and the others will be back by then. We can go somewhere faraway. You'll never have to see this place again, Sherin."

His breath is laced with grass and honey weeds, sweet and bitter all at once. I want to kiss him gently, hold him like a brother. But there's no time. There's a tension in the air, left behind by the one-time soldiers. The ripple of excitement and uncertainty that goes through a group of men before a battle they expect to lose.

I think of the dream I used to have. The one of Rin taking Oah into his arms and walking out into the desert with him. The way he turned back to me and held out his hand in salan. I think of Nif's belief in the stories dreams tell us, and feel as if my husband is with me. The gods have given me a gift, I realize. They've told me what will be and what I need to do. They've given me the assurance of Nif's presence, and his support of my actions. It's all as clear a feeling as the most basic human need. Like knowing what one must do to sate hunger.

"You're to take him," I say.

Rin shakes his head. "We will."

"No. Saru was right. Whether they take me to the barren lands, or I stay here with you. I won't make it."

Outside of the cave, I hear commotion. Raised voices and a lot of clamoring about. Packing up, arguing.

"If you leave with him now, you'll get ahead of them. If you take me along, they'll catch us and we'll all die. Roon would never stop looking until he found me."

Rin holds my face, grief stricken, like his kitten is burning all over again.

"Please," I say. There is a certain clarity in hopelessness, I'll give it that much.

His lips touch my nose, barely a kiss. I hear his resolve in his sigh and I'm glad. Reaching into his tunic, Rin removes the Lady of Life, placing her in my hand, and molding my fingers to her form. "You left her buried in Oah's linens."

She feels warm and comforting at first, then a little too warm.

"If you keep her with you," he says, "I will find you again. Someday."

Chapter 52

The Journey

IT'S SLOW GOING. Stifling hot under a cloak of canvas by day, and freezing cold by night. A typical early autumn. I sleep most of the time at first, my fever spiking again at the beginning of our journey, then coming and going. A few days in, I start staying awake longer, catching sounds, like a camel cooing and gurgling. Then words here and there—mostly complaints from Roon's men. Not of discomfort, they're too hardened for that. But of misery. The final chapter of my death sentence seems a waste of time—to them, to me, to everyone but Roon.

"Ugly as a hyena now," one of the men remarks as he looks me over.

I don't much care. In a few days I'll be dead, and can hold my brother again, enjoy my mother's love, hear my father's voice and Yina's laughter. I only wish Nif could be with me. Just to listen to the whisper of his tunic as he moves. That I could hold Oah and bring him to my breast one last time.

Fantasies. Far away, like clouds. But they help me pass the time.

Some days in, we camp near a tall dune the color of an orange. The sand changes hue as the day progresses—yellow like the coat of a lion in the morning, pale at high noon, then darker and glowing as we near sunset. Blushes of rose and cantaloupe are radiant with the last gasp of daylight.

I'm awake much of the time now, even if I can hardly move. The bumping and jostling of my tented cot keep me from the oblivion I crave. At the end of each day when they set me down, I melt into the sand.

Not this day.

While I do fall asleep to the sounds of the men eating their supper—chewing loudly on jerky and flatbread—I wake up to a feeling more than a noise some hours later. The camp is hushed with exhaustion, like it is every night. Loud snores and heavy breathing grind softly like an old, cracked saddle on a long ride. But every hair on my body stands up in alarm.

"I can't believe you're still alive," he says. I don't recognize his voice. "Maybe you are a witch."

He lifts the collar of my tunic, peeking at my wounds.

"What do you want," I whisper.

"He told me to do it," he hisses. "Pluck out your eyes and bring them to him."

"Who?"

He picks off my blanket with an odd sense of care, and I quiver at the icy touch of the desert night.

"Adamen," he breathes. "The hero of our realm."

A cold hatred snakes over every bone in my body—broken or not. I bite down and look right into his eyes. I do know this man. Not his voice, but his face. He's one of the guards who came for Toja.

"I'm not going with them," he says, slinking closer. "Not them. Not that Roon. I'm going back to the Palace City. There's at least something to live for there, I hope."

He reaches for his belt and slides his dagger from its strap. Breathing deeply, he holds it up to my eye.

"Don't curse me," he rasps. "I don't want to do this. I didn't want to do any of it. Not to you. Not to that old sorceress. And if I don't bring him your eyes, he won't let me back in the city. That's what he said. And he means it."

An odd feeling spreads through me, starting in my belly and bubbling up. One I've forgotten about. Something like joy. The joy of freedom. I haven't felt it since before the Vara. Only now, it comes from the power and candor of truly having nothing more to lose.

"You're a fool," I say, bursting into a laugh. "The worst sort, too."

The guard begins to pant. His breath, hot with decay, whistles through the gaping holes left by missing teeth. "I don't know what you are, but you're as crazy as he is."

He climbs onto me.

"You should never have looked at him, he told me. You should have never looked at me, either."

IT'S DAWN when my eyes flutter open. A honeyed hue lights up the canvas, making me feel like an ancient insect trapped in a piece of amber. For a moment, it's just another day, but then I remember.

My tunic has been tied around me again. Neatly, with a square knot at my waist. I'm covered by the blanket the guard tossed to the ground, and don't hurt any worse than I did the day before. My eyes! I reach up to touch them and find they're just as they were. He never took them. Of course not. I can see. But my last memory is of the pointed tip of a dagger coming so close and not being able to do a thing about it.

All around me it's as quiet as the night. Quieter. No snores or snorts. Neither are there sounds of morning—the grunts and clearing of throats. The clamor of a hasty breakfast and beginning-of-day chatter. About the stores, the condition of the animals.

My cot and its canvas shell judder, and I can hear the

crank and clap of it being hitched to the same camel that's been dragging me through the desert. The one they call Red Sun because of his odd coloring and quick temper. The rider huffs as he mounts Red, and I hear him click his tongue at the beast, gently kicking his side to go. With a sudden jerk, we're on the move. I clutch the sides of my cot, adjusting to the initial pains of travel, and breathe slowly to catch my rhythm. My canvas is undone at the front, as it always is to keep the air flowing. Someone has taken care to tie it back and make sure I can see.

Behind us lie the remains of Roon's camp, the scattered corpses of my people's animals spread about. Camp is still set up for the night, with some of the men lying in a circle. They've been killed in their sleep. Others seem to have gotten up to see what was going on, but were slashed and speared as they went to rise from the ground. They're all lying flat, motionless. Legs splayed, arms outstretched, or gripping a mortal wound. They're all facing the same direction, fighting a single enemy. Only Adamen's guard, the one who was after my eyes, has been propped up. Sitting against a pile of rolled mats and a couple of corpses, he's dead without a doubt, his throat slit from ear to ear. Mouth wide open, as if he was about to say something, but then thought better of it.

One man has done this. The only one capable of taking so many on alone. And the only one whose body I don't see because he's riding Red, pulling me further into the desert. Going along as quietly as he had when he used to take me for walks in the palace gardens.

Chapter 53

The Scorpion

WE DON'T SPEAK a single word to each other. Neither when he feeds me, nor tends to my wounds. Not as each day amounts to a week alone together. Having been a soldier, Roon prefers a routine, and we develop one.

In the mornings, he comes under my canvas and feeds me mashed barley sprinkled with salt. Next is watered down wine, which he tips into my mouth from a supple pig skin pouch that he leaves with me so I can slake my thirst during the day as we travel.

During the hours of high sun, we stop and Roon tents a thick quilt of Barbary sheep's hide over us—its furry wool a barrier against the harsh rays of midday. Flaps made from dorcas gazelle hides, much thinner, hang down like walls all around. They are open front and back to keep the air circulating, and make something resembling a comfortable space. For me, it's a break from the bumping and knocking of being towed across the sand.

Roon doesn't sit with me inside my canvas shell, but lies outside next to it, as he does when he goes to sleep every night. Our contact throughout the day is almost entirely during meals and I'm glad. As it is, I hate to go to my death in his company, and am grateful for silence. I hear only the chirr of the occasional silverbill, our camel's nasal bray, and the wind.

At night, we eat dried fish and spiced grasshoppers. He feeds me little bites of bread that I can suck, then mash against the roof of my mouth. Side by side under canvas like strangers in a roving caravan. After our meal, Roon sits out under the stars and whistles. I didn't know this is a habit of his. It seems like something he would have done when he was much younger, maybe when I first met him, and is an obscenely pleasant pastime for a man like himself.

There is a wind in the desert that speaks of eternity. That's what he's whistling.

On the fourth day of our journey to nowhere, our routine gets shaken up. It's during high sun, when we're sitting under wool and canvas. We've finished a small, silent lunch of flatbread and crushed seed nuts, when I see Roon stiffen.

"Don't move," he whispers.

It's strange to hear him speak after so many days, and I almost say so, but then I feel something. A light scrabble on my shoulder, much softer than fingertips, but with a creepy scuttle that makes my flesh crawl. I watch it inch onto my chest, coming into my sightline. A scorpion, a deathstalker the color of yellow lime and indigo is paying me a call. I observe it dispassionately, not concerned by the fact that its deadly venom could kill me in my condition. Given the fate I suspect Roon has in store for me—being left to die of exposure, alone in the most desolate place on earth—a scorpion sting is the better of my options.

Even if the pain of its sting is said to be like being flogged with fire.

As it raises its tail, Roon's hand swings down. He sweeps it off me, then crushes it with his palm. Grunting, he's stung for sure; I can tell by the startled look in his eyes. He brings his palm up to examine it, seizing it below his wrist as if to slow the poison's progression, then bites down on the pad of his thumb, sucking out as much of the toxin as he can and spitting it to the ground. His skin is already flushed a plum purple around the wound, and the base of his palm is swelling.

"Why did you do it?" I ask.

Gasping, he shakes his head hard, then kicks the dead scorpion out from under the canvas.

"Be fine in a few days," he rasps.

"Not that," I say. "Your men. Why did you kill them?"

Roon looks up from his hand, his eyes as golden as sunflowers and wanton with the morbid poetry of his emotions. He moves closer to me and I flinch, which seems to trouble him.

"You know why," he says. "I couldn't stand it anymore. What they'd done. The way they looked at you."

"And you look at me another way?"

"You could say that."

Roon leaves my canvas and goes to sit outside. We have no supper that night and he doesn't whistle. Cocooned in my little shelter, I fall asleep to the lonely sounds of a light wind, and the click and chirp of locusts.

The next morning, Roon rises as if it's any other day. He looks pale and his forehead is slick with sweat, but he packs us up as always, and mounts Red. Holding his bruised, bloated hand against his ribs, he rides on, towing me into a vast and yellow horizon. The most desert of the desert.

We travel for only three more days, then Roon dismounts in what is truly the center of nothingness. All sand curving in muscular recline like a sleeping warrior. A shelf of dune some ways to our right, but nothing else. Just the sky, nearing mid-morning, the sun, the hot wind, and us.

"Don't," I say. Roon has come under the canvas to help me out, but the spell of our journey is broken and I can't stand his touch any longer.

He says nothing, but stands there with the sun behind him. Black and featureless as a shadow.

Roon watches me struggle, rolling out from under the canvas and onto the hot sand. As I wheel onto my back, I can't help but take a hard look at him, expecting the stony expression he's learned as a soldier. The one I know well. But his face is turned inward, onto himself.

He whips the canvas off its shell, exposing my cot, then folds it up, packing the material onto his camel with his other supplies. He's set for a couple of weeks, I can see, assuming he knows where to find a water source somewhere along the way to wherever he's headed—the coastal plains, according to Saru. I find it hard to believe he'll make it after ridding himself of his men—strong and capable, if nothing else. Having destroyed all of the livestock, save for his camel, and taking with him only the most basic supplies from his caravan, he's lessened his already iffy chances by at least half. Bending over my cot, he takes the drinking pouch he's given me and waters his beast. The camel's sluggish, pink tongue curls around the mouth of the pig skin pouch, slurping up its contents. Even the incomparable Red Sun is thirsty.

"Do you think you'll make it?" I ask.

I don't even know why. To make conversation, I guess. Waiting to die is tedious, and it helps to have something to occupy myself.

"I'm not going to the coast," he says. "I have something to do, first."

"Out here?"

"I didn't think . . . " he begins.

Roon moves with a weary resignation. Securing his camel, he seems to be steeling himself to finish what he started to say. I want to save him the trouble, tell him not to bother, but before I can, he turns around. Roon looks at me for a moment, then falls to his knees. Like he's been cut down.

I don't move, but I do watch him.

Roon holds up his face to the sun. His eyes sweep over the

desert he hates so much. The one he blames for just about everything. "I didn't think I could still love you," he says, as if to the heavens. "But I do. More than ever."

Roon closes his eyes and pulls the turban from his head, letting the sun's rays absorb into his hair. Obsidian, raven feathered. Then he leans in, bending over me, still not touching me, but bringing his face close to mine. He says nothing, but hovers, taking me in. I can't help thinking that he's saying goodbye as much to himself, his former self, the one he was born to and believed to be his. Leaving the last remaining memory of that man to die with me.

"The gods will bring us back together," he whispers.

I fall into the titian hue of his eyes. They're eyes of fire and destruction. I should have known from the first time I saw them.

"I hope not," I tell him.

Chapter 54

To Die Once Is To Die a Thousand Times

MY SKIN IS TIGHT and peeling all around my eyes, making it a nuisance to keep them open, but I do. For a last look at the world, for hope, for the tiniest glimmer of joy I'm still able to garner from consciousness. I figure I'll have all of eternity to sleep a painless sleep.

I watch Roon walk away from me with a heaviness of muscle and bone. The sky is nearly the color of his eyes and the further away he goes, the less he looks like a man. More like a figure that's been cast in bronze. And cast away.

The air ripples with heat, giving the vista a hazy, jagged appearance. Like I'm viewing it's reflection in a metal plate that's been sloppily beaten into shape. Further in the distance, lithe and light, I see a pearly mist emerge on the horizon. A spirit, I think. It takes form, human, with arms and legs and head becoming more defined. It's swaddled in loose, white linens, the kind a priest might be buried in. Such a beautiful vision, I wonder if he's coming for me. To take me away to the next world with him, instead of leaving by body to the vultures.

Only the spirit stops a few steps away from Roon. Stiff as judgement, like it had been expecting him. Roon leans into the phantom—he must see him, too. Even from here I can see in Roon's comportment that his arms are flexed, his hands clenched in fury. In challenge. Perhaps the spirit has come for us both, and I don't like at all the prospect of traveling to the next world with Roon. I've had enough of his company to last me all of time.

Through a swathe of tears, I watch Roon stomp closer to the spirit, moving with a hatred I've never witnessed in him. Only Roon would quarrel with death himself.

They circle around one another and begin a long dance of leaps and twists. Their shadows wild over the desert floor, and their forms stark against the savage, orange light. Roon thrusts and rushes, pushes and storms. A beast of a man, he swipes at the spirit as if he's trying to kill a butterfly with a stick. The white specter slows and comes close to Roon, who takes it by the throat and throws it down. I watch it tumble in the sand, until it seems to sink into the grains, leaving only its linens.

Roon looks down on it, and his shoulders tremor, shaking off his rage. He steps over the cloud of linens, pushing his fingers through his hair, walking on. Not desolate, remote in his bearing like before, but flushed with the fleeting thrill of a victor who's been dealt a mortal wound, but will die with one last triumph over an enemy.

From out of nowhere, a wind starts to blow and the spirit's robes billow up. A hand comes up out of the linen, whipping a dagger low across the ground. I hear the rawhide whip of Roon's Achilles tendons as the blade severs them, flattening him to the ground. Roon's hand clutches at the sand, and he wrenches his neck, writhing in agony. The white figure rises up, glaring at the man he's cut down. He turns away from him, and Roon continues to claw after the spirit, raging at him. But the spirit moves on. Death must have plenty to do on any given day in a desert ravaged by war and Vara. And he has another death to tend to right here, I imagine. Mine. He continues his pilgrimage, coming toward me with the dagger still clutched in his hand. He takes the form of friends, animals, even the sultan himself as his robes flutter behind him. At last, as my eyes are able to make him out—the line of his face, the graceful arc of the way he holds his hands, I can see him for who he really is.

———— ✦ ✦ ————

"LOOK AT THE DUNES," Nif says. "They glow with the majesty of the sun." He's crouched next to me, his face misted with sand dust. Whatever shock he feels at my appearance, he keeps to himself.

I look out with Nif. What has been a barren wilderness to me begins to shimmer. The desert's lines are triumphant, and its air is sublime. The sky has the look of forever. Like the way I love him.

I can't say if it's been minutes or hours since Roon left me in the sand to waste away. The desert day warps the senses like a bad drug. But it doesn't matter. Nothing does. Nif is here.

"How did you find me?"

Nif shakes his head.

"Men like Roon's aren't hard to track in the desert."

I imagine that's true. He left plenty of evidence of camp as we traveled here together—charred torches, animal bones, things no longer of use that he didn't wish to carry with him. Nif and his men leave not a trace as they move along the sand hills. I glance out into the desert, but can't see Roon anymore. The wind has picked up and the horizon is full of brume.

"There was a spirit in the desert."

I run my hand over the white linens he wears. Not his usual clothes, he must have got them during his travels. Likely from the Palace City considering how fine they are.

"Not a spirit," he says. "Just a man who loves you."

"I must have imagined it."

I touch my forehead to Nif's, letting my mind revisit every moment we've spent together. But other thoughts come, too. Of Roon, of the Palace City and Adamen.

"Salan," I say. Of course, he knows. Nif went to the Palace City himself and returns to me empty handed.

I raise my fingertips to his face, still so perfect and handsome. Only a fresh cut near his brow and some emerging bruises on his throat.

"Oah's with Rin," I whisper. "I had hoped you would find him."

Nif's chest rises and falls with relief. Carefully, he wraps his arms around me. I should be mourning the fact that our son will grow up without us both, but in the moment all that matters is the feel of him, warm and alive.

"Rin will take good care of him," he says. "That is his destiny. You and I have other things to do."

I start to tell him of Roon. Not what he did to me. Nif doesn't need to go to his death with that in mind. What I tell him is how Roon killed his men, all of them. How he lost his mind and wandered out into the desert. Without animals and proper supplies, he was destined to die on that journey. I tell him about Saru.

"Our maker will welcome her, I'm sure," Nif says.

It's odd that he speaks of only one maker. It's our belief all of the gods await us after our deaths. But I suppose it hardly matters now whether there's one or a thousand. We'll find out soon enough.

"Yes," I say. "Saru was an angel, and the gods will make good use of her."

Nif kisses the crown of my head and takes a lock of my hair between his fingers, riding it all the way down my back. My hair, at least, is the same.

"Do you hear the wind?" he asks. "It sounds like the belly of a conch shell. Have you ever seen one of those? Held one to your ear?"

I have. In the Palace City. One of the vendors used to sell them and Toja had one decorating a table in her apartment. Salan thought it sounded like a distant storm when he gave it a listen.

"You shouldn't be sitting like this," Nif says. "It must hurt terribly."

I'd sat up when Roon started to go because I wanted to see out. I don't know why. Maybe part of me had some inkling that my life wasn't quite over. A lone wish was yet to come true.

"I'll lie down with you," he says.

When I pull away from the snug curve of his collar I see it. A dark wall of cloud advancing across the desert tide. I've seen tempests before, but never one like this. A Goliath taking up the whole horizon. Curling like smoke. Eating up what's left of the orange sky. I can feel pitters of sand strike, like the first, tentative drops before a colossal rainstorm.

"Nif," I say.

"It's all right." He strokes my jaw with his finger, and I incline my head to his touch. I can feel his callus, consoling and familiar.

It'll be faster this way, lashed and smothered by a violent rage of nature. To die from the desert sun is to die by inches. But I'm afraid. Even with Nif holding me. We'll die together, but will still die alone. We all die alone.

"I can't," I say.

The wind is stronger now—I can feel it coming. Settling into my wounds, forcing past my dry lips.

Nif puts his mouth to my ear and shushes me softly. Then he whispers, weaving his fingers into my hair.

"Did you know there was a day when you went to the

market with your mother and father? I was surprised to see you—you hadn't gone in some time, and rarely went with both of your parents."

He moves closer, shielding my face from the sand. His voice is soothing. Strong and steady like the burble of a river, but I can't stop shaking.

"You wore a pale yellow tunic and looked like a ray of light. Your father wore blue and I admired the way he held himself. Like a man certain of his place in the world."

The storm cloud has begun to eclipse the sun, making the wind feel cooler. I once heard that in the heart of a tempest, the sand grains feel like pellets of ice.

"Your hair had been plaited and tied up in a loop, making you seem much older. But you wore the smile of a girl."

He traces my lips with the pad of his finger and I can't help but smile. I hope Miriam and Abran will be waiting for us in the hereafter. I want them to know Nif.

"You had that smile when I kissed you in the Palace Gardens, and when I bathed you in the cave. Even then, when you were sleeping. When we wed. You had it then, too, and wore it after giving birth to Oah."

He kisses a small patch of pristine skin on my forehead, and moves closer. It's getting harder to hear him.

"You had it on the day I left to bring your brother home to you."

He kisses my nose with the tenderness of a breeze. "And you had it today, when I found you."

Nif puts his palm to my face and kisses my lips. "I promise you, Sherin, you'll smile like that again."

———— ◈◈ ◈◈ ————

AT THE MOMENT my soul is freed from my body, I see time

and all the world at once. From the microbes in the grass to the cold, thin air that makes up the upper atmosphere of the Earth, just where it breaks into outer space. I see volcanos at the bottom of the ocean, and the strange, alien creatures that live in those depths. Glowing like phantoms—blind, primordial. I glimpse each of my parents as they were born and as they had come together to make me and my brother. I witness as Nif enters the gates to the Palace City alone, but I can't see past them. They close behind him.

What I can see are the few who are strong enough to run away from the city. They try their chances in the desert, though most of them will die as we did. Some will make it to the dunes, outrunning the storm. Rin and Oah do. And Taran. They manage to survive there for a few years before moving on to the coastal plains. Some of their descendants end up in Egypt eventually, then leave with Moses.

The sultan's palace is buried dozens of feet below the desert floor. Where it belongs, I suppose. At least until Neville finds it.

I see so much—too much to understand it all.

"Nif?"

Did you hear that? No, of course not. I can swear I heard him—his soul's voice, like an echo. Distant, as if it's coming from somewhere else. Have I told you that souls have voices? I must have mentioned it. Not like speaking voices, or like telepathic ones you might hear in your mind. They're sort of a scent and a vibration mixed with a bright color, if that makes sense. The essence of a person. Nif's is so beautiful. Like fresh rain and an earthquake, all painted the deep purple of blood. When it's still in your veins, before it encounters the air and turns red.

Nif. He's there, waiting for me. I know it. Part of the life I'm going to.

I feel that pull, so strong. Like drowning, but magnificent. Falling so fast and free. Then a burst of light. Primitive, savage. Did I tell you that every life starts with its own big bang, just like the universe? Just like Rin speculated all those thousands of years ago. Then I'm there, a single cell. Like a dove appearing out from under a magician's hat. Energized, I divide and divide and divide. It feels like I'll never take a form that resembles anything human, but I do. Big head, small body—curled up like a shrimp. All at once . . . thump, thump. A heartbeat. I feel the spark of love for the first time in my new body. Love for my mother. And something else—love for Nif. That always comes with my first heartbeat. Ferocious growth . . . tingling everywhere, in every organ, every vein. Like I'm crawling out of my skin, but awesome. Better than jumping with joy, soaring above the clouds. My mind changes every day, too. I hear my new father's voice—I know it's his—and listen for it each day. Solid and steady, even when he's afraid. My heart knows to seek his love. My whole being knows when he's near. It's always that way.

At first I can swim, like I'm in a kiddie pool. Then a bathtub, one that feels smaller by the day, until I can hardly move. I start to feel restless. My eyes longing to see, my lungs desperate to gulp the air. It's loud in here. Blood rushing, heart pounding, heavy breathing. When my mother talks, her whole body pulses. Her laughter is like a song played at the highest volume. Although this mother doesn't laugh often. Neither does my father, now that I think about it. Maybe they're serious people.

One day, I wake up to find I'm upside down. Some hours later, I feel the first contraction, a tight squeeze that's almost unpleasant. The squeezes come closer and closer together—tighter and more commanding. Sometimes crushing me, then letting go right when I want to scream. That's new. I want to scream. I didn't know I could do that. But no, of course I did. I always do. Everything is old and new at the same time. I start to move, like shouldering through a dense crowd. It's become too close in here, uncomfortable. I feel something touch my shoulders—cool and smooth. Like nothing I've ever felt. Soft tubes—fingers! So big, though. Not like mine. Fingers touching my shoulders. I can hear voices again now—my mother's, my father's and another voice, too.

"It's ok, Bonnie," she says. "I can see her head now. Pretty dark hair."

"Like her daddy," Bonnie, my mother, says.

"Oh, God!"

"That's the ring of fire," the woman helping Bonnie says. "It's the worst part, and feels like one heck of a burn, but it's almost over now. Just breathe. That's better."

My mother grunts and pounds her fist into the side of her bed.

"You hear that cry?" the Lady says. "That's another baby. A boy. Born only a few hours ago. That's just how your baby's going to sound."

"Make it stop!" my mother screams. "It hurts so bad!"

"Just a minute more."

"Hunter!"

"Squeeze his hand, sweetie," the lady says.

Hunter must be my father. He's not saying anything, though, so I can't tell for sure.

All of a sudden, the big hands pull me by the shoulders and my head breaks free into the cold. I forgot how cold it is. Worse than the desert at night, or a cold lake in the Scottish highlands, or the first chilly wind as you ascend Mt. Fuji. My hands and feet break away from my mother's body, but I don't know what to do with them. I jerk and flail and it's scary.

"It's a girl," says the lady.

"We knew that," my mother says, irritably. Her voice is high and clear. She sounds like a bird.

I feel a tickle in my throat and open my mouth wide.

"Well, that's quite a howl," the lady says. "Maybe she'll be an opera singer?"

"If she's even normal," says a coarse voice from across the room.

"Shut up, Mama," says my mother.

"Stupid junkie," that coarse voice grumbles.

Drug addicts. Great. Well, I've had worse. My mother starts to cry.

"Dora, please," says the lady to my grandmother. "She looks good. A few weeks early, but sturdy."

"I haven't touched nothing," my mother cries. "Not one thing, since we found out! Neither one of us has."

My grandmother comes closer, bringing with her a whiff of hairspray and *Lucky You Body Mist*.

"Only because that asshole dragged you into treatment with him! I'll give him that much and nothin' else."

That asshole, I assume is my father. I can hear him breathing hard.

"Dora, why don't you go get some air," the lady says. "There's a smoking lounge outside, near the cafeteria."

My grandmother lets out an exasperated *ha* and scratches her head. She's got long fingernails and they sound like seashells scraping against the hoary husk of a coconut.

"As I'm payin' for all of this, I ain't goin' nowhere." My grandmother doesn't sound angry anymore. Just tired.

The lady is washing me. Tepid water that feels like heaven. Cooing, she blots me with a soft towel before swaddling me in it. She holds me close, smelling of tea roses and medicine. It feels so good to have a body again. One that's fresh and healthy.

"You want to see her?"

I hear a few tentative steps. As my grandmother comes near, she snorts up a wet gurgle of tears.

"She's beautiful," she finally says. A trembling finger brushes my forehead. It smells like a campfire.

"She looks like Bonnie did," she whispers. "All pink and skinny."

I hear her turn on her heel and run, the door whooshing back and forth after she slaps it open and rushes through. Her shoes—boots with a thin, high heel, I think—echo in the corridor as each hard step grows more distant.

When I open my eyes, most everything is a blur. Only when things come up very close to my face can I make them out. Otherwise not at all.

"Bonnie, would you like to hold her?"

"Not yet," my mother says.

The lady cuddles me closer and starts to walk toward my mother's voice.

"You poor thing," she whispers. "You're just a baby yourself."

"I want to hold her," a young man's voice says. It's my father.

I feel, rather than see, the lady nod. She bends over, instructing my father on how to support my head. Then they make the transfer. My father is almost hot to the touch, damp with perspiration. His chest is hard and slender, like a boy's. He doesn't seem slight, exactly, but not like the fully-grown men I've been held by in other times, other lives. I can still remember those. My memories from all of my lives are vivid at first, then fade in the first weeks of life, like a dream does in the early moments of wakefulness. Later, it's only in dreams that I'll be able to see what I've known.

"You're a daddy, Hunter," my mother says. "What do you think of that?"

I'm not sure what he thinks, because he doesn't seem to talk much. But he does hold me tight and close. His face is too far away for me to make out his features, but I can tell he's looking at me with a keen interest.

"Can I see her, too?" my mother says.

He remains silent and seems to hesitate, but then scoots closer to my mother, putting me between them. I like my mother's musky smell. One part fruit, one part wet soil.

Outside the door, I hear that baby again. Screaming and not to be ignored. Someone is pacing up and down the hospital corridor with him.

"I'm sorry," a deep voice says. "He seems to be a little excited."

I know that voice! It's Neville! That's Neville's voice!

I hear the clicking of my grandmother's heels again.

"Everyone doing okay in there?" Neville asks her.

"Just another glorious day of white privilege," my grand-mother snips.

Neville steps closer to the door and the baby stops crying. "He settles down whenever I bring him near your room. I guess he wants to pay you all a visit."

My grandmother reenters our hospital room taking one of those deep exasperated breaths. She lets the door close in Neville's face, and the baby boy begins screaming again right away. I join in the chorus.

"See what you did? He was just bein' nice and now our baby's upset, too."

"You don't need to make friends with every asshole you meet, Bonnie. That's what got you in this mess," my grand-mother snipes.

"It's all right," my mother says to the doctor. "He can come in. The babies were born on the same day, after all."

The doctor opens the door and Neville takes a tentative step inside with his son. I quiver all over and I can feel my father stiffen, holding me tighter to his chest. The infant isn't crying anymore, but I can hear him squirming in Neville's arms.

"Wow. My son seems to like it in here." He laughs a bit, still giddy at the prospect of fatherhood. It's the first time, I'm sure, he's referred to his son as just that. His son. "I won't stay long, I promise. My wife needs a few minutes with her doctor. We've had a big baby here, and she's not a big woman."

Everyone laughs a bit, except for my father. He's tense as a threatened panther, and doesn't seem to appreciate Neville's presence one bit. Or the other baby's.

"I'm sure she'll be expecting you back," my father says.

"Oh, come on, Hunter," my mother chides him. "We should let the babies meet. You heard the mister; his wife needs a few minutes."

"It's Neil," Neville says. "Cornelius Neville. Family name. Kind of funny, I know."

"I like it," my mother says. "I'm Bonnie, and this here is my mom, Dora, and my honey, Hunter."

I feel her elbow my father, but he doesn't budge.

"We're naming ours Ever, as in forever after. How about you?"

"Cornelius Michelangelo. Mickey for short." Neville laughs. "Even funnier name. See, uh, it's kind of a family tradition to use an artist's name as a middle name. Michelangelo was an artist."

"We know who Michelangelo is," Dora tells him.

"Of course." Neville's dark mass bends over me to get a look, but my father holds me tighter, curling me close. He doesn't want Neville to see me and I wish I could shout something, beat my tiny fists—anything. I want to see him! Opening my eyes wide, I belt one out.

My mother shushes me, taking my fingers in hers, leaning close to my face for the first time. She has pretty skin and a full set of lips.

"Well, will you look at that," she says. "Her eyes."

"Babies eyes often look cloudy when they're first born," the doctor lady says. "You probably won't know what their color will be for a year or so."

My mother takes a deep breath and I feel her bosom rise and fall at my side. Her breasts are soft and I can detect a faint, milky scent coming from them.

"But that's just it," my mother says. "Her eyes . . . they're so green. And bright. It's the damnedest thing. They're not supposed to be like that are they?"

"Well, every baby is different," the doctor says. I can hear her arranging things. Packing up. "And her father has pretty striking eyes himself. Perhaps it's a family trait."

My mother swallows, unsure.

"Hunter, take a look," she says to my father. "Have you ever in your life seen anything like our baby's eyes?"

My father takes a deep breath. He shifts and starts to come in close.

This time my father brings me right up to his face. I'm growing awfully tired. I forget how sleepy it feels to be so new. It's hard to focus, but I try just a bit and find my father is only inches away. He's young. So young. He can't be any older than fifteen. I'm looking right into his eyes and he into mine. Golden, like they're on fire. Ripe apricot deep in the center. I stop breathing altogether. I want to scream again but nothing comes out.

"Have you ever seen eyes like that in your whole life, Hunter?"

"Once," he whispers, raising his fingers to the side of my face. "Just once. In a dream."

Epilogue

I'M DREAMING OF NIF.

When I dream, I'm an angel.

With a small a.

I float above.

And can glimpse past lives.

Or look into the lives of others.

Neville.

"Looks like little Mickey's colic is pretty much over," he says.

Little Mickey is watching his father.

At only a few weeks old, I no longer remember much of who I am. I'm a tiny babe who needs milk and sleep. To be held. I know I was afraid of something. Someone. But I can't remember who that is. Except when I dream.

When I dream, I remember everything. There are times the tiniest detail comes to the forefront of my mind—a smell or brief flash of an event that I knew from many lives ago. This happens to Nif, too. Every touch, every whisper, every death is laid out like a hand of cards. There's so much there— a giant menagerie of images, feelings and ideas, mental bric-a-brac. Too much to comprehend. It's why I've become obsessed with dreams in each of my lives.

"He must finally be getting used to life here on Earth," my

Calliope says, yawning. Her hair is wild and she looks like a pretty Medusa.

"This one's an old soul," Neville murmurs. "He's yelling all night. It's like he's been trying to tell us something."

I yelled at first, too, only my mother couldn't take it. She'd cry and shake me, and then get so scared she was going to hurt me.

"Hunter!" She'd call.

He'd come in, quiet, still as a lake. Like he was on our walks in the Palace Gardens. She'd hand me over to him, and he'd look at my red, tear-stained face with that smile that isn't quite a smile. You can bet that put an end to my tantrum right there. When I'm quiet, my mother holds me.

Holds me.

In his arms.

Nif. So close—I know it.

His love flowing through me like electricity. Trying to protect me. I start to feel it again like I did with Roon and the soldiers at the guelta. Becoming a part of the current . . . surging . . . a lightning bolt.

We're on the cusp of a storm.

Not that storm.

Not the one that buried the Rah'a.

Another storm, another life.

A sky like a dirty sheet. Then clouds—so gray they're almost black. A vein of lightning that streaks all the way to the ground. Single drops of rain that could fill a teaspoon. Thunder that shakes the earth like the wrath of God.

So frightening. Like the end of the world.

"Sherin!" Calliope screams. "Run!"

My Calliope.

Is this a dream within a dream? That's never happened to me before. But how else would Calliope be here—and know my name no less?

And Neville, too. He has the statue and is holding it up high as a charge ignites the sky again.

The heavens open up and the rain comes down in sheets of glass. Through all this raucous nature, earsplitting as heavy metal, I hear someone else call my name. Not Calliope this time.

Roon. It's Roon. Damn Roon! I thought he was as dead as Adamen, as the sultan. As everyone in the Rah'a.

Everyone but Nif and me.

Roon is crouched low to the ground, calling my name—*Sherin*.

Roon, *Hunter*, my father.

No.

It's not the past I'm remembering. It can't be.

My God. It's the future.

Thank you for reading **BREATH**.

If you enjoyed the story, please take a moment to leave a starred review on Amazon or the platform of your choice. Reviews from readers like you not only let we authors know what we're doing right, but draw others to their next great story adventure!

JOIN ME ON SOCIAL MEDIA!
No politics. Just a great conversation.

Twitter: @vicdougherty
Instagram: victoria_dougherty
Facebook: @victoriadougherty.author
YouTube: youtube.com/victoriadougherty
Podcast: www.anchor.fm/victoria-dougherty
Web: www.victoriadoughertybooks.com
COLD Blog: www.victoriadougherty.wordpress.com

VICTORIA DOUGHERTY is the author of three acclaimed Cold War historical thrillers, *The Bone Church*, *The Hungarian*, and *Welcome to the Hotel Yalta*. Her epic historical fantasy series, including *Savage Island*, *Breath* and *Of Sand and Bone* are her newest works of fiction. Readers and reviewers have called Ms. Dougherty's fiction "breathtaking", "mesmerizing", and "genre-defying."

Her blog—COLD—features her short essays on faith, family, love and writing. WordPress, the blogging platform that hosts some 70 million blogs worldwide, has singled out COLD as one of the Top 50 Recommended Blogs by writers or about writing. Ms. Dougherty's new podcast, also called COLD, has been praised by listeners as "the storyteller's church."

I WANT TO THANK my family for putting up with the imaginary friends I've invited to live with us, my friends for their tireless support, and most of all my readers who make all of the blood sweat and tears worthwhile. I don't say this lightly — I know a lot of writers and their readership — and I can honestly say you're the best! A big, hearty thank you also goes out to Chris Bell and Brianna Harden, my designers, Faith Moore and Matrice Hussey, my editors, and all the many amazing and supportive people in my writing and research community. You answer my questions so patiently, give me such great ideas, and always have my back!

EMAILS ARE BORING. MINE AREN'T. You'll get a mini-magazine delivered to your inbox for free once a week. It's called Cold Readers Club and you're going to love it. To join, go to www.victoriadoughertybooks.com and click "Get in Touch" at the top of the page.

Here's what readers are saying about Cold Readers Club:

"I look forward to your email every week and often read it twice! It's like getting a little magazine."–Peggy H.

"I know I'm not the only one in your *Cold Club*, but I always feel like you're writing something personal just for me."–Roger B.

"You share the most precious moments and write so beautifully. Now I have to read your fiction!"–Terry M.

OTHER BOOKS BY VICTORIA DOUGHERTY

Savage Island: A Breath Novel

The island of Niue, 1944. Angelie, a 17-year-old Australian girl, is waiting out the war on the island, where warm tropical winds blow through her hair almost as gently as native islander Will Tongahai's eyes graze her body. But when a series of vivid dreams about deserts and long forgotten prophecies ensnares them, Will and Angelie discover not only their love for each other, but a powerful fate that began for them at the dawn of civilization.

What readers are saying about *Savage Island*:

"I love the author's way with words and her ability to wrap you into her story and entangle you in its threads. I'm going to be breathless with anticipation for the next installment of Breath."

"There are worlds within worlds [in this book], and time and space have no true meaning. Only the language of love."

"From the moment I opened its pages, I fell into an otherworldly, enchanting time and place that felt dreamlike and mesmerizing"

The Bone Church

In a time of danger and distrust, two lovers seek redemption...and a way back to each other.

What readers and reviewers are saying:

"In this case heavy is good, very good." Back Porchervations

"The Bone Church, by debut author Victoria Dougherty, is possibly one of the darkest and most sophisticated historical novels you'll be able to put your hands on." Mina DeCaro, Mina's Bookshelf

"This novel has it all...an addictive jaunt into a world of paranoia, deceit, distrust, and then the ultimate betrayal. I really, really, really loved this book!" Lit Bitch

"This FIVE STAR Cold War thriller is so highly recommended I would say beyond all doubt this would be declared the thriller novel of the year." —Amazon reader review

The Hungarian

Grinding her old life beneath the heel of her Dior stiletto, Lily puts her new one on the line, surrendering to fate, love and, for once, events bigger than herself. The Hungarian is a stylish and sexy romantic thriller you won't be able to put down!

What readers are saying:

"Absolutely brilliant, and readers will never regret getting it. I think it's one of the very best of its genre that I've ever read."

"Weighty, philosophical, poetic, with great knowledge of the literature and history of the Soviet Bloc."

"The heroine is fantastic and the story fast paced with lots of action."

"History and intrigue. Couldn't put it down."

www.victoriadoughertybooks.com

Cold: Essays on Love, Faith, Family and other Dangerous Pursuits

Daring escapes, backyard firing squads, communist snitches, bowlfuls of goulash, gargoyles, gray skies and bone-chilling winters—Victoria Dougherty comes from the ultimate Cold War family. Writing with humor and raw soul, she recounts the heart-pounding stories she grew up hearing at her dinner table and the two-hanky drama that played on in her home.

What readers are saying:

"I loved every page and didn't want it to end."

"These thought-provoking essays are among the best I've ever read in that I can relate to them so easily, like slipping on a sweater I've owned for years."

"This blew me away! Just give yourself permission to read this book; it is a blessing in disguise. It was an experience, not just a great read."